The Statue of the Mad Caliph

A Novel

Michael Tedin

The Statue of the Mad Caliph is a work of fiction. Names, characters, places, and events are the product of the author's imagination. Any resemblance to actual places, events, or characters living or dead is purely coincidental.

Cover Art by Mark Tedin

Published in the United States

ISBN: 1490374922
ISBN-13: 978-1490374925

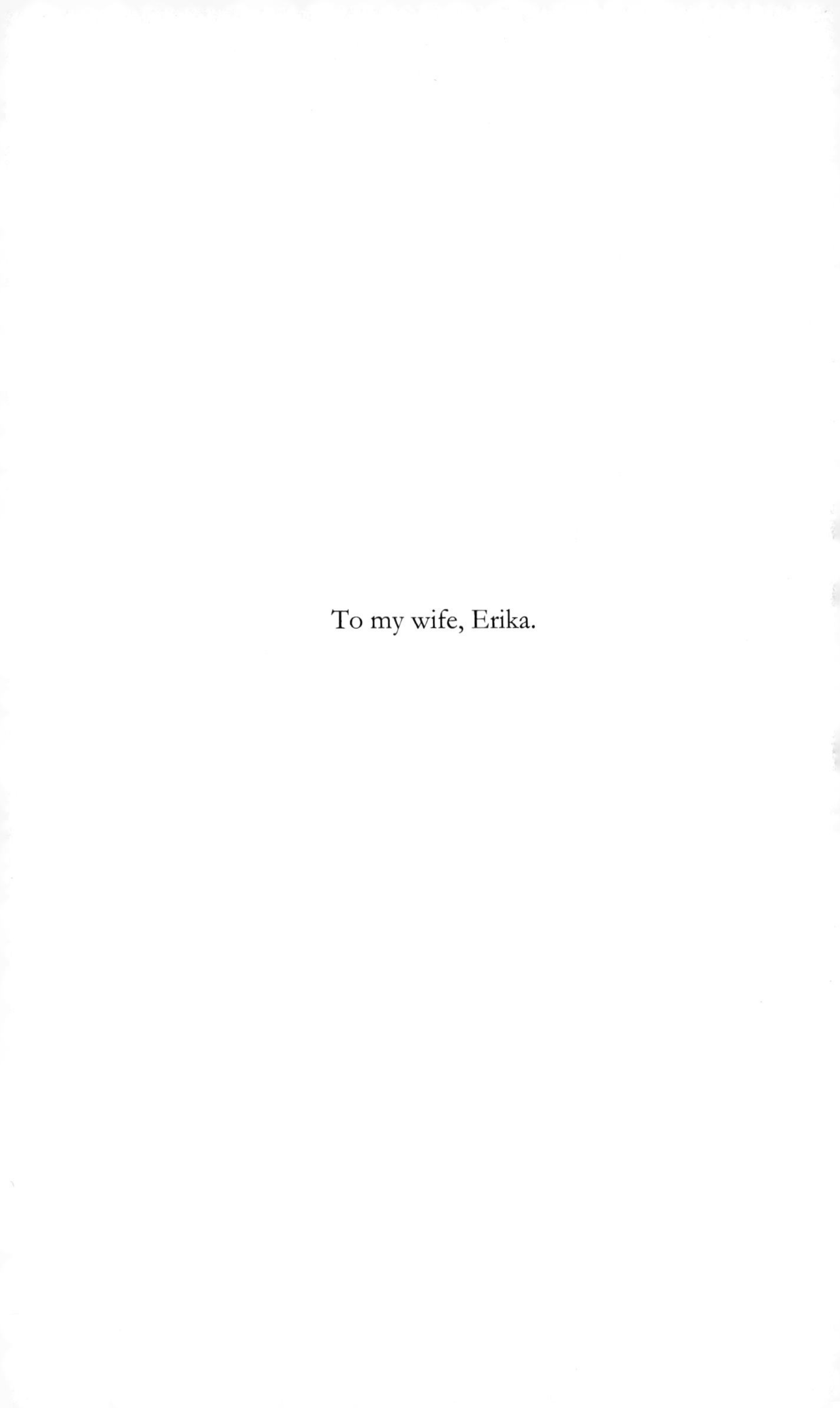

To my wife, Erika.

ACKNOWLEDGMENTS

Thanks to Erika Tedin, Sean Green, and Kim Nathan, who helped in proofreading and advice. Also thanks to my brother Mark Tedin, who provided the beautiful cover art. Special thanks to my editor Philip Athans, who provided the most valuable advice on correcting errors made by a first time novelist.

Deántika ghésos aiwes,
Ákemono úinoiko farakatar déprar.

Prologue

The moon had not yet risen and millions of stars shone bright through the clear desert air. Though the sun had long gone down, the star-dazzled sky provided enough light for Goron to move about. Inside the ring of tents, torches lit the area

The wizard had built a dais for the ritual he was about to perform. He stood at the center of the courtyard behind a pedestal. The lion statuette that served as the centerpiece of the ritual sat on the pedestal. Two children stood in front of it, chained to a short obelisk engraved with arcane symbols, the girl on the left and the boy on the right. A table stood to the wizard's left, holding the necessary substances and devices needed to perform the ritual. The wizard directed the preparations, giving tasks to his underlings while he oversaw the planning.

Goron snuck around the outside of the ring of tents. He had two objectives, but was uncertain he could accomplish both. How would he be able to prevent the ritual from proceeding and free the children? If he were to rescue the children, the wizard could still proceed with the ritual, though he would not be able to utilize the full power of the artifact. If he were to take the statuette, the wizard would be free to harm the children or use them to bargain for the statuette in return. Deeming it unwise to head directly across the tent-encircled plaza, he turned back to the exterior of the camp to take a circuitous route to the other side of the courtyard, behind the young prisoners.

Heavy boots thudded on the hard packed clay, coming toward him from his left. A sentry made his rounds, his leather armor creaking as he patrolled outside the circle of tents.

Goron crouched between two tents, finding the darkest of shadows in the lee of one of them. He calculated the time it would take to get to the other side before the next patrol came by. If there were only one sentry, he should reach the other side with time to spare.

The sound of boots and leather faded to the right as the sentry passed. Goron headed into the darkness in the other direction, to the left.

He passed a space between tents surrounding the circular courtyard. Within, the mage proceeded with his preparations. Beyond, the boy attempted to wriggle out of the cords that bound him until one of the Ushidian guards stopped him with a firm hand on his shoulder. Another guard stood close by, keeping an eye on the gap in the tents across the small courtyard from him.

Wanting to free the boy as quickly as possible, Goron continued on into the shadow of the main tent. He intended to get to the gap on the other side of the pedestal, nearer to where the Ushidians held the children. It seemed unlikely he could get the statue and the children, so he would get the children first. With any luck, the disturbance would delay the wizard's plans long enough for Goron to take the statue later. If the wizard wanted to perform the rite at midnight, Goron might have another full day to come up with a plan to stop him.

Distracted by his calculations, Goron was not paying attention when a sentry came around the corner of the tent and caught him by surprise. Drawing his sword, the scarfaced guard yelled an alarm in Ushidian.

Goron jumped back, instinctively shifting to a defensive stance. Having been disarmed earlier, Goron had no weapon to defend himself. He would have to fight an armed man in hand-to-hand combat. To succeed, he would need to get past the fat man's blade. A quick feint, grabbing at the swordsman's wrist, revealed his opponent's slow reflexes. Slowly working his way around the Ushidian, Goron calculated the difficulty of getting the heavier man down and silencing him.

Seemingly out of nowhere, another man ploughed into Goron's side, knocking the wind out of him and shoving them both to the ground. This one was quick and strong despite his thin, wiry frame.

Goron twisted away from his would-be captor, but the thin Ushidian twisted with him, denying his escape. The man knew a few wrestling moves. Executing a *kenous pleudou*, the "Sword of Water" wrestling move designed to escape an opponent's grasp, Goron twisted out of the attacker's grasp, rolling across the hard-packed clay, and moving to stand.

Now facing two men, he considered flight, but his opponents moved to flank him and cut off his lines of escape. The swordsman was the more dangerous of his two opponents. He would have to neutralize him first. He set himself up for a "Fox Against Wolves" move. If his opponents charged him simultaneously, he would use their momentum against them.

They did not attack simultaneously. The thin wiry one moved first while the fat man delayed.

Goron transitioned his stance into the "Plucking the Hens" move used to defend against one attacker after another. Turning to face his attacker, he set his balance. As the slim Ushidian reached out to grapple him, Goron shifted his weight to the left, grabbing his enemy and pulling him past. The man fell flat on the ground.

Goron had his back to the fat swordsman who took advantage of the opening. His new assailant's leather armor creaked as he charged.

Expecting this new assault, Goron shifted his weight again, listening for the pounding of boots on the hard-packed clay ground. He spun away from the approaching sound in time to miss being cut open by the Ushidian's short sword.

The sounds of fighting had alerted others. Four men carrying torches came from around the side of the tents. The wizard stood among them. Another man yelled at Goron's two attackers in Ushidian. The fat man drew back, sheathing his sword in response to his leader while the thin man, having risen from the ground, circled around behind him again. Two of the newly arrived men broke away from the leader to join the fight, circling him, each brandishing a rope with the obvious intent of using it to subdue him.

Goron spoke little Ushidian, but understood enough that the man was ordering them to take him alive and uninjured. This was a small piece of information he could take advantage of, but it was a small advantage. There were few ways to defeat four opponents without first surprising them. These men were seasoned and ready for him. He prepared to execute a "Rabbit Evades Wolves" move, hoping he would be able to escape the trap.

His opponents were too quick for him. Before he completed the move, the four Ushidians charged all at once. Goron had no time to react.

The Ushidians were apparently accustomed to fighting together in a group. Two of the men hit him hard, one low and one high from each side, knocking him down again. They held him tight while the other two tied him down, one slipping a snare around one wrist while the second tying a loop around his other wrist. Goron tried the *kenous pleudou* move again, attempting to escape, but there were too many men to escape from.

The four Ushidians subdued him, tying him hand and foot. He struggled in vain as they picked him up and carried him back to the sconce-lit courtyard in front of the pavilion. The wizard seemed quite pleased with his bodyguards.

"Excellent work, Valád, Brash." He nodded to the other two, whose names he seemed to forget. Then he turned to Goron and said, "I don't know how you escaped the tomb. I was certain you would not be able to cut loose your bonds, let alone move the seal on the airshaft. It is a shame Témopirz is not here. He would be pleased that we have captured his prey." To his men the wizard added, "Keep him under close watch. We don't want him to escape again."

Part I

Chapter 1

Wishing he did not have to visit him so late in the evening, Manoueka rode in his carriage to the home of Demodoi, one of the most powerful men in the city of Synnakon, perhaps in the empire. The old man was unavailable during daytime, preferring the cool of the night to the bright sun and oppressive heat of the daytime. Manoueka thought this odd since the summer this year had been unseasonably cool and pleasant.

He felt as if he were selling his soul to the old man, but he saw no other way. He had no students and his money was running out. He had incurred a great deal of debt when he bought his tower in the *Krolos Maholon*, the mage district of Synnakon. He also had to pay servants and guards.

Students sought out wizards, known as *maholoi,* with the freshest ideas and the newest spells. His ideas had all become stale, even the last spell, the *Korína* that set a watch on an area. His rival Senidimos had accused him of stealing the idea, claiming to have thought of it first. He had won the disupute but it was a pyrrhic victory.

Once the dispute became public, his students had abandoned him and transferred to Senidimos. He had proven himself the better mage but been beaten by his rival's political maneuvers. He would not make the same mistake again.

He needed a new idea to set him apart from his rivals. New spells, especially powerful ones, would attract the attention of new students and of the emperor's court. More importantly, they would attract the attention of the emperor's purse.

He had petitioned Demodoi for help to obtain a loan through the old man's agents. He had not expected to be invited to meet the strange old man himself.

Manoueka's carriage pulled through the iron gates into the narrow courtyard of Demodoi's large house. Unlike most of the rich in this city, the old man was not beholden to any of the ruling families or trading houses of the empire, though he had connections to most and spies in many. Demodoi's house was one of the largest and oldest in the upper Seniktikon, though no one knew how long he had lived there. Manoueka had searched the public records but could not find out who had built it or any of the previous owners.

Perhaps one of the merchant families that moved to the Neotikon, the newer neighborhood with larger mansions and estates, had sold it to the ancient aristocrat. Many families had made a fortune under the antarkanist dynasty only to lose it when the Emperor Kosyndeos set things right and gave the *maholoi* the freedom to practice their arts for the benefit of the empire.

Inside the courtyard, Manoueka observed the magnificent architecture; to call this place a house was to understate its grandeur. Most of the buildings of the city were built solidly of stone at the bottom in order to support the brick of the upper walls and tiles of the roof. This building was different. Its walls rose high but had the feel of the body of a young, graceful dancer rather than the solidity of a country farm girl. It seemed as though the designer of this building was a follower of Momados, who favored air, rather than Deihosos, the patron god of stoneworkers, who favored earth. The builders had carved the stone in graceful floral patterns. The mansion had no visible windows, but windows were not common in a city whose buildings were designed to keep the indoors cool and to keep the hot city air out.

Demodoi's servants took the carriage away and led Manoueka into the building through a remarkably open entry hall. The doorman instructed him to wait in a smaller salon off the hall, richly decorated with tapestries depicting stories of saints and myths as well as a few bronze statues. The statues looked like some of the ancient stone statues he had seen in stoneworkers' rock piles, ready to be broken up for building material.

He did not have to wait long before Demodoi arrived to greet him. The man did not look well. A frail man with a wisp of white hair, he had the bearing of one who was once strong and burly. The disease that he was purported to suffer from had made him thin and pale. Perhaps this was a consequence of never going out in the daytime and not being able to enjoy the sun and fresh air.

"Welcome to my home," said Demodoi in a frail voice. "It pleases me that you could come to me." He offered Manoueka a glass of wine. "I have yet a bottle here half-empty. I have consumed my fair share this evening. It would shame me to needlessly waste the rest."

"I could not impose on your hospitality, thank you."

"Please take some off my hands. We opened too many bottles at dinner and it would be a shame for such a fine wine to go to waste." The dance of courtesy that the higher ranks of society played required one to refuse a gift on the first offer and to reoffer after an initial refusal. The nobility of the Imperial court had raised this back and forth to the level of ritual, especially in regards to the emperor himself. However, both Manoueka and his host had ascended from lower classes and neither had patience for the game.

"If you insist, I will take some." In fact, Manoueka was eager to try a taste from what was rumored to be one of the finest wine cellars in the city. It was said that Demodoi's holdings included vineyards in Paphlagonia as well as the Allyrion hills overlooking the sea. Wines from those prized vineyards drew a high price.

Manoueka accepted the wine. Tasting it, he marveled at its flavor. He had tasted good wines before, but never one of this depth and complexity. Did Demodoi have such wines regularly or did he open this wine in anticipation of having a visitor?

"I suppose you wonder why I have asked you to meet me in person," said Demodoi. He held up his hand to ward off the mage's denials. "There is no need for false politeness. I am aware of my reputation for reclusivity. The fact is, I can help you, but I require a task from you in return. You contacted my agents seeking a loan. Per my instructions, my agent investigated your background and discovered much about you. Most prominent is the news that you pilfered the ideas of another *maholos*."

Manoueka felt the heat rising in his face. He calmed himself before speaking. "Begging your pardon, sir, but I was cleared of any wrongdoing by the *Nankisos Maholon*. They decided that Senidimos had conceived the spell first, but he did not implement it. I introduced my version before him. The spell is mine."

"Your dispute with Senidimos is irrelevant to my needs," he said, waving off Manoueka's protestations. "I only bring it up to clear the air. Your dispute has impoverished you. You need money and you come to me seeking it. If I were to loan you funds, how do you intend to repay me without a source of income?"

"I need time to develop new ideas. I am working on a few similar to the *Korína*. Also, I have an idea for..."

The old man turned, facing Manoueka. His eyes pierced the *maholos*, cutting his words off abruptly. "Your ideas are trivial, meant for merchants and shopkeepers. If you wish to attract the attention of the emperor, you need to set your ambitions higher, not these paltry notions you entertain. You want to set yourself apart from your rivals, conceive of grand schemes. Chasing minor spells will gain you nothing. If you cannot do so, then you are not the *maholos* for my intended designs."

Manoueka's eyes widened at the opportunity Demodoi offered. He almost felt his mouth watering. "But I am the man you are looking for!" he said. "My goal is to be the greatest wizard on the *Nankisos*. All I need is the idea that will raise me above my rivals."

A wry smile crept across Demodoi's face. "Very well, in the treasury of the emperor lies a gem by the name of Barashel with the ability to channel great power. It has long since been forgotten by most. The antarkanist dynasties of the past century purged the empire of much knowledge. The person that is able to return this powerful artifact to the imperial court would rise in fame, power, and influence greatly."

"Who must I speak to at the imperial treasury to gain access to this gem?"

Demodoi shook his head. "It is not so simple. The emperor's treasury is not a lending library and many officials still belong to the antarkanist faction. One cannot simply ask to study the emperor's artifacts. Only the most trusted and powerful of *maholoi* are allowed to even know the contents of the vaults."

Manoueka furrowed his brow at Demodoi's riddles. "How can this help me if I cannot gain access to the gem?"

Another wry smile formed on Demodoi's lips. "Barashel is only one of seven stones of power, the Shards of Kurovilos, a set of lost artifacts the Cokan emperors once used to maintain control of their far-flung realm. Barashel has six brothers. You must find another."

Manoueka felt as if the old man were toying with him. "How am I to find one of these other stones if they are lost?"

"I will grant you a gift that might help you on your way." He crossed the room to a table holding a book. He offered it to Manoueka. "This book is *An Account of the Wonders of the Caliph.* It should prove of great worth to you. This is the only copy extant; all others have been destroyed. It tells that Korefael, another of the the shards, was in the Mad Caliph's treasury."

Manoueka opened the book, glancing over its pages, "I have heard of the Mad Caliph. The stories tell that he destroyed all magic artifacts in the Merouin Caliphate."

Demodoi chuckled at Manoueka's understanding of the history. The frail sound disturbed Manoueka. "As always, the history is more complex than the story," Demodoi said. "The Mad Caliph did not destroy all artifacts. In fact, he did not even destroy all of his own. Some magic is too powerful to be overcome by non-magical means. As a fanatical adherent of antarkanism, the caliph did not have the means to destroy everything in his possession. Instead, he hid them."

"This book describes these artifacts?"

"Yes, but it does not tell where to find them. For that, you will have to do your own research. Many explorers have sought the location of Korefael but have not succeeded. The Tulkeen priests in Iskander have books from the reign of the Mad Caliph. Seek Dithaan among them. He knows of books that might lead you to the final resting place of Korefael."

Manoueka turned the book over in his hands. "Why are you offering me this? What do you gain from it?"

Demodoi examined Manoueka, his eyes scanning him, as if he were searching the mage's soul. "It would harm nothing to tell you of my plans, I suppose. I intend to use you as bait."

Manoueka's jaw dropped in shock. "As bait?"

Demodoi chuckled again in his disturbing manner. "Have no fear. You will be in no danger. I merely ask that you spread the word among your circles that you have a book describing the Korefael. I seek a man, Goron by name. He is an antarkanist determined to keep powerful artifacts such as Korefael hidden. The mere suggestion that someone might find a Shard of Kurovilos will draw him out of hiding. He travels alone. When he arrives in Synnakon to investigate your activity, you will capture him and bring him to me. When that deed is accomplished, I will lend you enough gold to finance an expedition to unearth Korefael from its hiding place."

Manoueka considered the offer. He had guards and magic to protect his property and person. Capturing one man should not be too difficult. "It is agreed. I will bring this man to you."

• • •

Once Manoueka left, Demodoi called his retainer Témopirz out of the alcove hidden in the corner of the salon. "The trap is set and baited," the old man said. He had sought Goron many times before, but the warrior had always eluded him, was always one step ahead.

"You are certain Goron will come?" asked Témopirz.

"He comes whenever one of the Shards of Kurovilos is threatened to be exposed," replied Demodoi. "This time will differ none from the others." He did not know why the stone was so important to Goron, but he knew that it was important enough to his prey that he would come out of hiding if the artifact were threatened.

"What of Morgenoi? You agreed to discover Korefael for them. Now you give him to this *molo*?" Témopirz used the old Ushidian word for wizard.

"The Morgenoi have allied themselves with us in this matter," replied Demodoi. "They will gain possession of the gem once Manoueka finds it." In fact, Demodoi had little use for magic artifacts. He had sought them out repeatedly in the past, but had found none that could remove his curse. Goron had the secret Demodoi was looking for, though he would not surrender it easily.

Turning back to Témopirz, he looked him in the eye. "Worry yourself not about the Morgenoi or the stone. We need Goron. This wizard believes he can capture Goron. I give him no credence, but perhaps he can. I wish to leave nothing to chance. If Manoueka fails to capture our prey, it will fall to you to bring him to me. I do not want him harmed, do you understand?"

A cloud crossed Témopirz's face. "I understand."

"If you need help, contact the Morgenoi," Demodoi said. "They have promised aid as part of our agreement. Ask for some men to watch some of the more likely places Goron will go when he arrives in Synnakon." The old man paused, pondering the various aspects of his plans. "Keep an eye on Manoueka as well," he said. "Make sure he stays motivated and focused. Too often, these wizards get distracted with some esoteric philosophy and drift off."

Being dismissed with a wave of Demodoi's hand, Témopirz left, heading into the cool night air of Synnakon.

Chapter 2

A few hours after leaving the inn in Kétekon, Goron once again checked the load on his wagon. The crate containing the silk cloth seemed untouched. It would be a shame to have brought it all the way from the province of Melissa only to have it stolen so near the end of his journey. He would have to ask Polous when he reached his destination why the dressmaker had not hired a regular caravan to transport the goods to Synnakon. Goron took the reins of his horse and checked the buckles on the traces of his harness.

Bason neighed in protest as he led the wagon away. Goron felt a pang of guilt at harnessing the horse to draw a wagon like a pack animal. After all, the steed had been trained in the arts of war and relished getting into a fight. Well, he was getting a little too old to be fighting any pitched battles these days anyway.

Traveling through the grassy hills east toward Synnakon, he smelled late-summer aromas of scrub oak and dry grass wafting through the air. He pondered the changes that had gone on over the past century: the loss of large provinces to barbarian and antarkanist armies; the decline in learning, especially of the arcane arts; the concentration of wealth in the hands of a few powerful families; and the hardening of the political stalemate. It would all lead to the end of the empire in time. Empires rose and fell. This one had risen on the ruins of the ancient Cokan Empire. How much longer Synnakon's decline would take remained to be seen.

Coming down out of the sun-drenched hills heading east, Goron spotted Synnakon miles in the distance before him. The midday sun glinted off the four gilt domes of the Eterodeihon, the largest church in the world and dedicated to the four gods. The towers of the Krolos Maholon, the mage district, pierced the skyline like needles next to the ancient acropolis of the Merkebios.

The Merkebios sat on a hill overlooking the Meginnikon River. It had been a provincial town when the emperor Cinnakariar I chose it for the site of his new imperial capital over five hundred years earlier. The emperor had fortified the hill and built a city at its base. It was in the lower city that one found the huge market plaza of the Megizikon, flanked by both the Eterodeihon and the Imperial Palace.

The fertile floodplain of the Meginnikon provided the city with its favorite foods. One found melons, cucumbers, and eggplant in the markets of the Megizikon and in the fruit and vegetable stands that dotted the neighborhoods throughout the city. The orchards of the floodplain provided dates, fruit, and nuts. Honey flowed from the apiaries throughout the region. But it was bread from grain grown in the dry, grassy hills around the city and nearby provinces that sustained the city and the empire.

Approaching the city, its massive walls rose up like the Manzakar mountain range, shoved up from below the earth outside Qamishli far to the south. The wall's bottom row of stones stood as high as houses. Past emperors encouraged legends claiming the walls had been built by giants before the history of man. Goron smiled to himself at the naiveté of those who believed such stories, knowing that Cinnakariar had built the walls when he founded the city. The triple set of walls and related defenses had repelled invaders since, including large barbarian and Ushidian armies in the time of the emperors Karokion and Jusicar as well as the occasional rebellious general attempting to take the imperial throne for himself.

From the base of the wall, Goron looked to the tops of the two towers flanking the main gates. He took careful notice of the sentries at the top of the gate-works, counting about a half-dozen on either side, each carrying a crossbow as well as javelins and armored lightly in leather. Studying the crowds waiting to enter the city, they could spot an undesirable person and signal the inspectors at the gate below to either refuse entry or even arrest him. A small group of personae non grata waited to the side of the gates, hoping for a change in their status and be allowed entry.

After a long wait in the queue, Goron reached the gate and produced his papers for the bored but attentive customs guards. One guard reviewed the cargo manifest, inspecting his crate of silks while another inspected him, examining his weapon permits. As hard as they tried, the guards could not find any flaws in the paperwork. Goron was as thorough as an imperial customs guard when it came to knowing which papers to carry for which items and activities. They let him pass and he entered the city.

It had been years since he had come to Synnakon. He remembered the scents and sounds of the city. The sound of the merchants calling out to potential buyers crowded out the silence of the road. The scent of spices sold in the neighborhood markets reminded him of earlier visits, the sight of brightly colored silks in the bazaars reminding him of the women he had known. The smell of perfumes reminded him of Aisarra, a woman he had lived with here. It was long ago, before he had left her to go off to war.

He forced the reminiscing from his mind. This time, the trip was for business, not pleasure.

He made his way through the crowded bazaars that had grown up a short distance inside the gate. Savvy shoppers avoided the unscrupulous peddlers and hawkers preying on unsuspecting visitors. Goron knew better than to deal with these dubious merchants and pressed past them, sometimes shoving the more aggressive ones out of his way. City dwellers knew prices dropped farther away from the main gates. He also kept an eye out for the light-fingered gutter snipes who would take his purse as quick as look at him.

Past the initial markets, crowds thinned and he relaxed a little and surveyed the city. It hadn't changed much since his last visit, but many of the houses looked run down. The aristocracy had traditionally kept their gardened estates on the outskirts of the city nearer the southwest walls. It appeared that many were now empty and more than a few had been parceled out into smaller apartments and rented to those of meaner income. Water conduits that once flowed to the area were probably broken. Goron saw misfortunates lugging buckets of water from wells on the grounds. Sheep or goats grazed on the grand lawns of some estates.

Toward the center of the city, the houses clustered closer together on the slopes of the low central hill. Many small but respectable merchants had established their shops along the broad thoroughfare coming down the hill toward the Megizikon to the northeast. The more well-to-do residents preferred to deal with the more reputable, longer established shops that faced the great market.

Goron led Bason down one of the narrower streets radiating out from the great square toward the Seniktikon, searching for Polous's workshop. Poorer merchants and craftsmen found less expensive real estate down these alleyways. Most had been here for generations and locals knew which ones provided quality goods and which did not. Some, like Polous, catered to a small, but exacting clientele. He provided gowns and robes of the finest quality to the nobility of the empire.

Goron's wagon fit on the street with enough room for one person to walk by. Many of the houses were in a poor state of repair. Few of them had been re-stuccoed recently, large empty patches revealing the underlying brick. The neighborhood seemed to have fallen on hard times. More than one unsavory character hung in a doorway along the way. He wondered which families controlled the area and which *esérgon* would get news of a visitor to the neighborhood.

The pseudo-official position of *esérgon* had a long, though less than savory history in the politics of Synnakon. Acting often as a ward boss and sometimes as a crime lord, the *esérgon* handed out favors to their own clients in return for services. The politicians in the city and in the imperial court relied on them to deliver support in crucial moments.

Goron found Polous's shop a couple blocks down the narrow street. The door stood open, so Goron left Bason and the wagon on the street outside and entered the shop. Inside looked very much the same as the last time he had visited some years ago. Half-finished garments hung on mannequins; swaths of material hung from racks, draping nearly to the ground; various tailoring tools lay spread out on workbenches: shears, measuring tape, pins, chalk.

The one difference from his last visit was the young girl in the corner. Intent on her work, she had not noticed him enter. She did not look up from embroidering a design into a large measure of fabric. Goron took a minute to study her. She couldn't have been more than ten years old but in a few years she would be a beauty. She had the classic Doran features: white skin, black curly hair and green eyes. If boys had not noticed her yet, they would soon.

"Is Polous in?" Goron's rumbling voice caused the girl to jump a foot and drop the embroidery hoop she held. She froze like a stone in water, gaping at him. Then, without a word, she rushed through the cloth-covered door to the back of the shop.

After a moment, an older-looking man appeared at the door, balding on top and pulling at a thin, white wisp of a beard, as if he had pulled the hair from the top of his head through his chin. Seeing Goron, his face brightened. Greeting Goron with a great smile, he kissed the visitor on each cheek. "Ah, you've arrived! It is so good to see you. I see you've met Kora. Please come in and sit." Polous rushed around, picking up bolts of cloth and uncovering chairs and a table. "Wait, you'll want to bring your wagon in. Kora, take the key and unlock the courtyard gate."

Heading back to the street, they led the wagon through the gate next to the shop and into the courtyard Polous shared with his neighbors. Before entering the courtyard, Goron noticed a shadow in the window opposite. When he turned to look, the shadow disappeared. Was Polous being watched? If so, by whom and why?

Polous waited in the courtyard. "You can keep your horse here for a little while." Polous pointed out a small shed with a feed trough. Goron brought Bason to the stable, his nose turning at the smell of stale straw and dung. "I know I need to clean out my stable," the old man said. "But I am too old for manual labor and too poor to hire stable hands."

Together, they unloaded crates of cloth from the wagon while Kora fed and watered the horse. "Tell me, Polous," Goron said. "Why did you have me bring this small amount of cloth all the way from Melissa? Why not purchase locally or have it shipped on a caravan?"

The old man waved away his question. "I can't buy fine silk locally because the Melissinos family controls the cloth trade and keeps the finest material for themselves. They wouldn't even agree to transport it for me. I serve mainly smaller, less powerful families, those allied with the antarkanist Morion or Goborous families.

"Antarkanism is out of favor in the imperial court." Polous spoke as if Goron knew nothing of the pro- and anti-magic controversies that had raged for decades in Synnakon. "Being out of power, they have fewer advantages and wearing a dress made from some of the finest Melissa cloth to the next imperial ball would be a social coup for a certain young woman. I may be poor, but I am the best dressmaker in the city and therefore in the empire and my clients recognize that." Polous puffed up with pride at his own reputation and skill.

"You may be the best, but you are not the most modest. If you weren't so stubborn, you might be the richest dressmaker in the empire as well." Goron set the crate down in Polous's storeroom.

Scowling, Polous brought out a crowbar and pried the crate open. He unwrapped the bolt of cloth and inspected the *zari* brocade. His scowl turned to a smile. "Oh, this is beautiful!" Taking a closer look, he examined the cloth. "I don't see a single break in the gold threads. The weave of the silk is so tight you can barely see the weft."

"I'm glad it's what you wanted," said Goron, bending over the cloth, trying to see what Polous described. "I only had vague descriptions in your letter, but the weavers seemed to understand exactly what you desired."

"Yes, this will make a beautiful dress." Polous carried the bolt of silk into his workshop. "I won't be paid nearly what it's worth, but it will cover the cost of the cloth and some of my and Kora's time."

Goron followed close behind with more cloth. "You would make more money if you gained the favor of the more powerful families. Surely you haven't burnt all your bridges with them, have you?"

"The arkanist faction is too entrenched, too dependent on the *maholoi.* I try to keep a low profile. I don't get involved in politics but I am not in the favor of the powerful families. I'm comfortable enough with my current business."

Goron looked around at the insides of the house. The walls needed a good coat of paint, the rugs were threadbare and the floors had shallow worn paths where the wood had been trod for decades. "Yes, you are very comfortable."

"Enough of this, you've had a long journey. Come inside and meet Kora properly. She'll prepare some tea and a hot meal, then you'll see how comfortable I really am."

• • •

Though the *bouloshke*, a simple dish of onion and eggplant, was meager fare, the spicy smell of roasting vegetables roused Goron's appetite. The tea was strong and fresh. Whatever Polous's failures in home maintenance, Kora made up for it with her cooking.

"Where did a girl so young learn to cook so well?" Goron asked.

Polous passed a plate of olives to Goron, who popped a couple in his mouth. "I'll admit, I taught her most of it, though she has a natural talent for flavor and aroma. I do enjoy good food. A little direction here and there and she learned how to cook exactly the way I like."

Kora silently laid out the plates of *bouloshke* in front of the men.

"She's my granddaughter, in case you were wondering," said Polous. "Her parents, Pitrous and Marja, were beaten to death by *makaphoi*." He spat the name of the Nankisos' paramilitary enforcers.

"They got caught up in the antarkanist riots when she was only five years old. Kora has lived with me ever since." Polous stared into his tea as if the tea leaves would tell him that his children would be coming back soon. He received no such message.

"Enough of the past, though," he said. "Eat some *bouloshke*. Kora picked out the freshest eggplants and onion this morning in the market. The herbs are fresh from the garden. I'm sorry we don't have any lamb, we ate the last of what we had two nights ago." The girl brought two plates of steaming vegetable stew on a bed of bulgur. The smell made Goron's mouth water. The two men dug into their dishes with gusto as Kora brought a smaller plate for herself.

After eating, Polous brought out a bottle of wine and poured a cup for each of them and a small, watered-down cup for Kora. "In years past, I would have been able to offer Paphlagonian, but the years have not been good to me and I can only afford local wines of lesser quality.

"I have to admit I had other motives for having you bring the silk. I had been trying to think of some way to get a message to you without explicitly stating my reasons. You see, someone has been watching me these past few years. At first, I thought it had to do with Pitrous and Marja, but it started long after they had died. I don't know what they want, but I thought it best not to put anything in writing." He took a sip of wine, savoring it before continuing.

"When I got the commission for this gown, I found my cover. I knew you were in Melissa, where one finds the best silk-makers in the empire. I needed to get you here and I needed some of the finest silk in the land. A fine coincidence, no?" Polous glowed with pride at his cleverness.

"In any case, I have heard news of the Gemstone Man."

At that, Goron sat up and his eyes narrowed as he focused on Polous's words. "About two months ago," said the dressmaker. "A priestess of Deihosos came to me. She said she knew you but not how to find you. She said she had news for you and that I was the only person she knew she could trust with the information. I don't know how she found out that I knew you or that I could be trusted. But she was right on both counts. She told me that you were looking for news of the Gemstone Man and she had information you could use."

"Did she tell you what she knew about it?"

"No, she only said that you would want to see her about it. She left her name."

"I think I know who she is."

Chapter 3

"Owwww!"

It wasn't the pain of the old nun tugging on the boy's ear that hurt so much as the humiliation of it. She had admonished him in front of his friends, then when he began to argue in his own defense, the old woman grabbed his ear, rendering him helpless to resist.

The crone dragged Iko into the main chapel. It was standard for the convent to put its unruly children in the chapel to wait until the Materssa Mérka of the convent had time to deal with the child and mete out an appropriate punishment. Unfortunately for the boy, the materssa was also his grandmother, or *amma*, and she was determined to make sure he kept in line.

"Ikomerakos, you are far too old to be playing such games with the girls." The old nun obviously blamed him for what happened, but the girls had suggested the game. Really, it wasn't his fault. Being the only boy in a convent made Iko the sole target of the girls' fun. Unfortunately, it seemed he was the only one to be blamed for their misadventures.

The old woman wagged her finger at the boy. "You stand here and meditate on what you have done. Your grandmother will be here shortly."

Without pews in the chapel, he was unable to sit. Instead, he inspected the statues and paintings reminding worshippers of the stories of the gods and saints. The lack of seating was in keeping with the attitude among many worshippers of Deihosos that sitting during service was decadent. Holy Maranna, to whom the convent was dedicated, was a follower of Deihosos and the beneficiaries of her generosity were all poor women. The order taught that it was immoral to sit during services when so many poor women and children could not afford to endow a pew to sit in at church. All Iko wanted right now was to sit down.

The sisters had formed their order in honor of Maranna, a holy woman who sheltered and fed women made homeless by the scorched earth campaigns of the imperial armies during the reign of Gurgulla over seven hundred years earlier. Now the sisters dedicated their lives to helping homeless and refugee women, widows, and otherwise destitute women. The convent provided a roof and bed and the sisters fed, clothed, and cared for the women and their children and helped ease their way back into society when necessary. Girls were allowed into the convent at any age, but boys were only allowed to live with their mothers until their tenth birthday, which was rapidly approaching for Iko.

That he lived in a convent with so many women and girls was an accident of his age and circumstances. Iko's grandmother, Aisarra, had given birth to his mother Kessia out of wedlock, shaming the powerful Morion family. Aisarra came to the convent with her daughter and became a sister of St. Maranna, eventually rising to the position of Materssa. Upon reaching maturity, Kessia had left to marry a rich merchant, giving birth to Iko in the province of Therakon. She returned to the convent after her husband had died.

His *amma* intimidated Iko, though he loved her very much. She was very strict, always telling him that he was of noble descent and that he should learn to act appropriately. He knew that his *amma* would disapprove of his most recent escapade. His behavior was "ignoble", she would say.

Aisarra Morion was descended from the Emperor Ikomerakos Morion, the founder of the antarkanist Morion dynasty. The Emperor Kosyndeos had overthrown the Morions twenty-three ago to begin a new dynasty. The coup was brutal, and most of the Morion family had been decimated in the purges when Kosyndeos consolidated his power. Only the few who pledged their allegiance to the new emperor or those who had left mainstream society, such as Aisarra, were allowed to live. Now, the family maintained its meager living and had few allies, with little chance of reclaiming the imperial throne.

The thought of being descended from an emperor excited Iko. He often daydreamed about wearing a crown or riding at the head of a procession. His mother and his *amma* made it clear he should keep quiet about his heritage. They were afraid that if the arkanist faction knew of a male descendant of the Morion line, they would seek him out and murder him. Consequently, he was not allowed to use his family name.

He had never seen the emperor, of course. He had never gone more than five miles from the convent, let alone to Synnakon. He had lived at the convent for most of his life. He hardly remembered his infancy in Therakon. A plague had ravaged the province, taking his father shortly after he was born and leaving Iko no memory of him. His uncle had taken him and his mother in, but his aunt was cruel so they left Therakon to come back to the chapel where his mother was raised. His mother was vague on the specific reasons, but what he had pieced together from the other women in the convent was that his uncle was a lustful man who desired his mother. His aunt became jealous of her husband's attention and forced Kessia out of the household.

Iko wandered about the chapel, inspecting the simple, hand-carved statues of Holy Maranna, Deihosos, and the other gods. The nuns used the statues to instruct the children in the religion of the four gods. Most children remembered the gods from a nursery rhyme:

Deihosos from the earth did rise
Motios in fire found law
Bodeihos in the water became wise
Momados in the sky found awe.

A large, ornate carving of Deihosos in his aspect of sacrifice hung on the main wall. According to the story, Deihosos was struck down by soldiers on midwinter's day and left lying in a fallow field to die, his blood pouring out from his wound into the frozen ground. A deep snow fell that night and covered him so that his body was not found until the thaw. The following spring, plants grew around where his body lay, fertilized by his lifeblood. Later he rose from the dead, revived by the warm spring sun as if he had only been sleeping.

The bas-relief above the altar depicted Deihosos being struck down by the soldiers. Rubies set into the carving augmented the carved flowing blood. Iko often wondered whether the rubies were real. It seemed out of place in a chapel of a saint dedicated to the destitute, especially one that disdained the use of pews. Perhaps they were colored glass?

In order to find out, he would have to get closer. But the sculpture hung on the wall high and out of reach. He scanned the room for a way to get up there. Standing on a chair might do it, but he could not find a chair. Also, there were no altars to stand on. Unlike in the churches of Motios or Momados, the followers of Deihosos did not allow altars. Worshippers did not sacrifice to Deihosos, Deihosos was the sacrifice.

With no chairs or altars, the only things to stand on to get Iko high enough to see the rubies were the pedestals that the statues stood on. The statues seemed rather heavy, carved from solid wood. Most were as large as he was, though the smaller ones seemed light enough to move. The pedestals stood fairly low, but one of them might be enough for him to at least get a hand on the carving on the wall. He could probably climb from there.

He took a look at a statue of Momados, the smallest statue on its pedestal. He grabbed the god under its arms and lifted. It was heavy, but he picked it up and set it on the ground with no problem. He tried to pick up the pedestal, but it was much heavier than the statue. Getting behind it and pushing, he slid it with some difficulty but was able to move it the ten feet or so to get it in place.

Once his platform was in place, he climbed up on it. He still could not get a good look at the rubies set in the blood represented in the carving, but was able to get a handhold on the figure. The carving had enough folds and furrows to grab onto and be able to pull himself up closer to the rubies. He had plenty of experience climbing apple trees in the convent's orchard or the oaks that grew in the countryside around.

He succeeded in pulling himself up high enough to get a foot in a fold in Deihosos's robes. Once in place, he stretched out to get a close look at the rubies. They had been cut in an oval, multifaceted and a deep red, but now that he had climbed up there, how could he tell if they were glass or ruby? If he could shine light through it, maybe he could tell. He would have to get one out though.

"Ikomerakos! What are you doing up there? Get down here at once!" The voice of his *amma* told him he was in deep trouble.

Chapter 4

Goron gave Bason free reign to run once they escaped the city walls. The horse did not like the cramped quarters of cities but loved the openness of the countryside. After the long journey pulling the wagon from Erminikon, Goron thought it only fair to give the animal a little playtime. When Bason ran, he ran hard. But he was well aware of his rider and knew his task was to carry him. He did this well, so even at a flat out gallop, Goron's ride was smooth.

They headed south from Synnakon for the Convent of the Sisters of Holy Maranna. It had been many years since Goron had seen Aisarra and even longer since she had entered the convent. The news that she had joined the order surprised him, but he should have foreseen that she would become the *Materssa Mérka* of the convent. She had always been headstrong and smart. And beautiful. The first two attributes were necessary to maintain an independent community of women in the patriarchal Doran society. The third gave her an advantage when dealing with society outside the convent.

The chapel of the convent appeared in the distance, visible at a greater distance than any other buildings. Being the most important building in a community of religious women, it was naturally the largest. Unlike most of the churches in Synnakon or provincial towns, it was built of plain brick, unadorned with the marble facing so common in other churches.

Next to the chapel stood a long, low building two stories tall, also of brick. From the outside it looked quite plain but he knew that plain outside walls often masked a more detailed and ornate interior. From the size and central location, he judged this to be the main living quarters of the sisters.

Other buildings surrounded these two main buildings. Some appeared to be stables and barns, others storehouses. Women walked back and forth among them.

Approaching the convent, Goron instinctively began assessing its defenses. The thin, low stone walls surrounding the convent provided little refuge against potential attackers. This close to Synnakon, the sisters would have little fear of attackers, of course. But if an Ushidian *perzal'* from the north decided to rally his followers and pillage the countryside, the convent would have nothing to protect itself.

The road led through an arched gate. Above the gate was carved the symbol of the order, a soup pot and ladle to feed the refugees that entered. At the foot of the gate a grey-haired and wrinkled old lady sat in the shade of an olive tree, cutting slices from a piece of fruit. She wore a white muslin shawl with a red border over her stooped shoulders.

Seeing Goron approach, the woman set down her fruit, but not the knife, and croaked out a warning,

"Stop! No man is allowed into the convent except on invitation. Whom do you have business with?"

"Your *Materssa*, Aisarra summoned me. Please send word that Goron has arrived to see her."

She gave him a scowl, looking him up and down as if to assess whether he was worthy to have been summoned by her *Materssa.* Apparently judging that he met her standards, she stepped through the gate, moving quickly for one as stooped as she was, and pulled twice on a rope, setting a bell to ring.

Shortly, two girls arrived. One girl took Bason toward the stables. The other girl led him into the low brick building. Watching her, he wondered what had brought a girl so young to a convent to be cloistered away from society. As if she felt his eyes on her, the girl stopped in front of a door and turned to face him. "Please wait here. The Materssa will be with you shortly." With that, she entered the door and closed it behind her.

Goron heard voices beyond the door. The girl who had led him here was speaking with an older woman. If he were more curious, he could probably have made out the words simply by putting his ear to the door. Instead, he inspected the painted walls of the corridor, depicting various saints and legends of Holy Maranna.

He had almost not come. He had left Aisarra years ago, heading off to war. He had wanted her to come with him, but she refused.

He had not seen her in years and now he was uncertain he wanted to see her again. Was she angry with him? She had not seen him in years and now she summoned him to her convent.

After a few minutes, the girl opened the door and beckoned to him. "You are requested to enter now."

• • •

"Welcome, Goron," Aisarra said. "It has been a very long time." She stood in the middle of the room to welcome him. Her once jet black hair had gone white and her skin, though still fair, was creased with the worries and cares she had born over the decades of her life. She maintained a noble bearing, as befitted her heritage as a daughter of the previous imperial family. Seeing her again after so many years rekindled in Goron memories of a happier time together.

"You are still as beautiful as your name implies."

She laughed at his compliment. "And you are still the silver-tongued fox that you always were. But I am older and wiser now and less susceptible to the charms of smooth-spoken men, least of all you. I do appreciate the compliment, however untrue."

"I have no hidden agenda. It was you who invited me. Your invitation surprised me," Goron said, glancing around the surprisingly small room. The furnishings were simple, a small wooden desk with some papers on it and a single candle to light it when it got dark. An icon of the Holy Maranna hung on the wall above the desk. Light came through the windows high on the wall but it was warm enough outside that there was no concern for weather entering. The only item that did not fit the furnishings of a simple religous woman was the small table with a carafe of wine and two glasses. "Are you no longer angry with me?" he asked.

Aisarra sighed. "I have long since forsaken any anger toward you or any others from my youth. The mirror of time reflects more of the good than the bad. Do you see me now? I'm an old woman and the worries of youth are long forgotten. The only anger I might have is for Holy Dantelos, the patron of fate, who has decreed that I wither while you stay as youthful as the day I first met you." She poured wine into the two glasses and offered one to him.

"Do not envy my fate," Goron said, taking the wine from her with a growl. "It is not as pleasant as you might think. But you did not call me here to indulge in self-pity and I did not come to relive the past. Polous told me you had information regarding the Gemstone Man. He said that someone had found a book but that you would not tell him more."

"Ah, to the point; you never were one to reminisce. Yes, I had two purposes behind my message. I'm sorry I could not confide in Polous. I wasn't sure where he stood after so many years. In fact, I almost didn't recognize him. I'm sure he didn't recognize me and I preferred to keep it that way."

"You do him a disservice. He is as loyal to me and my secret as he always was. So much so that he is one of the few I trust with my whereabouts."

"Nevertheless, I couldn't tell him anything because I needed you to come to the convent. As I said, I have two reasons for you to come. For my purposes, the information you seek is secondary." Aisarra paused, hesitating to tell him more. "The first involves a young boy. I wasn't sure you would come to see him without the book as bait."

"So you tricked me? There is no book? It has been a long journey from Erminikon." Goron's face reddened as his anger rose.

"Calm down. It was no trick," she said, her hands raised, palms facing him. "There is a mage in Synnakon that has found a book that will interest you greatly. I will tell you all you need to know about it, but I need a promise from you in return."

"Involving a boy?"

"Yes. This convent is dedicated to serving women. Children are also welcome when brought here by their mothers. There is a woman, made homeless by war and plague like the others who come here. She brought her infant child with her refugees from Therakon. Perhaps you remember the plague that devastated the cities of that province ten years ago?"

"Yes, but I do not see why you would have brought me here because of it."

"I'm getting to that." A slight tremble entered Aisarra's voice. She took a moment to recompose herself. "You see, the woman is my daughter, our daughter."

Goron's eyes went wide at discovering that he had a daughter. "But I never knew. You did not tell me."

"I'm sorry you have never met her. Her name is Kessia. She is a beautiful woman with much inner strength. She looks very much like you." Aisarra looked at him, her eyes moistened. "I entered this convent because you left us to fight against the Merouin, then the Ushidians. I waited for you to come back after the siege of Tulares, but you decided to stay in the emperor's service to fight in the Ushidian campaigns."

Goron offered her a cloth to dry her eyes. "Had I known, I would have returned," he said, avoiding her gaze. "After I left, I did not hear from you. I thought you were angry with me for leaving."

"I sent letters but received no reply. It was only later that I realized that my father intercepted the letters meant for you. I despaired of ever seeing you again. Kessia grew up in this convent until she was of an appropriate age to marry. She married into a minor merchant family from Therakon where she bore a son. A year later, her new husband and his parents all died in the plague. She lived with her husband's brother for a few years until Kosyndeos started purging the court of the Morion family. Kessia's sister in law suspected her; some say she was jealous. Her husband's family threw her out and she had no place to go, so she returned here."

Goron looked at the ground as Aisarra told the story. To find out decades afterwards that he had a daughter was a surprise, though it was not the first daughter he had. What was she like? Was she similar to the other daughters he had in his life or was she more like Aisarra? "I would like to meet Kessia," he told Aisarra.

"I'm sorry, you have come too late. She has taken the vow of *Seherain*. She can have no visitors other than resident sisters of the convent. She has been waiting for years to take these vows, but she has had a child to take care of. That child is now ten years old. When boys reach the age of ten, we try to find homes for them. Many are sent to schools in the capital, but those schools are nothing more than prisons. Most often, children are taught nothing other than how to dye cloth or produce paper or other lowly trades no others would willingly do. I cannot consign my grandson to such a fate." Aisarra paused and took a deep breath. "This is why I have asked you to come. I want you to take him and teach him some of your skills."

Goron's eyes widened and he stammered, "I... I cannot... Surely there is no place for a boy.... I am surprised you would ask me to raise him. Certainly my skills are inappropriate for a child his age. Would you have him be a soldier and a rogue, never to settle in one spot for years at a time? You might as well have him join the army."

"Your life is certainly not the life I would wish for my grandchild. It was to avoid that life that I did not follow you to Tulares. You said your actions were not always yours to decide. I didn't understand it at the time, but I did understand that you left for long periods and I wanted to be with you when you were gone." Aisarra sighed, a faraway look appearing in her eye. After a moment, she brought herself back to the present. "But I did not want to be bound to the road, a traveler for the rest of my life. In hindsight, I cannot say whether it was the right decision but the decision was made. Now I must give my grandson to you to follow the path I forsook so many years ago."

Goron set down his wine and shook his head. "Aisarra, I have little to teach him. I am a fighter and a seeker. As you said, my actions are not always mine to decide. I have not had a trade since long before I met you."

"Yet you remember everything that has passed before your eyes, even if you don't wish to speak of it. Surely you remember something besides fighting, enough to pass something on to your grandson."

"Yes, I remember much. I can teach him something, but the learning is old and he must find out himself how to make it useful."

"Good. Then we are agreed. You will take the boy and teach him. It is up to you to decide what to teach. I'm sure he will have much to say about what he wants to learn, though."

Goron felt he had no honorable choice but to reluctantly concede. "I will agree to take the boy." He immediately regretted conceding to Aisarra, but he had always had difficulty telling her no. What was he to do with a young boy?

He was still pondering his new dilemma when Aisarra interrupted his thoughts. "I suppose you are wondering about the second reason I asked you here." He was not. His decision to take his grandson under his protection had driven all other thoughts from his head.

Aisarra paused as if deciding where to start. "Have you heard of the *maholos* by the name of Manoueka?" She glanced at Goron, who shook his head.

"He is a young and ambitious mage who recently gained a seat on the Nankisos Maholon," she said. "Like many of his type, he is hungry for power, but has little regard for the risks and dangers inherent in that power." Aisarra turned to face Goron, who listened idly while he inspected a painted icon of Holy Maranna that sat on a rough-hewn table near the door.

"Rumor has it that he has found a book in a library in Iskander that contains information about the Seven Shards of Kurovilos."

Goron's head whipped around. "Are you sure?" he asked quickly. If it were true, it would be an important find. "Most of the books regarding the Seven Stones were burned during the reigns of Ulosian and Deihodosos four to five hundred years ago. Those that remained were destroyed by the Amr aw-Wanaj when he conquered Iskander about two hundred years ago. Scholars and mages have been searching for copies ever since. It would be remarkable for someone to have found one now."

"Is that why you have been spending so many years in Erminikon? It is said that many tomes of magical learning still exist there."

"I can assure you there are no books that even mention the Shards of Kurovilos in the libraries of Erminikon." He omitted the fact that he had taken the books from the libraries himself and altered or destroyed them to conceal the information they contained.

"Very well. It is said that Manoueka has a book. It contains information that is important to you." Aisarra drew herself up, the tone in her voice signaling that the discussion was at an end. "Now, would you like to meet Ikomerakos?"

• • •

Aisarra led Goron down the hall to the chapel. Inside stood a young boy of not more than ten years old. Much like Goron, he had straight black hair and light brown skin. However, he also had the blue eyes of the Morion clan, similar to Aisarra. There was no doubt the boy was descended from the two older people. He wore a finely woven wool tunic not quite long enough to cover his knees, as was the fashion among children. The borders at the collar and cuffs were simple, as befit a resident of the convent.

Aisarra bent down and gave the boy a kiss on his forehead. "Ikomerakos, this is the man I told you about. He is your grandfather; he will take care of you from now on. He has agreed to teach you a trade that will allow you to maintain a living and perhaps marry. What trade he will teach will be up to you and him." Aisarra shot a glance at Goron, who looked grim.

A look of fear passed across the boy's face, as if he were about to cry. Goron felt the boy's apprehension. He was being sent away with a stranger and might not see his grandmother again. Iko seemed to have a strength he would not have expected in a boy so young. In that, he took after his grandmother. "But Amma, I don't want to leave," Iko complained. "I promise I won't get in trouble again. I'll be good."

"We have discussed this, Iko," Aisarra said, straightening his hair. "This is a women's convent and you must learn to become a man. Goron will teach you how."

With that, the boy's face took on a look of steely determination. "All right, I'll go with him. But can I come back to visit you and mama?" His steely determination softened as he pleaded for a compromise.

"Yes, you can come back at the Feast of Holy Maranna, but your mother has taken the vows, so you might not be able to speak with her."

"I understand," he said as his eyes moistened, tears threatening to replace the determination in his face.

The older girl that had led Goron to Aisarra's study entered the room with a satchel. It did not seem heavy, so could not have been very full. Taking it from the girl, Iko looked up to her. "Goodbye, Rosetta. Amma says I must go away. I'll miss you and the other girls. Please say goodbye to them."

The girl, who had the same steely determination on her face as Iko, began to cry.

"Don't be sad, Rosetta, Amma says I can come back at the Feast of Holy Maranna, so we'll see each other again." Then the dam broke and Iko began to sob as well. He reached up to the girl and hugged her. Aisarra eyes also moistened, swept up in the emotion of the moment. Goron looked at his feet as Aisarra threw her arms around the boy and girl.

After a moment, Aisarra withdrew from the embrace and dried her eyes on a silk cloth. "Come now, Ikomerakos. Goron is waiting and you have a long journey ahead of you." She turned to Goron, drawing a deep breath to compose herself. "You probably don't have a horse for him, but he is an accomplished rider already. I can loan you a pony to get you to the next town."

"We will be going back to Synnakon. I must attend to the business that we discussed. The journey is not far; we should arrive there by mid-afternoon. Thank you for the pony. I will deliver it to your chapter house in the city when we arrive. I promise I will take good care of Iko. Come," he told the boy. "It's time to leave."

Chapter 5

Annissa set up the table with the broken leg in the afternoon sun of the east side of the square that served as home to the morning market. She discovered the broken table she usually set up thrown in a corner with some other rubbish. She carried it to her favorite spot and found a crate to prop up the broken leg. It wouldn't hold a load of vegetables, but it would be sufficient to lay down the cards she used as foci for telling fortunes.

Annissa sold her services as an unlicensed *alutsa*, mostly telling fortunes or performing minor hexes. She kept to the markets in the poorer parts of town, avoiding the richer markets and the greater risk of garnering the attention of the *makaphoi*, the enforcers of the Nankisos Maholon.

The morning air rose cool from the river, but the sun had already struck the upper walls of the surrounding houses. Soon, it would burn off the remaining chill in the air. The early risers among the vegetable merchants set up their stalls on the east side, leaving the west side to the afternoon merchants.

Kalanolite priests were blessing the stalls as the farmers set out their wares. While Deihosos was the most popular of the four gods among those that worked the land, Holy Kalanolos the Farmer was the most popular of his saints. Annissa thought it made more sense to seek the blessing of Bodeihos. Wisdom was more important for a merchant, but farmers were a conservative lot. If Deihosos had blessed them with a good harvest, it made sense to them that he would continue blessing them with good sales.

She greeted Nikos the fruit merchant in the corner where she usually sat in the morning. Nikos was a good man, raising two teenaged daughters alone since his wife had died in the plague that swept the empire ten years earlier. Annissa trusted him and the majority of the working men and women of this neighborhood not to turn her in for illegally practicing magic but she did not want to take too many chances.

Preparing herself for her first potential client, Annissa pulled out a small silver hand mirror from her *rokota,* the robe favored by *alutsai* and *maholoi* and worn over a dress or tunic. The one luxury she retained, the mirror reminded her of her grandmother who had given it to her when she had died. The mirror revealed Annissa's face and green eyes. Her lightly tanned skin was no longer young but still smooth, years away from the creases of old age. She ran a broken-toothed comb through her sandy-colored curly hair to remove the tangles that had crept in. Her finely woven full length wool *stola* required cleaning, but the *rokota* was clean enough to cover the stains on the *stola.*

She extracted the inherited deck of cards from her *rokota* and reviewed them. The once stiff paper had become as soft as cloth with use through the years. All of them had rounded corners where they had once been sharp. The Sun card had a corner missing, ripped when an unhappy client had tried to grab it from the table. Sometimes a client did not like to hear what an *alutsa* had to say. Practicing magic was often as much about managing clients' expectations as it was performing the magic.

As she did every morning, she started by telling her own fortune, slowly laying down and reflecting on each card. The first card she turned over was the Judge. That was not a good sign given her situation with the *makaphoi*. Of course, the Judge wasn't always about legal matters; it could mean a decision needed to be made. It really depended on all the cards taken together.

Repression by the *makaphoi* had put a strain on her income. They were not only arresting practitioners, but also threatening their clients, often poor or working class citizens who could not afford to hire a *maholos*. Fewer and fewer came to visit her or ask for her services. She had taken to setting up this table in the market in order to let people know she was still available to do a couple of spells or tell a fortune. It was risky, though. If a *makaphos* caught her performing any magic at all, she would join her close friend and sometimes lover Geotheris in the dungeon of the Domous Nankisou Maholon, or Domous for short. If she only faked her way through a fortune, she risked being branded a charlatan and would get no clients at all.

Most citizens still used magic in some small way. They would come to Annissa for a potion to help heal a sick child or for a fortune-telling to find out if a marriage prospect was promising. She usually counted on someone coming to her, but the last few weeks had been difficult.

Her second card was the Beggar. It probably referred to herself. She lived a marginal existence, barely making enough to feed herself and put a roof over her head, modest as it was. She rented a small room from *nutha* Menetsa in a boarding house in the poor, working class neighborhood. Annissa made barely enough to pay for a private room; a small window was something of a luxury.

Though the meals in the house were meager, *nutha* Menetsa was a good baker. The small breads made up the standard morning meal for the residents of Synnakon's working class neighborhoods. It was not much, but it was fresh and Annissa looked forward to it every morning.

"Not telling fortunes, are you, *kibona*?" Askulas' shrill voice made her jump. Her face flushed with anger that he insulted her in her native Catacalonian, but she could do nothing in return. Braxas, his Ushidian enforcer stood behind him, arms crossed and muscles bulging. "You have been warned that casting spells without a license is illegal," the *makaphos* said.

Recently, somebody in the Nankisos had given a directive to put an end to public sorcery by the *alutsai*. Askulas seemed to target her specifically. The last time she had seen him, he had warned her that if he caught her practicing her art, she would be imprisoned. He had already arrested a number of her colleagues, including Geotheris.

"No, of course I'm not," Annissa answered, trembling. "I am simply playing a card game."

Askulas chuckled to himself, setting Annissa's teeth on edge. "By yourself?" he asked.

"Not all games require a partner, though they are more enjoyable with two or more. Would you like to join me?" She flashed the cards at him, offering to split the deck.

"I have time none for frivolous pastimes just as yours," he said, his Catacalonian accent thickening. "I give you warning. The penalty for violating the law has risen. If I catch you in spell casting, I will arrest you to the Domous."

Signaling to Braxas, Askulas turned and left. Annissa turned back to her cards. Should she continue? She could not afford to be imprisoned. She did not have the money to pay the restitution fine to be released. In order to pay it, she would be sold as a slave to a work camp. She looked at the soft skin of her hands. She would not survive long as a slave.

Nor could she afford not to ply her trade. In order to raise the five silver *archoi* Menetsa charged for her room, Annissa needed to come up with seventy copper *sestroi*. Five years ago, a silver *archos* cost twelve coppers, but the cost of the silver coin had increased since then. Menetsa did not accept the baser coin and her clients often did not have the more valuable silver.

Deciding that the vague threat of prison was less than the certain threat of vagrancy, she sat down at her table.

She next laid down the *Maholos*. Did it refer to Annissa herself or someone else? Although the card was called the *Maholos*, it really referred to any practitioner of magic. Whereas the distinction between *alutsai* and *maholoi* had developed within the last ten years, the *Maholos* card had been named since ancient times.

The *maholoi* had grown to become one of the most powerful segments of Synnakian society. Centuries ago, they had merely been magicians for hire, no different from the *alutsai*, common street sorcerers. Those who were able to gather wealth reinvested in research. Better learning meant better spells, leading the nobility to rely on them for many everyday functions. The richer *maholoi* used their connections to the nobility to increase their influence in the imperial court.

The loss of the eastern provinces to the Merouin Caliphate increased resentment of the *maholoi*, leading to the antarkanist backlash of the past century. Beginning with Leonos III nearly one hundred and fifty years ago, successive emperors initiated policies restricting the use of magic. During the reigns of the antarkanist emperors, the *maholoi* began to organize, forming the Nankisos Maholon, the Council of Mages.

A mere twenty-two years ago, Emperor Kosyndeos III had promulgated the *Lumos Maholon*, ending the antarkanist period and creating a license system to regulate magic use. The law granted the *maholoi* a monopoly while branding those without a license as *alutsai*, subjecting them to various imperial sanctions, including fines and imprisonment.

It was sad that she had come to this, telling fortunes for a couple of *sestroi*. Her ancestors had been powerful *maholoi* before Leonos had them arrested. Her family continued to practice in secret afterwards, serving those who could not find or afford assistance from the priests who continued to practice legally. She had inherited only a few spells and a deck of fortune telling cards from her father and grandfather. They did not have the resources or connections to be able to afford a *maholos* license.

Annissa drew the next card, the Daemon, but reversed. Normally, the Daemon refers to control. She often interpreted it for others as the control they had over their own life. Reversed, it indicated a loss of control.

The final card was the One of Fire. That indicated a new beginning for her. Annissa shivered. A card indicating a new beginning immediately after one suggesting a loss of control could mean many things. It might mean Askulas' threat of imprisonment would come to pass. It was hard to tell without an actual spell to view the future probabilities.

With the cards laid out, she began to chant her spell quietly to herself. "*O póntonízuva wániz, digímaviz, niz, okuvuz. Akilód wíkiz kapirikaviz mivi.*"

Finishing the chant, future probabilities began to unfold before her eyes like a blooming rose. People standing in the market square appeared to stretch out, extending along their probable future paths. The possibilities unfolded and overlapped. It required some discipline and focus to be able to understand the revelation. She slowly blocked from her mind those other occupants of the square not involved in the fortune she laid down. It seemed more people had come to the market since she began, but perhaps that was only one of the probable futures. Filtering the extraneous people out of her vision, she focused on her own path and those people who might be standing in front of her table today. Faint ghosts of people who might ask her advice today passed by. A small boy seemed to be important somehow, but he would not come to her table, only watch from afar. Two girls would likely ask her for a fortune regarding a young man one of them was romantically involved with. Askulas might come by and give her trouble.

Then as suddenly as a whiplash, the visions disappeared and the market came back to normal. Nikos finished a sentence he had started when Annissa had begun casting the spell. Nothing in the market seemed to have changed even a bit. It was as if she had seen everything in the blink of an eye. It was difficult to become accustomed to.

The visions she had seen did not seem unusual. The clearest visions were the most probable; they were things she expected and had prepared for. Perhaps the boy was Askulas's spy and the two girls would be sent to trap her. She decided that she would not cast any more spells. If the two girls came asking for a fortune, she would lay the cards and interpret them as best she could, but not cast the spell showing the true future.

Chapter 6

Iko watched in fascination as Kora counted out change. He had not needed coins at the convent, so had seen very few of them. The pictures and words stamped on the small copper disks fascinated him. They were stamped with the picture of the man's head and an inscription around the edge: *Kosyndeos III Enepranos Gendou Cokanes.* Kosyndeos was the current emperor. It must have been his face on the coin.

Kora finished counting the coins and took a basket down from the wall of the kitchen. Iko had met the girl the day before when Goron brought him here from the convent. She and Polous had been very polite in welcoming him, though Polous seemed surprised that Goron brought a boy back with him. With a disarming smile, Kora had shown him a storeroom for him to sleep in, setting up a cot among dressmaker's mannequins and bolts of cloth.

The following morning after finishing breakfast, Polous had gone to his workshop while Goron excused himself, going into the city to meet with business associates. Iko was left alone with Kora, who began preparing to go out as well, throwing a muslin shawl over her shoulders to keep the sun off.

"Where are you going?" Iko asked.

"I go to the market every Friday to get food for the week," Kora said with a smile. "Do you want to come? I could use some company."

Eager to spend some more time with her, Iko accepted. While she was not particularly outgoing, her attitude was more easy-going than the girls that had grown up with him in the convent.

Kora and Iko headed down the street to the market square. It was a warm day and for the first time in a long time, Iko relaxed. He laughed at Kora's remarks and told her some stories of his adventures when he lived in the convent with his mother and *amma.*

A half-dozen produce stands stood in the market, some specializing in fruits, others in fresh summer vegetables, others in onions and stock vegetables. Iko's mouth watered at the sight of the fresh fruits. Kora headed to the nearest vegetable stand and began inspecting eggplants and summer squash.

Iko wandered through the crowd, investigating what else the market had to offer. Keeping Kora within view, he found jugglers and tumblers performing in one corner of the square wearing brightly colored, tight-fitting clothing intended to attract attention. They had gathered a small crowd and seemed to have gathered some coins as well.

Nearby, a sandy-haired, tan-skinned woman sat at a small table with two girls. She turned over cards from a deck one by one. As she turned over a card, she brushed her curls out of her eyes, speaking to the girls while pointing at a card. As she spoke, the girls variously giggled or gasped at what she had to say. This was apparently an *alutsa*, a street magician and fortune teller. Having never seen one before, Iko drew closer to find out more about her, but one of the girls scowled at him. He obviously was not welcome at the table while the girls had their fortune told. Iko stood back a bit and watched as the *alutsa* laid her cards on the table and the silly girls laughed to each other.

Feeling put off and bored with watching and not knowing what the woman was saying, he headed for the nearest fruit stand. His hunger had risen since he and Kora had left the house. He noticed the fruit seller speaking with a demanding customer on one side of the stand. The merchant was busy filling the customer's basket with various wares. While the man was distracted, Iko snuck a peach from the stand and hid it under his cloak as he walked past. He did not uncover it until he found Kora at a butcher's stand, picking out some lamb for the night's dinner.

"Hungry?" Iko asked Kora. "I found a peach. Would you like some?"

Kora pulled him aside. "How did you get that? I thought you had no money to buy anything."

"You don't always need money to get things." The thought crossed his mind that Kora might be very naïve.

"You shouldn't steal from people," Kora said with a scowl. These people have very little. If you take from them, they only get poorer. You need to pay for what you take. They work very hard to get food to us."

Iko had not thought that these people might be poor. "But they have so much food on their stands. Surely they won't miss one piece of fruit." He bit into the peach and it tasted sweet and juicy.

"In order to earn enough to support their families, they must sell a lot of food," Kora explained. "Look, that one peach costs one copper *sestros*. They would need to sell about fourteen peaches to buy a silver *archos* and the landowner charges ten *archoi* for them to set up their stand here in the market. If everyone simply took the peach instead of paying for it, they couldn't pay the rent on the stall and wouldn't come here to sell anymore."

Kora fished a *sestros* out of her coin purse and walked over to the fruit merchant. "My friend Iko wanted to buy a peach, but didn't have any coins on him." She handed the coin to the stocky, dark-haired fruit seller, who accepted the coin with a smile. He smiled and waved at Iko, who stood bashfully a few yards away. Kora continued talking with the merchant and inspected some lemons. Iko took another bite from his peach, which no longer tasted as sweet.

After finishing his fruit, he headed back in the direction of the fortune teller. This time, two men stood at her table with the two giggling girls behind them. Only now, they weren't giggling. A smaller, thin faced man with long dark hair, spoke to the sorceress with a Catacalonian accent. The other man was much larger, had short-cropped blond hair, and stood menacingly nearby. Iko had learned to recognize the traits that typified the Ushidian minority of the empire. The rich and powerful men of the city who needed guards and enforcers sought them out for their larger size and low wages. Iko drew closer to the scene even as the rest of the crowd tensed and moved away.

"I warned you to practice no magic without a license, Annissa," the smaller man said.

"But I wasn't using magic, Askulas. I was only advising a couple of girls on their marriage prospects."

"We spoke with the girls a few minutes ago and they told to us you cast a spell to tell their fortune. Either you were in unlicensed spellcasting or you were defrauding them. Either way, you broke the law, exactly as you have in the past. Braxas, let's arrest her to the *Thunolohoi* for sentencing."

The larger man stepped forward to grab the woman, knocking the table over. Grabbing her cards, Annissa stepped around the table, keeping it between her and the larger blond. The girls backed off as Annissa started off at a run through the crowd, which split in front of her. The Ushidian lumbered after her, pushing his way through the crowd that reformed behind her like water.

It looked as if Annissa would outrun Braxas but the thin man uncovered a small gem from a bag hanging around his neck and began chanting. *"O póntonízuva wániz! Yasigód kélsham mam!"* He gesticulated a pattern in the air in front of him and the air began to shimmer and bend, slowly growing into the shape of a grasping hand. When it grew to a certain size, it shot through the air past Braxas toward Annissa, grabbing her and stopping her dead in her tracks. Annissa stood in mid-stride like a living statue.

Striding over to Annissa, the Ushidian threw her over his shoulder like a sack of onions. The two enforcers carried her out of the marketplace toward the Megizikon and the Thunolohoi.

"Why did they take her away?" Iko asked Kora.

"She is not supposed to tell fortunes to the public without a proper license. They say that without the proper training she could do harm. Polous thinks it's because they don't want anyone besides *maholoi* selling magic. That way, they can charge more."

"What is that gem hanging around the man's neck?" asked Iko. "It looks valuable."

"It probably is," answered Kora. "Mages use them to concentrate the you-son."

"*Ousion*. It's pronounced *ousion,*" a deep voice told them from behind. "It's the substance that *maholoi* and *alutsai* use to wield magic."

Iko turned to see Goron behind them. He had cleaned up, shaved, and put on a fine tunic and dalmatic. "Where are they taking her?" Iko asked.

"To a dungeon under the Domous," said Goron. "It is very difficult to break out of because of the magical locks, though it is fairly easy to get into the building. There is a door between the Eterodeihon and the Domous which is locked with a fairly simple lock. Let us not speak of such matters here. It is best that people do not know how much one knows of magic and discussing such matters in public can be dangerous. Let us go back to Polous's home."

Chapter 7

Sitting at his writing desk, Manoueka wrote in a folio with newly pressed leaves while studying the tome he had received from Demodoi, his right hand buried in his straight, dark hair.

He rubbed its polished surface, thinking of how the desk symbolized his rising fortunes. He had bought it recently from a member of the Morion family who had fallen on hard times. He had no sympathy for the traitorous fool. If the family hadn't taken sides against the emperor and the *maholoi* years ago, they wouldn't need to sell off their heirlooms now. As it was, he now had a finely crafted writing desk, large enough for his height and with plenty of room to spread his papers and books while he studied.

His recent admission to the *Nankisos Maholon* foretold a prosperous future. The richest and most powerful mages in the empire filled the council. Simply being a member allowed him to make connections giving him access to imperial libraries. He hoped to get access to the imperial treasury as well, where some of the greatest magical artifacts were said to be stored. He would be able to make a name for himself in history if he were able to rediscover lost spells or artifacts and put them to use for mankind.

The tome he read troubled him greatly. Entitled *An Account of the Wonders of the Caliph*, it told of the shards of Kurovilos, the Seven Stones of Power. The writing suggested the Mad Caliph had buried one of the stones in an ancient Hikuptahn tomb.

The stories of the Mad Caliph Harun, a fanatical adherent of antarkanism, were well known, as were the many stories of the lost final resting place of his treasury, most of them pure legend. When a resurgence of antarkanism swept the Merouin Caliphate, the caliph ordered all magical items removed from his possession. He could not give them to others to use, so he had returned them to their original owners, provided that owner was no longer living. He had ordered his servants to exhume the graves of those owners and rebury them with the magical artifacts. This strategy backfired on Harun when robbers easily found most of the burial sites and excavated the artifacts. Almost all the sites had been found except the site of some of the most powerful items. The Mad Caliph considered these items the most dangerous, so he had the servants who hid them executed so the sites could never be found.

Demodoi's book claimed one of those sites was located in ancient Hikuptah. Manoueka had written to the Tulkeen, the priests of Motios who managed the library in Iskander. They had confirmed that they had in their possession *An Inventory of the Treasuries of the Caliph Harun* and *An Account of an Exploration of the Tombs of the 27th Dynasty of the Kings of Ptahmel.*

The *Treasuries* should confirm whether the Caliph Harun had buried the wealth of the caliphate in the tomb of the Hikuptahn pharaoh Thamses the Great and whether one of the Stones was buried with it. The *Exploration of the Tombs* should lead him to the tomb he sought. Further exploration of Thamses's tomb should reveal Harun's treasure. The tomb was well known and very little of value had been found there recently. Grave robbers had plundered the ancient pharaoh's riches long before. But perhaps Harun had hidden Korefael in a hidden chamber that the grave robbers had overlooked. After all, there would be no reason to rob an already empty tomb.

Manoueka turned a page to read more about Korefael. Like all magical gems, the stone was a magical focus that allowed one to cast a spell more easily. Few *maholoi* completely understood the working of gems as magical foci, but sometimes using a gem allowed a magician to cast a spell without needing to call on the gods and spirits. They had become central to the crafting of magical artifacts. The sparse literature he found on the subject described the stones as magical gems but the text of *Wonders of the Caliph* seemed to say they had a world trapped inside.

The account given in the book told that early Cokan emperors divided the Stones of Power among the kingdoms and *comitati* that made up the empire, using them to communicate amongst themselves. The stones were lost over time as one by one the kingdoms and *comitati* broke away from the empire or were conquered by invaders such as the Amr aw-Wanaj, who destroyed or hid many magic items and books when he founded the Merouin Caliphate.

According to the book, the stones were some of the most powerful magical foci in history. If that were the case, they might be too powerful for one man to control. Manoueka thought it would be prudent to enlist the help of another to perform the *seganaion*, the activation ritual, on the stones for the first time, but he did not want to share his discovery with any of his colleagues or any students, all of whom would be as ambitious as he. Any of them could easily use his discoveries for their own ends, furthering their own agenda and power. Perhaps Demodoi could help him find a young wizard who had no political connections to use to exploit the discoveries.

The book had been written in an archaic form of Doran, but that should have been no problem. Manoueka had studied ancient Doran at the academy and gotten a perfect score in his exams, something no one had done in nearly a decade. This text seemed older. The language was similar enough to ancient Doran, but it made use of words that were not familiar to him. It was as if the text had been translated from an older document and when the writer did not know the meaning of a word, he left the old word in place. Many of the old, non-Doran words seemed familiar to Manoueka, yet unknown. He felt as if he were on the verge of a breakthrough, as if the meaning were about to become clear.

Manoueka jumped in surprise when Mirán, the Ushidian *perekhe*, or head of his private squad of guards, entered the room. The large brown-haired and bearded Ushidian looked like a bear, which would have made him happy to hear. Ushidians were proud of the frequent comparison to bears. Some blonds even dyed their hair brown or black to improve the comparison.

"Manvecze, please forgive interruption, but we have news of dressmaker Polous. He has visitor who has arrived from Erminikon. It is Goron, man you are looking for." Mirán spoke Doran slowly and poorly with a thick Ushidian accent. Most of the Ushidians hired as guards, soldiers, or mercenaries lacked even the basic education that most Doran Synnakians received.

Manoueka snapped at his guard. "Damn it, Mirán! You've broken my concentration. Now I might never get that train of thought back. And my name is pronounced Manoueka. Man-u-E-ka. I don't want to hear another word of Ushidian again. When you and your men work for me, you speak Doradic, do you hear?" Ushidians made his blood boil sometimes. They wanted to be full citizens of the empire and enjoy the benefits of civilization, but refused to speak the common tongue of the empire. If he could have found Doran or Volish guards, he would have hired them. But when the Ushidians arrived after the emperor Deokekos made them full citizen of the empire, they underpriced all other guard companies and put them out of business. Now he must tolerate Ushidians in his household.

It would not be so bad if they did not smell so bad. Their diet consisted mainly of cabbage, onions, and pork, including a favorite of theirs made of onions and rancid pork fat. Manoueka's stomach turned at the thought. It seemed every one of them smelled of this putrid dish and no amount of bathing could wash it out of them.

The news of Goron's arrival pleased him, though. Demodoi would be happy to learn that his bait worked. He still did not understand why the strange aristocrat wanted this man, but he would have to find out. "Keep a watch on this visitor. Listen to whatever conversations you can. I want to know where he goes and whom he talks with. If he has any conversations with any other known antarkanists, let me know immediately."

"Yes, sir. Manweka." Manoueka let the error pass. At least the dolt was trying. "We were tracking him. Yesterday, he traveled to Convent of Holy Maranna where he spoke with convent's Materssa. He came back with boy."

"Have someone keep an eye on the boy as well. Who is he? He might be running errands or messages for traitors." The sect of Maranna was known to harbor antarkanist women who had rebelled against the emperor, and the widows of traitors.

When Mirán turned to go, Manoueka turned back to his table. Who was this Goron? Were local antarkanists making contact with Erminikonian secessionists? What was Demodoi's interest in it? Rumors circulated about the old aristocrat's powerful connections, though he did not participate openly in the imperial court.

He looked at the book and his notes and suddenly felt tired and discouraged at his lack of progress in studying it. The possibility that he may have uncovered a threat to the empire captured his imagination and replaced the study of ancient artifacts in his mind.

Manoueka rose to leave his study for his bed chamber. His research should be safe enough in his own private study, but he had created a *korína* specifically to protect his research from intruders. There were three components to the spell that needed to be put in place in a certain order. First, the trigger to detect if someone other than himself entered the room. If he put the other two components in place before the trigger, then the effects would strike him and he would not be able to complete the remainder of the spell. He began chanting the ritual. "*O póntonízuva wanuvuz, binimath komikava tilipava wikiz kaz nimiviz...*"

The trigger was in place, now he needed to create the effects if the condition were met. First, render the intruder unconscious, "*...yad kinimam sippatanaiy...,*" then raise an alarm. "*...ki yakúd kikegam.*"

He brimmed with pride at his creation. The conditional form of spell had been around for hundreds of years, but only recently had *maholoi* begun creating nested spells where the condition triggered a second spell. Manoueka had gone one step further and nested a second spell inside the first nested spell. Few *maholoi* had thought of developing spells of such complexity. He had not gone one step further, but he suspected spells could be nested within each other infinitely.

The *korína* was quite powerful given the types of spells most *maholoi* had developed in his lifetime. Even so, it was generally thought they were living through a renaissance in magical scholarship. So much learning had been lost during the antarkanist period. Most of what passed for progress was merely the rediscovery of lost knowledge.

Yet Demodoi thought his achievement petty. Manoueka frowned to himself at the thought. Perhaps it was petty compared to the potential of the Stones of Power. If he could get his hands on the one described in Demodoi's book, it would solve many of his problems and even propel him into the circle of the most powerful *maholoi* in Synnakon.

He must capture Goron in order to get Demodoi's support, though. If the man did attempt to break into Manoueka's study to find the book, the *korína* would catch him.

Leaving his papers open on his new desk but taking the book with him, he blew out the candle and headed to his bedchamber, plunging his study in darkness, confident that his *korína* would keep his research safe.

Chapter 8

The Agos Deihikos lay in a poor Doran neighborhood in the lower Seniktikon near the harbor. Mirán felt uncomfortable meeting people in an *índomos*, a wine house frequented mainly by the Doran and Catacalonian residents of the city.

He would have to be very careful; the older, more established working classes of the empire still harbored a resentment of the northern race. Too often, poor Dorans accused the barbarians of stealing work, causing hard times and the poverty they suffered.

As a young Ushidian first arrived in Synnakon, he had gotten involved in many brawls with the working class residents of the neighborhood simply by trying to order a beer in a local *índomos.* His thick accent had gotten him into trouble with the native Doran speakers. It bothered him that people assumed he was dense simply because he could not speak well. Reading and writing were not important skills in his native Ushidia, but the ability to read another man's thoughts in his voice and bearing were considered essential.

Few Ushidians would be found in an *índomos*. Their beverage of choice was beer or mead rather than the wine favored by Dorans and Catacalonians. A northerner would more likely drink in an *eludhzim'*. The beer-serving taverns often formed the center of community life among the Ushidians, reflecting social traditions in their northern homeland.

He had left his village in Ushidia as a minor member of the house with no prospects. He had left to seek his fortune. Traveling with his cousins Valád and Barász, and other desperate men from his homeland, he found a ship in Peršati and sailed south to Berdov in the Synnakian Empire.

He had impressed the other men with his strong will and determination to succeed and upon arrival in Synnakon, they chose him as their *perekhe*, or leader. He found employment for himself and his men as guards for powerful men. Eventually, Manoueka heard of him and hired him to manage security for his tower and his interests in the city.

Now, he thought of Berdov as a far northern outpost. He and his companions had so adapted themselves to city life, the idea of returning to his small village seemed impossible to him. What would he do there with no lands?

Dusk approaching, Mirán headed down into the Doran Seniktikon, the walls and towers of the Merkebios looming above. The inhabitants gave him no trouble as he passed, but he felt their watching eyes on him. Seeing the painted image of Deihosos eating purple grapes on the wood sign of the Agos Deihikos, the guard master took note of his surroundings, watching out for the *esérgon*'s men. If anyone were to give him trouble, it would only be with the knowledge and consent of the district boss.

When he entered the wine house, the few customers turned to eye the unfamiliar visitor warily and began murmuring amongst themselves. Silently thanking the Four Gods for his brown hair, he hoped he would not be immediately identified as an Ushidian before meeting his contact. The black sword hanging above the bar made him nervous, though.

Scanning the room, he spied the man he sought in a booth near the back. A silent sign from the man instructed the locals to stand down, relieving the tension in the room.

"The gods be with you, Ushidian," his host said, standing and clasping Mirán's hand.

"May they walk with you also," he responded in the Doran fashion. "What have you found out about newcomer?"

"First, there is the matter of payment," his host said with a crooked smile. "I require more. Dedosos, our *esérgon*, has heard of our arrangement and is levying a fee of five percent."

Mirán pulled out a small pouch containing five silver *archoi*, the amount that comprised a standard fee for information. Frowning at the man's extortion, he also pulled out another pouch. He calculated the extra charge slowly while the informant watched, counting out four *sestroi*. He added the coins to the first pouch and handed it to his informant.

The Doran smiled, taking the fee. "It seems Goron has expressed an interest in your patron, Manoueka. He met yesterday with some men in an *índomos* near here. The older ones remembered him from their youth. It seems all his contacts are ancient, mostly men from houses that were once powerful under the antarkanist emperors."

The spy continued to relate Goron's conversation with his old associates. The old men had seemed bitter about the reversal of fortune of their houses. Goron's contacts pressed him for help in restoring their fortunes and a return to antarkanist rule. He apparently had no interest in their rebellious schemes. "Such plans would fail," he had told them. "Focus more on your mercantile concerns; that will be the route to renewed wealth." The younger men had seemed disappointed, but the older ones nodded in agreement.

Goron's own interest lay solely in Manoueka and his connections. They told him where to find his tower and about his recent, rapid rise in power and recent admittance to the Nankisos Maholon, albeit as a minor member. They also mentioned the wizard's connection to Demodoi, the old aristocrat. Goron had seemed very interested in their relationship.

The old men remembered Demodoi well. "I seem to remember that he played a role in politics since before I was a young man," recollected one of the ancients. "I have never been certain where he gained his wealth or influence," he added.

Goron continued to press the men on how the tower was guarded, where inside the house lay the wizard's study, and other specific information about Manoueka's security. They told him about the *korína* the wizard had invented, though he seemed unconcerned with it.

Mirán's eyes widened, concerned at his informant's description of Goron's line of questioning. It seemed the mysterious visitor planned to break in to his employer's study. Perhaps to steal the book Manvecze had received from Demodoi or even to cause harm to the wizard. It could happen tonight. Deciding that he had found out enough, he cut the interview short in order to bring the news to the magician.

"Manweka will be grateful for your help," said the Ushidian. "I must report to him at once. It is possible he or his property is in danger. I assume extra fee for your *esérgon* will assure my safety on my return this evening?"

"Have no fear," the Doran said, smiling his crooked smile. "Nothing happens in the Seniktikon without Dedosos's knowledge and approval."

Chapter 9

Iko and Goron stood at the base of the tower, looking up its curved brick face stretching into the darkness. The small window Goron planned on climbing up to faded into the darkness as a blacker patch in an already dark night. A slender crescent moon had shown only the faintest sliver of white that night, but it had already set less than an hour after the sun.

Most of the towers of the Krolos Maholon, Synnakon's mage district, had been built a hundred years before by merchant families during the reign Synnakarious V. Until about a decade ago, it had been known as the merchant district. Not every building in the neighborhood boasted a tower, but there was at least one on every block. Like the other buildings in the city, the merchants who had built the mansion-sized houses in this area had kept them stuccoed and whitewashed, but the mages were more careless about maintaining their palaces' unadorned exteriors, the stucco cracking and flaking in many places. The bare brick tower of Manoueka's mansion rose above the main bulk of the structure.

Merchants had built the towers in an age when they had no other way to communicate at long distances. Since the restoration, merchants had been using spells to track their ships and caravans from a distance, no longer needing the towers. Since then merchants had moved closer to their warehouses and mages moved into their towers.

Iko seemed happy to be brought along on this errand. Goron felt a pang of guilt. If Aisarra knew Goron would bring Iko along to break into a wizard's tower, she likely would never have put him in his care. He knew his grandson had a tendency to get into trouble. He didn't want to lead him down the wrong path, but he needed to find out about the book in Manoueka's study she had told him about.

Goron saw nobody alive on the darkened street other than Iko and Bason. Most *maholoi* and their servants did not leave their towers except during the day and the common folk avoided the Krolos Maholon, especially at night. Stories circulated in the lower town about people who had come up here, never to be seen again. Goron didn't believe most of them, but the common folk's fear of the mages made for a quiet street in the dark of night.

Still looking up, Iko whispered, "I don't see how you are going to climb the face of this wall. That window's got to be a hundred feet up there."

Having retrieved what he wanted from his toolkit, Goron loosened a pair of spooled silken ropes from the horse's saddle. "Do you see the crack that spirals up the side of the tower?" He pointed upwards. "I will use that and it will be like walking up stairs."

"But that crack can't be more than a quarter inch at the widest spot," said Iko, craning his neck to see in the darkness. "You won't be able to get your fingers in."

Goron removed a set of small tools out of a bag he retrieved from the horse's saddlebag. "That is why I will use these expanding spikes." He displayed a set of very narrow metal tubes with small buttons and a hook at the end. "These were made by the finest craftsmen of Castria. The steel is the strongest in the world and will hold up to five hundred pounds. When I drive these into the crack in the wall, they will expand to create a solid wedge that will hold my weight. I will attach a hook to them and pass a rope through the hook. That is to catch me if things go badly."

Goron began tying knots in the silk cords. An Erminikonian climber's bend joined the two ropes together, making the full length one hundred feet, the length needed to reach the top of the tower. Next, he folded and coiled cords around his waist and thighs, attaching a metal ring and tying multiple half hitches to fashion them into a harness. Finishing his handiwork, he threaded the extended line through the ring.

"What I need you to do is stay here with the horse," he said to Iko, taking the line and passing it through a loop on the saddle. "Hold the rope tight. You don't weigh enough to hold my weight if I fall, but you can use this saddle loop to increase your leverage. Keep it relaxed so long as you feel it pulling gently, but if you feel it suddenly go tight, I probably have fallen and you will need to react quickly. Pull the line against the saddle loop and use it as a brake. Got it?"

The boy looked at the rope in his hands skeptically. "Are you sure this is going to work?"

"Do not worry, Melissene silk makers craft the strongest rope in the world. I've done this many times."

Goron respooled the remainder of the line on the ground next to the horse. "Keep it there and I will pull it out of the spool as I need it. It should be long enough for me to reach that window. When I am ready to climb down, I will give three sharp tugs on the rope and you pull it in. Keep it taut but not tight. Spool it back onto the ground as you pull it in. This should not take long."

Goron found a small crack in the stuccoed wall about chest height and drove one of his expanding spikes into it. Attaching the rope, he climbed up using whatever cracks and rough edges he found to hold himself against the wall. Every ten feet or so up the wall, he drove another spike into a crack and continued up.

Every once in a while as he climbed, the cord would go tight as if Iko had used the brake, afraid that the man had started falling. He had to gently tug on the line to let the boy know he was okay and needed more rope.

A few cracks spider-webbed the ancient wall, but the brick had worn unevenly, leaving fingernail wide ledges for Goron to hang from. The spikes worked well, but he did not think he had enough of them to make it the hundred feet up, so he began placing them farther apart than he would have liked. Luckily, the wall provided better hand and footholds farther up due to increased weathering. Perhaps the wind had eroded the bare brick and they had stuccoed the wall near the street in the past to deter climbers such as him. Was it a commentary on the hubris of the *maholoi* that they feared burglars so little they did not protect against them or was it a comment on the burglars that they feared the *maholoi* too much to try to break into their towers?

Coming up beneath the small window, he peered in on a stairway spiraling up along the inside of the tower wall. Climbing into the darkened stairway, he untied his harness, looping the rope on a nearby sconce set in the wall so it would not fall back down to Iko below. He stood halfway up the stairway and could go either up to the right or down to the left, but his instincts told him to always go right when given an even choice. Most *maholoi* prefer to have their studies on the top floor; he would likely find what he was looking for by going up.

The stairway climbed about ten feet, ending in a locked door, but a locked door had never stopped Goron before. He pulled his lock-picking tools out of his bag but to his surprise, the door opened as if it had never been locked. No noise stirred the darkened room. Fumbling carefully, he found a candle in the dark and lit it.

Warily, he entered the dimly-lit room. A large table spread with books and papers stood in the middle of the room; about a dozen workbenches lined the walls. Another desk overlooked the central table, allowing the *maholos* to keep watch over the younger apprentices. Books, scrolls, vials, and ceramic containers stood on the shelves above the workbenches. The room reminded Goron of many others he had been in during his youth. It was the public study. According to centuries-old tradition, the *maholos'* assistants and apprentices worked in the public study while the *maholos* himself worked in the private study. The desks and workbenches looked fairly clean; few books and scrolls lay about for study, indicating that Manoueka had few students or apprentices.

A wrought iron stairway in the middle of the room led up to the next floor. The fine workmanship of the stairway indicated that the owner of this tower had plenty of money and power. It likely led to Manoueka's private study.

Climbing the stairway into a slightly smaller room filled with books, he began to feel drowsy; perhaps a nap this afternoon would have been a good idea. He glanced across the bindings of the books to see if he could find anything of interest. He recognized most of the books and had read many of them, albeit in earlier editions. Most books these days were poor copies and had lost their proper meanings. The transcribers often drew the symbols poorly and transcribed the spells incorrectly. It was a wonder any *maholos* could learn anything from them. Most learned what they knew as apprentice to a master. Although the *maholoi* had recovered some knowledge in the past two decades, more had been lost in the preceding centuries. Mages these days merely tried to recover lost spells. They were more conjurers and technicians than ancient wizards. In ancient times, wizards were seekers of knowledge, experimenters and investigators. The *maholoi* of today were able to create great works of magic only by discovery. They had little interest in understanding the why and settled for simply implementing the how.

A large writing table stood to one side of the room, smaller than the common table of the apprentices downstairs but finely carved and inlaid with woodwork. A simple wooden chair sat carelessly pushed out in front of the desk, as if the person sitting at the desk had gotten up intending to come back shortly.

Sitting down at the desk, the desire to lay his head down and sleep grew on him. Resisting the urge, he searched the numerous documents scattered on the desk but could find no book. He found a letter written in an archaic form of Doradic addressed to Manoueka from Dithaan, a librarian in Iskander. It confirmed that they had in their possession two books: *An Inventory of the Treasuries of the Caliph Harun* and *An Account of an Exploration of the Tombs of the 27th Dynasty of the Kings of Ptahmel.*

Some of the papers were letters to caravan companies inquiring about rates and whether they would travel into the countryside away from established trade routes. In one letter Manoueka mentioned that he wished to travel to the area of Amonkhareb. Certainly that was significant; the tombs the wizard sought were near Amonkhareb. Goron remembered that city, though few would know of it these days. Once, it stood as the capital of an independent Kingdom of Hikuptah. The Pharsi overthrew the kingdom; Aranel the Great subsequently conquered it and later so did the Empire of Coka. The city of Amonkhareb lay in legend, a once great and powerful city buried beneath the sands of the desert. And now Manoueka wished to travel there and possibly unearth some ancient artifacts.

A fresh parchment lay below the correspondence. Glancing at it, he read a few words scrawled in fresh ink: The Seven Stones, Ashaphael... Dux of Viktra, Adranael... Karlstejn, Korefael... King of Ptahmel. This paper explained what Manoueka sought. Aisarra was right; he sought the lost shards of Kurovilos, the Stone of Power.

"*My brother*," a voice spoke in the darkness. Goron started to turn to look, wondering who had spoken.

It was the last thought that crossed his mind before everything went dark.

• • •

Manoueka sat in the dark waiting for his prey with Mirán and two of his men. What were their names? Curls and Velsid? In any case, Manoueka had cloaked them all with an invisibility spell he had learned from a colleague. In addition, he silenced them with the basic spell learned by every apprentice. The four of them stood undetectable in the public study, waiting for Goron to arrive.

He had only slept an hour before Mirán woke him. The guard leader had seemed certain Goron would come tonight, though he did not know how he would break into the tower.

Goron was coming for the book Demodoi had given him, *The Wonders of the Caliph.* Manoueka returned it to his private study. If Goron were looking for the book, he would enter the study and be subdued by the *korína* without his guards risking themselves in a fight.

The silence and darkness made Manoueka sleepy. He could not see or hear his guards, but he hoped they remained awake. A sound from outside the silenced area penetrated the room, bringing him awake. Someone was coming up the stairs from lower in the tower.

A moment later, Goron entered the room and lit a candle he found nearby the door. He spent little time searching the big room, focusing on the stairs to Manoueka's private study. The *maholos* felt a surge of excitement as Goron climbed the stairs. He had never actually watched the korína activated on an unsuspecting target. The intruder should be knocked unconscious at the top of the stair just as he entered the study.

Nothing happened.

Manoueka's jaw dropped. Goron had entered the room apparently unaffected by the korína. Had he cast the spell wrong? Going back over his memory, he was certain he had done it right. Why hadn't Goron been knocked unconscious?

He pulled himself together, glad nobody had seen the stunned look on his face. He canceled the invisibility spell and signaled to Mirán and his men to go up and capture the man. He kept the silence in effect. It would help them sneak in on Goron from behind. If he were alerted to their presence, he might fight back and someone would be hurt. Manoueka didn't want to have to pay for a *kailotos* to heal unnecessary wounds.

The three Ushidians climbed the stairs, with Curls in front. Or was that Velsid? It didn't matter, they would capture their prey soon.

The moment Curls entered the room, he fell over, unconscious. No alarm rang out, likely because of the silence spell had had cast on the guards earlier. Hastily, he climbed the stairs to cast the counterspell, canceling the *korína.*

Goron stood hunched over his reading table, unaware of his presence at the entrance to his study. Just as Goron sat to begin reading, Manoueka began casting the sleep component of the *korína.*

The spell had no effect on Goron. Manoueka was puzzled. Even in silence, so long as the *maholos* spoke the words of a spell, it should still take effect. Had he found some spell or artifact that canceled other spells? That would be a valuable piece of magic. He would have to figure out the problem later. Right now, he had an intruder in his private study reading his research.

He signaled to Mirán and the other guard to go in and capture Goron. Mirán obeyed immediately. Quickly and silently coming up behind the intruder, he knocked him unconscious with a blow to the head from a small club. Mirán was not a master of subtlety. He preferred the most direct solution to a problem.

As the Ushidians bound their captive, Manoueka looked at the unconscious man's face. Demodoi wanted the man, but Manoueka wanted some questions answered first.

Who did he work for? Not antarkanists, if what Mirán told him was true.

What was his connection to the Stones of Power? Was he hunting them as well? He had been studying the book and the other documents on the desk, probably for clues as to the stones' whereabouts. It made no sense. In any case, the intruder would learn the cost of stealing someone else's research.

The mage began rifling the intruder's pockets, searching for any clues as to his purpose. Sadly, he found nothing, not even gems or pendants. He wanted answers before turning his prisoner over to his patron, but he would have to wait for him to recover first.

"I'll need to interrogate him in the morning," he said to Mirán. "We must bring him to Demodoi tomorrow; make sure he is kept in a secure location."

"Okay, Boss. Do you want me to put him in cellar?"

Manoueka thought for a moment, running his hand through his hair. "No, he might find a way out of there or be discovered by Margera or one of her kitchen girls. Take him to one of the cells under the Domous and put a guard on him. I'll go to Demodoi, tell him we have captured his man."

"I understand. I will have Valád watch him. You two," Mirán barked at Velsid and the reawakened Curls in Ushidian. "Grab him, we'll have to carry him down stairs like this." The burly Ushidians manhandled the unconscious Goron down the stairs toward the base of the tower. They headed through subterranean tunnels to the Domous prison .

Manoueka needed sleep as well. He had not slept that night; the anxiety of waiting for the trap to be sprung had kept him awake. He could not rest yet, though; more work needed to be done. After the guards carried the prisoner out, Manoueka went down to the carriage house to wake the coachman. It would take some time for the grooms to get the horses ready for a late-night visit to Demodoi.

• • •

Iko waited at the bottom of the tower, watching Goron climb. Bason let out a quiet whinny and Iko patted his nose, calming him. “It's okay, boy. He knows what he's doing. I hope.”

Soon, Iko could only see Goron as a dark spot on the wall in the night. He gave up watching him and focused on the rope, making sure it was not too tight, but still keeping hold of it in case Goron should fall. He felt the older man pull on it as he climbed to the next level of his spike ladder, sending messages to Iko that Goron was still there. After a while, the rope went slack, as if the climber had reached his goal.

Iko had not known his mother's father was alive and now he stood at the bottom of a mage's tower as the older man climbed the wall and broke in. It seemed odd for this man to be connected in any way to his *amma*. She was very strict about observing rules whereas Goron seemed to observe only those he did not find inconvenient.

Iko waited, assuming Goron had made it inside, searching for the book Aisarra had told him of. After what seemed like a long while, he thought Goron should have found what he was looking for. Suddenly, the rope moved and he prepared for Goron to start climbing down. Instead, the rope went slack and started falling, pooling at his feet as it hit the ground. He stepped back to avoid getting hit by the end of the rope as it flailed to the ground in front of him.

Iko stood there, mouth agape. How would his grandfather climb down now? Did he plan to come through the front door? Had something happened? He examined the end of the rope and found that it was not cut; it still had the end splice intact. Someone had dropped it intentionally.

After a few minutes, he decided he needed to climb up to find out what was happening above. He had seen Goron tie the harness out of the end of the rope, so he set to creating his own harness. If he held the other end of the rope himself, he could probably belay himself. In any case, he did not plan on falling.

Iko grabbed onto the first spike where Goron had inserted them between the bricks in the tower wall. He was shorter than his grandfather, so it was harder to reach the next spike, but he was strong and wiry and used to climbing walls. It took longer than it had Goron, but he reached the base of the tower window. This must have been where the older man climbed in. He reached up to grab the windowsill and climb in as well when he heard voices above him.

A high-pitched voice with a Doran accent spoke with an air of command. Much of what he said was muffled, as if they spoke on the other side of a wall.

"Take him through the sub-cellar tunnel to one of the cells under the Domous... tell him we have captured his man."

Another voice spoke with a heavy Ushidian accent though it was difficult to make out what he said. "...grab his legs, you other his arms. We'll carry him downstairs like this."

Goron had been caught!

Iko heard a door open and the voices got louder as they got closer. They were struggling with a heavy burden. The high pitched Doran yelled down at his underlings. "One of you close the shutters on that window and lock it. That's probably how he got in. It must have been a long climb."

Two other voices spoke in a foreign language. Iko thought they sounded Ushidian, though he had never heard the language.

A head poked out of the window a few feet above Iko. In a panic, he froze, saving himself from being discovered. Had he climbed away from the window, the guard might have seen him. He waited, frozen against the wall in the dark for what seemed like an hour, though it was closer to a minute. The guard pulled his head back in and closed the shutters. Iko heard the sounds of a crossbar dropping into place and the guards' conversation in Ushidian fading as they continued down the stairway.

After he could hear no more, Iko slowly let out his breath. He needed to climb down, but climbing down looked a lot harder than climbing up. He could not see the spikes below him in the dark. Holding on tightly to the rope with one hand, he groped around with his foot. His foot slipped off the spike he stood on and he fell. Grabbing the rope hooked through a spike driven into the wall, it slid through his hands, the silk strands burning skin off his palms. His body pounded against the wall as he fell. Straining under his falling weight, the top spike popped out of the wall. The next three spikes from the top popped out as well.

Plummeting, his hands began to bleed; the ground rose at him rapidly. Desperate to break his fall, he took the loose end of the rope, wrapped it under himself and around the taut rope holding him. He yanked on it as hard as he could and rocked backward. The friction of the rope against itself acted as a brake and brought his fall to a halt. One more spike popped out of the wall and his heart skipped a beat. Then he stopped falling and hung in the air, holding on tightly to the rope.

Regaining his breath, he looked down. He hung twenty feet in the air and the nearest spike stuck out of the wall about twenty feet to the right of him. He loosened the braking rope enough to allow him to slide slowly down the wall. He kicked against the wall on the way down in order to avoid banging up against the brick again. Reaching the ground, he relaxed, rubbing his bruises. He drew in the rope and pulled as many spikes out of the wall as he could reach and put them in Goron's saddle bag. He would have to figure out how to free Goron.

Part II

Chapter 1

Manoueka's carriage once again entered the narrow courtyard of Demodoi's house. Climbing down from the carriage, he followed a footman to the small salon off the main entry hall where he had met the old aristocrat earlier. Having more time to wait, he inspected the tapestries more closely than before. He had assumed they were of the saints, but upon closer inspection, they did not look like any icons or carvings he had seen. He was not a religious man and had spent little time in the presence of religious artifacts, but there was something about these depictions that were different from others. They felt more ancient. Perhaps Demodoi collected ancient art. After all, artistic styles had changed over the centuries.

When Demodoi finally arrived, he looked even more frail than their previous meeting. He held out his hand in greeting. Taking his host's hand, Manoueka noted the strength of his grasp conflicted with the old man's frail appearance.

"Welcome to my humble abode. I hope you did not have to wait long. My servant can offer a glass of wine, if you would like."

Eager to try the old man's wines again and impatient with the dance of courtesy normally required, Manoueka took a silver goblet from Demodoi's servant. "I have come to discuss our arrangement and the next stage in our plan."

"Have you captured the renegade?" Demodoi asked. "I will not finance your scheme unless I have him."

"The trap you set for Goron worked," replied Manoueka, sipping his wine. "He took the bait and is now in the dungeon of the Domous. I can deliver him to you tomorrow. I would like to begin outfitting my expedition immediately. I will need some initial capital to begin hiring." A sense of accomplishment came over him as he described Goron's capture.

"Excellent. I am pleased," said Demodoi with a smile. The old man's smile unsettled Manoueka, making him want to leave the old man's presence as soon as he could. Demodoi continued, "I can give you a small sum to get you started tomorrow, then more when Goron is safely in my hands."

"If I may ask, why do you want the man?" asked Manoueka.

"As you may have heard, I have an affliction that prevents me from going out in the sunlight." Demodoi held up one hand to forestall any questions. "It makes me pale and weak, as you see me now. The treatment is horrifying. I will not burden you with the details. Goron has knowledge that may lead to a cure. I wish to discover his secrets. You have heard of the Gemstone Man?"

"There is a children's song, isn't there?" Manoueka tried to remember a song he had heard once as a child.

"Yes, you have probably heard it." He began to recite in a sing-song voice:

They made a man of gemstone
Who opened up the gate.
He let out all the old sheep
So with the black they'd mate.
The old ewe had a white lamb
The black ewe had a beast.
He sent them to their pastures
With two lambs for the feast.

The sound of the decrepit old man singing a children's song disturbed Manoueka. "I don't understand what a children's rhyme has to do with Goron and the book you gave me."

"Perhaps you will find out in the course of your research," Demodoi said with a chuckle. "The *Account of the Wonders of the Caliph* was helpful, then?"

"Yes, much more than I imagined," said Manoueka as he looked into the contents of his wine glass. "It describes all the stones."

"Shards. Remember, they are but shards of a single stone," said Demodoi, holding up a finger as if correcting a schoolchild. "If you were able to find all seven, you would be able to reassemble them."

"Yes, the book lists the location of all the shards but one. Some of the tales seem very fanciful, though. I have inquired with the imperial treasurer regarding Barashel. He would not confirm that it is in the treasury. He told me that any questions regarding the Stone - his words - would not be answered."

"You are certain, then, that the book gives the correct location of Korefael?"

"Nothing is certain when it comes to such things. The book is a summation of legends and stories surrounding the shards. It tells that the Second Jewel of the Kings is encased in a lead statuette, the Lion of Ptahmel. Its last reported resting place was in the treasury of the Merouin Caliph."

"You mean the *Amr aw-Wanaj*," said Demodoi, raising his finger to correct the mage again. "If you are traveling in their lands, you should address them in their language."

"*Amr aw-Wanaj*, then," said Manoueka, his lips tightening with annoyance. The old man corrected him too often. He was a fully licensed *maholos*, not some apprentice. Besides he needed no other language than Doran and old Doradic. Though he did not speak Kukrili, he read it well enough. He would be able to find translators in Iskander and Hikuptah. He could not be expected to learn every foreign language in the world.

"As I was saying," Manoueka continued, "the shard was last reported in the treasury of the *Amr aw-Wanaj*, but that was before the Caliph Harun had the riches of the caliphate buried some hundred and fifty years ago. I don't know whether he did so in a fit of paranoia, if he worried about a grand theft, or was swept up in a religious fervor, hiding his riches to make himself a pauper in the eyes of Momados.

"In any case, most of the treasury was recovered. Some of it could not be found, including the statuette. Harun had the treasure buried in multiple locations, then had the diggers executed so they could not tell where they had buried it. Afterwards, grave robbers and thieves were able to find the locations of all of the hoards but one. The records I have found indicate that the last hiding place was back where Korefael started, in Hikuptah."

"Why there?" Demodoi asked.

"It is believed that he buried artifacts as close as possible to where the original owners held them. Korefael was the jewel of the King of Ptahmel, so I am looking for a king's tomb large enough to hold a large portion of the Merouin treasury but secluded enough that nobody has found it in a century. I plan to dig at the tomb of a king from the Twenty-seventh Dynasty of Ptahmel. The tombs are certainly large enough and it is widely believed that the shard was encased in a golden lion during his reign. All I need now is a small sum to begin preparations for my journey."

"You have done well. I look forward to the results of your expedition and to seeing Goron here in my house tomorrow night. Please arrive shortly after sundown." Demodoi signalled to his servant, who picked up a small coffer and handed it to Manoueka. "This should be enough gold to get you started putting together your expedition."

Chapter 2

"Kora!" Iko called out in the dark. He could not call too loudly for fear of waking Polous. If he were to be caught in Kora's private room, he would be in big trouble. "Kora, wake up."

"What is it? Iko, what are you doing in my room? You shouldn't be in here." She pulled the bedclothes up to maintain a measure of decorum.

"I need help. Goron has been taken to the prison under the Domous." He still found it difficult to imagine the man as his grandfather. Grandfathers were supposed to look like Polous, with grey hair and beards. Goron had dark, black hair. "I'm pretty sure I can get into the building, but I need something to put the guards to sleep."

"Okay, I'll help." She yawned. "But you need to get out of my room so I can get dressed. I'll be out in a minute

"Okay, but we don't have much time."

After a few minutes, Kora met him outside her room. The two children snuck through the house, determined not to wake Polous. Entering the kitchen, Kora went straight to the spice cabinet and began digging through the powders. "I have some *trempious*, a sleeping potion that will put anyone to sleep. I give a little to Polous when he has trouble sleeping. A larger dose will knock your guards out. The problem is that it has to be swallowed. I don't know how to get the guards to eat it."

"Can we put it in their beer?"

"It doesn't work as well in beer and how are we going to get beer to them anyway?"

"Was there any food leftover from dinner? We could bring them something to eat and put the potion in that."

"That would work, but how do we get them to eat it?"

Thinking for a minute, Iko brightened, remembering the conversation he had overheard in the tower. "One of them mentioned somebody by the name of Margera and that she had kitchen girls. I can get us into the building. Maybe you could pose as one of her kitchen girls and bring them a plate. If they're pulling late duty they're probably hungry."

Kora opened the pot that stood on top of the stove, full of last night's dinner, still warm from the coals inside the oven. She spooned out some of the lamb stew onto a ceramic plate, then put the plate over the firebox of the ceramic oven. She opened the door to the firebox, loaded a couple of small sticks of wood on the coals that still glowed within, then blew on them to light them. "It will take a few minutes to get the plate warm enough. We can't be serving the guards a cold plate of food. We have to be sure they will eat it."

She placed a ceramic lid over the plate. "That will keep the food warm while we carry it to the Domous.

Hand me that basket." Iko grabbed a basket woven from thin reeds and passed it over to her.

When Kora decided that the plate was warm enough, she loaded it into the basket and covered it with a thick kitchen towel. She took a warm shawl from a hook in the kitchen and wrapped it around her. She then took a key down from a hook hidden behind the stove. "Are you ready?"

"As ready as I'll ever be," answered Iko.

Kora used a hidden key to unlock the front door and pushed it open, trying not to make any noise at all. When they had both exited, she closed the door just as carefully, re-locked it, and hid the key in her skirt.

Kora knew the way well. They crossed town under a dark sky lit only by stars. Leaving the narrow side street of their neighborhood, they crossed the open Megizikon for the Eterodeihon church. The church stood to the left of the Domous on the northeast side of the square, the Imperial palace stood to the right on the southeast side. The huge market square was empty this late at night, only the folded tents of the merchants lay in the center. No creatures could be seen or heard.

"I seem to remember Goron telling me that they keep the church open at night, so it should be fairly easy to get in," Iko said as he headed for the western entrance. They climbed the stairs to the great carved, wooden doors. Iko looked up at the bas reliefs of the saints. There must have been ten panels up and four across, each one foot square. The sisters in the convent had taught him about the saints and he could name them all. This door only portrayed saints of Motios.

"I'm sure the gods will condemn me for breaking into a church at night with the saints watching," said Iko, hesitating before opening the door.

"The church is a public building, so there's no crime in entering it," said Kora.

"But I'm going there to break Goron out of jail. Isn't that a sin?"

"It might be a crime, yes. I can't speak to what will offend the gods. You have a strange sense of morality for someone who was willing to steal a peach from a merchant today. Besides, I don't think the gods condemn a person to eternal torment for a single sin. Like Holy Embersion says, man must walk down a long road to make it to hell or heaven."

She stepped past him and pulled on the huge handle of the door to open it. The church was dark inside except for a few votive candles in front of icons of saints, but it was enough light to move around. The builders had laid the church out in four sections, one for each of the four gods, Motios, Deihosos, Momados, and Bodeihos. A partial dome topped each section with a huge dome in the center unifying the four quarters. The circumference of the central dome passed through the center of each of the surrounding partial domes. The central dome sat atop a ring of pillars made of a green marbled stone with four massive pillars at the intersections of each of the surrounding domes. Giant chandeliers hung from each of the four partial domes, but were not lit this late at night. There were no priests or clerics in the church, which by day was normally crowded with worshippers and holy men and women.

The children had entered the building in the section dedicated to Motios. Icons of the god surrounded them, some of his avatar the Sacred Bull, others of Motios himself presenting a book to the people, instructing them in the law.

Kora interrupted Iko's contemplation of the icons with a whisper that echoed throughout the church. "I think we need to get to the lower levels to find the passageway to the Domous. I have seen priests coming and going through doors in the chapels before. I think they keep their vestments down there."

Kora tried opening a nearby door but it was locked.

"I can unlock that, I think." Iko pulled out Goron's lock picks and began to work at the rudimentary lock. "This is a simple one. I don't think they have much of great value down there." The door opened easily.

"You were worried about going to hell for entering a church at night, but you pick locks and enter places you are not supposed to be," said Kora with amazement. "As I said before, you have a strange sense of morality."

He shrugged and went through the door. Immediately inside and to the right, a stairwell descended into darkness. "Light one of those candles on that votive shrine over there," he said.

Handing a candle to Iko, Kora lit another for herself. They headed down the stone stairway a short distance before it opened into a small vaulted room. The stairway continued down on the opposite side of the room and a hallway stretched out beyond an open doorway on the right side of the room.

"We'll need to be on the eastern side of the church, nearest the Domous. I think we are on the western side of Motios's dome." Iko prided himself on his sense of direction. "Should we go back up and find a door in the eastern dome?"

"That is Deihosos's dome, but I have never been to that one, so I'm not sure where the door is," said Kora looking around to get her bearings. "Besides, I think the chambers down here are all connected."

"Then we should go through that doorway to get to where we need to go."

They went through the open doorway to another room with corridors leading in every direction. Iko led them to the center of the church, figuring that if the chambers below the church were all connected, they were likely connected in the middle.

They traveled through a series of chambers to the central vault. Four hallways radiated from it and a giant spiral staircase ascended to the main church above. In front of the entrance to each hallway stood an altar dedicated to one of the four gods: Bodeihos to the north, Momados to the south, Motios in front off the western hall they had just come from and Deihosos on the eastern side. Iko led them past the altar to Deihosos and down the eastern hallway.

Going through another series of chambers mirroring the chambers on the west, they came to a vaulted room similar to the one they had entered when they first came down the stairway. The difference here was that the icons portrayed Deihosos. Iko saw icons of the god, some of his avatar Manmel, others of Deihosos himself with his blood flowing onto green fields. The most ornate icon showed the god's rebirth, with him rising out of the field he had just irrigated with his own blood. The other difference was that a door opened on the opposite wall where there was none in the western room.

"This must be the door to the Domous." Iko pulled out his picks once again and set to work on the lock. "This one is a little more difficult. Like the saying goes, 'the path of most resistance leads to the greatest reward.' "

In a couple minutes, the lock was open. He opened the door to darkness. He raised his candle to reveal a hallway leading away from the door. It smelled musty, as if few had ventured past the door. "You need to go alone so it seems you came from the wizard's household," he told Kora, waving her into the hallway. "The holding cells are under the Domous, which should be about a hundred yards down this way."

"Can't you come with me part way?" asked Kora, hesitant to go through the doorway. "At least until the hallway goes into the jail?"

"I can come, but if there is a door or even a turn in the corridor, I'll stay behind."

The two of them started slowly down the hall as it zigzagged right then left. The passageway was built of worn stone. It seemed much older than the walls of the foundation of the Eterodeihon. In places, the cracks between the stones were so worn the soil behind them spilled through to the floor of the hallway. Unlike the basement of the church, water seeped through the walls here, leaving chalky deposits.

After a short distance, the corridor ended in a T-intersection. "Which way now, Iko?" Kora peered into the darkness to the left.

"It's to the right," said Iko. "I see a door. I'll stay here while you see if that's the one we want." Kora relaxed visibly when she heard she didn't have to turn left. He understood her concern. There was nothing he could name, but he had a bad feeling about what lay in the darkness to the left. Even facing prison guards to break out of jail seemed less dangerous than what lay down the left corridor.

• • •

As Kora crept forward, dinner basket in hand, she checked to see that the food was still warm. Though it was important that the guard find it tasty enough to eat, she was actually delaying. A wave of apprehension rolled over her. What if someone had already brought him some food? Not only would he not eat hers with the *trempious* in it, but she might be exposed as an impostor.

She stopped in front of the door and took a deep breath. She could explain herself enough to avoid the second problem but the first, well, if he didn't eat enough for the *trempious* to put him to sleep, there wasn't much she could do. There was enough in the dish to put a horse to sleep.

Trying the door, she found it unlocked. She pushed it open and saw a guard sitting on a stool in front of jail cells. A tall, heavy-set man with bright blond hair, he might have been attractive as a younger man, before acquiring a large scar across his face and a broken nose. The scar ran from his left forehead across his now broken nose and split the right side of his lips. It was an intimidating visage and probably useful for someone in his line of work.

He sat in front of a gate of iron bars. The hall beyond him was lined with similar gates. The stonework of the hall was cleaner than the hall she and Iko had just left.

The guard looked up immediately when she opened the door, freezing her in place. "I, uh..." She stopped and took a deep breath. "Margera sent me to bring you some food. She said you had not had anything in hours and were probably hungry after being up all night. I brought lamb stew and beer."

"*Kadzh*! Yesh, I'm hungry," he lisped from the scar on his lip. Thank you, girl! I have dreamed of breakfasht, but I don't know how long until new guard arrivesh. It'sh hard to tell time down here."

Beyond the iron bars in the cell behind him, a group of half a dozen sleeping men and one woman began to wake from the noise of their conversation. Kora looked past the guard as he took the basket from her and saw first Annissa, the street sorceress, then Goron. Her eyes met Goron's and a silent understanding passed between them.

The guard must have seen fear in her eyes. "No worry about them. They can't hurt you. Shells are magically locked. Only I have key." He pulled a neck chain from beneath his shirt and showed her the gem attached to the end of it. Then he pulled a spoon out of the food basket and began to shovel the vegetable stew into his mouth. Kora took that opportunity to back down the corridor to where Iko lay hidden.

"Leaving sho shoon, little girl? Don't you need to take utenshils back?"

"Uh... You can bring them back in the morning when you are finished," she said, backing away from him. "I um... I'm tired and need to get to sleep."

"Oh, shtay little while," the Ushidian said between bites. "You can shleep here if you want. Here, come putcher head on my lap. Sshheee... I'm sshhleeepyy toooo." With that, the guard slumped forward, spilling the stew on his trousers and onto the floor.

Kora turned and headed for Iko, who sat behind the door where she had left him. "The guard is asleep now," she told him in a rush. "He has a gemstone key on a chain around his neck. You can get Goron out. I'll go home now before Polous knows I've left."

Chapter 3

Iko headed into the jail where Goron and six others, five men and a woman, were held. He bent over the sleeping guard, searching for the pendant that Kora had described.

"He put it in a pocket inside his *yelya*," Goron pointed from behind the bars at the woolen jacket common among Ushidians. "You can see the chain around his neck."

"Found it!" Iko pulled the stone out from the folds of the guard's clothes and over his head. "How do I use it? I've never seen a key like this before."

"It's a magical key, as you might expect a *maholos* to use," said Goron. You have to take the stone in your hand and touch the lock while commanding it to unlock the door. I don't know the command."

"I heard it when they brought you in," offered a long-haired mage. "Repeat after me," he told Iko. *"O póntonízuva digímaviz! Niyasigód kélsham darám!"*

Iko started off uncertainly. "Uh... *O ponto... nízuva...*"

The mage encouraged him, having him repeat the next words.

"...digímaviz..."

"That's it, the next phrase starts with *Niyasigód."*

"Niyasigód... kélsham..."

"...da..." coached the mage.

"...darám."

With the last word, Iko felt a strange feeling inside him and heard the sound of metal rubbing against metal within the lock. The iron gate swung open an inch. Goron took no time opening it wider and stepping out of the cell. The other prisoners were a step behind him.

"Let us get out of here before this one wakes up." He nudged the guard with his boot. With that, the guard began to moan. "Quickly, now!"

Afraid that the guard was about to wake, two of the prisoners panicked and ran through the open door that led out of the jail, turned left down a corridor, and headed for the stairs that led up to the street.

"Not that way!" The two did not hear Iko's warning. Loud voices and the sound of a struggle came down the hallway from the direction they ran. They had encountered guards up the stairs.

Led by Annissa, the sorceress Iko had seen arrested earlier that day, the remaining prisoners pushed past Goron and headed for the door. They heard the guards coming down the stairway to the left sounding an alarm.

"We have to hurry, *Ketos*! It must be morning. I think replacement guards are coming," Annissa grabbed the long-haired mage's hand, addressing him with a term of endearment. She turned to the child who had released them. "Which way out?"

Iko pointed down the hallway he had come from. "It's one of the passages ahead on the left."

Mumbling some words, a light sprang forth from Annissa's hand and she ran forward into the dark hallway, the others following, Iko included.

"Wait! You can get lost in the catacombs if you do not know your way." Goron tried to stop them but it was too late; the others began to run down the hall following Annissa. Goron and Iko followed.

In the rush, Iko lost count of the number of passages on his left that he had counted on the way in. Was it this one or that? Farther down the hall, the group came to a T-intersection. Misunderstanding Iko's instructions, Annissa led the group left. After short distance, the hallway turned right into the darkness.

Behind them, they heard voices and the din of hobnailed boots on the stone floor.

"The door should be up here on the left." Iko tried to remember how he got to the prison from the Eterodeihon, but this passageway no longer looked familiar. Perhaps they had passed his corridor. They were going deeper into the catacombs. It was too late to turn back at this point, though.

Where the passageways in the prison were constructed from close-fitting stone, these passageways looked as though they'd been tunneled out of rock and soil itself. Water dripped from the ceiling about ten to fifteen feet above them, depending on the section. Weaker sections had been shored up with beams that looked as if they had been there a very long time. Some of the beams seemed to have rotted away. Passing an opening on the right, Annissa shone her light into it and Iko only saw more chambers; nothing looked familiar.

Goron made his way to the front. "They will be close on our heels," he whispered. "Keep quiet and go straight ahead. It's too late to turn back. Follow me." Goron led the group farther down the hallway, past another passageway on the right that led to a single chamber. After another distance, the passage turned to the right and dead-ended in a single door.

Goron tugged on the door handle, but it did not budge. "Iko, did you bring my lock picks?"

Iko dropped his shoulder bag with the soft sound of leather sliding and a light crash on the ground. He rummaged through it the bag a bit then said, "Here it is."

Taking a small leather wallet from Iko, Goron went to work on the lock. It took a couple of tries before the lock was undone.

Goron tugged on the door again, but it did not move.

"Perhaps it is enchanted as well," suggested the long-haired man who had helped Iko open the jail cell. "If there are many thieves in the catacombs, there are likely to be a few lock pickers among them. Someone probably wants to keep them out of the Domous. Picking magical locks is much more difficult."

"Can we use the gem we took from the guard? If it is a key, perhaps Geotheris can adjust it to open other locks," suggested Annissa to the long-haired man.

"The magic of key gems can be altered to open locks lesser than the ones they were designed to open, but almost never greater locks," replied Geotheris. "The lock and key are attuned to each other. A trained mage can detect the eldritch emanations from *sep* fields of lesser locks. Give me the key, let me see if I can attune them." Iko wondered what eldritch *sep* fields were.

"Are you trained in the magic of key gems?" Goron asked the thin mage.

"I have experience with it, yes," Geotheris reluctantly replied.

"They imprisoned him for lock picking," offered Annissa. "So if anyone can do it, he can."

With a pained look on his face from Annissa's comment, Geotheris took the gem from Iko and crouched in front of the door. Concentrating on the lock, he mumbled some words Iko did not understand. "Yes, there is an enchantment here. The *sep* emanations are clear. I have seen the fingerprint of this particular field before... There it is." The door popped open and stood slightly ajar. With a smile, he pulled open the door and bowed, beckoning the others to enter.

Goron went through first and led the group into a tunnel wider than the one the had been traveling. A door stood directly across from them but Goron headed left.

"Geotheris, close the door behind you and wedge this stone between the door and the jamb." Goron picked up a wedge-shaped sliver of stone that had fallen from the hewn side of the passage and handed it to the long-haired man, who was the last to come through the door. "I think I see doors ahead. We will go through there and try to hide in the dark."

The group moved more slowly now, trying to stay quiet. They did not see or hear anyone chasing them and each silently hoped they had lost their pursuers. Farther down the corridor, they found a set of double doors ajar, went through and closed them behind.

• • •

"Annissa, you will have to put out your light," said Goron with a tone of command in his voice. The chaos that ensued when they all ran from their prison cell convinced him that this group needed strong leadership. If he and Iko were to get out of the catacombs alive and safe, he felt he should take control.

"It will be very dark, so everyone grasp hands and we will make our way down this hall. If our pursuers are using light, we will see them first and be able to hide. I have not heard anything for a while so it is possible they will not pursue us into the catacombs. Nevertheless, stay silent."

Each of the group grasped each others' hands, Iko holding on to Goron and Annissa with Geotheris and the other man in a human chain behind her. She extinguished her light and the group was plunged into darkness. Underground, there is not the faintest reflection of a dim light. Indoors, light tends to find cracks in shutters and windows. Outdoors, even on the darkest night outdoors, starlight or moonlight provide enough light for the human eye to adjust to the dimness. But underground no light penetrates to aid the eye.

Goron had been in these catacombs before, long ago. Strange creatures lived in the dark places under Synnakon. He did not wish to meet any of them this time. His main goal was to get out of the tunnels. The most obvious route would be to go up, but finding a stairway up was difficult.

The group moved more slowly in the blackness. They sensed passages open to their left but moved past them. After slowly and quietly feeling their way down the hall, they came to another set of double doors in front of them. Goron touched the doors silently, noting to himself the fine workmanship that had gone into crafting them. It seemed out of place in these rough hewn corridors. Given their position and the direction they had come, this was probably the main door to the catacombs under the Merkebios. Most of the treasury of the empire was stored in those catacombs. It would be irresponsible to try to open the door for the sole reason of seeing what riches lay beyond, but it was the most likely direction to find an exit from the catacombs.

A voice in his head disagreed with his decision. "*Leave the door. I feel my cousin beyond; you must avoid him. He wants to be freed to find his brothers.*"

Goron had heard the voice before and dreaded its return. Why did it always appear when he had the least concentration to resist it? He could not afford to give in to its demands now. Too many people depended on his judgment. Its will was great but he summoned the strength to resist the call. He would try to open the door.

Feeling his way across the door, he found no handle. He tried pushing, but it was locked. He took out his tools again, searching for a keyhole. Sight is not a necessary sense when picking locks. The master lock picker will feel the mechanism at the end of the tools as it if were at his fingertips. Master lock makers often hid the keyhole, requiring great skill on the part of the person searching for it. Goron had great skill, but this lock was well hidden and it was dark. Perhaps there was an enchantment on this door, which meant that there might be no lock to pick at all. Whatever was beyond it must be very valuable.

"I cannot seem to open this door." Goron turned to where he thought the others were standing. "Geotheris, can you open it?"

"I can give it a try, yes." The sorcerer took out the gem he got from Iko and turned to the door, feeling his way along the wall. Concentrating, he extracted a dim glow from the gem. The shape of the door appeared in the faint light. Craftsmen had carved the stone with ornate floral motifs and bas reliefs of war scenes depicting past emperors vanquishing their foes. After spending a couple of minutes chanting quietly and concentrating on the door, he turned to the others and the light in the gem dissipated.

"I can find no handle or keyhole," said Geotheris. "It is indeed magically locked, but the enchantment is finely crafted. Someone with greater skill than any I have ever seen locked these doors. I can sense the *sep* emanations, but they are constantly shifting and I cannot concentrate on them. We will not be able to go this way."

"We will have to go back to the last passageway we passed," Goron sighed, relieved that he would not have to test his will against the demands of the voice he had heard.

Goron had the group grasp hands again and doubled back. Turning right into the passageway, they came to another intersection. Goron led the group to the left. After short distance, the hall ended and a stairway led downward.

Knowing what lay in the lower levels of the catacombs, Goron was wary of facing those challenges with this group, though he saw no better alternative. He had spent time among the beggars that made the catacombs their home. Many of them had come from Catacalonia looking for a better life than the hardscrabble existence they left back home. Hopkassenes, Melissenes, Dalassenes, and Hadassenes all spoke the Catacalonian language and had darker skin than their Doran neighbors They had all come from their home in the mountains to the west. Life was hard there trying to raise a crop or a small flock of goats in the thin soils of their homeland.

Unfortunately, the stories told back home of the riches of Synnakon did not match the reality. Most of the Catacalonian migrants who found work ended up as menial laborers in the households of men far richer than they. Those were the lucky ones. They all remained in poverty. Those who could not find work either sold themselves into slavery or had to find shelter wherever they could and an income however they could. Most found shelter in the catacombs. Many turned to thievery.

The Catacalonians spoke of unnamable things living in the depths beneath the city. Many of the less fortunate disappeared in the dark and were never seen again. Some that did return could not remember what they had seen but in the back of their minds, they knew something had happened to them. Those were the lucky ones. Others returned unable to remember where they had come from or even their own name. A few unlucky ones were incapable of anything beyond babbling of evil creatures in the dark.

Aside from the potential pitfalls of interacting with the gangs of thieves and beggars, if the stories were true, Goron would be putting Iko and the others in danger if he led them down deeper into the catacombs. He knew that he would never be able to face Aisarra ever again if he let any harm come to Iko.

"We have a choice now," said Goron, lighting the torch he had taken from Annissa. "We can go down and see if there is another way back up and out or we can continue to wander around up here. I have been through this layer of the catacombs before and the only way out I know is through either the Eterodeihon or through the Merkebios. We have missed our turn to get to the church and the doors we were unable to open likely led to the Merkebios."

"At this point, every *makaphos* in the city has been alerted of our jailbreak," said Geotheris. "They will have every exit from the Eterodeihon, the Domous and the Merkebios watched closely. I think we have a better chance to get out if we go down through the catacombs. The thieves and beggars who use the catacombs as their lair have their own exits.

"That path is dangerous," said the mage with closely cropped dark hair, very out of style in Synnakon lately. "They fight over turf underground as much as they do above ground. Terrible things happen to people in the dark. Shouldn't we try to exhaust every avenue above before we go deeper?"

"What is your name?" asked Goron.

"Kyrion of Attalia."

"Well, Kyrion of Attalia, we could spend hours wandering in the dark on this level. I have spent time among the beggars below and have searched the upper catacombs for ways into the vaults beneath the Merkebios. The only exits are the ones I spoke of. Do you want to risk being caught exiting through the Domous or take our chances among the inhabitants below? I am sure we can limit our contact to the human inhabitants only."

Annissa spoke up, "Geotheris said that every *makaphos* in the city must be looking for us by now. You know that half of the beggars in the catacombs are Ushidians, don't you? Ushidians work with the *makaphoi* to round up Catacalonians. That is why Ushidians are taking over the city. If the *makaphoi* are looking for us, we will find no shelter among them in the catacombs."

It had been a long time since Goron had visited Synnakon. The last time he had been here, Ushidians were rare. At the time, the Ushidian Kagan Krum had been pillaging the countryside in the western provinces. Ushidians were the enemy and none would have been allowed in the capital city. Now it seemed that they made up most of the security apparatus of the city and the Krolos Maholon.

"The Ushidians and the Catacalonians do not get along," Annissa continued. "I am Hopkassene and I know the brutality of the Ushidians. Merely opening one's mouth as a Catacalonian these days can get one tossed in jail. What angers me most is that we have been in this city longer than the Ushidians and speak better Doradic too!"

"The Ushidians are helping keep the peace in the city," replied Kyrion. "If you *kassoi* weren't thieves, you wouldn't have any trouble with the law." Kyrion addressed her with a derogatory term for a Catacalonian.

"Is that why they threw you in jail?" came Annissa's retort.

Enraged by her insult, Kyrion pushed his way through the others and threw himself at Annissa. He grabbed her by her *rokota* and tried to slap at her. She got her right hand in the Attalian's face and pushed back, trying to get the aggressor off her. Kyrion did not let go, ripping the sorceress's robe. At that, Annissa began punching with her left, her fists glancing weakly off her opponent's right shoulder.

"That's enough of that!" thundered Goron as he stepped in to separate them. "You are acting like two schoolchildren." He grabbed Kyrion's wrist and squeezed, forcing him to let go of Annissa. Kyrion's eyes blazed with anger at Goron's rough treatment. At the same time, Goron pushed Annissa away with his left arm, knocking her to the ground.

"We are not going to get out of here by bickering. Kyrion, I am aware of the stories told about the dangers in the dark. You, girl..."

"My name is Annissa. I am a woman."

"Annissa, I was not aware of the extent to which the Ushidians have taken over the catacombs."

Brushing the dirt off herself, Annissa had an answer. "I know where the Catacalonian quarters are. I was going to suggest we go down, but you must follow my lead. The Ushidians are to the northwest and the Catacalonians are to the east. If we stay to the right side of the grand corridor, we should find a welcome reception."

"How do we know that they won't turn us in for a ransom?" asked Kyrion.

"If I know the Catacalonians, they will not do anything to help the authorities or the Ushidians. I think we will be safe with them."

Kyrion appeared to weigh that in his mind. Geotheris and Iko, who had been quiet to this point as the two loudest argued it out, agreed to descending the stairs.

"I think we are decided," concluded Goron. "Down we go."

Chapter 4

Manoueka hated the dungeon. He normally hated coming down below the earth for any reason. The hollow sounds of voices, footsteps, water dripping, all made him feel claustrophobic. The smell of mildew and rot pervaded his nostrils. This time, though, he hardly gave any thought to his discomfort. His anger struck him dumb; he could not get any words out of his mouth. Any time he tried to form a word, only spittle came out. The guards that had brought him the news of the jailbreak backed away toward the door when he turned his reddened face to them and stammered. "Wh... Bbb... You mean... How did this happen?"

Mirán tried to explain that the guard had fallen asleep next to the cell and somehow the prisoners had taken the key from him. It only raised Manoueka's ire. He had no patience to wait for the Ushdian to find the correct Doradic words. If he ever earned enough money, he would hire exclusively Doran guards in the future.

"Valád is a fat fool," Manoueka said, directing his venom at his guard chief. "Why do you hire these oafs?" He knew that Mirán had only hired the sleeping guard Valád because he had married his sister. Ushidians overvalued their family, thought Manoueka. Of course, their families were less likely to drag them down as raise them up than a Doran family such as his own.

The Doran magician shoved at the guard's sleeping bulk with his boot. Still the Ushidian did not wake. He bent down and smelled the sleeping guard's breath. "He was drugged, otherwise he would be awake by now. Most sleeping potions only last an hour or two; he should be awake soon. Take him to a cell to sleep it off. I'll be along to question him when he wakes up."

Mirán directed Vélszid and Darzo to pick up the large body. "Be careful not to drag him, you'll disturb the pattern of footprints," Manoueka warned. The two, struggling with the weight, carried him out.

Manoueka scanned the packed dirt floor where the guard lay. He noticed the half-eaten plate of food and full cup of beer. "This beer is full, had he been drinking?" The magician asked more to himself than anyone else.

"Guards are not allowed drink when they are on duty", responded Mirán. "Valád did not normally drink, even off duty."

"Who brought him this lamb stew?" Manoueka asked, bringing the plate to his nose. "*Trempious.* He's been drugged with *trempious.*"

"Margera and her girls are not awake yet. We haven't questioned them."

"Get them awake! I want to get to the bottom of this. Those prisoners could be miles away. Find out who helped them escape and we'll likely find out where they are going."

Continuing to examine the footprints, Manoueka found those of the guards who had come in last, including the two who dragged Valád out. Ignoring those, he studied the footprints leading out of the cell. The pattern split, one set heading up the stairway to the street and another pair leading down a darkened corridor heading for the catacombs.

There was another set of prints, different from the prisoners'. These were smaller, childlike. They could be those of a serving girl bringing food to a hungry night guard. But they did not come from the right, to the tunnel back to Manoueka's tower. They turned left, down another tunnel. Looking closely, he spotted two sets of children's footprints coming in from this tunnel, but only one going out.

"Mirán, where does this tunnel lead?" he asked, pointing down the corridor.

"I believe it leads to Eterodeihon. But door has been locked for many years."

Manoueka suspected as much. "It has been locked for years but is unlocked now." He opened the door to peer beyond. "This is where they came in, but they did not leave this way."

Relations between the *maholoi* and the religious orders had never been good. The faith of the people swung like a slow, century-long pendulum between faith in religion and faith in wizards. The tunnel had probably been built during one of the low points in the fortunes of the magicians and at the high point of religious influence, perhaps as long ago as the reign of Hastor I, when the buildings above were built. In any case, it had been dug long before the Emperor had given the Domous to the Nankisos Maholon.

"I want a guard detail at every door of the Eterodeihon. Contact the Stegoi for assistance. Kerimeros Paleologus owes me a favor." He had done a favor for the captain of the emperor's guard a while ago by creating a *korína* to protect the captain's chambers from intruders. "You'll need them to deal with the priests. Question any priest who was in the church last night. Ask whether they saw any children in the church. Probably a boy and a girl.

He turned to the fleeing prisoners' footprints. "Put together a group that can track underground, have Brash lead them," he ordered, mispronouncing the name of Mirán's best tracker. "Follow them into the catacombs. Hire someone who knows the tunnels. Hire people to watch the exits and have them report anybody coming and going. I want Goron found alive if possible."

Demodoi would not take news of Goron's escape well. In fact, he was likely to be very angry. Manoueka would have to accelerate planning for his expedition. If he could not recapture Goron, he would need to travel to Iskander immediately, leaving too little time to properly prepare for the journey. He would have preferred to outfit the entire company in Synnakon, where he could take better measure of his hirelings, but Goron's escape made that more difficult. He could try to explain the situation to Demodoi, but he did not want to face the older man's wrath. According to rumors, he did not tolerate failure. Manoueka could respect him for that, but Goron was merely a means to an end for the mage. If he could find the stone, he could protect himself from Demodoi's revenge.

"Mirán, once those orders are given, find a ship. We must sail for Iskander before sundown."

Chapter 5

If it were possible for a tunnel in the darkness to get more miserable than the ones they had traversed above, then the catacombs below were worse. A fetid aroma assaulted their nostrils as the five jail breakers headed down the stairs. Annissa rekindled her light to help navigate, but the slime on the steps made every step treacherous. Supporting herself on the walls did not help, it appeared the green algae could climb and had covered the walls and part of the ceiling. More than once, something wet and gelatinous dripped on Goron's shoulder or back. He used a glove to wipe it off.

"Be careful of what might fall from the ceiling," warned Goron. "We are below the level of some of the sewers here."

Iko also wiped something black and slimy off himself with his bare hand, grimacing as he worked out how to avoid stepping in any wet spots while descending the stairs.

The stairway ended in a T-intersection. The floor of the corridor was wet but no algae grew on the walls. "Which way now, oh great leader?" Kyrion asked Annissa, sarcasm dripping off every word.

Looking to the right, the sorceress saw the corridor open up to a larger room. "We'll go right." The confident tone of her answer disguised her uncertainty. She had never been in the catacombs and did not know the way. She wished she had not said that she knew the Catacalonians who made their home in these tunnels. Her one consolation was that none of the other fugitives knew the way either.

Down the corridor, the passage did indeed open into a large chamber. The corridor appeared to continue through the chamber, lined on either side by a double set of columns. A pictorial relief had been painted on each column, depicting stories of men and women.

Iko stopped and inspected the faded painting on one of the columns. It showed a man in a tunic with no leggings, playing a flute on a hillside. Another panel showed people coming to the flute player from a nearby town and threatening him, a warrior carrying a black sword leading them. On another one, he herded his flock of sheep to a cave in the hills while a great storm destroyed the town.

"Are these pictures of the lives of the saints?" Iko asked. "They look like the icons at the convent but I don't recognize them."

"They are very old," said Goron, coming over to look at the pictures over the boy's shoulder. "Many of the stories of the saints are actually based on the lives of these men and women. In some cases, we now venerate the saints instead of these holy men. These are stories from the time of the Elder Gods. This chamber was once a temple, long before the priests of the Younger

Gods condemned them, accusing them of being demons and devils. The people continued to use this temple, so the priests of the Younger Gods turned it into a temple for their saints, changing the stories slightly to fit their own theology."

Goron's companions alternately looked confused, doubtful, or incredulous. "I've never heard of any gods other than the Four," said Iko.

"There are very few these days who have heard of them," Goron said with a faraway look in his eye. He looked down at Iko with a smile. "As I said, they are ancient."

"We can enjoy the sights later," said Annissa. She wanted to get out of this dark hole as quickly as she could. "Come, I see a door ahead to the right."

Annissa led them toward the door, which was unlocked. They entered a great hall, wider than any other hall and extending into the darkness. To the left and right, torches set in sconces lit the area. "It is as I suspected," said Goron, looking down the hall, "this is the *Megipurton*, the grand corridor. Like the one above, it bisects the entire catacombs."

As he finished his sentence, Annissa noticed two men standing across the passageway near a doorway lit by two torch sconces. They seemed as surprised to see her as she did to see them. Drawing their swords, the men yelled into the open door behind them, calling two more guards armed with foot-long paramerions. Each wore a leather jerkin but no other armor. The four armed men moved out to surround the group.

"Who are you and why have you come to the home of the Melissenes?" they asked.

"Be calm," Annissa warned her companions, then addressed the guards in Doran laced with a heavy Catacalonian accent. "We are fugitives from Ushidian brutes who have been pursuing us through the catacombs. Will you give us aid?"

With her explanation, the armed men relaxed their stance. "Ushidian thugs are no friends of ours, it is true," said the guard leader. "However, we do not have authority to grant shelter. We will take you to our Emilios. He can decide whether to grant shelter. Follow me."

Leaving the two guards behind, he beckoned the group into the open doorway. They followed him into a corridor built of stone blocks. These blocks were larger than the ones a level above and covered even more with mineral deposits that trickled from above.

The five fugitives followed the guard to a medium-sized chamber well-lit by glowing stones. Annissa's eyes were not accustomed to the brightness of the stones after traveling through dark corridors for the past few hours. Her eyes adjusted slowly to the dim light. A small, thin man reclined on a pile of large pillows, smoking a hookah. Another thin man, slightly taller, sat behind him and whispered to him as the escapees entered the room. Two guards stood on either side of him, and another stood at the entrance to the room. The room was much drier than the corridors and other chambers they had seen. The aroma of scented tobacco smoke and the perfume of wildflowers filled the air. Plates of food drew the escapees' attention immediately. Cheeses, sliced sausages, flatbread, and *mavos*, a fava bean paste, lay in front of another set of pillows.

"Welcome to my home," the man greeted the five visitors. "I am Giannas Melissene, Emilios of the Catacalonians of the Rock. It is rare for us to receive visitors here. Please forgive our meager fare; we have little to give and are more accustomed to receiving."

"I am sure I speak for my four companions when I say we appreciate whatever hospitality you offer."

Annissa bowed with a polite flourish. She knew that Catacalonian beggars were poor, but they were proud and any respect she could show would not hurt her cause. "We do not mean to stay long, but we must be sure we are not being followed by any Ushidian thugs that might be on our trail."

Giannas chuckled. "I can assure you, we would not allow Ushidians near our catacombs. Your predicament is known to us. We have many watchers under the surface. Please, sit." He directed them to the pillows at the side of the chamber.

Annissa followed the others and they all sat. Eyeing the food, she realized she had not eaten since the day before. Her hunger rose as he began spreading the *mavos* on the flatbread. Even Kyrion's hunger overcame his suspicion of the Catacalonian food.

"Tell me," Giannas asked, "how did you escape the guards in the Domous? It appears they did not pursue very far after they lost you."

With a mouthful of bread, Iko answered, "We ran faster than they did!"

This set everybody to laughing. "It is true, we did run fast," Goron said between bites. "Faster than we intended, for we missed our exit and entered the catacombs instead. It helped that they were overconfident in their magic and the one guard they left behind fell asleep."

"It's because Kora put some *trempious* in his food," interjected Iko.

"That was good thinking on her part," replied the Emilios. "So if you did not intend to enter the catacombs, surely you must be anxious to leave."

"I wish to leave as soon as possible," Kyrion exclaimed. "I warned against coming so deep in here."

Annissa frowned at Kyrion's lack of manners. If he were allowed to keep talking, he might offend the

Emilios and they would all be thrown out and possibly turned in to the *makaphoi* for a price. Tension was rising between Kyrion and Giannas, and she had to try to calm them quickly.

"Yes, we all wish to leave," said Goron before Annissa had a chance to say anything. "But it would be best if we could do so in as discreet a manner as possible. It would be best if we could find a way outside the city. I am afraid it would be too dangerous for us to remain and I have business in Kupria."

"Discretion be damned! I'm getting more and more claustrophobic the longer we stay underground," Kyrion practically yelled.

"Certainly, if you wish to leave immediately, I'm sure we can find an escort." The Emilios nodded to the guard behind them, who put his head out the door and gestured down the hall, calling someone to lead the fugitives out of the catacombs.

Goron acted fast to recover the situation. "I am in no rush to leave the gentleman's hospitality. If Kyrion or any of the others wish to leave now, there is nobody to stop them. I prefer a more circumspect exit from the passages. I would be most grateful to the Melissenes for whatever help they might provide."

Annissa shot a distasteful glance at Kyrion. "I wish to stay with Goron, if I may." Both Geotheris and Iko nodded in agreement.

"It is settled then," said Giannas as another guard entered the room. "Those who wish to stay under my protection may do so as long as they wish. Others may follow Marchion, who will lead you out by the most direct route." He gestured at the large, muscular guard who had entered, wearing a large knife belted to his waist.

"How can I trust this *kasso* brute?" Kyrion inspected his escort doubtfully. How do I know he won't knife me in the back once we've left this chamber?"

Annissa's jaw dropped. The Emilios's face slowly started to turn red as the others turned to face him, shocked at Kyrion's accusation. "You have spurned my hospitality and insulted me in front of my guests. By rights I should eject you from the halls of the Catacalonians, but that would be as much a death sentence as the knife you fear. Melissenes are men of honor, much more so than you Doran dogs. I have promised you safe passage to the surface, but you are no longer welcome here. If you are seen here again, you will face my wrath and next time, I will not be so merciful." He gestured to Marchion, the burly guard. "Take him safely to the surface. You need go no further than that. It does not matter how you take him or where he exits. He is to come to no harm, in spite of his insult."

After Marchion left with Kyrion, Giannas turned to his remaining guests. "Now that that business is done, perhaps we can have a more pleasant discussion. Tell me, how can I help you? You said you wish to return to the surface in a discreet manner. Do you wish to return to the city to conduct business or do you simply need a place to hide?"

Goron took a moment before answering. "I have business outside the city and the boy is with me." He looked sideways to Annissa and Geotheris. "If my other companions wish to join me, they are welcome. My main concern, however, is my horse and possessions, which remain at the home of a friend here in the city."

Annissa considered Goron's offer. Remaining in Synnakon would be dangerous for her and Geotheris now that they were fugitives from the supposed justice of the *makaphoi*. But was this rough man planning on living in the wilderness? How would she fare outside the city?

The Emilios continued, "Ah, so you need passage out of the city and wish someone to retrieve your horse. These things can be done, of course. Getting you and your companions out of the city should be simple enough. Getting the horse may prove more difficult, depending on the nature of his current custodian."

"I can provide a letter of guarantee," Goron offered.

"That would be most helpful." Giannas turned to the tall, thin man behind him, who was writing on a tablet. The two whispered together before the Emilios turned back to Goron. "I will need to hire escorts for you out of the city and a teamster to gather your horse and belongings. Of course it will also require me to find a cell with dinner for you for the stay, which might last a few days. It will cost about fifty *nomastoi.*"

Both Annnis's and Geotheris's eyes widened and they opened their mouths to protest. After all, fifty *nomastoi* was nearly three pounds of gold. Goron raised a hand to prevent them from interrupting the negotiation. Turning to Giannas he said, "I understand the value of your men and the service you provide, but I and my associates are poor. I can afford no more than fifteen *nomastoi.*" The two mages looked with surprise at Goron, not expecting him to counter with so rich an offer.

"I appreciate your generosity, but my men are also poor. Would you be able to consider twenty-five *nomastoi*?"

"It might require me some time to gather the coin, but I have deposited a small amount of gold with the Rimkai Manon Kroatou. I can write a letter of promise that you could redeem with them."

Annissa had heard of the ancient warrior society's banking system which extended throughout the former Cokan Empire from westernmost Acilia as far east as Harabia. She had no need for a bank herself, having no wealth and not knowing anyone who did or who traveled far beyond Synnakon.

"Excellent, then we have a deal," said Giannas, clapping hands and smiling. "I will have Arthetos begin the arrangements." Giannas nodded to the tall, thin man behind him, who bowed and left the room. "In the meantime, you may have this room at your disposal. Help yourself to food and wine. If you require more, simply ring the bell." He pointed at a bell sitting on a table next to the front door. "When you do so, someone will attend you shortly. I do not recommend wandering or exploring beyond this room. Please make yourself comfortable and rest before your journey."

After the Emilios left, Annissa turned to Goron. "How are we to pay a pound and a half of gold? I barely have two copper *sestroi* to rub together." She hoped Goron would not demand that she pay a share of the ransom he had agreed to.

"Have no fear, I have gold enough to pay," said Goron, waving off her concerns. "I could have paid the fifty, but that would have been highway robbery and Giannas would have had no respect for us if I had not bargained with him. He would have accepted the offer of fifteen if I had pushed it, but I wanted the business done with. Plus, it honors him to pay more. It seems we will have some time to wait here. Eat and rest." He pointed at the food their hosts had left for them. "We will need our strength when the time comes to leave."

Sitting down to continue their repast, they attacked the food ravenously. Iko did not eat, but slumped into a large pillow nearby, muttering, "I'm not hungry anymore." He scratched at his left arm.

"How can you not be hungry?" asked Goron. "You have not eaten anything since yesterday and now you only had a few bites of bread and *mavos*." Grabbing a piece of bread, he spread some spiced *mavos* across it and laid a slice of cured meat on top, offering it to the boy. When Iko pushed the food away, Goron moved over to him and laid his hand against the boy's face.

"You are burning up. You must drink." He poured some wine, diluting it with water.

"My hand itches."

Goron grabbed Iko's hand; a black crust had formed between the fingers and a matrix of black spots appeared underneath the skin. He pulled back the sleeve, exposing a network of black veins extending up to his elbow.

"He has the *mordigenon*. He must have gotten it from the mildew on the stairs coming down." He rang the bell Giannas had provided. A servant arrived shortly. "My grandson is ill. Call for a healer at once."

Chapter 6

Seabirds screeched overhead in the morning air, fighting over offal scraps a fisherman threw into the harbor from a recently caught fish. The presence of seabirds gave the impression that the Seniktikon harbor lay on the sea, when actually the birds followed seagoing ships almost a hundred miles up the Meginnikon River from the sea to the harbors and markets of the Emula, a tributary of the great river. The Seniktikon lay on the Emula, which was said to separate gold from water. In fact, it only separated gold from the merchants who rode the ships that entered the bay. A small stream fed the natural harbor but the meager volume of water from that stream did not fill its depth. The Meginnikon River flowed past on the east side of the city, doubling back into the sunken vale of the small stream on the northwest, creating the Emula. The river and its tributary created a peninsula of the ancient acropolis of the Merkebios, the impoverished Seniktikon neighborhood, and the Krolos Maholon, the mage district with its tower-adorned skyline.

Millions of tons of trade goods poured through the ports of Synnakon, either through the Seniktikon, the Old Harbor on the Emula, or the Neotikon, the New Harbor to the east on the Meginnikon. A number of ships lay anchored in the deeper water of the Emula, shallow-draft barges from upriver as well as seagoing ships. A few smaller boats plied the waters propelled by pole or oar.

On the docks near the screeching gulls, Manoueka supervised dockworkers loading his belongings onto the *Morspena Ula.* Mirán had done well to find this ship on short notice. Few enough ships made the journey to Iskander from the empire; finding one ready to sail that day had been a stroke of luck. His baggage loaded, the wizard asked a nearby sailor for directions to the cabin he had reserved.

Finding his cabin, he set a small bag containing his personal belongings on a bunk to be unpacked later. He had a number of tasks to complete before making himself comfortable. The small chair and table furnished with the cabin were small compared to the table in his study that he had recently acquired, but they were adequate for his needs. The journey would take a couple of weeks, so the furnishings would only be temporary.

A knock on the cabin door announced Mirán's entrance. "Boss, *makaphos* Askulas is here with escaped *alóze.*"

Manoueka sighed, exasperated. "He is an *alutsa.* Please learn some Doradic for once."

"Yes, boss." Mirán led Askulas into the cabin with an abruptness making plain his distaste for the Catacalonian *makaphos.* Having employed Mirán for over a year, Manoueka knew that most Ushidians did not like Catacalonians. Their lack of understanding of more civilized cultures led them to distrust the polite formalities of conversation between Dorans and Catacalonians.

"Welcome, dear Askulas." The *maholos* greeted his thin-faced visitor with a smile. Braxas, a hulking brute of an Ushidian, stood a step behind the *makaphos*, holding the tether to a disheveled, filthy prisoner. Manoueka's nose wrinkled unconsciously at Kyrion's odor.

The wizard had notified the *makaphoi* early that morning of the jailbreak. They certainly were not happy with the escape of so many prisoners. Two had been captured attempting to leave the main exit of the Domous, but Goron and three others escaped through tunnels under the Merkebios. Askulas had blamed Mirán for the fiasco. The Ushidian resented the accusation, but the *makaphos* was correct.

In compensation for the harm done, Manoueka had offered to aid Askulas in recapturing his prisoners. As part of his offer, he asked him to turn one fugitive over to him if he paid the offender's fine. He needed a mage with the ability to awaken the Stone of Power once he found it. Everything he had read warned of the artifact's danger and the risk of it overwhelming the user. He needed a man with no political connections beholden to him alone. Kyrion met those criteria and had the added bonus of having been with Goron when he escaped the dungeon.

"So this is one of the fugitives," said Manoueka. "Tell me, how did you find him?"

"After you informed the *makaphoi* of the jailbreak, they stationed men at every known exit from the catacombs. They were able to pick up two runaways but the rest eluded them. Given where the fugitives entered the catacombs, I surmised they would encounter the Catacalonians first and ask for protection. I made some inquiries with my contacts among them and discovered my guesses to be true." Askulas smiled and puffed his chest in pride at his cleverness. "I learned that one of their number would be ejected from the sewers, so I waited for him as he climbed out of the grating in the middle of the Megizikon."

"You must realize that, as soon as the prisoners escaped, a bounty was put on their heads," Askulas said, narrowing his eyes and leaning towards Manoueka. "Because your man was responsible for their escape, you will be responsible for paying the bounty to the man who captures them."

Manoueka cringed at the thought. The jailbreak was costing him more and more. He would have to find the stone quickly in order to cover his costs. "Did you question him regarding the others?" he asked Askulas.

"Of course. I found out that they had indeed sought the protection of the Emilios Giannas. However, this one quarreled with the Catacalonian leader, even called him a derogatory name. He wouldn't say much more to me. It seems he has an intense dislike of any non-Doran. It is no wonder he quarreled with the beggar king. It was not the smartest tactic." Askulas sneered at his captive. Kyrion scowled in return.

"Perhaps you would be more comfortable answering my questions," Manoueka addressed the Kyrion. "Do you understand that Askulas is turning you over to my custody? I have the power to put you back in prison if I wish. Or I can solve all the problems you have had with the Lumos Maholon," referring to the law regulating magic use in the empire.

"I have made some inquiries into your situation and I am surprised that a mage of your caliber is not able to obtain a license. My investigation revealed that it was a simple problem of missing payment for the license. I have taken care of it for you. It is a small debt. You have been kidnapped in a prison break with some dangerous felons, dragged through crypts under the city then mishandled and slighted by beggars only to be dragged again through the sewers to be arrested again. It has been a bad day for you, hasn't it?

"But no mind, I have arranged for your release and the reinstatement of your license. In return, I ask you to enter my service."

Askulas's jaw dropped at the wizard's generous offer to this filthy *alutsa* smelling of the sewers.

Kyrion's eyes also widened at the offer. "That is a charitable view of the events of the past few days, sir. You will protect me from prosecution for unlicensed magic use and breaking out of prison?

"I know my view of events sound like either willful ignorance or plain stupidity," said Manoueka. "Trust me, I am not stupid. I have need of a mage such as yourself."

"What service are you asking for?" asked Kyrion.

"First, I would like to know the whereabouts of one of the men who broke from prison. You would know him as Goron. Of course, if you don't know where he currently is, it would be helpful to know if he gave any indication of where he would be heading."

Kyrion hesitated, glancing first at Askulas, then back to Manoueka. Manoueka knew that the valuable *maholos* license would be too great to pass up and Kyrion would decide that cooperating would be the less risky path.

The *alutsa* spoke carefully and deliberately. "The Catacalonians were going to help Goron escape from the city. He mentioned wanting to go to Kupria, but nothing really beyond that. I assume he meant Iskander, but I didn't give it much thought. Nor did I have time to ask him much more before I was ejected from the beggars' hole."

"How many others escaped with him?

"There were five in the cell with me, but we lost two as we fled. I don't know what happened to them. Two *alutsai* escaped with us, Annissa and Geotheris. The boy who opened the cell fled with us."

Manoueka nodded. Kyrion's story matched what he already knew, suggesting the captive told the truth. "Indeed, how was he able to open the cell?"

"A girl named Kora came and gave the guard some food laced with *trempious*. The idiot didn't even finish the meal. He fell asleep almost immediately." Mirán bristled at the insult to his cousin Valád, but said nothing.

"After that, the boy came and used the guard's key gem to open the locks. Geotheris gave him the command words. After opening the door, we headed for the tunnel the boy came from, but the whelp got his directions mixed up and the sorceress led us into the catacombs instead, where we met up with the Catacalonian beggars. The beggar king himself bargained for their release."

Pleased with Kyrion's story, Manoueka turned to Askulas. "It appears Goron plans on leaving the city with your other two escapees."

Askulas thought for a moment. "You have paid me to turn over this one to you but I spent a great deal of resources to capture the others and I will not get paid for them until they are tried and found guilty. If they are going to Iskander, perhaps I should travel with you. I would bring Braxas as well." He gestured to his Ushidian companion.

Scowling, Manoueka silently calculated the added cost of including the bounty hunter and his retinue to the voyage.

"I am willing to help track your Goron as well," the *makaphos* added, sweetening the pot. "It seems that where we find one, we will find the others."

Reluctantly, Manoueka agreed to the deal. "We sail before sunset. Be on this ship an hour before then."

Shaking hands with Manoueka to seal the agreement, Askulas and Braxas left the cabin. Mirán escorted them off the ship, returning minutes later.

Manoueka scrutinized his newly-acquired captive. The smell would easily wash off. "You certainly have been treated poorly today. I don't think these bindings will be necessary." The moment Mirán returned, the wizard instructed him to remove the ropes around Kyrion's wrists.

"You have provided me very useful information, but I have one other request of you in return for paying for your wizard's license. I need help with an artifact that I expect to come into my possession soon. It is a complex and little understood item and I need someone with the utmost discretion. If any other *maholoi* were to know of its existence, they would attempt to take it from me and turn it to their own uses. I need you to help me activate it and bring it under my control. If you are successful in the attempt, it could bring you great rewards, perhaps admission to the Nankisos."

In spite of his surprise at the offer and his wariness of Manoueka, Kyrion licked his lips at the bait. The story sounded too good to be true, but the prospect of increased wealth and prestige tempted him. Gone would be the poverty of an *alutsa*. He could practice his craft as his grandfather had.

"You are obviously weary and we will need to be traveling soon. Please accept my hospitality for the day. My household staff will escort you to my residence and draw a hot bath. You will need rest and clean clothes." Manoueka again wrinkled his nose unconsciously at Kyrion's smell. "We must sail before sundown."

The wizard gestured to a servant, who led the filthy-robed sorcerer out of the cabin to accompany him to his bath, leaving Mirán alone with Manouka in the cabin.

"What did you find out about the dressmaker?" Manoueka asked once the foul-smelling prisoner left. "Did Goron return there?"

"We have not seen him. I stationed Darzo there to keep watch. Neighbors reported traveler came two days ago. One tall, dark-haired man brought wagon. His papers list silks from Melissa. He left following day and brought boy back with him. They stayed two days. Nobody has seen him since last evening."

"All this we know. I want to know why Goron is here."

"As I told yesterday evening, Goron met with known antarkanists, old men from Zalakarios, Berids, Morion families. They wanted help to rebel against emperor. Goron was interested only about you and Demodoi, not in rebellion. He planned to enter your tower, but we know that."

Manoueka considered the information. If Mirán believed the antarkanist connection was incidental, he was probably correct. If he was more interested in the stone, what did he want with it. Did he know of its powers? "What did the old man say? Did you question him?"

"I have questioned dressmaker. He is in cells under your tower. We get little from him. He is very weak old man. If we question too hard, he might not endure it. Young men have died under this kind of questioning."

Manoueka did not care about the old man's health. He instructed Mirán to press him harder. "He is more likely to tell us what we want to know if he is afraid of dying. What did Goron do in the city?"

"After Goron arrived, he visited Convent of Maranna south of city. The boy was raised there by mother. That is, by Materssa, mother of convent. She is his grandmother." The Doradic word confused Mirán. They should not use the same word to mean different things.

"I understand what a Materssa is."

"We have not gone to convent, but old man says Materssa sent message to Goron through him." He emphasized the strange word, getting a feel for its use. "She summoned him to collect child, who is now too old to live in convent."

"So both children are ten years old." Manoueka mused out loud, remembering that the girl was the same age.

"Prepare the girl for the voyage. She may be useful to draw out Goron in Iskander." Once the stone is found, she might be useful as well, Manoueka considered, remembering a passage in a rare book regarding incantations that would increase the power of certain spells.

"Has anything else happened at the dressmaker's house since Goron left?"

"Catacalonian horse merchants bought Goron's horse early this morning before we arrived."

The mention of Catacalonians sparked Manoueka's memory. Kyrion had said the Catacalonians were going to help Goron escape the city.

"Mirán, send men to question the beggar king immediately. That horse was Goron's. The Catacalonians know where he is. We must find him before he leaves the city"

Chapter 7

A man returned to the chamber as Goron inspected Iko's arm. The blackness did not seem to be spreading very fast. "Are you the healer?" asked Goron.

"I'm sorry, but no. I am Diotheros Iogeboros. You can call me Diothos. Giannas sent me to escort you out of the catacombs to a place of safety."

"The boy needs the hand of a *kailotos*. He has the *mordigenon*; it will get worse without a healer's touch."

"We have no *kailotoi* here. I have brought a tincture of renaskuta. It is well known to help all manner of disease. The medicine works best when the afflicted has time to rest. Without rest, the disease may progress." He handed Goron the tincture and a pitcher of water. "Use the water to clean the black crust from his hand. We will be going to the river; he will be able to clean again there."

Goron administered the renaskuta and cleaned as much of the black crust off his grandson's hand as he could. The skin was raw and grey below; black veins formed a network below the surface. "I'm afraid the

Emilios would not be willing to shelter us for as long as it will take for the boy to heal." Goron understood how Catacalonian contracts worked. Giannas would abide by his agreement to the letter, but would exploit any loophole for an extra profit, even if it meant selling out Goron and the others. "Our best option is to move while he is still strong and we can find a place of safety outside the city. Let's go quickly."

"You should know that our men found your horse and belongings exactly where you described them, but it appears that Polous was taken away forcibly by Manoueka's men shortly afterwards."

"What of Kora? Did anyone see Kora?" the boy asked wearily.

"I have no knowledge of any girl. Only that Polous has been taken. The rumor is that he has been taken in for questioning by the *makaphoi*." Diothos beckoned them to enter the hall and led them back to the broad corridor they had crossed previously, leaving the warrens of the Catacalonians.

Diothos led the four remaining fugitives down a stone ladder into the sewer. The tunnel ceiling was a stone vault with platforms wide enough for three to walk abreast on either side of a central channel. A brown colored liquid smelling of human waste flowed in the channel. The platforms were mostly dry, but large puddles had formed when the central channel overflowed, probably from a thunderstorm that had swept through the city the previous afternoon.

"Ach, whad a horrible sbell." Iko appeared as if he were about to retch.

Diothos smirked at the boy. "I did tell you we would be going through the sewers to exit the city, did I not? Come, the quicker we go the sooner we leave."

Goron steadied Iko, who appeared to weaken as they proceeded. The two mages followed closely behind. They passed a few side tunnels discharging effluent into the main channel. The sewer was fed mainly by spouts of water pouring from pipes overhead into a conduit below, which then flowed into the main stream. This water seemed cleaner, but none stopped to test it. The group had to skirt around the spout, moving near the central channel to avoid being spattered by the discharge. Once in a while, the spouts would erupt suddenly and without warning. Those were harder to avoid.

"I wish I had worn sturdier shoes," complained Geotheris. "These are getting soaked through."

"Keep them on and I will loan you some boots when we meet up with my horse and equipment." The linen shoes might be uncomfortable to walk in once they got wet, but it should be enough cover to keep the black crust off his skin.

"Do you have an extra *stola* as well?" asked Annissa, jumping over a pool of brown water. "I think my *rokota* is ruined." Her wool robe and dress were drenched, but not stained. She had been caught in a surprise gusher from one of the overhead spouts. Luckily, the water had been somewhat clean. A washerwoman had probably dumped her washbasin into a sewer grate above. After that, they had given all the spouts a wide berth.

"You probably needed the shower," Goron laughed. He thought he could probably loan the sorceress something more suited to travel in than a torn *rokota*. He did not have a *stola*, but could probably loan her a man's tunic, if she did not mind cross-dressing for a while. All of them could use clean tunics. After overnighting in a dungeon cell and crawling around in the sewers, they all probably reeked of sweat and shit. It was a wonder their Catacalonian hosts had not thrown them out sooner. On the other hand, Diothos did not seem to notice the rankness of the sewer. Goron wrinkled his nose at the thought that perhaps, the Catacalonians smelled this way as a result of their underground lifestyle.

After about an hour of slow travel, the tunnel began to brighten. Near the tunnel mouth, sunlight reflected off the harbor waters where the sewer discharged its waste. A few hundred feet from the entrance, Diothos set his lantern down and began to make strange squeaking sounds. "I am signaling our boatman with the call of the sewer badger," he whispered, noticing Annissa's curious look. "It is not so common as the rat, but would not arouse suspicion to hear one here so close to the river."

As if in response to the explanation, a man came into view, poling a flat-bottomed wood boat into the entrance of the sewer. Diothos signaled the group forward to get into the boat. It was wide enough to hold all six and fairly stable when the passengers sat on the deck. It had a shallow draft in order to ply the backwaters of the Meginnikon River. The boatman directed where each person should sit in order to balance the craft. Diothos and Goron sat forward next to a pair of oars. Annissa and Geotheris sat close to each other next to another pair of oars. Iko sat in the center of the boat and the boatman sat aft next to a tiller. Once they were all in position, the boatman pushed off from the sewer entrance, steering the craft across the surface of the natural harbor of the Emula.

The late morning sun shone down on a number of ships anchored in deeper water. Goron saw the shallow-draft barges that brought goods downriver from the south. Caravans bearing spices, ivory, and exotic perfumes across the bandit-ridden deserts from the southern city of Qamishli loaded at Trapezus where the river became deep enough for the barges' draft year round.

The barges brought their cargo to the Emula to be loaded onto seagoing ships headed to Dellys in the Ponaji Levant, Pinos, Iskander in Kupria, sometimes even to Coka, the old capital of the empire, conquered by barbarians centuries earlier.

Goron thought he saw a ship in the harbor bearing a Cokan banner. The thought of it brought back nostalgia for earlier times. It was not that life was easier or any better back then, he thought. He felt uneasy looking back on what had been lost. To him and to the world in general.

As their small craft headed out to deeper water, the boatman interrupted Goron's contemplation as he drew in his pole and instructed the passengers to grab an oar and how to pull on them. "When we reach the main channel of the Meginnikon, the current will be strong and the river is too deep to pole across. I will steer, but I will need at least two of you to row. It will be much easier if all four row."

The four oarsmen propelled the boat out of the shadow of the Merkebios and into the main channel of the great river. They faced aft while Iko and the rudderman faced into the rising sun.

"Are we heading to that shore?" Geotheris asked as they made the turn into the main channel, pointing to a stretch of willows growing down to the water on the shore across the river.

"No, that is an island in the river. There is no good landing there anyway. We are heading for a dock almost due east of the city on the far shore. The current will take us downriver to that inlet you see to your left." He pointed downstream to a break in the line of willows. "When we get there, the river will be much shallower and the current weaker. We can then row upstream to the dock."

The four oarsmen pulled hard, leading the boat almost directly across the river. "Very good rowing. You needn't pull so hard. Ease up a bit and let the current take us down some." Relaxing their pull, Goron felt the boat being taken downstream by the current. As they approached the inlet the boatman had pointed out, he ordered them to pull hard to enter the inlet.

"If I had you four on my boat all the time, I would have no problem crossing the river." The boatman laughed, pleased with their progress.

"How will you get back?" Annissa asked.

"I will pole back up one of the slower moving side channels to an inlet upstream of the city. I can then row across and the current will bring me back to the city. Have no fear, I do it almost daily."

Goron believed him. The size of his upper arms and powerful back was evidence of the man's ability with the oars.

The four rowers propelled the craft lightly upstream in the gentler current. The eastern channel was narrower than the main channel, and willows and cottonwood crowded the river more closely. Goron noticed Iko staring aimlessly at the woods, absentmindedly scratching at this arm. He pulled his oar in and moved closer to the boy. The blackness had spread farther up his arm. "Come, wash your arm in the river."

The boy gave him a blank look, so Goron lifted him to the side of the boat and reached his arm over the gunwale and began scrubbing the black crust that had formed on his hand. Most of the crust came off, revealing pale skin beneath. The blood poisoning created dark black blotches and a network of black veins radiating outwards from them.

"We need to get somewhere that the boy can rest." He moved Iko back to the center of the boat and sat back in his own place, picking up an oar. "Pull faster, let's get to shore as quickly as we can."

Shortly, they came to a break in the willows revealing a dock on the eastern shore. The ferryman instructed them to bring their oars in so he could pole them the final way to the dock.

The boat bumped up against the dock on the port side. The boatman jumped out and tied a quick hitch around a wooden cleat. He then grabbed a line from the stern and tied another half-hitch to secure the craft.

Chapter 8

Goron helped Iko from the boat. He seemed to have weakened during the journey across the river. Climbing the pathway past scrub oaks, up the low rise from the dock toward their meeting place, Iko walked slower and slower until he finally sat down, too fatigued to continue.

"Iko, we must go on," said Goron.

"I don't want to walk any more," said Iko, his entire body limp and lethargic. "I'm too tired. Can't we go back to Kora's?"

"We cannot," said Diothos, their guide. "My master warned that we might be followed. I must get you to your meeting place soon."

Goron lifted the boy's sleeve and saw that the black veins had gone as far as his upper arm. The situation had become urgent. He suspected that if the disease reached Iko's heart, his grandson would die. He scooped up the child in his arms and hurried to catch up with Diothos. "We must hurry. Is it far, and will your man be there with my horse?" Goron had given specific instructions to Giannas as to where his men would find Bason and his belongings. He had more of the healing *renaskuta* in his saddlebags. If he retrieved it quickly, they would make camp and Iko could rest.

The party of three men, a woman, and a boy hurried up the slope to the road road. Diothos led them a mile farther north to a rise looking down on a shallow valley between two hills. A man with a horse stood next to a lemon tree at the bottom of the glen. Relieved to see Bason, Goron ran down the hill, carrying Iko. As he approached the lemon tree, the other man ran away up the other side of the basin, the large warrior charging at him frightened him away. Goron ignored him. He gently set Iko on the ground under the lemon tree and began to dig through the horse's saddlebags. Geotheris and Annissa walked down the hill together toward the meeting place.

Before Goron found the *renaskuta*, he heard the sound of galloping hooves. The two mages stood in the middle of the road looking around for the source of the sound and four horsemen came at them, one pair over the hill to the north and one pair over the hill to the south. Each pair carried a net between them. The attackers wore lamellar shirts, their blond hair marking them as Ushidians.

Seemingly without thinking, Goron stopped his search and drew the sword hanging from the side of his horse. "Get off the road," he bellowed at the two mages, moving into a defensive stance in the middle of the road between the two sets of attackers.

He faced the charge from the north as the southern riders veered off the road toward the mages, who had moved over to the lemon tree. The two horsemen on the road charged toward Goron as if to capture him with the net they carried. The lamellar the Ushidians wore made it difficult for Goron to use the direct attack tactics of the Rimkai Manon Kroatou. The pure defensive strategy of the Setikos Stegos warrior society could have protected him as the attackers wore themselves out, but he had no armor available and did not have the advantage of time. The Kenous Pleudou society's evasive tactics seemed to be his best approach.

The moment the two horsemen were almost on top of him, he bolted to the right. He drew his sword across the throat of his enemy's horse as he passed out of the way of the net.

The horse fell twitching, throwing the rider ten feet away, where he lay unmoving. Goron turned to the other rider, who had dropped the net, drawn his sword, and was preparing to charge again. The attacker rode past, swinging his sword left handed.

Goron deflected the blow. He pulled back out of the way of the horseman's blade using the Sword of Water move. Finishing the move with Scorpion's Tail, he spun around and sliced the horse's flank as it passed.

Meanwhile, the other two horsemen charged directly at the two mages. The course of study for the magical arts did not include such topics as defense in battle, so Geotheris was at a loss as to what to do. When Annissa moved to split the two and make a more difficult target, Geotheris followed her, nullifying her tactic. Obviously, the sorcerer had never been chased by the *makaphoi*.

Annissa's quick thinking saved the two from the net, however. They moved closer to Bason and the lemon tree, making it harder for the horsemen to maneuver their net. The Ushidian on the left dropped it and drew his sword, leaving the net for the other. The other twirled the net in the air, preparing to toss it at the pair of wizards. The swordsman circled around Bason to flank his prey.

Although the two wizards had no experience in the art of war, Goron's horse did. He understood that the attackers were attempting to flank them and he would have none of it. Rearing up, the horse kicked up with his front hooves to attack the net-wielding Ushidian. Neither he nor his horse expected the attack and were caught by surprise. Bason came down hard on the other horse, knocking him off balance. Frightened, the other horse also reared, throwing his rider.

By this time, Annissa had regained her wits and spun to face her flanker. *"O póntonízuva wániz! Yasigód kélsham mam!" Ousion* flowed around her as her spell formed the clenching grasp that would stop a person dead in his tracks.

The spell had worked for her in tight spots before as well as against her, so it was the first she thought to use. It seemed to slow the man down, but it did not work on both the horse and rider. She ducked out of the way of the still charging horse in time to avoid being run down, but the spell had slowed the swordsman enough that his swing missed widely.

Seeing Annissa using spells, Geotheris thought quickly. All he really knew were lock picking skills. He knew how to form and shape keys and locks, and he could probably do the same to the buckles holding the saddle and reins on the horses. Quickly, he shaped out of air a key he thought would unbuckle the horse's saddle strap. He was used to fine work, but here the horses were moving quickly. He got his key close to the strap but the horse moved and lurched so quickly that he only gouged its belly.

"Make it sharper, *Ketos*," yelled Annissa, who had noticed what the other was doing.

Geotheris understood quickly and sharpened the key into a knife. As the horse turned for a second pass, the mage extended his spell beyond what he had thought he could reach and, following Goron's example, slit the animal's throat. Its knees buckled and it fell to the ground. This rider was more agile and slid off his horse at it fell, landing on his feet.

The remaining rider turned his horse again, ready to trample Goron. The standing warrior had avoided the first two attacks, but the rider was not about to be tricked a third time. He charged his horse toward Goron, who moved into the same stance as before, ready for the attack. As soon as he drew up in front of Goron, the rider lurched his horse left, preventing Goron from executing another Sword of Water move. Doing so, the horseman swung his sword into his opponent's left shoulder, slicing it open and leaving his tunic hanging.

The two unhorsed Ushidians closed on the mages, swords drawn. The one closest to Annissa charged. Panicked, the sorceress reacted to block her attacker. *"O póntonízuva digímaviz! Miyakistigád!"* A mound of earth heaved up between the two combatants, creating a small hill the barbarian had to climb. She was surprised that she had created the hill almost without thinking. Quickly rising from flat earth, it formed a wall between Annissa and the Ushidian faster than the attacker could climb, tumbling him over backward.

The armored man moved to get back on his feet more quickly than Annissa expected. She knew little about spells of earth and knew even less about fighting against a man intent on killing her. Barriers could keep the man away for only so long before the effort of casting wore her out. Moreover, she did not know that her spells were so malleable, but she sought a way to make it work to her advantage. Annissa needed something that would make him go away for good. *"O póntonízuva digímaviz! Kikilúd lígish kélshai mámai!"*

She manipulated *ousion* to open a crack in the ground below her opponent, who was still gaining his footing from falling off the mound she had created. He tumbled into the hole, falling face down at the bottom of the newly formed ditch. He turned himself over to climb out of the hole. Annissa was ready. *"O póntonízuva digímaviz! Yapligrivád kélsham kilam!"* She directed the hole in the earth to close, engulfing the barbarian in the ground. The Ushidian fought his way against the collapsing hole as the soil cascaded around him, burying him alive. It was not the most elegant way to kill a man; he would likely suffocate slowly beneath the ground. Annissa wouldn't have wished such a fate on someone, but she felt she had no choice.

Meanwhile, Goron had his hands full with the horseman, who had turned again to charge. The Ushidian had not counted on Bason coming to the aid of his master. The warhorse plowed into the horse and rider's right side, avoiding the sword on their left side and forcing them off the road.

Bason circled back to Goron, allowing him to climb on his horse's back. His injured shoulder made it difficult, but he climbed on his horse quickly enough to avoid the Ushidian's charge from off the road.

The two riders faced each other. Now that he was on horseback, Goron focused on the mounted combat tactics of the Étikai Manon Kroatou. The tactics were out of favor in the Synnakian Empire because of their close association with the Merouin Caliphate, so the Ushidian would probably not know how to counter them.

Goron held his sword tightly in his right hand. The wound on his shoulder made it difficult to hold on to Bason's reins with his left hand. He would have to rely on his horse's instincts. They had fought well together in the past under worse conditions. This should be no different.

The Ushidian charged again, steering his horse to keep Goron on his left. Goron prodded Bason forward and the horse charged directly at their opponents. With Goron's sword on the wrong side of his horse from his enemy, it appeared that the barbarian would have the advantage. Bason was a smart horse, having had experience in jousting and knew when to avoid an opponent's sword. Knowing that Goron's weapon was on his right, Bason veered left at the last second, putting the other horse and its rider on his right.

Goron and his horse knew each other well. Each of them had prepared the move, having practiced and executed it many times before. Now he had his enemy and his sword on his right side. The maneuver put the Ushidian at a disadvantage. His sword was now on the opposite side, away from Goron.

Now that he rode at the same level as his opponent, Goron could more easily avoid the other's sword as he charged past. He swung hard at his adversary's neck, above his chain shirt and struck a clean blow.

The Ushidian's head snapped back at the force of the blow. His neck muscles severed in front, nothing held the head forward. The carotid artery sprayed blood about a foot away under the pressure created by the warrior's active heart. As the horse charged past, the semi-decapitated rider slowly leaned sideways and fell to the ground. The horse continued galloping on without the rider's active direction.

With one swordsman gone, Annissa turned her attention to Geotheris and his opponent. The barbarian pressed the sorcerer hard, sword drawn and slashing vigorously. The magician attempted to block each swing of his opponent's sword with the knife he had created out of air. The warrior was faster than the mage.

The moment Annissa was about to bring her own magic to the fight, the swordsman feinted left when Geotheris blocked right. The Ushidian's sword stabbed deep into the mage's belly, spilling his insides. The sorcerer grabbed at his stomach, vainly trying to put the contents of his abdomen back where they belonged. As Geotheris fell to his knees, the swordsman stepped back with a smile of grim satisfaction.

Enraged, Annissa struck out at the warrior. *"O póntonízuva digímaviz! Kikilúd lígish kélshai mámai!"* If throwing her previous opponent into a hole had succeeded in killing him, then the same trick should work here.

A hole began to open in the ground beneath the Ushidian, but he had seen what had happened to his fellow countryman and tried to step aside. The hole opened quickly and he tumbled over the edge. Unlike Annissa's previous victim, this man fell partway in, clutching the edge of the fissure up to his armpits, and then he attempted to climb out.

Annissa had to close the hole quickly before the man got back to his feet. *"O póntonízuva digímaviz! Yapligrivád kélsham kilam!"* The opening closed around the barbarian's legs and waist, confining him in an earthen restraint. His arms and head remained above ground, allowing him to yell and grab at what ever came near.

Annissa grabbed a fist-sized rock and threw it, striking the Ushidian directly between the eyes, knocking him unconscious. She ran to Geotheris, who was lying on the ground, bleeding profusely from his abdomen. "I'm not going to make it, Annissa." He grabbed her hand tightly.

Annissa began to cast as tears formed, *"O póntonízuva... O póntonízuva..."* She was at a loss. Which spells could possibly heal such a deep wound? She held

Geotheris's hand. He tried to speak, taking a deep, rattling breath. His grip loosened and the light went out of his eyes.

Chapter 9

His footing uncertain due to the rocking of the ship, Mirán entered Manvecze's cabin with a knock. He had come to deliver the bad news of his failure to capture Goron. He expected a dressing down by his superior, but it was the loss of two of his men that hurt him most. Czúlirz and Vélszid had been with him for years. Both had traveled from the cool forests of Ushidia across the northern sea to this hot, foreign land, only to be buried in the dust with only one tree to shade them. Érzopirz and Czoszín returned late in the afternoon with their tale, licking their wounds.

Giannas, the Catacalonian beggar king had told them where to find the fugitives, albeit reluctantly.

Mirán had brought Kyrion and five men with him, including Barász, his best tracker, to find the *kasso* leader. He did not like the idea of bringing Kyrion on the expedition; the Doran *alóze* was far too arrogant to obey an Ushidian's orders. The value of bringing the man to identify the men involved in Goron's escape outweighed whatever misgivings he had about the sorcerer's arrogant attitude.

He had been skeptical of Barász's ability to track underground; the man had learned his skill in the forests of northern Ushidia. After arriving in Synnakon, the tracker had thrived in the city environment where the others failed. The city was not so different from the forest, he said. All you had to do was recognize the signs of your prey. A footprint in the dust of a dried puddle or graffiti marking the territory of a neighborhood gang were the signs of the city-dwelling man.

It was similar inside the catacombs. According to Barász, the catacombs were merely an extension of the city underground. The dampness of the tunnels caused strange things to grow, increasing the chances of a man leaving a track to follow.

Using these methods and the tracker's contacts among the Ushidian gangs, Barász led the team to the *kasso* lair. More used to knife fights and minor skirmishes among rival beggar gangs, the two Catacalonian guards stood little chance against six well-armed and armored soldiers. Knowing they were outnumbered and vulnerable, the defenders broke ranks and ran.

Following his instincts, Barász led the Ushidians in pursuit of the fleeing guards hoping they would lead him to the beggar king. Keeping the Catacalonians in sight, they were easy to follow. They passed doorways on either side of the passageway before the fleeing guards turned right down a wider corridor. As the fleeing men turned the corner, one of them grabbed a rope hanging from the wall and pulled.

Barász stopped short, recognizing the trap. His quick instincts saved the pursuers from serious injury. The rope unleashed a rock fall, pelting the Ushidians with small rocks and dust. Evading the trap, they avoided larger boulders intended to crush an invader's skull.

Picking their way through the loose rubble, the Ushidians continued their pursuit. Barász found the guards' trail beyond the rock fall in the settling dust.

Farther down the hall, ambushers emerged from the doorways in front and behind them, pelting them with stones. The missiles bounced off the invaders' lamellar armor, but a few well-placed hits bruised and battered the Ushidians. Mirán charged the rock throwers, setting them to flight.

Barász followed the fleeing rabble, hoping they would lead him to their Emilios. As expected, they ducked into a doorway leading to a well-lit chamber defended by armed men.

The guards stood in front of a thin man to defend him. They held their short swords before them as if they were large knives. Érzopirz and Czúlirz, Mirán's two best fighters, quickly disarmed them, using their swords to slap the weapons from the defenders' hands. Two other guards already in the room carried large knives similar to the paramerion of the imperial army. Vélszid and Czoszín removed their weapons effortlessly as well. Another man stood behind the thin man. His shaved head designated his role as a scribe, his eyes betraying a look of sheer terror.

Quickly, Kyrion identified the smaller man as Giannas and the bald one as his advisor. He also pointed out a third, the guard that had escorted him out through the sewers, humiliating him.

"Greetings, Giannas," Mirán addressed the anxious Melissene leader. "We summon you to answer questions regarding harboring of fugitives from justice of Thunolohoi Maholon."

"Leave at once!" The diminutive man recognized Kyrion. "This man has been forbidden to return here. You have no right to invade my home."

Ignoring his shrill objections, Mirán directed his men to seize the small man as well as his taller advisor and the guard Kyrion had pointed out. Binding their wrists, the Ushidians tied the three men together in a chain, leading them out.

Leaving the underground lair, Kyrion did what he could to insult and degrade the captives. Mirán grew more annoyed at Kyrion's increasingly self-important and condescending attitude.

They brought the detainees to the sub cellar under Manvecze's tower. Situated below the kitchen cellar, the wizard had converted the dark rooms to a dungeon of sorts. He rarely used it, but as a member of the Nankisos, he had the right to detain violators of the Lumos Maholon before turning them over for trial. Mirán doubted whether he had the right to imprison Giannas and his followers, but Manvecze had argued that the right extended to capture of those aiding and abetting fugitives from the justice of the Thunolohoi.

Giannas remembered Kyrion and refused to talk to him, no matter how much the mage ordered the Melissene beaten. It irritated Mirán that Kyrion assumed command of his own men, commanding them to torture the old man unmercifully.

Still, Giannas would not talk to the sorcerer. The small man's resistance to Kyrion's harsh interrogation surprised Mirán. It was only after he interrupted his counterpart's questioning that he gleaned something from their subject. Grinning through bloodied lips in mockery of the mage's failed questioning, he responded to Mirán directly, ignoring Kyrion.

"You want something from me, but nothing comes for free. I honor my agreements and Goron was an honorable man. He paid well. If you want to know anything, you must match his offer. I will tell you as much as I can without betraying our agreement with Goron."

Mirán laughed to himself at the offer. Catacalonians, especially the poorest in the city, were known to be mercenary, but he had never heard such a bold request. He would have ended this farce of an interrogation long before if he had thought that a payment of gold would get the results he sought.

"Goron offered me a bag of gold in return for safe passage out of the city. By now, he should be beyond the walls. I have honored my agreement with him. I can tell you where to find him in return for fifty *nomastoi*."

The thin man was sly. He had planned to give them the information all along; he only waited for enough time to pass to meet the conditions of his agreement with Goron. Once he fulfilled his promise and Goron was safely out of the city, he was free to make any other agreement with anyone else, using the valuable information for profit.

Once Mirán agreed to the payment, the Melissene revealed everything. The Catacalonians had agreed to meet Goron at a common rendezvous point on the eastern shore of the Meginnikon River. Giannas had them bring in his advisor, the tall, thin man they had captured with the beggar king, introducing him as Arthetos. The advisor described the spot with great clarity, down to the size of the lemon tree and the slope of the road descending into the small basin.

With no time to delay, Mirán had ordered four men to take horses across the river and ambush the fugitives at the designated spot. The *kasso* beggar king was true to his word. Mirán's men had found Goron and the others, but things did not go well for them. On returning from their defeat, Érzopirz and Czoszín described the skirmish, reporting that Goron had killed both Vélszid and Czúlirz. He had underestimated the warrior's fighting skill. He would not make the same mistake twice.

The rocking of the boat brought Mirán back to the present. He entered hi employer's cabin. "Boss, Goron escaped." Facing him, the Ushidian saw his disappointment. "My men tried with nets to capture him," Mirán continued, "but he fought back with weapons from his horse. He killed Vélszid and Czúlirz." It was difficult to admit that last part. It was never easy to deal with the death of one's comrades in arms, but he was a soldier and death in the line of duty was to be expected.

Manvecze's response was calm and measured, though he made plain his disappointment at Mirán's failure. "We will need to finish preparations for sailing. Get your men in their cabin. Kyrion and the girl have already boarded. We will not wait for Askulas to be ready and on board. If he wants to join us, it is up to him to be on time."

"Askulas and his man are in a cabin with Kyrion. I have made sure my men are on board as well. We are ready to sail."

"It is nearly dusk. Tell the captain we must leave immediately." Mirán left.

• • •

The ship's cabin grew dark in the oncoming dusk. Manoueka would have to light a candle. The subtle rocking of the ship made it hard to write, but if he steadied himself, he could check off the final items on his task list. He had hoped to get more done before sunset, but he still had many chores to finish and errands to run. He had no choice but to leave them undone.

Mirán's failure to capture Goron before he left the city worried the *maholos*. He had hoped to avoid a hurried flight from Synnakon by delivering the fugitive to Demodoi today. The news that his prey had escaped the trap and killed two of his men frustrated him.

In spite of the bad news, the name of the ship, *Morspena Ula*, was a good omen. If it flew as fast as the petrel it took as its namesake, they should arrive in Iskander before Goron. Demodoi would be angry for not bringing the fugitive to him before sunset, but given enough time in Iskander, they should be able to set a snare and capture him for the old man, smoothing over any possible dispute regarding his patron's demands.

"You have not delivered Goron." A thickly-accented voice spoke from the gathering darkness as if reading his mind.

The mage jumped at the sound, startled by the interruption. "Who are you? How did you...?" The door to the cabin had been closed, one guard stationed outside it.

"How I arrived matters not." Manoueka saw the man's outline in the gathering shadows, but not his face. "I am Témopirz, my lord Demodoi's faithful servant. You have failed him. He expected seeing his old friend Goron at his home this sunset, yet I am finding you aboard ship skulking out of town."

"There were complications," said Manoueka, stuttering. "We had him under lock and key, but his accomplices organized a jailbreak."

Témopirz moved out of the shadows to loom over the *maholos*. "I have heard of these friends, one ten-year-old boy and one young girl you captured. Your abilities are lacking, my friend."

"I must leave town quickly, Goron has already left for Iskander. I plan to capture him there."

"I am bringing my lord's message: Bring Goron back to him or men will be dying." Témopirz paused a moment to let the threat sink in. "Have you heard of practice called vampyr? It is one feared by Ushidians such as ones you employ. It was practiced in old Ushidia for centuries. Stories tell that it is done by dead men come to life." He paused again to make sure Manoueka was listening. "First, one man still living is captured and hung upside down by his ankles. All blood is flowing down to his head. Slayer then cuts one vein in his neck." He sliced a finger across his neck in imitation. "Blood is flowing out. Blood can be captured in pail or let flow into ground. Man dies and body is placed in public place. It instills fear in men, especially Ushidians. It is difficult for men to obey when fear is gripping them. You will not be seeing me again soon, but I will be present. Do not forget." He stepped back into the shadowed corner from which he had appeared.

Scrambling to find and light a candle, Manoueka illuminated the corner the strange man disappeared into. He found no doors or openings. He would have to ask the captain about secret openings in the cabin.

Part III

Chapter 1

Goron sat by the fire, listening to Iko's rough breathing and mending his own shirt, cut when the Ushidian wounded his shoulder. He threw another stick of dry juniper wood on the fire, sending a piney smell into the air and a cascade of sparks up to join the uncountable stars in the clear sky above the roofless villa where they had taken shelter.

Favoring his injured shoulder, he read again the letter that he had found on his foes after the fight. It was from Kyrion, giving specific instructions as to where to find Goron, Annissa, and Iko. The information was too specific to have been guessed at. Giannas himself or someone close to him must have provided the information. Kyrion's betrayal did not surprise him, but he had hoped for more discretion from Giannas.

Staring back at the fire, Goron began to doubt his promise to Aisarra to care for her grandson ... *his* grandson, he reminded himself. His road was dangerous. He risked danger to himself regularly. He had lived so long he doubted anything was able to kill him. Such a life made it easier to face risks that would kill any other man. But to have a boy by one's side needing protection changed everything. It had been a very long time since Goron had traveled with others. How long before Iko came to his end? And would it be because of choices he made for him?

And what of Annissa? Was she now to become a traveling companion, too?

As if she knew Goron was contemplating her and her fate, Annissa came over to the fire. Geotheris's death seemed to have affected her greatly. She had spoken little in the time since she had buried him. She had offered up a grudging thanks when Goron found her a set of ill-fitting clothes to replace her own, the *stola* soiled during their escape through the sewers and her *rokota* torn in her fight with Kyrion.

"Where do we go from here?" she asked. "I understand that we need to stay here for a couple of days, but I don't think we can go back to the city. Are you planning on staying here longer than it takes for the boy to heal?"

Annissa's inclusion of herself in his plans surprised him. It appeared she had already assumed she would be accompanying Goron on his journey. He had assumed she would want to return to Synnakon. Should he take her under his protection? He had been unable to protect Geotheris or Iko from danger.

Goron knew where he planned to go next, but thought carefully before speaking, not knowing how much to tell the sorceress or whether he should include her in his plans or not. "It will take a few days for Iko to recover, at least to the point that his fever breaks and he will be able to ride. Once he has regained his strength, he will be able to walk." He poked the fire again, sending another shower of sparks skyward.

"You are correct that is too dangerous for us to reenter Synnakon," he continued. "Every gate and port will be alerted to capture us. I plan to travel east to Iskander, one of the great cities of the Caliphate of the Amr aw-Wanaj. It is a long journey and I am not sure you will want to join me. You would be out of place there. Few people there still speak Doradic and most of them are scholars and old men. Your Doradic accent would mark you as a Synnakian immediately."

Annissa shook her head, her face stern and determined. "I have cast a spell with my cards, trying to determine my future path but I don't see the probabilities. It's as if something is blocking the spell, at least in regards to us. Not knowing what will happen if I go back to Synnakon or if I continue on with you, I can only guess. I know I am in danger in the city, so the least dangerous path appears to be with you."

Goron pondered Annissa's offer. "The journey will likely take longer than a month, perhaps two months, depending on how well Iko recovers," he told her. "Life is hard on the road. You are city-born and know nothing beyond Synnakon's streets. Sleeping under the stars and foraging for food in the wilderness are not skills you understand."

Annissa appeared to accept his warnings."I'm willing to travel with you, if you will have me. I've never traveled far beyond Synnakon. I took a trip to Ikerea when I was younger, but it was only for a few days."

She might become useful but that remained to be seen. She seemed to have undergone a subtle shift since Geotheris died, outwardly harder, more determined. Besides, he would enjoy the company.

Looking at the mage's linen shoes, he frowned. "You will need stronger footwear. Calcea are appropriate for city life, but the linen will fall apart soon after a day of travel. Perhaps we can find something in the next village."

Iko let out a low moan from his bed next to the fire. Goron moved closer to him and placed his hand across his forehead as the boy opened his eyes. "Your fever seems to have abated somewhat. How are you feeling?"

"I'm cold," Iko said, shivering.

"You need to rest." Goron pulled the wool blanket tighter around the boy's small frame. To continue traveling might kill him. The three survivors had traveled a couple of hours east into the rich farmlands of the province of Allyrion. The hills provided grass enough for grazing sheep and cows, but it was disconcerting to see how many villas had been vacated recently, probably due to the crushing tax burden imposed by the empire. On the other hand, the number of failed farms made it easy for the travelers to find an abandoned villa suitable to a couple days' rest.

He had given the boy a draught of *renaskuta* that he kept in a small healer's kit. The medicine was useful against infections, but the *mordigenon* had progressed quickly. There was no furniture in the abandoned farmhouse, so Goron fashioned a bed for the boy, cushioning the ground with some dry grass he and Annissa harvested from a nearby field.

"We should warn Kora," said Iko, as if he were dreaming. "I don't know if she made it home last night."

"It has already been two days. If any harm has come to Kora and Polous, it has already happened and there is little we can do now." Goron frowned, thinking of the fate of his old friend.

"If she's captured, we have to go back and free her." The boy started to rise, but could not find the strength and fell back to his hay cushion.

Goron laid his hand on the boy's shoulder. "Sleep now. We can discuss this tomorrow if you have recovered." Goron watched the boy until he fell back to sleep, his breathing becoming low and regular.

• • •

Goron prepared a breakfast of dried bread and sausages in the bright morning sun. They would need to find more food at a farm or village soon. His provisions would not last long among the three of them.

Iko slept late into the morning, waking occasionally for some food or water. When he did wake, he struggled to rise but had questions. He asked again about Kora, whether they should go back to Synnakon for her.

"No. We have important work to do in Iskander," Goron answered. "We must prevent Manoueka from finding the artifact."

"What artifact?" Annissa asked, returning from gathering wood for the small fire Goron cooked breakfast on.

Goron poked at the sausages, checking their doneness. "I believe he is looking for a shard of Kurovilos, the Stone of Power. There are seven shards, all pieces of a single stone that was broken over a thousand years ago. There were originally two stones but few know where the other is now. The Cokans gave the shards the names they are now known by. Ancient rulers such as the Cokan Emperor and other kings used the seven shards to communicate with their subordinates and maintain their power. They are much more powerful than simple communication devices.

Manoueka is very ambitious and would find uses for the stones that were never intended."

"But gems are only as powerful as the spells they channel. What is it that makes these so powerful?" Annissa asked. She added more wood to the fire, trying to avoid kicking ashes onto the cooking breakfast.

"The best explanation I can give is that, like all magical gems, they are portals to an alternate plane of reality," Goron explained. "Unlike other gems, the Stones of Power can open those portals and keep them open."

"Gems are portals to alternate realities?" Annissa said with a scoff. "It is well known that gems simply channel spells that mages attune them to. They are simply magic focusing tools."

Goron sighed at Annissa's lack of knowledge. Too much knowledge has been lost over the past centuries. "Yes, most gems are magic focusing tools, but all spells create alternate realities. To most mages alive today, spells and artifacts are building blocks or tools, but they do not understand how they operate. The entire universe, including the alternate realities, is made up of *ousion*. It is the eldritch energy that all matter is composed of. Everything you see and most of what you do not is created from patterns in *sep* fields and it can all be reduced to *ousion*."

"All mages know about *ousion*," said Annissa, " it is simply the substance that creates the magical effects."

Goron's lips tightened in annoyance at the sorceress' quarrelsome mood. "In a limited sense, this is true," said Goron. "But in a fuller sense, magic works by bringing alternate realities into our own reality through a transfer of *ousion*. When a magic-user casts a spell, he creates a *sep* flow. He is transferring magical energy to make a less likely reality more likely. His or her own perception and force of will determines the specific outcome. The *ousion* imposes that perception on the reality around him."

Annissa furrowed her brow, confused by his explanations. "Like my fortune telling? My spells allow me to see probabilities. Shall I show you?"

"Yes, please!" said Iko, listening in on the conversation from his bed.

Goron nodded his assent. Annissa had said she had already cast the spell last night and did not see his future, so doing it again now should not be a surprise.

Annissa began chanting, "*O póntonízuva wániz, digímaviz, niz, okuvuz. Akilód wíkiz kapirikaviz naviz.*"

As she finished the last word, she and Iko appeared to stretch out, extending along their probable future paths. The possibilities unfolded and overlapped, the various possible futures attenuating and fading into shadows. The landscape around them remained virtually unchanged while Annissa variously cleaned the camp, stoked the fire, and gathered more wood. Iko sat watching the display, his mouth agape, at the same time that he lay on the ground sleeping and rose weakly to gather his things.

Goron sat alone among the shadows of the others, no probabilities revealed, as if he had no future and he were forever fixed in the present.

Annissa glanced over at Goron. He sensed her confusion. The spell had no effect on him and she would see none of his possible futures. A sense like a whiplash hit him as she ended the spell, bringing everything back to normal.

"Can't we see more?" asked Iko? "Maybe it will tell us how to find Kora."

"No, I had only planned on quick demonstration," explained Annissa with a timid tone to her voice. "We've seen enough. It can get very confusing to watch if you don't know how to determine which action is the more likely."

"Why didn't we see Goron stretch out like us?" the boy asked.

Annissa turned to Goron as if to ask him the same question.

Goron hesitated. It would be unwise to tell them the whole truth. How much could he trust Annissa? He had just met her days ago. He measured his next words carefully. "I... carry an item that masks the probabilities. It will be difficult to cast your spell when I am near and you will never be able to forecast my probabilities."

"How does the spell work?" Iko asked Annissa, apparently satisfied with Goron's explanation.

"The spell shows what would happen to people if they were to do one thing instead of another," she explained. "Only you see both happening at the same time, extending into the future as long as I care to watch. It's like watching people live many lives all at once."

"Yes, that's it," said Goron. "Every decision point and every possible outcome of an action creates a separate potential reality. The universe is made up of infinite potential realities. All those alternate realities actually exist alongside each other. It is our perceptions, all taken together, that determine the reality we observe."

"But when I am finished casting my spell, only one of the probabilities becomes real," Annissa said.

"That's not completely true," said Goron. "Every one of these realities actually exists alongside the others and is connected to the others, but we can only perceive the most likely outcome. Your spell allows you to see all of those alternate realities."

Annissa pondered this while she munched on some dry bread. "None of this explains why the stones you are searching for are so powerful," she said. "If it is the caster's force of will and perception that determines the outcome of spells, then the gems should have no power beyond that of its user."

Annissa had a great deal to learn about the magic she wielded so freely. Few mages these days understood how the process of channeling *ousion* works. Much was forgotten during the antarkanist period and now mages simply worked with spells like recipes or gems like tools. "The transfer of *ousion* and manifestation of alternate realities is very tightly controlled by what were once called daemons," he explained to her.

"Demons?" she said, sitting up straight in alarm. "Then the antarkanists are right?"

"Not demons," he corrected her, "daemons. Daemons are not living creatures, though most magic-users these days think of them as spirits or gods. Daemons are the patterns that create *sep* flows. Spells invoke the daemons by calling on spirits and gods, but daemons also reside inside the gems. When you call on the gods or on the spirits of elemental power, you are also calling on a daemon to create a *sep* flow to transfer enough *ousion* to complete your spell. In a similar way, when you activate a gem, you activate the daemon that the gem's creator has imprinted on its crystal structure. There has always been controversy and debate about how these processes actually work. The *monousion* and *biousion* controversy under previous emperors is a good example." That was before the antarkanists won the debate.

Annissa sat shaking her head, bewildered. "I'm not sure I understand everything you're talking about. Daemons, alternate realities, and *ousion*? Nothing in my studies mentioned anything about alternate realities or daemons."

"Your studies did include invoking spirits and gods, and viewing probabilities. These are different names for the same phenomena, but your understanding of them is limited to how they are used in particular spells. In fact, they underlie all magic and all spell casting. Manipulating *ousion* is easier than most people imagine."

Annissa thought for a moment. "In the fight with Manoueka's soldiers, I was able to take spells I had previously used and changed them. Was it simply the force of my own will that changed them? What you are saying is that I summoned energy with my spell and shaped it the way I needed. Geotheris shaped his keys for opening locks, but he shaped a knife as well when he needed it." She frowned at her mention of her dead friend.

"That is correct," Goron replied, laying a hand on her shoulder to comfort her. "The possibilities of manipulating *ousion* are limited only by your imagination and your strength of will."

Annissa gave him a sidelong look. "If what you are saying is true, then we would need no spells to perform magic. If so, why do all mages cast spells? Why don't they simply call forth the reality they want?"

Goron nodded in agreement. "Casting spells is definitely easier. It takes a discerning mind and a strong force of will to imprint your own version of reality on the world. Spells have the effect of invoking a particular daemon, that is, a particular *sep* flow, as well as focusing the caster's mind on the specific outcome he or she desires."

Iko yawned at the discussion of daemons, *ousion*, and *sep* fields. "So we have to go to Iskander to prevent Manoueka from using a stone of power?" he asked. "Because he can change reality with it?"

"The danger with very powerful gems such as the Stones of Power is that they lay open the ability to perceive and alter many possible outcomes," Goron replied. "To discern or decide which reality will prevail becomes very difficult when wielding such power. It is like drinking from the Megizikon fountain in the great market square in Synnakon--the one that shoots great streams of water. Some water will land in your mouth, but you will also get drenched and possibly knocked over by the stream. Only the most discerning mind can handle such a flood of perception, let alone control it. Someone such as Manoueka who is very intelligent but does not understand the underlying processes would be overcome. Like most *maholoi*, he only works with pre-prepared spells, like a recipe book. He does not understand how these spells work or how to manipulate *ousion* for his own purposes, only that of his spells. Activating the shard could release forces far beyond his control."

"When we are done, can we go back and find Kora?" asked Iko.

Goron laughed at his grandson. "You are a persistent child. If we are able to succeed in our task, we will try to find a way to get back to Synnakon." He pulled a sausage from the fire and, testing that it was not too hot, handed it to the boy. "Have something to eat and then go back to sleep. Annissa's fortune telling showed that you need to regain your strength. When you wake this evening, you should be strong enough to start for Iskander." He looked at the sky, judging the height of the sun. "The moon will be bright enough to allow us to travel by night, at least for a while. The journey will take three or four weeks. We will have to find provisions in a village or farm along the way. There are no cities in Allyria between Synnakon and Iskander, so do not expect the comforts you are used to." He grinned at Annissa, knowing well the sorceress's poor living conditions at home.

Chapter 2

Iskander had fewer residents but was more spread out than Synnakon. Al Jebr, a low hill rising to its west, shaded it from the evening sunset. In a city with so little shade, one would welcome any respite from the heat of the day. An ancient, compact Kasbah topped Iksum, a smaller hill next to the Copper River. Iksum lay in the center of the city, with the classical Doradic city laid out at its base like a skirt sprawling as far as Al Jebr.

Aranel the Great had founded Iskander, building a small citadel less than a mile from a harbor at the mouth of the Copper River. Protected from the sea to the north by a natural sand reef that acted as a breakwater, Aranel used the harbor for his fleet and built the city on its shores. As the city grew, the Doradic residents reinforced the sandy spit with rock, dredged out the lagoon behind it, and made it into the largest port on the northern coast, larger even than the Ponaji cities of Palma or Dellys at their height.

Like in Synnakon, merchants came through the port, trading the agricultural products of the river valley that led inland from the city. Also, ships laden with copper from mines in the hills surrounding the valley left the port daily to be traded for Castrian steel in Burgos, gold from Bottia, or oak for shipbuilding from the Duchy of Devone.

Dominating the skyline, still catching the rays of the setting sun, rose the golden temple of Momadou, as Momados was known in the local Kuprian language. Nearby and more humble in stature, sat the antique library run by priests of the religion of Moshou, as Motios was known in the Caliphate of the Amr aw-Wanaj. The Tulkeen priests of knowledge who managed the library were more prevalent the closer one got to the Ponaji Levant, hundreds of miles farther to the east.

No walls hemmed Iskander in. Only the Kasbah on Iksum still had its ancient walls, repaired by the residents with brick where the stone blocks had been damaged or fallen. It was as if the primeval citadel kept a silent defense against the encroaching city surrounding it.

Manoueka approached the city from the sea, tired from the long voyage. He was not by nature a seagoing man and the incessant rocking of the waves and the *Morspena Ula*'s creaking timbers had kept him awake and restless throughout the journey. After three weeks on the waves, he faced the prospect of putting his feet on solid ground eagerly. His flight from Synnakon was hastily planned and hastily executed. Mirán had found only this small boat to take him and his Ushidian guards down the Meginnikon River to the Outer Sea and thence along the coast.

The *Morspena Ula* was less like its namesake, the petrel, than its captain liked to think. Unlike the seabird, it sailed slowly and its owner had little gold, as evidenced by its poor state of repair. Water leaked through the wooden boards separating its passengers and cargo from the sea. Everything Manoueka owned was damp. He had wrapped his most precious book, *Wonders of the Caliph,* in oilskin, so it had remained safe, but most of his notes and other books had been damaged. There had been too little time to properly prepare for a sea voyage the day he left Synnakon.

His fear of Demodoi had driven him to flee so hurriedly. The old aristocrat was determined to capture Goron, though for what reason Manoueka did not know. Perhaps Demodoi would have understood that the prisoner's escape was beyond his control, that Manoueka had done everything he could to turn him over to the ancient Ushidian, but something about the aristocrat unsettled the mage. Rumor had it that Demodoi became vicious when angry. Mirán had heard stories that he had drained his underlings of blood for offenses that most would punish only with a severe beating. Manoueka did not know if this were true but given Témopirrz's warning before they left Synnakon, he did not want to find out.

Demodoi's insistence on only meeting after sundown was but one of his strange habits. He also, apparently, had an irrational fear of boats. This was the main reason Manoueka decided on a sea journey to Iskander rather than overland. It should have been faster as well if Mirán had found a faster boat, but in their haste, the *Morspena Ula* was all he found.

Fleeing from Synnakon with Demodoi's money was a risk Manoueka had to take, but he expected the rewards to be great. The smaller amount of gold that he had received from Demodoi would be enough to get an expedition started. He did not want to sit in Synnakon waiting for another opportunity for more gold. A second payment from Demodoi would not be forthcoming without Goron in return. The warrior had escaped the squad Manoueka had dispatched to recapture him. Goron was likely in Iskander. Both Giannas and Kyrion had confirmed the fugitive had planned to travel here.

Kyrion lay below in his bunk. Apparently, the *alutsa* was less fond of sea voyages than Manoueka. He spent the first two days hanging over the side, emptying whatever food he put in his stomach. Since then, he ate little and stayed below where the pitch and yaw of the waves were less noticeable. He would be happy to know that they were arriving at their destination.

It took a couple of hours to get permission to enter the port and Manoueka was anxious to disembark. He intended to spend as little time in this city as possible. All he needed to do in Iskander was to find the books that confirmed the location of the stone and hire men for an expedition to find it. The sooner he could accomplish those goals, the sooner he would be on his way.

Finally coming down the gangway, he got a good look at the city. Iskander's port looked impressive on the surface, but it was nearly deserted. Warehouses and market buildings stood boarded up, a sign of the decline of the city in recent years. Few other ships stood at anchor in the harbor, suggesting that very little trade now came through the port. Apparently, the port bore the brunt of the lack of funds.

Waving his hands in the air, the *kupthaan* of the port, a rotund, bald man with a light goatee, came striding over to the *Morspena Ula* when Manoueka and his men disembarked, demanding a letter of transit from the emir.

"We don't have one," said Manoueka, surprised at the offical's prompt appearance. "They are hard to get in Synnakon these days. Damn these bureaucratic obstacles!"

The *kupthaan* stiffened at Manoueka's outburst. "The emir himself has decreed this law. I cannot let you or your crew off this boat without the proper letters."

Manoueka composed himself and spoke slowly, enunciating each word through gritted teeth. "I had hoped to obtain one when I arrived here. Here I am, now how can I get the required paper?"

The *kupthaan's* bristled even more when faced with Manoueka's condescending tone. "You can apply for one with me, but you will have to wait on your ship until the letter is prepared and approved. It might take days or it might be available this afternoon." The port official examined Manoueka. "I am no expert in Doradic clothing, but you dress like a *djenkiin*, a Synnakian wizard. That might raise some concern with the *am'mustari baydiir*." He referred to the Committee for the Prevention of Malevolent Magic, the organization that enforced the prohibition against non-sanctioned magic. "That might add some time, perhaps a day or two."

Manoueka was concerned that, if Demodoi had agents in the city, they would soon find out that his ship had landed. It was dangerous to stay here too long. "Perhaps we can come to some arrangement to speed up the process. My men and I are violating no prohibitions on illegal sorcery, I assure you. But we wish to avoid any delays." He produced two gold *nomastoi* coins.

The bald man's eyes lit up at the sight of gold. "I think we can speed up the process somewhat. If you will come with me to my office, I believe I can grant you an expedited letter that will allow you into the city on a temporary basis. Of course, you will have to come back later today or tomorrow for the permanent letter," he explained as he led the wizard to the customs bureau.

• • •

From the rise at the southern shoulder of Al Jebr, Goron surveyed the city of Iskander laid out before him. He and his companions entered the city on the main road, traveling downriver from the west. On the outskirts of town, they passed a number of inns. Men stood outside them beckoning them to come to this inn or that tavern.

"There are many places to spend the night here. Shouldn't we stop? We have been walking for weeks and sleeping on the ground." Annissa looked forward to a soft bed and a warm meal.

"Do not let these rat traps fool you." Goron walked past the hawkers, waving off a particularly persisent one. "Many travelers stop at one of these because they are the first ones they see. You are more likely to get robbed here than anywhere, possibly raped as well. Besides, they are overpriced and have uncomfortable beds. We will go to a place near the Kasbah. I know of one that is very comfortable and safe."

The three of them continued on, past the carnival-like atmosphere of the edge of the open city. The smells of roasting meats and spice from the booths that lined the road drifted through the air.

"This city is a lot different from Synnakon," said Iko, leading Bason. He licked his lips in anticipation of a cooked meal after days eating dried traveling food. "There are no walls or gates. Aren't there any guards to check people when they enter?"

"No, the emir has no guards," said Goron. "But do not let your guard down. Farther into the city, *am'mustari baydiir* make their rounds."

"Are they the *mustaroi*? I've heard of them," whispered Iko, drawing closer to Goron as if for protection. "They kill people for casting spells."

"That is not far from the truth," said Goron, putting a hand on the boy's shoulder. "You have likely also heard of Malmud, the first Caliph."

"Everybody's heard of him," said Iko. "He was an evil preacher."

Goron laughed to himself how people viewed historical events through the prism of their own culture. "That is what they teach in the Synnakian Empire. Malmud founded the sect of Wanaj, an offshoot of the Momadist cult of Hadrianism, preaching that any magic other than that granted by the four Younger Gods was derived from the evil Elder Gods and was therefore heretical."

"That is foolish," said Annissa. "You said that all magic is controlled by daemons. When I cast my spells, I don't invoke evil gods."

"The people of the caliphate believe differently," said Goron. He stopped in front of a man tending a grill of skewered meat and vegetables. Speaking a few words in Kukrili, he ordered a skewer for each of the travelers, paying with a few copper coins. The vendor wrapped a flatbread around the skewers and slid the meat and vegetables off into it. Pouring a creamy white sauce over each of the breads, he handed them to the three travelers.

Annissa examined her food carefully, picking the meat out to inspect it. Iko devoured his, filling his mouth with large bites.

"It is *tesoki:* grilled lamb, onions and peppers," Goron said, laughing at Annissa's anxiety. "It is perfectly fine to eat. Have no fear. They are not trying to poison you. They deal with mages differently here."

The three travelers ate in silence for a short while, enjoying the first meal not made from dried bread and sausages for some time.

The first to finish, Iko interrupted the silence. "What happened to the wizards here?"

Swallowing his mouthful, Goron answered. "Once, this city was not so different from Synnakon. Two hundred and fifty years ago the western Cokan Empire ruled as far east as Thelonia and the Ponaji Levant. *Maholoi* and *alutsai* cast spells the same as they do now in Synnakon." He reached into his bag and found some dried apples and gave them to Iko. "In their zeal to rid the empire of heretics, Malmud and his followers overthrew the Cokan governors of this region. They founded a theocratic caliphate and named him the Amr aw-Wanaj, or leader of the Wanaj sect. In order to prevent use of non-sanctioned magic, Wanajjis slaughtered many wizards and sorcerers and forced the rest into exile or hiding."

"So the *mustaroi* killed the wizards?" asked Iko, feeding the dried apples to Bason.

"Not exactly. The Caliph Yazd appointed the Committee for the Prevention of Malevolent Magic to enforce the prohibition against non-sanctioned magic nearly a hundred years after Malmud's conquest of Hikuptah and Kupria. Many wizards had already left long before. The committee is commonly called *am'mustari baydiir* or *mustariim* for short because of their habit of wearing white to honor Momadou. The *mustariim* derive their authority directly from the caliph, not from local emirs. They exercise this power throughout the caliphate, even in emirates not directly controlled by the caliph such as here. They are generally considered fanatics by the majority of the populace."

Goron had hoped to avoid any trouble while in Iskander, but trouble was heading for them in the form of two *mustariim* who had spotted them. He had hoped to find some local clothing for Iko and Annissa to change into; the cut of the tunics and dalmatics they wore marked them out as Synnakian. Annissa's recently cleaned and repaired *rokota* was enough for a well trained *mustari* to suspect the wearer as a magician. Residents of the caliphate never wore such robes for fear of being accused of being sorcerers.

"Zün! Yajunane fahasaya matqala. A'tab-bat'qulu al-maharumaat?" The darker-skinned one stopped them, addressing Annissa directly.

Annissa looked at Goron for help, not able to speak a word of Kukrili. It sounded like gibberish to her. Luckily, Goron was able to intervene. "Please, my friends do not speak the language here. Do you speak Doradic?"

"Yes. We must see in your bags. You must not carry forbiddens. She is *djenkiin*. She wear *djenkiin* clothes, very bad."

Annissa looked at her dress. Goron should have known her clothing might be conspicuous in Iskander.

He stood between the two *mustariim* and Annissa, "No, she is no sorceress. This is the style of clothing in Synnakon, where we come from. Since the wizards rule there, all people have adopted their clothing style. We are merchants," he lied. "We come to buy copper to trade."

"She must not wear *djenkiin* clothes here. We see in your bags now." The lighter-skinned one looked Doran, with blue eyes and curly brown hair. He was probably descended from the race that had ruled Kupria from the time of Aranel the Great until the Merouin overthrow.

"Suit yourself, you will find nothing." Goron remembered the key Iko wore around his neck, the gem that Geotheris had used to release them from the dungeon of the Nankisos. He hoped Iko would do nothing to call attention to himself. That little gem could cause them a great deal of trouble.

The *mustariim* opened Bason's saddlebags while Goron steadied the horse. They emptied the contents on the dusty ground, including their extra clothing, bedrolls, and the dried fruits and meat jerky they had been eating since purchasing the food from Allyrion farmers not far from Synnakon.

The other enforcer, who apparently did not speak any Doradic, rooted through their belongings, searching for evidence of illegal magic. After searching for a couple minutes, he found nothing. Leaving the contents of the saddlebags in the dust, they turned to Annissa.

"We look in your clothes, take them off."

Annissa looked to Goron for help.

"That won't be necessary," the older man protested. "Would you require a woman to undress in front of this crowd of men?" He pointed out the small crowd that had gathered to watch the incident. "Perhaps she can take off her outer tunic and you can see that she is not carrying anything else."

The lighter-skinned of the two agreed, and with a nod ordered Annissa to comply. In order to prove that she was no mage, she removed her robe and stripped down to her thin woolen *stola*. With a vulgar leer, the other *mustari* stepped up and patted her down thoroughly, not omitting her breasts. When done, he nodded lewdly to the other, telling him Annissa was not carrying anything under her dress. "You go now. Tell us inn you stay at so we visit you again."

"We are staying at *Lasd al-Tha'ab*, The Golden Lion." Goron pointed east towards the Kasbah, the old neighborhood on Iksum. "It is run by Lazaar. He has known me for years."

With that, the two *mustariim* left them, though they stayed a short distance away. The crowd around them dispersed while Annissa dressed, fuming at the humiliation. "Why did you tell them where we are staying? I don't want them showing up at our doorstep to ransack our room."

"Because they will follow us and find out where we are going anyway. I would rather not antagonize them any more than we already have. I warned you that people here are hostile to magic-users."

"Next time you want to avoid antagonizing someone, you can be the one to strip to your underwear."

"I'm sorry, I forgot that you were wearing a *rokota.* That alone is enough to raise suspicion here. I will warn you again not to use any spells while we are here. Or any magic items," he added, looking at Iko. Iko moved his hand to the gem hanging from his neck, but immediately took it away, looking around to make sure the *mustariim* did not see him.

Sensing that Annissa's clothing had attracted the *mustariim* attention, a garment peddler came up to them and displayed some robes in the local style. "Five, five. Nice. You buy?" It seemed he had reached the limit of his Doradic and began pantomiming changing clothes. Goron encouraged Annissa to choose some clothes. She picked out a striped cotton dress and a simple *abaya* while Goron paid the man. She packed away the dress but changed from her *rokota* into the new *abaya.*

They reached the *Lasd al-Tha'ab* at the base of Iksum, followed conspicuously and not far behind by the two *mustariim* who had not gone far from them. The inn was a small place, its stone-paved courtyard not quite large enough for the three of them and the horse. In the center stood a tall date palm with a small pool at the base. A comely young woman swept at the entrance to the house.

Goron called out in Kuprian, "Is Lazaar here? We come seeking rooms. Tell him Garoun is here to visit."

The woman stepped into the house, calling for Lazaar. After a minute, she came back with a white-bearded, bald gentleman wearing a finely embroidered tunic and shawl against the approaching coolness of the evening.

"Garoun! I did not expect you. Had I known you were coming, I would have reserved my finest room. It has been a long time," the innkeeper said, speaking in a nonstop chatter. "Come in and rest. I will have my boy take your horse to the stable. It is run by the son of a close friend, may he rest in peace. You and your companions must be tired after your journey. Have you come far? Of course you have--you will want to wash the dust of the road off. Except your friend with the new *abaya*. Will she be staying as well or is she local?"

Goron removed his saddlebags from Bason and handed one to Annissa and one to Iko. He laughed at his old friend's rapid-fire conversation. "Lazaar, it is good to see you. We are three. We purchased the new *abaya* today to cover my friend. Apparently, two *mustariim* thought she dressed too much like a sorceress. We would like to avoid any trouble," he added with a wink and nodded to the two *mustariim* who followed them.

"Ah, those two," Lazaar said, looking out the gate at the two. "You encountered a couple of the more fanatical members of the committee. Not to worry, they won't bother you here." Letting a younger boy out to take the horse, he closed the gate on the two *mustariim*, who had already started away down the street.

With a wave, he led them into the house. The interior was cooler than the city outside and the scent of jasmine and sandalwood drifted in the air. The young woman came in offering a tray with four silver cups and a plate of pastries. Iko took a pastry eagerly. It tasted of nuts and was sweet and crunchy. He washed it down with the water, which smelled of lemon and roses and was cool and refreshing after the long day of travel.

Lazaar showed them to a pair of adjacent rooms, each with a washbasin and clean linen towels. Goron and Iko's room had two beds. He gave Annissa her own, smaller room. Both rooms were much larger than one might expect given the size of the house. "Please make yourself comfortable. Take some time to clean up and rest. We will be serving dinner soon, and I would be honored to have you join us." He turned to Goron. "I would enjoy a conversation with you. I have not had the pleasure in a very long time."

Annissa went to her own room, heading directly to the washbasin, smiling in pleasure at the rose-scented soap and white cotton towels. Iko splashed around in the water a bit until Goron pointed to the soap and told him to clean himself more thoroughly. Goron himself cleaned absentmindedly, pondering his next move.

Manoueka had been corresponding with the library in Iskander regarding the treasury of the Mad Caliph Harun and a book describing the tombs of the Twenty-seventh Dynasty of Ptahmel. He wondered when Manoueka would mount an expedition to the tombs and whether he had begun already. Certainly, he had questions he needed answers to.

Tomorrow he would visit the library of the Tulkeen. The library had first been built at the founding of the city by Aranel the Great, who also went locally by the Kuprian name Xander, whence the name of the city. The library had later been taken over by a sect of the priests of Motios called the Tulkeen, dedicated to law and learning. They had tended the ancient texts like they would a great treasure. Few uninitiated were allowed to view the books. Goron had not visited the library in over fifty years, but he remembered a young priest he once knew there. Perhaps the man would remember him as well. He hoped it would be enough to permit him access.

Tonight, he would visit with Lazaar. It had not been so long since he had visited this city. Hopefully, Lazaar had kept faith with the Menthani in that time.

After finishing cleaning himself and donning a fresh tunic, Goron left the other two lying on their beds, Annissa having already fallen asleep in her room, and went to find Lazaar. He found the older man in the dining room reading some letters.

"Have you come for dinner, then?" asked Lazaar, setting down his reading. "My daughter Abiir will be out shortly. She found a nice lamb a few days ago and we have been eating it roasted and stewed. Tonight, she is directing the cooks to prepare spiced meatballs with rice and cucumber. It should be very tasty."

Goron pulled up a chair and took a seat across the table from Lazaar. "I look forward to it. My companions will as well, we have had nothing but dried fruit and meat since leaving Synnakon."

"That is a long journey," said Lazaar, offering Goron a bowl of pistachios. "What trouble brings you here from so far away?"

"Can an old friend not simply stop for a visit?" Goron asked, taking a nut and eating it.

Lazaar smiled wryly at his visitor's question as if it were a bad joke. "All the members of the Menthani say the same thing: Goron only arrives when there is trouble. If there is none to be had, he will bring it with him."

Goron sighed. "I suppose that is true and just as true in this case. I must visit the library of the Tulkeen. There are books there that might lead someone to one of the Stones."

Lazaar's eyes went wide with the mention of the Stones. "Shhh... You must not be heard speaking of such things. Abiir is trustworthy, but I have told her nothing of the Stones. I don't trust the stable boy to stay quiet, though. My cousin Meshaal who owns the stables sent him. The boy loves telling stories and sometimes I suspect Meshaal's sympathies lie with the *mustariim*."

"I will keep it quiet, and warn my companions as well," said Goron. "Tell me what you have heard these past few years."

"I do not need to go so far back for news to tell you. I suspected you might arrive soon after we heard about the Doran magician who arrived by boat. The customs officers gave him a bit of trouble, but found nothing incriminating so let him go. He arrived yesterday and as far as I know, he has not left yet. He seeks to visit the Tulkeen as well. "

"Do you know whom he seeks among the priests?"

"I thought you might ask; it is a man by the name of Dithaan. He is wanted by the *mustariim* for giving aid to magicians, but he is protected as a priest of Moshou. They cannot touch him in the Library of the Tulkeen. It is from him that your Doran friend seeks help. If the magician seeks the stones, then Dithaan has unwittingly associated himself with dangerous powers."

"What would it take to convince someone in the emir's court that the ship is not welcome here?"

"As you know, magicians are undesirable in the realm of the caliph. It would not take much to convince the right official to rescind his entry documents. A couple of pieces of gold would do it," Lazaar said, rubbing two fingers against his thumb.

"I am sure we can find something that will suffice," said Goron, patting a pouch hanging at his side. "As for the Tulkeen, do you have contacts among them?"

Putting a finger to his mouth, Lazaar leaned back in thought. "I know one or two among the Tulkeen who would be sympathetic to our cause. Ashaar is the sedormatos of the library. He has helped us in the past. I can write a letter to introduce you."“

Abiir entered with two servants carrying plates of meatballs, rice, and vegetable, interrupting their conversation . "Ah, here is dinner!" said Lazaar. "Let us summon your companions to eat and speak of business later."

Chapter 3

Having obtained the letter from the *kupthaan*, Manoueka reflected on the venality of minor officials. Perhaps they were worse in these backwaters, but even in Synnakon, gold seemed to smooth the official machinery. Not that he was happy giving up even two coins. Those two coins probably meant one month's worth of labor for a man in this country. Hopefully it would not be necessary to hire too many men for too long. There was still the matter of paying the captain of the *Morspena Ula* the remainder of his fare and unloading the ship.

His most precious cargo besides Demodoi's gold was the girl. Somehow she had helped Goron escape the dungeon with the rest of the prisoners. Mirán had traced her back to Polous, the old man the traitor had first contacted when entering Synnakon. He did not understand the warrior's connection to the old man and his granddaughter, but since the old man had not survived the questioning by the *makaphoi* interrogators he decided to bring the girl with him. Perhaps she would prove useful after he found the stone.

Returning to the ship, he summoned Mirán. "I will need you to do three things for me. First, get this ship unloaded and find me lodging. I will need finer accommodation than we will likely find in the port area." Manoueka was tired of the dampness of the boat and needed to stay on dry land for a while, at least long enough to air out his manuscripts. "Get the girl a small, secure room attached to my own. Find something cheaper for yourself and your men. Kyrion can stay with you as well. I want a man posted with the girl at all times and one with me at all times.

"Second, I believe Goron is coming to this city. Brash is a hunter, isn't he? Have him hunt the man down. Make sure he does not confront Goron; he is dangerous and resourceful. You heard what he did to your squad outside Synnakon. When he finds him, report back to me and we will figure out how to capture him and return him to Demodoi. Coordinate with Askulas. He will no doubt be looking for the *alutsa* he seeks and she will likely be with Goron.

"Finally, get me something to eat that doesn't make mewant to retch. I'm sick of hardtack and dried fish. I'll be going to the library for research. I may be there all day. Get a message to me when you find me lodging."

Mirán directed Czoszín, one of his better fighters, to follow Manoueka as the wizard left and the large, blonde warrior carrying a two foot blade fell in behind him.

"Kyrion!" the *maholos* beckoned the other mage, who was standing around looking completely useless. "Come with me."

Eager to be of service, the short-haired mage followed.

The library lay between the port district and the small hill of Iksum. The great temple dedicated to Momados also lay in the same neighborhood. Reflecting on the potential difficulty he might run into if he encountered the *am'mustari baydiir*, Manoueka avoided the temple on his way to the library. Hopefully, the priests of Motios would not have the same attitude toward magic-users that the *mustariim* had.

Approaching the library, he pondered its similarity to a temple. Of course, technically it *was* a temple to Motios, managed by the Tulkeen sect. It was here that he would find the final clue in his search for the shard. He suspected from *Wonders of the Caliph* that the Mad Caliph Harun had buried it in an ancient Hikuptahn tomb in Ptahmel. He needed to see the books held by the Tulkeen to confirm the story and find the specific location. He would be able to determine which king's tomb the Mad Caliph had buried the stones in by studying the *Treasuries of the Caliph Harun.* His understanding of *An Exploration of the Tombs* was that the book located in specific detail each of tombs of the kings of the Twenty-seventh Dynasty. Together those two books would provide the key to the mystery of Korefael, Second Jewel of the Kings.

Manoueka and his two subordinates approached the great doors of the library, which were carved with various scenes of the life of Motios. The scenes depicted Motios teaching his followers, judging disputes, and giving law to civilization. One scene showed him holding an ancient book written with the first laws. The carvings must have been quite ancient, the book in the scene having been written in ancient Doran. Few in this city nowadays could read the script; most everyone who could read at all had been taught in the Habric script.

The wizard instructed Czoszín to announce their presence by banging a large brass knocker hung from the center of the door. After a few minutes, a wispy-haired man, shrunken by age, opened a smaller blind door built into the larger doors.

"Hello. What business brings you to the Temple of Moshou?"

"I have come seeking two books in your collection. I have a letter from one of your members, a certain Dithaan." Pulling the letter out of his dalmatic, he unfolded it and presented it to the wrinkled priest.

Hearing his colleague's name, a look of concern crossed the ancient cleric's face. He took the letter, and holding it close to his straining eyes, read it. "Please wait here," he instructed, taking the letter inside and closing the door behind him.

"Come back here with that letter!" Manoueka shrieked. He was not about to be put off entering the library after his long journey. Talisman-like, the letter was his only license to enter the library and access their books. He knew the Tulkeen were very protective of their collection, which is why he had written to them in the first place.

He banged on the door with his fist then thought better of it, the rough surface being carved in bas-relief. He began to inspect the surface, searching for a latch or handle to open it from the outside.

Finding nothing after a short search, he considered a spell to open the door. Such spells were common in Synnakon, but strictly forbidden in Iskander. After looking around to make sure no onlookers saw him, he began casting.

Kyrion interrupted him immediately. "Is it wise to be casting a spell here? You were very clear about the dangers when you explained about the *mustariim* earlier."

Manoueka closed his eyes to compose himself before turning to Kyrion, addressing him as he would an impudent child. "Do you see anyone wearing a white cloak here? In fact, do you see anyone here that would be able to accuse me? Czoszín, keep an eye out for onlookers."

The Ushidian nodded in assent as the wizard turned back to the door, beginning the spell again. It was a simple and short spell, one of the basic spells known in Synnakon. Most doors in the city of wizards had been counterspelled against it, but in Iskander, where most magic was forbidden, he did not expect such countermeasures.

He was correct. The door opened before them.

As he and his companions entered the building, the old priest returned with another wizened cleric, this one only slightly younger than the other, and two younger, larger men. The two Tulkeen priests stopped short on seeing the intruders.

"How did you enter?" the second priest asked Manoueka, his voice creaking with age. He turned to the other priest. "Did you leave the front door unlocked?"

"I told your door warden that I have come seeking two books in your collection," said Manoueka, evading the old priest's question.

"I'm afraid we cannot help you," the old priest answered, handing Manoueka his letter. "Dithaan was beyond his authority in offering you access to our volumes. Only I can grant entrance to the library to outsiders. I am the Sedormatos of the Order."

"Well, then you can now grant me entrance. I have come very far on the assurances of your agent. He presented himself as having authority to permit me entrance and I relied on his guarantee. I have traveled over a month from Synnakon at great expense to study two books, both of which he assured me are in your possession. I do not want to have to spend the time and money to appeal to your superiors in Damash."

Blanching at the mention of Damash, the two elderly scholars looked at each other nervously. Nevertheless, the old man was adamant. "I must refuse your request. The books you have requested are restricted. If you must appeal to the head of the order, then so be it. I must ask you to leave."

The two larger men stepped forward to escort the Synnakians out. Manoueka was too close to his goal to be turned away now. He needed those books to find Korefael. Without thinking of the consequences, he fell back on the spell he knew best. "*O póntonízuva wanuvuz, yad sippatanaiy kelsha mama!*" he chanted.

Simultaneously, the four Tulkeen priests lost consciousness, collapsing to the floor. Kyrion's jaw dropped. "No good can come of this," he said, almost to himself.

"Come quickly," said Manoueka heading towards the door leading into the library. "We must find Dithaan quickly.

Following a short passageway, the two mages and their Ushidian guard came into an open courtyard surrounded by a collonaded arcade. A priest in the robes of the Tulkeen order hurried toward them. Czoszín stepped forward to defend Manoueka.

The priest stopped short. "I am Dithaan," he said. "I heard you had arrived and came as quickly as I could. Did the Sedormatos allow you entrance?"

"Not exactly," said Manoueka in a loud whisper. "We decided a more direct approach would be better. Your superior is sleeping by the front door. We are in a hurry. Can you show us the books I wrote you about?"

Dithaan's eyes widened at the implication. He waved them back. "Go back into the corridor before you are seen."

The intruders stepped back into the relative cover of the passageway, followed closely by Dithaan. "Do you realize the trouble you may have caused?" asked the priest. "If I am seen to be helping you, I might be expelled from the order. And you will certainly bring the wrath of the *mustariim* down on you."

Manoueka grew annoyed at the priest's delay. "Yes, I understand the problem. That is why I said we must be quick. Find us the books and we will be on our way."

Dithaan headed down the corridor, motioning for them to follow. He lead them to a small room with a table and a pair of chairs. "Stay here while I get the books. Nobody should find you here." He ducked out of the room, leaving the three of them to wait.

Czoszín stood guard by the door while Kyrion and Manoueka sat. "Can we trust him?" asked Kyrion.

"We have little choice," answered Manoueka. "I need those books."

Dithaan returned a short while later carrying two large tomes. He laid them on the table in front of Manoueka. "You don't have much time. They have found Ashaar unconscious at the front door. They are searching the library now." He opened the first book. "I have done some research on the books. I believe you will find what you are looking for in this section.

Manoueka practically licked his lips in anticipation of discovering the location of Korefael.

Reading the *Treasuries of the Caliph Harun*, he found that it was written in Kukrili, as he expected. It was the dominant language of the court of the Amr aw-Wanaj, having supplanted Doradic and Cokan when Malmud conquered this portion of the Cokan Empire. He had studied the language specifically for this purpose. Though he could not speak it, he could read it well enough.

He opened the book from left to right in the Doradic fashion, only to curse the strange customs of Habric writers when he remembered they wrote from right to left.

"The writer organized the book as an extensive list," continued Dithaan. "He documented each item and its worth. Rather than being organized according to the final location of each item, the book is organized according to the vault it was found in at the caliph's palace, with its eventual destination listed after each entry."

Manoueka nodded in understanding. It might take a while to find the correct entry. He needed to find it quickly, before the priests alerted the *mustariim*. "The stone was deposited somewhere in Hikuptah, so we merely need to scan the list for Hikuptahn names."

"I had the same thought," said Dithaan. He pointed out a few entries. "Three come up regularly in the lists. There is Ptahmel, after whom the later kingdom was named, as well as Selene, one of the last rulers before the Cokan conquest. Finally, there is Thamses."

"Thamses the Big?" asked Manoueka, reading the entry and cursing himself for not having studied Kukrili more thoroughly.

"I believe that is Thamses the Great," said Dithaan, correcting him.

It would stand to reason that the Mad Caliph would bury his treasure in the tomb of the greatest king of the Twenty-seventh Dynasty. He could eliminate the other two, both of Doradic descent and both from the thirty-third dynasty.

Quickly scanning the lists, he came across mention of the shard. Exactly as he expected, it was listed next to Thamses. "This is the confirmation I need," he said. "Now I only needed to find the specific location of the tomb."

Closing the *Treasuries*, Dithaan turned to *Exploration of the Tombs*. "The ancient Doran scholar who wrote the book organized it better than the authors of the *Treasuries*, which had been written hundreds of years later."

Manoueka found the logical Doran order much easier to understand than the disorganized thoughts of the Merouin scholars. A table of contents listed the various tombs and an illustration at the beginning mapped their locations in the necropolis.

Without paper and pen to take notes, Manoueka would have to remember the specific location of the tomb of Thamses the Great, at least long enough to get out of the library and write it down. He did not expect it to be difficult; he had mastered far more complex intellectual challenges before. He turned to the section describing Thamses's final resting place and began to read.

• • •

"We have run out of time," said Dithaan, looking out the door of the small chamber as Manoueka read. "They are beginning to search this section of the library."

Czoszín drew his paramerion, prepared for a fight. "Put that away," ordered Kyrion, waving to the Ushidian to put the long knife away. "We don't want any more trouble than we have already caused."

"I have everything I need," said Manoueka, closing the great tome. "We can leave."

Kyrion had been pacing the floor, eager to leave the confines of the small room. "I know of a spell that allows us to pass undetected," he offered.

"It would be for nothing. They have have brought *mustariim*," said Dithaan. "The adepts of that sect can perceive spells being cast."

"They are probably watching every exit," said Kyrion, his voice rising. "How can we leave this place undetected?"

"Have faith. Ashaar has performed searches such as this in the past and he conducts them the same every time. He always starts at one end of the building and sweeps through. This will be the last place he will look to find us. We can circle around the searchers and exit on the opposite end of the library."

Dithaan stepped toward the back wall of the chamber and pushed on the wall in a pattern. A section of the wall slid back, exposing a narrow tunnel built into the thick stone walls of the library.

Manoueka's opinion of this priest rose considerably as someone who obviously planned ahead.

"Ashaar is far too honest a man to lead a priesthood dedicated to keeping secrets," said Dithaan with a wry smile. "It simply never occurs to him that there would be hidden passages in the temple of secrets." He led the three Synnakians into the tunnel, Manoueka first, followed closely by Kyrion and Czoszín.

Chapter 4

Iko found it difficult to sleep once the sun had risen. The noise of the new city waking crept through the open window, urging him to rise. The morning was still cool, the sun still low enough that it did not shine directly on the courtyard of the inn. Feeling his hunger growing, he wondered when they would eat breakfast. Goron snored lightly in the bed next to his; the boy wondered whether all men snored and if he would when he grew up.

Trying not to wake his grandfather, he climbed out of bed as stealthily as he could. He wanted to explore the city. He washed quickly, though not noiselessly, causing Goron to stir in his bed. He dug through his bag, looking for a clean tunic to wear, but the few that he owned had been sent to be washed by the innkeeper's staff. He decided on the one he had worn yesterday. It was old and decidedly out of fashion, but it was still mostly clean. As he pulled on the tunic and cinched the belt closed, a pillow flew across the room at him from the direction of Goron's bed.

"Why don't you go out and see if they have some breakfast for you in the kitchen." Like an arrow released from a bowstring, the boy shot out the door for the kitchen.

He found Abiir there directing the kitchen staff. With a smile, she offered him a breakfast consisting of bread with a white labneh-like cheese and a plate of cucumbers and melons. He had not had much in the way of fresh bread or vegetables since he left Synnakon, so he wolfed the food down.

A couple of minutes later, Abiir returned and laughed. Saying something in her language, she put out another portion of bread, but admonished him in broken Doradic, "You eat fast and much. No more."

He didn't mind so much, the breakfast was sufficient. He ate more slowly this time, watching the woman as she went about her work with the kitchen staff.

After he finished his breakfast, he sat longer. He had nothing much to do but watch Abiir. She was pretty, so watching her was pleasant. He perked up whenever she turned and smiled at him.

After a while, Goron and Annissa entered. The man greeted Abiir in her language while Annissa smiled and nodded. After exchanging a few words, the Kuprian woman brought more bread, labneh, and vegetables for the two visitors. When Iko looked at the food, she laughed at him again. "No more for you."

"She says you have already eaten a day's worth of breakfast, lunch, and dinner," Goron translated for the boy. "She speaks a little Doradic, but she understands much more. We should teach the two of you a bit of Kukrili. She speaks the Kuprian dialect of it, but you would do well learning the language of the caliphate. I cannot translate for you all the time."

He continued his conversation with the young woman in Kukrili while Iko and Annissa sat quietly, not being able to add anything to the discussion.

Turning to the boy, he said, "It is settled. Abiir will look after you today while Annissa and I visit the library of the Tulkeen."

Iko brightened at the prospect until Goron added, "You are to help her with some chores. It will reduce the cost of our visit here, but more importantly, it will teach you the value of work. There is much to be done in running an inn such as this one. Your help will be valuable to Abiir and Lazaar."

The prospect of working all day deflated Iko. He had hoped to explore the city but now Goron had saddled him with chores. "Couldn't I go with you and Annissa to the library? I can read, perhaps I could find some books for you."

"I'm afraid not. It is not a lending library and most of the books are in ancient Doran, Cokan, or Kukrili. Some are in languages more exotic than that. You would be bored there. Abiir has a more interesting day planned than you expect. You can help her carry goods from the market."

That did not seem as bad as he had thought. He looked forward to spending the day with Abiir. The other two rose from the table and Goron bowed, saying something in the way of thanks in Kukrili. Annissa copied him awkwardly and they left.

With a smile, Abiir beckoned Iko over to a large basin full of dishes. "You work now? First wash, then market, yes?" She handed him a cloth and a bucket of hot water.

When the washing was done, Abiir brought out two baskets and handed one to Iko. "We go to the market now. You carry one for me, yes?"

The boy was glad to be done with the washing and eager to get out to explore the city. They left the courtyard and headed up the slope of Iksum into the Kasbah. The entire city seemed to be built of sand. The buildings were not painted at all. They were covered with tawny-colored mortar that seemed to have been mixed with the local sand. If it weren't for the straight lines and sharp angles, the whole city would like exactly like the landscape surrounding it.

The streets became narrower and the buildings seemed to loom higher over the two shoppers as they approached the bazaar. The houses were so close together that it seemed as though the street was another room in the residents' homes. Iko did not remember any streets in Synnakon that were as narrow as the ones here.

"You stay close," warned Abiir as they approached the crowded bazaar. "Easy to go lost in the Kasbah."

The boy agreed to stay by her side at all times.

This market was different from the Synnakian markets as well. Back in the empire, the markets were built in wide plazas. The booths were spacious with the wares spread out in wide displays. Here the market was built on a wide street. At least, it was wider by the standards of Iskander. It was narrow by Synnakian standards, with barely enough room for two people to pass between the booths.

Iko passed fruit sellers, butchers, cloth vendors, and hardware merchants selling knives, spoons, and the like. One merchant roasted meats, dousing them in a sauce and selling them on flatbreads ready to eat. It seemed dangerous to have a fire in such cramped quarters, but everybody at the market seemed to take it in stride.

Abiir stopped at the butcher to haggle over a piece of meat. It had already been skinned, so Iko could not tell whether it was lamb or goat or some other small animal. He could understand nothing that the people were saying to each other. He had never been in a place where nobody spoke Doradic at all. At home, it was the non-Doradic speakers who were foreign but here he was the foreigner.

After a while, he became tired listening to people talking when he could not understand. He found it easier to tune out the voices and became lost in his own thoughts. Certainly he had had many adventures since he left his mother and grandmother in the convent. His *amma* had probably not wanted Goron to bring him on any adventures like the ones he had in the last couple of months, but she must have suspected something like this would happen.

He noticed a few other boys his age and younger running through the market. He could not tell if they were playing or running errands. They seemed to congregate around one particular merchant who sold what looked to him like sweets. An older boy seemed better dressed than the others and was buying sweets and handing them out to the other children. When handing out sweets to the boys, he would give them some kind of instructions and they would run off, candy in hand. He would also give out some sweets to the prettier girls, but would keep the girls close by.

At one point, he noticed Iko watching and called him over. Iko approached him, but could understand nothing the older boy said. When Iko did not respond, the Kuprian questioned him more sharply. Iko still did not understand. The other children crowded around, touching his dalmatic as if it were an exotic costume. One of the other boys said something and they all began laughing at him. He recognized one word, "*djenkiin.*" It was what the *mustariim* had called Annissa when they ordered her to strip to her undertunic.

Worried that they might turn him over to the *mustariim* or search him right there, he absentmindedly clutched at the gem he wore around his neck. The other boys and girls laughed at him, causing him to turn a bright red from humiliation and anger. He wished they would stop and leave him be.

The leader of the pack of children began coughing, apparently having inhaled a piece of candy that he had been sucking on. The other boys, concerned that he was choking to death, stopped their laughing and turned to help. They bent the older boy over and began pounding on his back to get him to cough up the confection. In the confusion, Iko slipped away between two ladies who came to see if the boy needed help. He made a note to avoid other children until he learned more of their language.

Running away from the other children, Iko flew past merchants selling everything from spices and vegetables to ironsmith goods. As he ran, people yelled at him, though he didn't understand what they were saying.

After a few minutes, he became aware that people were looking at him and he felt very out of place. He decided that he needed to attract less attention, but had to change out of his dalmatic into something more suitable for the area. He spotted a clothing merchant selling tunics in the local style. He didn't have any coins to purchase it, so he would have to steal it. Kora wasn't here, so she would not be able to object. He began to worry about her. Was she all right? He felt guilty for dragging her into the jailbreak in Synnakon. He hoped they had not punished her too severely.

As the clothing seller spoke with another customer, he walked slowly past the booth, hoping the merchant would not notice him. He had scoped out the tunic he wanted before approaching. It was small and not too showy, exactly the thing for a boy trying to blend in. As he passed, he took the tunic with one smooth move and bundled it under his dalmatic. The merchant never noticed as he walked slowly away. He also attracted no attention from other shoppers or the merchants.

Away from the bazaar, he found a side alley hidden enough for him to change unnoticed. He formed his old clothes into a pack that he could easily carry.

He headed back to the market in the direction he had come, thinking he could find the butcher where he had left Abiir, but the merchants seemed different to him from before. He walked unnoticed past the clothing merchant he had stolen the tunic from. Beyond that, he recognized nobody from earlier in the day. Perhaps they had changed shopkeepers over the course of the day, similar to the markets in Synnakon. He looked for Abiir, but the crush of the crowd made it difficult to see anyone beyond the people directly in front of him.

He looked around for a sign that might point him in the right direction, but everything was written in the loopy, flowing script of Kuprian rather than the blocky lettering of Doradic. He could read it no better than he could understand the spoken language.

Reaching the opposite end of the market, the booths ended at the bottom of a hill. Only a residential street lay beyond, broader than the streets on the hill. He could try to find his way back to the inn from there. He continued down the street, making sure to take better care in remembering landmarks.

Walking for a while, perhaps a half-hour, the smell of salt air grew stronger. He smelled fishmongers and heard the cry of the gulls and the creak of wooden ships as they rocked on the waves. That would mean he had headed closer to the port, in the wrong direction from where he wanted to go. Perhaps he could find foreign sailors who spoke Doradic and get directions back to the inn.

Reaching the waterfront, he turned left, toward what looked like the center of the port. A few sailors and merchants milled about. They looked rougher and a bit more intimidating than those at the bazaar. They reminded him of the vendors and innkeepers on the road into town that they had traveled the previous evening.

Farther down the wharf, he noticed blond-haired men loading a ship. Figuring that they must be Ushidian, he thought they might speak Doradic. He approached them, excited that he might be able to communicate with someone. As he approached, he heard a familiar voice as Kyrion came on deck.

Iko stopped dead in his tracks.

Like a malevolent preacher addressing a hated congregation, Kyrion stood on the deck of the small ship. "Hurry with the loading, you cabbage-eating Ushidoi. Manoueka wants everything on board at once. We must sail immediately."

The men grumbled their displeasure at this arrogant magician giving orders. Mirán stepped forward and addressed the mage. "We have now finished unloading. We prepared for overland trip and suddenly Manvecze returns from his errands and changes his mind. Now we must reload. We are landsmen, not men for long sea voyages. Perhaps you understand my men become upset."

"You can explain to them that the emir did not give us permission to hire men and take them overland to Hikuptah. We have to go to Ptahmel. The emir there cannot prevent us from hiring men to work within his borders."

From the group of men, Valád shouted, "Why do we leave so fast? Can we not stay one more hour? I want to say goodbye to girl I met."

"There is no time!" Kyrion shrieked. "You'll meet more whores in Ptahmel. You can do you drinking and womanizing there."

The men grumbled louder at Kyrion's vulgar reply. "Maybe we can content ourselves with Manvecze's girl during voyage." The grumbling turned to crude laughter at the suggestion.

Kyrion's face flushed red. "The dressmaker's daughter is none of your business! If any one of you men so much as touches her, you will get a chance to find out what lives at the bottom of the sea. The old dressmaker died under your rough treatment. If he had lived longer, Manoueka would have been able to get some useful information about him. The master will not allow the same thing to happen to the girl. You are wasting time with this idle chatter, now get this ship loaded."

At the mention of the dressmaker's daughter, Iko thought of Kora. He turned his attention from the men loading to the wooden barque itself. Was she on board? If old Polous had died because he and Kora freed Goron, then he had caused the old man's death. The guilt hit him like a blow to the stomach, taking his breath away.

The men were loading toward the center of the ship; the cargo hold was likely there. The ship had a small stern castle with a cabin below. He had seen most of the men coming in and out of a forward hatch. Nobody entered the stern cabin. If Kora was on board, Manoueka likely kept her prisoner far from the other men. He needed to find a way to get her off the ship.

The boy continued past the men loading the ship. He spotted a couple of windows in the rear cabin.

Perhaps he would be able to see her through a porthole. He saw nothing from this vantage. He would have to get closer, but the only way onto the boat was the gangplank being used to load it.

A number of lines hung off the stern of the craft, including the one mooring the boat to the dock. He thought about shimmying the rope up to the deck, but he would be too exposed.

Farther down the dock, someone had tied up a small skiff. Figuring out a plan, he sauntered down to the skiff, trying not to attract attention. Climbing in, he cast off and started rowing toward the *Morspena Ula.*

As he had hoped, the skiff was below the level of the dock, out of sight of the Ushidians. He had some trouble with the oars at first, having never rowed a boat before. He had seen Goron and Annissa row across the river when they fled Synnakon. He remembered little because of his fever at the time, but with a little practice, he brought the craft under control.

He directed the small boat to the stern of the larger one, directly alongside a line hanging over the rail. Grabbing the wet line, Iko climbed up high enough to grasp the lip of the porthole and pulled himself up to look in.

Inside the cabin, a head of long, black, curly hair faced the other direction. "Kora!" he whispered loudly, trying to catch her attention without Kyrion or the Ushidians noticing.

Her face brightened when she turned and recognized him. "Iko! How did you get here? Can you get me out of here?"

"Shhh! There are men on deck above us," he whispered. "I have a boat below." Looking down to his borrowed boat his heart fell. It had drifted away. To get Kora out, he would have to swim to bring the skiff back and he was not a good swimmer.

He looked back into the porthole toward Kora. She looked desperate, he thought. He hoped she was safe and unharmed. At that moment, she turned her face away from him. Someone had entered the cabin. Iko saw two large hands grab her and pull her away from the porthole.

Loud voices erupted on the deck of the ship outside his view. He had been spotted hanging from the side of the boat. The men who had been loading the ship all turned to face him. For a moment, he froze in place like a hunted animal.

He could not remain hanging or he would be taken too. He could drop to the water, but they would be waiting for him at the dock while he swam ashore. His other option was to shimmy down the line mooring the *Morspena Ula* to the dock. It was just out of reach.

He grabbed the line he had climbed to get to Kora's porthole and drew back enough to let him swing out toward the mooring line. An arm shot out from the porthole, snatching at him as he flew past. He reached out at the end of his swing and caught the line tying the ship to the dock. He let go of the other line to hang by one arm over the water of the harbor.

The Ushidians watched in amazement, astonished at the boy's leap. One of them began to cheer at his success. The crowd of them took up the cheer as Iko slid down the line to the dock.

Manoueka and Kyrion appeared on the rail of the *Morspena Ula*. Manoueka sputtered in anger, unable to speak, his face red. "Don't stand there cheering the little brat, you idiots!" screamed Kyrion. "Get him!"

Iko ran. As if waking from a sleep, the Ushidians, realizing the boy had been trespassing on the ship they were supposed to be guarding, began to pursue him.

Farther down the dock, a pair of longshoremen loaded cargo onto a ship and a fisherman unloaded his catch while buyers surrounded him, ready to take fish to the nearby market. He ran past them all, followed closely by a pack of Ushidian fighters. He deftly slipped past the barrels, crates, bins, and baskets. His pursuers were not as agile. The containers the small boy was able to slip past became obstacles for the cluster of large brutes pursuing him. Barrels overturned, stacked crates crashed to the ground, baskets were destroyed. Still, the men gained on him.

The port became more crowded the farther he ran. He dodged men carrying heavy loads. People tried to move quickly out of the way of the oncoming pursuers but not all were able to do so. The Ushidians jostled people in order to get past them, knocking over their freight. The boy turned onto a side street into a bazaar where merchants had set up booths, selling their goods to customers. A few shoppers stood nearby.

The crowd slowed him down somewhat but it slowed the Ushidians even more as they had to shove their way through, overturning merchant booths and destroying their wares. Not looking behind him, Iko heard the clamor of the angry mob as it pursued the foreigners as well. The boy left the noise of the crowd behind as it stalled Manoueka's men in the market place. He heard the sound of men screaming in Kuprian and arguing with the foreign warriors, who yelled back in Ushidian.

When he had lost his pursuers, he slowed down and began to take in his surroundings. He was still in the port neighborhood and took a chance at heading back toward the docks. Warehouses and offices lined the wharf, but the Doran boy could not read any of the signs until he came across one in Doradic. "Customs," it read. If someone here spoke his language, perhaps he would be able to ask directions.

The office consisted of one man seated at a desk amid piles of paper. He scribbled away at one with a quill pen and a vial of ink.

Iko introduced himself. "Do you speak Doradic? I'm lost and need directions."

Taken aback by being addressed in Doradic by a young boy, the man looked up from his documents. He examined Iko for a minute, trying to match up the vision of a boy wearing a Kuprian caftan with the sound of colloquial Doradic coming from his mouth. "Yes, I speak Doradic. Are you from the *Morspena*? They are sailing today, as soon as they finish loading."

"No, we came overland." Iko omitted the fact that the crew of the same ship had stopped loading in order to chase him through the port market, destroying much of it in the process. "I thought I could find someone in the port who speaks my language. Can you tell me how to get to the Golden Lion inn? It is near the Kasbah and not far from a large market."

"Yes, if you follow the next street down, it takes you to the western road," the customs officer said, directing the boy back to the main road into Iskander and avoiding the confusion of the bazaar. "Perhaps you should stay here. I can call someone to bring you back to your parents."

"No thank you," Iko said with a bow and ducked out the door. He did not want to stay any longer at the port and be identified as the boy who caused the disturbance in the port bazaar. With the help of the man's directions, he ran back to the Golden Lion as quickly as possible.

Chapter 5

On his way to the library, Goron regretted rising as early as he had, but it was no use trying to sleep once the boy had woken him. For the older man, even with the sunrise and sounds of people beginning their day in the courtyard outside, it felt good to sleep in a soft bed after the long journey. Now, hours later and wide awake, he and Annissa headed to the Tulkeen library to see the books Manoueka sought. Curious about whatever magical treatises they might have, the sorceress had wanted to go with him to the temple library.

It was afternoon before he found Lazaar and asked him to write a letter to introduce him to the *sedormatos* of the Tulkeen. The foot and horse traffic had grown since the morning, consisting mostly of merchants carrying their wares to sell in the nearby bazaar. The sun had risen high enough to shine down into the narrow, curved alleys of the city, designed to cast shadows and ward off the oppressive heat of the afternoon sun.

Arriving at the doors of the library, the older man warned the enchantress, "It is possible you will not be able to enter the library. The Tulkeen are very protective of their books. If you are allowed entrance, you will likely be restricted to remain with me at all times. This is not a browsing library. One must know specifically what book one wishes to see and ask for it by title."

"I understand. It'll be enough to read the books you are asking for. You say that you've been welcomed here in the past. Do you know if they will remember you?"

"It is difficult to tell. I was here long ago. Even if the priests I knew then are still alive, it would be a wonder if they remembered me."

Approaching the carved wooden doors, each panel a scene from the legends of the life of Motios, Goron picked up the great brass knocker and announced his presence.

The same shrunken wispy-haired old man who had greeted Manoueka earlier that day opened the blind door built into the larger doors. He greeted the two in Kuprian. "What business brings you to the Temple of Moshou?"

"May you live in the light of the law." Goron greeted the ancient priest in Doradic with the formal greeting of an initiate of the Tulkeen sect. "I have come to be instructed in the teachings of Moshou." Although he did not necessarily believe all the legend, lore, and ceremony that had grown up around the life of the Scholar God, he still respected the beliefs of others, especially when it eased his interaction with them.

"May the law be always in your heart." The old doorman opened the door and invited them to enter.

"I seek Ashaar," said Goron, handing the old priest the letter of introduction Lazaar wrote for him. "He was young when I was here last. Is he still in residence here?"

"Ashaar? If you mean our *sedormatos*, he still resides here," said the priest, reading Goron's letter. "I know of no other and I have been here a very long time. He has been very busy today. Follow me and I will see if he is receiving now."

Refolding Goron's letter, the elderly cleric led them to a comfortable room, books lining the walls, a large table occupying the center of the room, and comfortable chairs enticing them to sit and read. Goron took a book off the shelves and encouraged Annissa to do the same. "They are mostly instructional, about the life of Motios and the laws governing the lives of believers. There is nothing here revealing any secrets of great value. They are the only books accessible to those outside the sect. Please take a book and read. It would be impolite not to."

The diminutive door warden returned with another priest, interrupting Annissa after only a few pages of *The Life of Motios*. Though younger than the timeworn guardian, the other priest carried his years on him like baggage.

"You are Garoun?" asked the *sedormatos*, taken aback upon looking at the visitor. "You cannot be. Lazaar's letter says you visited here fifty years ago. If you had, you would be as old as I am." The old priest studied Goron, as if trying to solve a puzzle.

"I assure you I am the same man," said Goron with a smile. "We met during my last visit. You were the assistant to the *sedormatos* then. Bashaad was his name, was it not?"

Ashaar nodded, "I remember the visit. You look exactly the same. How is it you have not aged since then?"

Noticing Annissa's look of surprise and inquiry, Goron quickly changed the subject, "I would much rather speak of your books. A mage from Synnakon has been inquiring after two books, *An Inventory of the Treasuries of the Caliph Harun* and *An Account of an Exploration of the Tombs of the Twenty-seventh Dynasty of the Kings of Ptahmel.* This wizard was in contact with Dithaan, one of your initiates."

Ashaar nodded gravely. "We are aware of Manoueka and his correspondence with Dithaan. He arrived here earlier today and forced his way into the library. It caused us some trouble with the *mustariim* and they are influential in the emir's court. It reflects poorly on the Tulkeen when a Synnakian wizard arrives with a letter from one of our own admitting him to our library, especially when that member is already under suspicion for collaborating with *djenkiin*. I spoke with Dithaan and found more about what Manoueka was looking for." The old priest turned and looked at Goron, asking him bluntly, "Can you please tell me more about the Stones of Power? I can find nothing in the written record."

"There should be nothing in the written record," answered Goron, surprised at Ashaar's directness. He weighed how much he should tell this old man. Deciding that he could trust a priest of secrets to keep his own, he explained. "The existence of the stones is a secret entrusted to very few. They are powerful artifacts interwoven with the legend of the birth of the Gods. I have taken it as my mission to make sure the stones stay hidden. Manoueka is on the verge of discovering one of them. When he does, he will attempt to bend it to his own use, but he does not have the strength of will to subdue the power of the stones. These stones have a force of their own that resists any attempt to subjugate them to another's devices."

Ashaar took in the information Goron gave him, his eyes darting back and forth as if the stones were about to manifest in front of him. "How do the books relate to his search?" he asked.

"He sought the books to find the location of the last resting place of Korefael, the Second Jewel of the Kings. *Inventory of the Treasuries* names the tomb where the Mad Caliph buried his treasures and *Exploration of the Tombs* specifies the location of the tombs of the kings of Ptahmel. Manoueka likely has all the information he needs to find the stone. We are here to find the same information and get to the tomb before he and his crew find it."

"It is as I suspected," said Ashaar with a sigh. "It is a powerful secret you carry. Secrets as powerful as this must remain hidden." The *sedormatos* looked old at that point, his shoulders sagging as if he carried a great weight. "I have bought you some time. In order to improve relations with the *am'mustari baydiir* and the emir, we told them about Manoueka and recommended he be ejected from the city. I received a message an hour ago that the emir issued an edict prohibiting Manoueka from hiring any diggers here in Iskander and instructing him to leave the city immediately. He also wrote a letter to the emir of Hikuptah recommending the same. It is unlikely to have much effect. The Hikuptahn will not do anything that the Kuprian supports. The two block each other at every turn. Rather than working together to support the caliphate, each acts to prevent the other from gaining any control over it.

Goron considered this information, wondering if Lazaar had provided a bribe to the emir to ensure this outcome. He changed the focus of the conversation, thinking it unnecessary to inform the secretary of the bribe. "May we see the books?"

"Certainly. In fact, I have another book to offer. I think it will help. *Exploration of the Tombs* actually contains many volumes. Manoueka only asked for the volume regarding the twenty-seventh dynasty, but no others. Dithaan only had time to provide him with the books he asked for. Having reviewed the books he read here, I think the exploration of the thirty-eighth dynasty is more relevant to your search."

Ringing a small bell, the sedormatos summoned three acolytes, each carrying a tome. They placed them on the central table and left. The two men continued talking as Annissa took the topmost book and began studying its contents.

"Having some curiosity regarding our impolite visitor, I decided to do some research regarding these books. After questioning, Dithaan offered up the information you have now confirmed. Manoueka is seeking the treasure of the Mad Caliph. However, he may have come to the wrong conclusion. I read *Inventory of the Treasuries* closely and it appears there has been some confusion over the years regarding the identity of the tomb where Caliph Harun buried his treasure. There was more than one pharaoh named Thamses. Most know Thamses the Great of the Twenty-seventh Dynasty, but few remember his successor in the thirty-eighth, Thamses the Fat." He opened the book and pointed out the name of the pharaoh listed.

"The ancient Hikuptahns used different words to describe 'great' and 'fat,' exactly the same as one would in Doradic or even Kuprian. Kukrili, however, uses the same word when written, but it is pronounced differently depending on the context. When writing Kukrili, small marks above the letters distinguish the vowels. Careful spellers use these marks, but often the meaning of a word is understood without vowels simply from the context of the sentence.

"However, it appears that the scribes of Harun's court were not careful spellers. Sometimes they spelled it properly, but most of the time, they were lazy and wrote quickly, leaving out the marks. There are a few entries where they actually wrote 'Thamses the Fat' in the ledger." He pointed out the entries written long ago. "Perhaps it seemed obvious to them which Thamses they were referring to, especially after spelling it properly a few times. After a while, they dispensed with the vowel marks and a careless reader would still read 'Thamses the Great.' "

"The stone is not old enough for a king of the Twenty-seventh Dynasty to have owned it." Goron studied the entries in the ledger. "It was created in the Phersi Empire before Aranel's conquest. If the Mad Caliph buried the stone in the tomb of Thamses the Fat from the Thirty-eighth Dynasty, why would the legends and literature point to the twenty-seventh?"

"It is the curse of the careless researcher." Ashaar sighed, as if weary from correcting the mistakes of poor researchers over the years. "Thamses the Great is more famous and one would expect the greater king to have the greater treasure. A good researcher wants corroborating evidence before coming to any conclusions. That is, when he finds some evidence of something, he should find another source that confirms the evidence. But when all the sources of information are based on the same mistake, then the mistake is confirmed as fact. Legends have long told that the Mad Caliph's treasure is hidden somewhere in the tomb of Thamses the Great. Manoueka did not come across any original discovery there. Other expeditions have sought the treasure before but come up short. Like all treasure hunters, Manoueka's greed clouded his intellect and he read in the texts what he wanted to hear: that the treasure is in the tomb of Thamses the Great."

"But it is not, is it? It is in this smaller tomb of Thamses the Fat."

"I would bet my books on it."

Chapter 6

Mirán's tracker Barász returned to the *Morspena Ula* before the emir's men arrived. Mirán had been waiting for his cousin's return. Manvecze was eager to set sail for Ptahmel and leave this city behind him. Just a few hours before, he had been planning on staying at least a few days. Mirán noted to himself how a person's actions can have consequences far different from what he planned.

Upon receiving the tracker's news, the *perekhe* headed directly to Manoueka's cabin. His cousin Barász was a good man, having adapted his talents well to life in Synnakon. He found it difficult to follow anyone in this strange city, though. In a city, the same as in a forest, one needed to understand the inhabitants. The Kuprians of Iskander were a foreign race to Barász; he was not familiar with them. Nevertheless, he had found Goron. The Dorans had left an obvious trail through the Kuprian populace, he had said. It was like tracking an elephant in the Ushidian forest. It was so foreign to the place that it would leave a trail plain enough for any to follow.

Mirán had travelled far from home, farther even from Synnakon to a yet more foreign land. Soon, the ship would take him the farthest from home he had ever been. He wondered, if something were to happen to him here, if he were to die here, would news of it reach his mother or his beloved back in his homeland? He had received regular news from Antasza through travelers from Ushidia, but few of them came this far to the east.

Having reached the door to Manvecze's cabin, Mirán hesitated before going in. Askulas had informed him a few minutes earlier that his man Braxas had been found dead, killed in a manner that gave Mirán nightmares. Askula had been apoplectic, blaming the Ushidians for the killing. Mirán would have to inform Manvecze of this as well.

Mirán forced himself to focus on the task at hand: delivering news of Goron to his boss as well as informing him of the more terrible news regarding Askulas's companion. He knocked and entered after hearing Manvecze's reply. The mage was behind his desk in the small cabin reading a letter. Much smaller than his study back in Synnakon, it was still the largest cabin on the ship, having been appropriated from the captain for the duration of the journey.

"Barász has found Goron," the *perekhe* reported. "He found him at inn near old city. He followed him and Askulas's girl to library early today."

"It will do us no good," said Manvecze. He looked up from his letter and spoke with a firm voice. "We sail immediately. Your hunter has done well, but neither we nor Askulas can catch our prey here. It is good to know they are heading in the same direction as we, but we will have to hope they follow us to Hikuptah."

Manvecze folded the letter he had been reading. "The book in the library showed where the tomb we are seeking is buried. The author mapped out the locations, but could not enter the tomb of Thamses because it had been filled with sand. I plan to hire local workers in Amonkhareb, a short distance from the site. I had hoped to hire them here and make an overland journey to Amonkhareb, but the emir here would not allow me to do so." He waved the letter. "Due to events at the Tulkeen library, the *kupthaan* has rescinded our letter of transit. We must leave Iskander immediately. It will be more expensive to travel to Ptahmel and go overland there but we have no other choice."

"Yes, Boss," said Mirán. He and everyone on his crew had heard how their employer had cast a spell knocking the head librarian unconscious, thereby incurring the wrath of the Tulkeen as well as the *mustariim* and the emir. He laughed to himself at this self-important man's arrogance. Did he think there would be no consequences from his actions?

In any case, Mirán wanted to get as far from this city as he could. He hesitated bringing up the matter of Braxas and the gruesome manner of his death, but felt he had to. "Everyone is on board and ready to leave except Askulas's man Braxas. Vampyr killed him last night. *Kupthaan* of port found him with throat slit and hanging upside down in alley near docks." Mirán shuddered just from speaking the word. "Askulas blames us for his death." Like many Ushidians, Mirán believed a supernatural being caused such deaths.

"Vampyr?" Manvecze said, cocking one eye at the guard. "I have heard of the practice. It originated among you Ushidians, you know."

"If one did follow us here, he threatens us." Mirán whispered his fears, as if one of the creatures stood nearby, listening.

"There is no such thing as a vampyr," said Manvecze, waving his hand as if the story were an irritating insect. "It is a tactic of terror, used by men. When the killer wants to send a message to someone, he will slit the throat of someone close and leave the body drained of blood in a public place."

A shiver ran down Mirán's spine. His eyes darted around the small cabin, scanning each dark corner. "But Braxas was not in public place. Vampyr hid him in alley."

"I tell you, it was Demodoi's agent who did it. He is warning us that we need to follow Goron rather than pursuing the stone," Manvecze said, pounding his index finger on the desk for emphasis. In a softer voice, he said, "I'm sorry for Askulas's loss. Explain that it was none of your men who killed Braxas. Tell him that Demodoi is following us somehow and neither his men nor ours should go anywhere alone. Also, tell Kyrion the same thing. Let your men know that I don't want anything to happen to him before we find what we are looking for. I need him once we find the jewel we are seeking."

"Kyrion is important for jewel?" he asked, stiffening at his mention. He had no love for the Doran magician. "My men grumble about him. He gives orders like we are slaves." Ushidians had a strong sense of their own freedom and bristled at any attempt to be subjugated, seeing any loss of autonomy as a personal humiliation.

"Yes. He's arrogant but useful. There is no need to pass on this information, but I plan to have him activate the stone when we find it. The artifact is very powerful and any attempt to use it could be very dangerous. I would rather find that out when someone else makes the attempt." The *maholos* smiled maliciously. "Your men can have him once he has completed the task I brought him for."

Shouting above deck interrupted their conversation. He made out a few words: "Soldiers on the docks!"

Mirán opened the cabin door in time to find a sailor standing there, out of breath from running. "The captain says we must cast off. If you have any men still ashore, we must leave them behind."

Mirán nodded. "I understand. All men are aboard and accounted for."

At that, the ship lurched sideway as the crew loosened the lines mooring the ship to the dock. Mirán took his leave of Manvecze, heading above deck to speak to Askulas again, then his own men, as the ship set sail, leaving the Kuprian city behind.

Chapter 7

Iko ran all the way back to the Kasbah, following the directions the official in the port gave him. He found the western road they had arrived on, but from the other direction. He gathered the courage to ask locals the direction using only the one word. Kasbah. People were polite, pointing him in the right directions with a few words he did not understand.

He would have liked to have taken some time, wandering the city. There was so much yet to discover in the city, especially the strange language and writing.

When he found the narrow gate into the old city, his anxiety melted from his shoulder. He recognized his surroundings and was able to find the Golden Lion.

Abiir stood in the doorway, wringing her hands. Seeing Iko, she ran to him with a cry of joy. Wrapping her arms around him, she squeezed him tight, chattering away in her native language. He did not mind the hugs from the pretty young woman, though he understood nothing of what she said until she changed to broken Doradic.

"Thanks to Momadou you come here," Abiir said, tears in her eyes. She held him close, as if he would disappear if she let go. "You lost in market. I come here to find you. Servants go away to find you. If grandfather know I lose you, he is very angry." She began wagging her finger at him. "I said you stay close, but you wandered. You find trouble."

He did not mind the lecture from the pretty young woman. Even if she were angry with him, her face did not show it. He grinned when she took him by the hand and led him into the kitchen.

Feeding him a plate of freshly made lamb stew, Abiir continued lecturing him in Kukrili. He understood very little of what she said, recognizing only a word or two. Switching to Doradic, she said, "I worry when you leave. I hear rumors of a riot by foreign sailors in the port. I hear it is a boy. Some say beggar boy. Some say foreign boy. I worry it is you."

She looked at him, her eyes piercing his own, scanning for some truth to the rumors. Iko grimaced at hearing the news of his flight from the Ushidian soldiers. He felt he should be honest with the young woman. He owed her that at least.

"I am sure that was me," Iko said. Remembering why they had pursued him, he grew more animated. "It was Manoueka's men, the Ushidians! They have Kora. I tried to get onto the boat to talk to her or to get her out of there but they saw me and I ran. She's still on the boat with Manoueka who is leaving. We have to get to her as soon as possible or they are going to leave Iskander and take Kora with them!"

Abiir stopped chopping, surprised by Iko's outburst. "I do not understand," she said. "Who is Kora?"

More slowly, Iko explained how he and Kora had helped Goron and Annissa escape the jail in Synnakon.

"Manoueka must have captured Polous and Kora because they were helping Goron. Polous died and now they have Kora. We have to find Goron as soon as we can so we can stop them!"

"Stop whom?" asked Goron, stepping into the kitchen with Annissa and Lazaar close behind him.

Seeing Goron, Iko launched into his appeal for help for Kora. "We must go now, before the boat leaves port! Kyrion is with them, so they must know we are here."

Goron studied the boy with a blank face. "I had received news that Manoueka had arrived by boat and that Kyrion was with them. Rescuing Kora would not be an easy thing. He has a contingent of Ushidian guards with him."

"In any case, it is too late," said Lazaar. "I have just returned from the Emir's palace. He sent soldiers to arrest the foreign *djenkiin*, but his ship has already sailed."

"But if you knew Manoueka was here, you could have done something to save Kora!" said Iko. "She is more important than your books!" Didn't Goron care about her? He had squandered an opportunity to save Kora from Manoueka and his thugs.

"We will find Manoueka in Hikuptah," said Annissa. She knelt down to him, putting her hand on his shoulder to calm him. "He is going there to dig in the tomb of an ancient pharoah. We must prepare to leave today. It is another two weeks walk through the desert."

Goron nodded in agreement. "When we find Manoueka, we will find Kora. She is not in danger so long as he has not found the stone."

Another two weeks of walking? He had hoped they were going to stay in Iskander. He liked sleeping in a bed with clean linens. He liked having a washbasin in the morning to clean himself. He liked the hot meals he ate while staying at the inn. He especially liked Abiir. He could have stayed with her, helping her with kitchen chores and trips to the market.

Why could they have not rescued Kora in Iskander? They had lost an opportunity when she had been so close here. Instead, they would have to find her at the tomb of some dead king.

• • •

They had already walked two days from Iskander. This landscape seemed drier than the journey from Synnakon to the Kuprian city. The road through Allyrion had traveled through hills of scrub and grass punctuated by the occasional oak tree. Palm trees lined the road they traveled today. They followed the river, plots of irrigated green farmland lining its banks. Wind blew sand down from the barren hills above. Infrequent bushes and spots of dry grass dotted the slopes.

Passing out of the shade of a tall palm tree, the heat of the sun beat down on Iko. He silently thanked Deihosos for the light fabric of the tunic he had stolen. Though Abiir and Goron had looked askance at his new attire, they had not said anything. In any case, it seemed more appropriate to the heat than the Synnakian tunic and dalmatic he had worn on the journey to Iskander. Also, Abiir had bought him a cap and a headscarf, a *kaffah*, so he would look even more like a Kuprian boy. She showed him how to wrap it like a turban when he got hot or how to wear it down to cover his neck in the hot sun. He would blend in so he would not get into any trouble with local boys.

Goron had told him and Annissa that they were heading south for the market city of Syre, though they seemed to be heading west. The sorceress explained that the Kupria River flowed north out of the desert hills then turned east shortly before it reached Iskander, so they had to travel west toward Synnakon for a couple of days before the road turned south again.

They would not be staying in Syre. Goron had explained that they would head east from the desert city through dry hills and canyons to the city of Amonkhareb. The older man also warned the two that the crossing from the caliphate into the realm of the emir of Hikuptah would be dangerous. Tensions between the Hikuptahn and the emir of Kupria were at a fever pitch because of the tolerance of magicians in the former. As a result, Kupria watched their borders closely, allowing nothing even hinting at magic to cross out of Hikuptah. Travelers going in the other direction were given less scrutiny, so Goron did not expect any trouble on the way.

In spite of his disappointment at leaving Iskander and his apprehension at the dangers of the route, Iko was looking forward to seeing Hikuptah. Annissa had told him that it was even more exotic than Iskander. It was many centuries older with ancient monuments to long dead kings littering the desert, sands blowing over them, sometimes uncovering forgotten ones.

Traders from the south came across the deserts through Sinopia to Syre, where they then traveled north to Iskander or headed east through Hikuptah. In Iskander or the Hikuptahn port city of Ptahmel, merchants from the kingdoms of the old Eastern Cokan Empire bought the traders' silks, gold, spices, perfumes, and ivory to sell in far away lands.

He did not remember seeing any of those goods or the exotic black-skinned traders in the market in Iskander, but Annissa explained that Abiir had taken him to a food market that catered more to local inhabitants rather than the port market where the foreign traders bought and sold their wares. He had been through the port market, but with Manoueka's Ushidians pursuing him, he had not had time to pay much attention to what was sold or who was selling it.

Numerous caravans passed them along the road, but all of the merchants in them wore the plain tunics and *kaffa'at* of the local Kuprians. Some were dark-skinned, but none so dark as the men from the forests south of the desert that he had heard of in stories. The caravans carried bushels of grain, wool, dates, copperwares, and other local goods. He had hoped to see gold and ivory, but Annissa told him that, even if they did carry such things, they would not be transported openly for fear of attracting the attention of highwaymen. She told him bandits waited in the hills for rich travelers that they could rob.

From that point on, Iko kept a close watch on the hills.

• • •

Walking down the well-travelled road toward Syre along the Kupria River, Annissa reflected on the events of the last month. She had been arrested by Askulas the *makaphos* and thrown in jail with Goron and her beloved, Geotheris. After the boy helped them escape from jail, they had left the city only to have Geotheris killed by soldiers of a powerful Synnakian *maholos.*

She still choked up when she thought of him, sometimes breaking into tears. She had known Geotheris since they both were young. Though she had left the prospect of marriage behind her years ago, he had been her greatest love for most of her life. Even after each of them had taken other lovers, they always came back to each other, sometimes as lovers, most often as friends. Somehow, deep within her, she had harbored the hope that their circumstances would change. Now that hope was gone and she had to find another hope to anchor her future to.

In the days after Geotheris' death, something had hardened within her. While he lived, she had always looked to him for support; she depended on him like a rock. Without him, she felt adrift and would have to find her own foundation.

Now, she journeyed through foreign lands with this warrior and a boy, his grandson, on their way to find an ancient powerful artifact sought by the same *maholos* that had Geotheris killed.

Why had she come along on this adventure? There were too many nights sleeping on the ground with nothing but a thin blanket wrapped around her. For the first week or so, her legs had felt like they were going to give out from under her from walking so far each day. Even the blisters on her feet had healed into hard calluses within the new boots Goron had given her. Surely, she would have been more comfortable staying in Synnakon, but given the circumstances of her arrest and subsequent jailbreak, the danger of staying would have been too great.

Besides, Goron intrigued her. He seemed to be driven by a single-mindedness regarding the stones he had spoken of. She did not understand why he had agreed to have her accompany him on this journey. Certainly, she burdened him more than she helped. He had obtained extra food for her as well as boots and clothing, since she had only brought the single *stola* and *rokota* that she wore. She felt next to useless if it came to a physical fight, notwithstanding the skirmish outside Synnakon when Geotheris was killed.

A certain question prodded at Annissa's thoughts. It had been with her since leaving the library in Iskander. Goron had said that he had been there long ago, but was unsure if any of the priests he knew then were alive. To be sure, Ashaar remembered him, commenting on his agelessness and not having changed in fifty years.

She interrupted the quiet among them. "Goron, at the library, the old librarian said that it had been centuries since you first visited the library. How old are you?"

The warrior raised one eyebrow at her question. "Whatever your abilities as a magician, you certainly are adept at getting straight to the point. I am afraid I cannot answer your question so directly. The best I can tell you is that I was born in the Phersi Empire, long ago."

Annissa thought for a minute, trying to remember the histories she had read as a girl in her father's library. Her realization turned to surprise. "So you were born around the time of the emperor Heraclion?"

"You misunderstood me. I was born in the Phersi Empire, not the Pharsi Empire. The first empire was conquered by Aranel the Great."

After a short calculation, Annissa's face registered surprise. "But the Phersi Empire existed centuries before Heraclion's wars against the Pharsi. Are you saying you have been alive for centuries?"

"Somewhere around fourteen centuries. I was born shortly before the Phersi conquered Hikuptah and the Ponaj. I lived in the capital, Pharsakandor, studying magic. It was an era of experimentation and learning. Much of what magicians now know is merely copied from that time. In fact, most of the spells you learn are in the language I was born with. Nobody understands the ancient language other what they learn from their teachers as spells, which they repeat like parrots. The job of a wizard these days is preserving knowledge that was uncovered long ago rather than finding new knowledge."

"How is it you have been able to live for such a long time?"

Goron's shoulders stiffened. "I was conducting an experiment that failed, creating a powerful surge of *ousion*. That surge preserved me much as I am now. It also left me unable to perform any magic or use any magical devices. It is also why your spellcasting does not work where I am concerned. That is all I need to say about this topic," he said with a growl.

The discussion brought many other questions to Annissa's mind, but Goron's tone of finality stopped them in her throat.

Part IV

Chapter 1

Manoueka shaded his eyes against the glare of the cerulean sky. Looking out from the camp, he narrowed his eyes against the sun reflecting off the sand-colored hills. No trees broke the horizon in any direction. No clouds broke the smooth expanse of sky.

By the Four Gods, it was hot, even in the shade of the tents he had ordered erected at the base of the low hills that contained the tombs of the kings of the Twenty-seventh Dynasty. The flat lowlands had once been a small lake but its clay bottom had been baked to brick by the unrelenting sun and scoured clean by the unceasing wind. He had at first thought tents unnecessary due to lack of rain, but after one day on the lakebed, he sent Mirán back to Amonkhareb with some local men to buy something to provide shade and a windbreak.

Named after some ancient, forgotten god and lying about a two hour journey from the tombs of the kings, Amonkhareb had stood since the time of the kings buried here. If the books he had read about the Twenty-seventh Dynasty were correct, it had been a city of gardens, palm trees, and fountains. The kings had carved it out of the desert, bringing water from the river and faraway hills through aqueducts. Manoueka had expected to find it as it had been described in his books, but the reality was now far different. Time had not been kind to the city. Springs had dried up while overuse and lack of maintenance had ravaged the city's water system. When Manoueka arrived, he found no public fountains, trees, or gardens. The desert had slowly claimed the city back, drying it out in the heat like a wet cloth laid across a rock.

It had taken nearly two weeks to get to the Hikuptahn port city of Ptahmel from Iskander by ship, then another week from there to Amonkhareb. He had been here a week already, exploring the tomb area, searching for the right one. It was a shame that the Tulkeen had not allowed him to take notes while inspecting their books. He had written down his research immediately after leaving the Tulkeen library, but all memory is incomplete. Even as good as his intellect was, he could not remember everything.

It had taken him a couple of days to find the tomb he sought. Overlooking his camp on the dried lakebed and nestled at the base of a windswept hill, a tall porphyry stele half-buried in sand and engraved with cryptic hieroglyphs of birds, dog-headed men, and other pictures marked the site. Their excavation had uncovered similarly carved stone pots surrounding the site, broken in pieces. No doubt some ancient stonemason had carved them and the stele to honor the dead king's ancient esoteric gods.

The workers he had hired in Amonkhareb walked the two hour long journey back and forth from the town while the sun was still low in the sky. While they slept in the cool shade of their homes, the wind blew sand into the tomb they had excavated the previous day, forcing them to excavate the entrance to the tomb daily. There was nothing in this godforsaken desert to block the wind. Only a few shrubs and grasses grew among the cracks of sheltered rock; even those got buried in sand so often they did not live long.

Mirán interrupted Manoueka's reflection, bringing his midday report. It had become a ritual for them on this expedition and the wizard had become more reliant on the Ushidian throughout the trip. It was unfortunate that he could not depend on either of the Dorans that had come with him on the journey. Though he had a strong intellect, the wizard Kyrion had no skill at motivating men. Manoueka had put him in charge of a group of diggers, but his arrogant attitude and authoritarian personality had forced most of them to quit. Askulas was more of a natural leader, but he had no obligation to the *maholos*. The bounty hunter's goal was to track down his escaped prisoner, not help search for ancient artifacts. In addition, he had seemed to grow resentful of Manoueka since Braxas had been killed in Iskander. Askulas had left the camp to hunt his prey in Amonkhareb. Lacking any dependable Dorans, Manoueka had turned to his Ushidian *perekhe*.

"Boss, there is man found dead. It looks like vampyr again," said Mirán.

"I have told you before, there are no vampyrs," said Manoueka. "Don't call it that. You'll only upset the men."

"Yes Boss, but man's throat was cut and blood drained, that is vampyr." The Ushidian led his employer toward the scene of the murder.

"We discussed this before, Mirán. Vampyr-style killings are Demodoi's trademark. He wants to strike fear into you Ushidians, hoping you will desert me. He has a man following us. He wants Goron and expects us to find him. This, like the man in Iskander, is a warning that he is watching."

Mirán led his boss up the hill to the burial site. Approaching the tomb along a broad, grass-punctuated lane, one could imagine the entrance had been placed in such a way to give the spirit of Thamses the Great a peaceful vista in the afterlife. It had been lined with trees and pots planted with roses, jasmine, or other fragrant flowers. But the trees and flowers had long vanished, parched to ash on the side of a sun-baked hill and buried in shifting sands. It was a sad commentary on the impermanence of the power of kings.

It had taken longer to find the tomb and dig it out than he expected, putting a greater burden on his diminishing treasury. A few men stood outside the entrance. All the hirelings were poor and worked for a pittance, but the enormity of the task had surprised him. The tomb had been filled completely with sand, forcing him to dig out every foot as they made their way into it. It was larger than he had expected, making the job even more enormous. He wondered if the Mad Caliph had buried it purposefully or whether sand had invaded the underground cavity naturally. The cool, subterranean air on his face was a welcome relief after the midday heat outside. He contemplated whether he should move his entire camp into the recently excavated tomb, but his dislike of being underground overcame his dislike of the heat of the open desert.

Mirán led Manoueka to where the dead body lay in a corner of the central hall, a group of Ushidian and Hikuptahn men gathered around it. Their excavation had revealed a large central chamber with smaller rooms on either side. The walls of the burial chamber were brightly painted with images of creatures with the bodies of men but with the heads of animals all gazing down. Lizards with long rows of sharp teeth, long-snouted dogs, birds, and cats with human eyes peered down at him as if judging his actions. He wondered if they would condemn or absolve. The tableau unsettled him, adding to his unease at being underground. It inspired fear in both the Ushidians and the Hikuptahn diggers. More than a few locals had quit working after seeing the pictures, walking back to Amonkhareb in the hot sun muttering about temples of the Elder Gods. Only the promise of generous pay motivated those that remained to continue.

Manoueka heard raised voices. Tension rose between the two groups. Each spoke in their own language. He understood neither Ushidian nor Kukrili, but he heard the word vampyr mentioned a few times.

He raised his hand for silence and the small crowd quieted. Inspecting the body, he found it to be one of the Hikuptahn men. His throat had been cut precisely, with an inch-long slice lengthwise along his jugular. Blood had soaked the man's tunic but none had soaked the ground.

"Calm down, please," said Manoueka, the Hikuptahn foreman translating for his crew. "This not the work of a vampyr, so please stop spreading rumors."

Bashr, the foreman, addressed him with the Hikuptahn term of respect in an accented formal Doradic. "Please *Sidhi*, Musa has been drained of blood. It is not on the ground here. Never before has one of our own been slain in such a manner. The Ushidians are here and they have woken a demon, a servant of the Elder Gods. They call it 'vampyr.' We should have left the pictures hidden. No other explanation is possible."

"On the contrary, Bashr, other explanations are possible. I don't know why this man was killed. Perhaps it was a fight over a woman or a gambling debt."

Manoueka lied, knowing that Demodoi's agent had chosen his victim at random. "Perhaps someone robbed him for his pay, which I might point out has been generous. Perhaps the robber killed him in a manner which would lead people such as yourselves to blame our Ushidian guests. In any case, the robber probably killed him elsewhere and brought here. If you search around, you will likely find a spot with a large pool of blood soaked into the sand."

The crowd of men mulled this over, each group discussing it amongst themselves.

"There is no such thing as a vampyr," Manoueka continued. "The superstitious among you may want to leave. Remember that there are more men in the city who would be happy to do your job and take your pay." He gestured to the paintings towering above them. "Do not be foolish. The Elder Gods are long dead."

Then pointing at the dead body at their feet, he added, "Let's get him shrouded. I'll need some volunteers to return him to his family in town."

A trio of men stepped forward, the foreman explaining that the three were the victim's cousins and would bring the body back to his wife in Amonkhareb.

"Admirable. Mirán, give each of these men a bonus of one copper." Though it pained him to be giving away his rapidly dwindling coin, he knew that by offering coin to the native workers as a token of respect for the dead, he would remind the men that there was money to be earned, enticing the other laborers to remain on the job.

"As for the rest of you, get back to work. Time is growing short, and I need a larger area cleared so I can conduct my search."

In addition to the time required to dig, Manoueka had to search for secret chambers where the caliph's treasure might have been hidden. He could not allow the men within the tomb to excavate while he cast the divination spells intended to reveal hollows behind the stone of the walls. Drawing on the power of the earth, the spells were powerful but very slow, requiring a solid layer of foundation spells in order to work. Before he dared cast any spells, he had to make sure all the Hikuptahn diggers left the cavern. Though the emir of Hikuptah was more tolerant of magic than the ruler of Iskander or the caliph, Manoueka considered it unwise to test the boundaries of his patience or that of the locals. Most of the magic used in Ptahmel was done by petty fortune tellers, not full Synnakian *maholoi*. In any case, all his caution had been for naught; the spells he had cast so far had revealed nothing.

He looked up at the larger than life sized portraits of the Elder Gods. Their painted grins appeared to mock him for his futility. Cursing them silently, he left the enclosed, cool darkness of the burial chamber, exiting to the outside heat of the sun.

Finding a broken bench near the mouth of the tomb, Manoueka sat, watching workers push wheelbarrows full of sand up the ramp rising out of the tomb to dump them down the hillside. In addition to the Elder Gods, he cursed his luck as well as Demodoi, who had likely sent his assassin Témopirz to terrorize him here and in Iskander. The message was clear: Deliver Goron as the powerful aristocrat had demanded or suffer the same fate. The problem now was that he had left Goron in Kupria when the emir had forced him to sail on to Ptahmel. He could only hope that Goron would continue following him here, where he would have a chance to capture him.

The thought struck him, why would Goron follow him? What was the connection between the old warrior and the stone? Demodoi knew something but had neglected to fill him in on the secret. The old Ushidian had given him the ancient tome, *An Account of the Wonders of the Caliph,* as bait to lure in Goron. The warrior's interest was strong enough to lead him to break into the wizard's tower and to draw him from Synnakon to Iskander. It was likely strong enough to draw him to Hikuptah as well.

Hikuptahn voices rising from the nearby tunnel interrupted his contemplation. Close behind the sound, a line of men streamed out of the tomb, followed by his Ushidian overseers pleading and cajoling them to go back into the tomb and continue working.

The local foreman came forward and addressed him in accented Doradic. "I am very sorry, *Sidhi*, but my men will no longer work for you. The cutting of Musa's throat has frightened them mightily. Rumors abound of another Douraadii in Amonkhareb who is paying well for a dig north of the city. I am very sorry."

After the foreman left, Mirán ran up out of the tomb. "Boss, all diggers quit." The Ushidian was out of breath. "They talked among themselves. When we demanded they work, they refused and argued, then left. I cannot convince them to stay."

"It's all right, Mirán. Let them go." The Doran smiled slyly, reflecting on the news the foreman had brought him. "I think we have found the solution to our vampyr problem. Get the girl and a squad of men. We are going on a visit."

Chapter 2

The route from Syre to Amonkhareb led through a canyon slicing through the hills between the two cities. Long stretches of gravel interrupted by rocky pools of water lay in an otherwise dry creek bed at the bottom of the canyon. The road, a simple path for much of the way, wove its way through the creek bed. In places, the path had been washed out by a flash flood, though Annissa wondered when it had last rained. Apart from the occasional spots of moisture between the rocks of the creek bed, everything here was so dry it seemed rain had not fallen for years.

The black-stained red sandstone walls of the canyon hung over either side of the travelers, as if some prehistoric giants had constructed a narrow basilica open to the sky. Having lived her entire life in the city of Synnakon, Annissa had never seen natural wonders such as this. She craned her neck to see the top of the canyon. The closeness of the walls felt simultaneously protective and constricting.

The one saving grace of trekking overland at the bottom of a ravine was that they traveled in shade. Only occasionally, when the path turned and sunlight made its way to the canyon bottom, did Annissa feel the bright light and heat. Otherwise, the air at the canyon bottom felt relatively cool.

"Keep a close eye out for bandits." Goron eyed the canyon walls. He led Bason while Annissa and Iko strode alongside and behind the horse. "More than a few live in the hills around here. Once we start seeing tunnels dug into the sandstone, the danger increases. When the path rises out of the canyon into the open hills, the danger will subside."

Only a few hours journey into the canyon, the travelers saw caves dug into the stratified sandstone high on the canyon walls. Annissa worried about Goron's warning, keeping her eyes on the dark openings above. Certainly, there would be no reason to be mining the sandstone. Precious metals and jewels would be found in hard rock, not among the layered sandstone that made up the hills and canyons of this desert. The only purpose of caves and the tunnels that connected them would be for bandits and highwaymen to ambush travelers on the narrow road between Syre and Amonkhareb.

Having seen the caves, the three were ready when the first arrow flew at them. It landed among the baggage slung over Bason, directly in front of Annissa where she marched alongside the horse. Observing the poor condition of the feathered flets, she speculated that the archer was too poor to repair his arrows. Suddenly she understood what was happening.

"Attack! Bandits!" she yelled. Following the line of the shaft backward up the wall of the canyon, she spotted a bowman hidden in the shade of a cave and pointed him out to her companions.

Goron wasted no time. "Stay close to the wall and keep moving forward." The slight hollows and ridges in the rock wall would provide a meager shelter from above. "Annissa, can you reach him from here with a spell to collapse that cave?"

"I can try." She needed to see the cave better, which meant that the archer would see her better as well. Having seen mages create shields of air, she decided such a spell would be helpful now. *"O póntonízuva digímaviz! Miyakistigád!"* Shaping the *ousion* from a *sep* flow, she manipulated the energy into a screen broad enough to protect herself, Goron, and Iko. She stretched it from one canyon wall to the other.

"I have created a shield to protect the bottom of the ravine," she said. "Take Iko and Bason farther up the canyon. I will see what I can do about the archer." Remembering what Goron had told her about manipulating *ousion* to create her own reality, she imagined the stone above the archer collapsing on him and decided to try a spell to make it happen.

Stepping out to the other side of the ravine and getting a better view of the bandit, she cast a spell to shatter the stone above him. *"O póntonízuva digímaviz! Yadirplúd kélshim kavím!"*

The *ousion* flowed through her as the ground shuddered and cracks grew in the sandstone above the ambusher's cave. The bowman, surprised by the sudden earthquake, stopped in his tracks and braced himself against the walls of the tunnel. It did him little good. The roof of his den collapsed on him, burying him in a pile of stones.

Turning to join her companions, she found them facing a group of six gaunt brigands, swords drawn. The attackers seemed a seedy lot, sweating in the radiant heat of the stone walls. Few of them had washed or shaved, and none of them recently. Their caftans and *kaffa'at* were stained and dirty, presumably from crawling in their tunnels. Their weapons, on the other hand, looked clean and well-cared for; the short swords and scimitars reflected the bright blue sky above the canyon walls.

Drawing his sword from Bason's saddlebag, Goron also pulled out a shorter paramerion, the hand-length dagger used by soldiers in the Synnakian army. He handed the knife to Iko and instructed him on its use. "Hold it with two hands and keep the pointed end in front of you."

The boy complied, waving the blade, nearly a short sword for his size, but not swinging it.

Hearing the sound of feet on gravel behind her, Annissa turned to see another band of four men behind her breathing hard from climbing down from the caves. They cut off any chance of retreat. Knowing there was no way that a sword and a half would be able to hold off ten men ahead and behind them, she began her call to the daemons of air. She channeled a *sep* flow of eldritch force, shaping it into a shield as she had done before, intending to buy some time for her companions.

Goron needed help quickly. Iko would be little assistance against the six men facing the two defenders. Goron could defend a narrower gap between the rocks if he faced only a couple at a time. Knowing that she could only hold the shield a short time against her ambushers without concentrating, she began a similar incantation, this time to the daemons of earth. She had to work quickly. The effort of controlling the *sep* flows was beginning to wear on her.

"*O póntonízuva digímaviz!*" She called on the earth daemons. Hesitating, she struggled to remember the words of the incantation. "*Yairád... Yairád...*" What was the word for a wall of rock? Summoning up childhood memories of her father's lessons on ancient incantations, she had to cobble together a word for a cleft in the rock. She suddenly remembered, "*Yairád stípigaviz mírim!*"

The volume of *ousion* necessary to break the walls of the canyon was more than she had ever manipulated before. The strength required to control such a large flow was almost beyond her, but she focused her resolve on her intended result. Slowly, the rock on one side of the ravine cracked, sending boulders tumbling into the gap between Goron and his attackers.

Not understanding what was happening, half the bandits moved back, leaving only three in the gap. The rock continued falling, cramping the attackers and forcing them out of their carefully planned line. As Goron moved forward to engage the remaining thieves, one slipped past him to menace his flank. Iko charged forward with his paramerion and stabbed the unsuspecting outlaw in his thigh.

Shrieking, Iko's foe turned to face his unexpected attacker. Being a clever judge of circumstances, the boy realized the scimitar-wielding brigand outmatched him. Having scoped out possible routes of escape, he quickly turned and ran, making for a section of cliff with enough handholds for him to climb to a nearby cave for refuge.

Slowed by the wound in his leg, the boy's pursuer could not catch him before Iko began his climb. From the bottom of Iko's ascent, the man leaped to grab the child, who would have been within his grasp had he retained the full strength of his leg. As it was, Iko was able to scramble out of reach and managed to make it to the cave entrance where he began pelting his already wounded pursuer with rocks from the mouth of the cave.

The sounds of the bandits' rearguard struggling against her makeshift barrier drew Annissa's attention away from the boy's battle. The enchanted shield would not hold out long against their exertions. She needed a more permanent solution, like the one she used against the archer in the cave earlier. She noticed that only three were left, leaving her to wonder where the fourth had gotten to. The thought quickly left her mind. She had little time to figure out that puzzle.

It would be more difficult to cause a cave-in without rock directly above her enemies, but perhaps a well placed rockslide would do the trick. Weary from the earlier exertion of channeling high volumes of *ousion*, she began to chant again. "*O póntonízuva digímaviz! Yadirúd sitíya kélshaiviz máiviz!*"

She felt the *ousion*, but the *sep* flow was weak. Concentrating harder, she enlarged the flow, pulling more *ousion* from the extra-dimensional *sep* field. Directing the magical energy at the sandstone above her enemies, she imagined cracks in the rock near the rim of the canyon, dislodging a shower of fist-sized stones onto their heads, followed by a large boulder. The smaller stones pelted the bandits, knocking one unconscious and wounding the others, forcing them to run. The boulder came down on the unconscious man, crushing him with a sickening crunch and effectively blocking the path back to Syre.

By the time she turned her attention to her companions, Goron had already killed three of his enemies and set another two to flight. Iko's pursuer lay unconscious at the base of the canyon where a well-aimed stone had cracked his skull.

• • •

Iko still felt the excitement of the chase after having knocked his bandit out cold, but he was no fool to go back down to the canyon floor. He knew he could not help Goron, who had four men bottled up in the narrowed gap of the canyon and had already killed one. Awed by the power Annissa wielded to shape the rock walls of the canyon, he realized he would be even less help to the sorceress.

Feeling safe in his sheltered cave above the fighting, he heard a sound behind him. He realized he had not bothered to check the back of the cave. Goron had mentioned tunnels; what if one of the bandits came upon him from behind? He pulled out the long knife he had stuck in his waistband, brandishing it before him as he crept deeper into the cave.

Sure enough, he found a hole in the floor of the tunnel farther back. He crawled to the edge to peer over in time to see a man climbing a ladder not a foot below him. The face that looked up at him glistened with sweat and the blood of recent battle. The odor of weeks without washing assaulted Iko's nose.

Whipping his paramerion in front of him, Iko sliced the unsuspecting bandit's face, causing him to shriek in pain. Letting go of the ladder rungs to protect himself, the bandit fell down the shaft to lie motionless at the bottom.

Waiting a few minutes to make sure the man did not move, the boy built up enough nerve to climb down the ladder to investigate. Inspecting the body, he recoiled when he realized the man was dead. It was the first time he had come face to face with a dead man fully aware of what had happened. A wave of guilt washed over him, realizing he had killed someone. Was there some other way he could have protected himself?

He didn't mean to kill the man, only to make him go away, but there he lay, a corpse in a dark tunnel.

Beginning to feel sick, Iko stumbled down the corridor looking for a place to vomit. After emptying the contents of his stomach in a corner, he looked around at the tunnels carved into the sandstone. Shafts had been drilled through the walls of the caverns, bringing light and air to the interior passageways.

Investigating farther down the tunnel, the boy found chambers excavated on either side of the shaft. For the most part, they appeared to be store rooms filled with ceramic urns and vases covered by a thick layer of dust. The dust covering the floors of the chambers lay undisturbed as well. It was apparent that the bandits had not used these chambers for a very long while, if they ever had.

What, then, did the urns contain? Curiosity getting the better of him, he opened one, expecting to find a long-lost treasure, perhaps the treasure of the Mad Caliph that Goron sought. Disappointed, he found only old scrolls. Every one of the urns he opened contained only scrolls. He pulled one out to see if he could read it, the edges of the material crumbling as he handled it. Unfortunately, it was not written in the block letters he had learned from the nuns at the convent of Holy Maranna where he had been raised. It appeared to be the same flowing script he had seen in Iskander and Syre. He had learned a little bit of that lettering from Abiir simply by asking what the signs in the market had read. She helped him through a few words of her native language, though these words were different. He recognized some of the letters, but many of them he did not. He put the scroll back into the urn. He would ask Annissa about them later.

Remembering his companions, he climbed back to his cave, stepping over the corpse with a silently muttered apology to the dead man. He arrived at the cave entrance in time to see Goron wiping the blood off his sword and Annissa examining the unconscious bandit below him.

"Hey, there's a tunnel back here with some scrolls stored in it," he called down to his elders. "They look like they've been hidden a while. We should look at them. They might lead to treasure."

Goron looked up at the boy, catching his breath. Though he had won his fight, he had suffered some injuries, bleeding from cuts on his arms and a deep gash on his thigh. Iko had never seen so much blood. He could not tell how much of the blood was Goron's and how much was that of his enemies. Annissa looked shaky, as if she were about to pass out on her feet. The sorceress leaned against a rock to steady herself.

"We will need to rest before we do any exploring." Goron sheathed his sword and put his arm around Annissa's waist to support her, wincing from the pain in his thigh. "Annissa is too weary to go on. We will need to find someplace protected and easy to defend."

"There are rooms back here that we could hide in for a while," Iko called out from his cave. "I can go back in and look for another opening to bring in Bason."

Before either of the adults could object, Iko ducked back into the tunnel. Avoiding the bandit he had killed, he looked for another entrance to the catacombs. Heading east up the tunnel, away from the storage chambers he had found earlier, he passed a couple of other shafts going up from the tunnel, neither of which had a sturdy ladder to climb. Not far past these, he discovered an entrance emptying out onto the canyon floor with multiple tracks coming and going from the cave opening.

One set of tracks headed back up the tunnel in the direction he had come. Presumably, they had been made by the bandit he had killed. The thought of the dead man again caused a pang of guilt. Brushing it from his mind, he ran back to where Goron and Annissa rested.

"I found the tunnel entrances," Iko said, coming up short when he saw the gash in Goron's leg. "I think the bandits came from there. They turned right from the entrance but there are chambers to the left. Maybe we can rest there."

Assessing the situation, Goron took one look at Annissa and agreed, directing his grandson to lead the way. He picked up Annissa, throwing her arm over his shoulder to support her. Carrying her along, he limped as they followed Iko to their refuge.

Passing the dead man in the tunnel, Goron looked at Iko with a quick appraisal. The boy felt the older man's eyes on him and felt ashamed of what he had done to the bandit. After arriving at the chambers, Goron prepared a bedroll for Annissa to sleep on. Lying down, the weary sorceress fell asleep immediately, leaving her two companions to prepare a defense of the chamber. Goron instructed Iko how to build a barrier farther down the tunnel out of assorted rubble to protect them from intruders to the west. Goron intended to leave the eastern passage they had come down open so they could exit when Annissa had rested fully. Coming back to the chamber, Goron bandaged his wounds as he probed the boy about the dead man in the tunnel.

"Iko, this is the first time you have killed a man, am I correct?"

"I didn't kill him," Iko said, his voice quavering. "I cut his face and I think he broke his neck when he fell."

Though he felt the guilt of causing the man's death, he could not admit it to Goron.

"It is all right," said Goron, putting his hand on the boy's shoulder to comfort him. "Sometimes you have to do unpleasant things to protect yourself and those you love. I had to kill three men this day. Each of them had a family... at least each had a mother who loved them. Who knows what friends and family will mourn for the man who died here. Taking the life of another man should never be an ordinary occurrence. You should remember the man. Let's go and find a place for him. We shouldn't leave him sprawled in the tunnel like a dead animal."

Finishing tying off his bandages, Goron helped his grandson bring the man's body to another chamber where he could be laid to rest. When they had positioned the body for its final repose, Iko felt the need to say a prayer to Deihosos in the man's memory.

"O Father of Life and Death, take this man into your arms. Seal him into the soil to give life to new life." It was the opening prayer of the Deihosian funeral rite. He had heard his *amma*, the Materssa Mérka of the convent, chant the prayer. When one of the sisters died, she would say the funeral prayers and he would often have to sit with her. Once he laid the man to rest and said the prayer, he felt better.

The two of them spent the rest of the afternoon in the chamber with Annissa sleeping. Goron studied the hidden scrolls in the urns. He set a few aside but most he put back into the vases that he found them in. Many crumbled in his hands when he tried to open them. The light from the air shaft dimmed as afternoon turned to evening and the boy grew sleepy from his earlier exertions.

Iko woke a few hours later, a lantern burning in the corner and Goron snoring against the opposite wall.

Annissa was awake and poring over scrolls she had taken from the urns.

"What do they say?" the boy asked, his natural curiosity aroused.

"They appear to be the notes of grave robbers or treasure hunters, probably hundreds of years ago. See here?" She pointed at a crude diagram that looked like a floor plan of a house. "This is the tomb of a rich or important man, perhaps a king or pharaoh. It has more than one room, like a house, but this word written here is ancient Doran for 'grave' or 'tomb.' "

She reached for another scroll she had set aside, unrolling it carefully. "I think this might be a diagram of the tomb we are looking for, that of Thamses the Fat. My understanding of ancient Doran is not very good, but I think this is the word for Thamses the Fat, not Thamses the Great."

The conversation between the two woke Goron. "May I see that scroll?" he asked, yawning and rubbing the sleep from his eyes.

Not wanting to pick it up and risk damaging the fragile papyrus, she moved out of the way so he could see it, pointing out what she had already read. "See, the tomb has air shafts. That's how the robbers entered. We could probably enter the same way."

Reviewing the writing, Goron agreed. "We could drop a rope down the shaft and climb. This is a very valuable find. It must have been written by tomb robbers before the coming of the Wanajjis, so it predates the Mad Caliph. The robbers would have found the treasure of the ancient pharaoh, but not that of the caliph.

Iko didn't understand. "Wouldn't the bandits that attacked us have read these scrolls and found the caliph's treasure?"

"These scrolls are very old," said Goron. "Outlaws have used these caves for centuries. Nobody around here speaks ancient Doran other than scholars and there are few of them. It is certain that our attackers yesterday were not able to read these scrolls. Annissa, do you know how to preserve this scroll?"

"I'm not sure how to do that," she said. "How does one prevent something so fragile from falling apart?"

"We'll have to take some time to copy it." He looked for scrolls in better condition, scrolls that would not fall apart when carried. Having found one, he began copying the old scroll onto the back of the new one. Annissa read from the original while Goron wrote.

Iko, thirsty from the dry air and somewhat bored, went through the baggage that Goron had already unloaded from Bason the night before, looking for a waterbag. What he found upset him. A small hole in the side of the bag had nearly emptied it. Running back to the two adults, he announced that the waterbag had been drained.

Annissa seemed surprised, but Goron confirmed that he already knew. "Yes, it had been hit by an arrow from the bandits yesterday," he said. "Take a half of a cup now and we can have more after midday. We will have to ration water for a few days until we get to the other side of these hills. We can fill our waterbag at the next spring. It will be a rather dry journey for the next few days, I'm sorry to say. The sooner we can copy this scroll, the sooner we can leave and reach those springs."

He turned back to the scroll, writing what Annissa had read to him. Iko's thirst raged up inside him like a fire with fresh wood thrown on it. A half cup would not be nearly enough to slake it. Pouting, he tromped off to the waterbag to get his tiny ration. He wished he had never come along with Goron. He had gotten into nothing but trouble since he left his *amma.* She would not be happy with the way his grandfather had treated him.

Chapter 3

The journey east to Amonkhareb was long, hot, and dry. In spite of Iko's grumbling, Goron had rationed the remaining water well. There was enough water to last them the few days it took to reach the first spring at the headwaters of the Kolovi River. They all drank their fill at the spring. The water soothed Annissa's parched throat like cool, sweet nectar after days of dusty travel. Filling the waterbag, she inspected the repair she had made. It seemed to hold water. The fresh water seemed to lighten the boy's mood, which relieved her. Iko's incessant pouting grated on her.

By the time they came down out of the desert hills separating Hikuptah from Kupria, the river had grown, fed by springs that discharged stored water from the few rains that fell in the area. It grew large enough to water fields for a few farms. Lined with date palms, the road followed the river closely, passing farms watered from an irrigation canal paralleling the road and fed by the river. The farms seemed poor, with only small mud huts for the farm workers to live in, children dressed in simple homespun tunics playing outside, one or two goats in a pen next to the home.

There were no inns on the road and few travelers. The only traffic they seemed to encounter on the road were men leading donkeys carrying vegetables, straw or other goods.

After a few days following the road, the large, water-filled irrigation ditch that had paralleled it for a distance took a turn northward, diverging from the main road. A smaller side road forked off the main road, rutted by wagon wheels, tufts of grass growing between the ruts. The main road continued to follow the river east, a sign pointing the way along it. Annissa could not read the curved letters of Kukrili that the inhabitants of Hikuptah used, but she assumed it pointed the way to the next large city, which would be Amonkhareb. Goron indicated they would take the smaller road to their destination.

"Are we not traveling to Amonkhareb?" she asked.

"No, the tombs we seek are to the north," answered Goron, pointing in that direction. "There is nothing we need in the city. We should have all the supplies we need. The notes from the scrolls we copied as well as what we found in Iskander should be able to lead us to the tomb we're looking for. If the scroll you found is correct, we should be able to enter the tomb with little problem." With that, he took Bason's leads and turned onto the smaller road.

The road passed through what appeared to Annissa to be the ruins of city blocks. She spotted the occasional colonnade of a destroyed temple, arena, or market. The columns were different from the ancient Doran temples still found on the Merkebios in Synnakon. These were carved in an unfamiliar but simpler style, yet massive compared to the slender, elegant Doran and Cokan styles. Once, she spotted the bottom half of a massive statue in the distance, the top having been destroyed. Perhaps it had been a statue of a king, smashed by his enemies after his overthrow, or a shrine to an Elder God, defaced by followers of the Younger Gods. Maybe time had merely taken its toll, claiming its due through earthquake or erosion. In any case, the memorial was lost to history, to be remembered only in the dusty pages of books, buried in libraries and jealously guarded by the Tulkeen sect.

In places below the irrigation canal where the land was low and flat enough to grow crops, farmers had restored the land to fields punctuated by the lone stone-built shrine or colonnade, having dismantled the brick residences of the former inhabitants of the city. On the hillside above the canal, the ancient residences' truncated walls still stood at the base of sandstone outcroppings, flocks of goats and sheep grazing on the meager grasses between them.

The canal ended at a large reservoir but the road continued around it on the north shore. Annissa spied a structure on the south shore of the artificial lake with a colonnaded aqueduct leading away. She strained to see where the colonnade led, whether it might go to Amonkhareb but it appeared to end a short distance away from the reservoir. Hoping to have seen the city of gardens, she was disappointed that they were going around it. "Does the aqueduct water the gardens of Amonkhareb? I have heard stories about their beauty."

Goron shook his head. "Sadly, reality is much different from legends. The water system is in ruins and the gardens have dried up. The colonnade once held the main aqueduct, supplying most of the water for the ancient city. Lack of maintenance and natural causes destroyed it. The water system was once the wonder of the world, allowing Amonkhareb to bloom in the desert. After the ancient kingdom was conquered, kings and emperors turned their attentions elsewhere and they no longer attended to the needs of a city far from the centers of their power. Once it fell into disrepair, the city shriveled. Now the canal is used for irrigation. Water for drinking and washing is brought to the city from smaller canals closer to the river. Few gardens are left."

"Then the ruins we passed were once part of the city?" asked Iko.

"Yes, that is correct," said Goron. "Here is a map of the area." He drew a circle in the dust of the road to represent the city and a line showing the road passing north of it. "The river passes through the center of Amonkhareb," he said, drawing a wavy line through the middle of the circle. "The road we are on once skirted the outer edge of the city. When the population shrank, there was nothing to sustain residences and markets on the outskirts. People moved away and left the buildings behind."

They continued on through the afternoon, past the ruins of brick buildings, stone temples, and what remained of Amonkhareb. Looking backward, Annissa saw the sun lowering in the west, turning dark and red through the dusty haze that hung over the rocky, sunburned hills they had spent the last week traveling through. Goron led them down a side road toward a sandstone outcrop. "According to the books we read in Iskander, the ancient necropolis is to the north of the city a short distance beyond those rocks."

The sun was just touching the western hills when they came upon two obelisks on either side of the small road. The road continued past the pillars, falling away as it descended into a darkening valley. The reddish rays of sunset hit the rim of the sandstone gorge ahead, painting the golden-brown rock the deeper crimson of blood.

Goron stopped at the obelisks. "This is the entrance to the necropolis. It is too dark to continue into the valley below. Let us set up camp in the remaining light." They found a sandy, flat place off the side of the road, protected from the steady wind by a low, rocky bluff, perfect for a campsite. As they had not for weeks, they did not pitch tents, having no fear of rain from the cloudless sky.

Goron sent Iko to his regular chores, gathering whatever wood he could find, though no trees could be seen. All the boy was able to bring back were sticks from the dried shrubs that covered the surrounding hills. Meanwhile, Annissa fashioned a fire pit in the center of the site while Goron unloaded bags from Bason's back.

With a fire going and the bags unpacked, the three sat down to a meal of thin broth made from dried meat rehydrated in water and a dried biscuit to soak in it.

"Why didn't we go into Amonkhareb?" Iko wondered aloud. "We could have had some real food."

"We will go there when our business here is finished," said Goron. "We have to complete our task quickly before Manoueka knows we are here. He is digging at the grave of a different king."

"Manoueka has Kora!" Iko exclaimed. "I saw her on the ship in the port. We have to rescue her. She helped me get you out of prison in Synnakon."

Annissa was surprised at Iko's determination to free the girl, but Goron refused.

"I understand your concern, but we do not have time to free her," said Goron. "For one thing, we are not certain where he is. We must find the stone before Manoueka finds out we are here. Once we have it, we can figure out how to free Kora." A growling tone in Goron's voice ended the discussion. It was not the first time she had heard him use that tone to end a conversation, Annissa noted.

After finishing their meager dinner and cleaning their bowls, Annissa drew from her pack the parchment she and Goron had copied from the scrolls they had found in the tunnel in the hills a few days before. Unrolling it, the two of them bent over the notes, paying close attention to the map he had drawn with her assistance.

"We should be somewhere here, to the southwest of the tomb area," Goron pointed out a pair of marks on the lower left corner of the map that to Annissa looked like a gate. "Tomorrow, we will enter the necropolis and follow this road down the gorge here." He traced a meandering line from the lower left upward to the right.

"If the grave robbers' notes are correct, the main entrance to the tomb we seek is here." Annissa pointed at a spot on the line Goron traced. "The air shaft would be at the top of the gorge behind it fifty to a hundred feet, depending on the size of the tomb."

Goron examined the map intently, as if he were trying to discern the path of his own life in it. "After we enter, it should not take long to find the stone," he said, as if to himself. "When we locate it, take nothing other than the stone." Coming back to the present, he turned to her, his dark eyes fixed determinedly on her. "We cannot afford to waste time with trinkets that are likely to cause us more trouble than assistance. When we retrieve the stone, we will need to find a new place of safe-keeping where it will not be found by inquisitive wizards."

It struck her then, if Goron were as old as he said, was this what had sustained him through the centuries: the need to keep others from using the stones? How many times had he sat here with another person, reading a map to retrieve a stone? How often did someone threaten to find a stone? Perhaps decades or even centuries flew by before he felt the need to protect one of them. This time it was Manoueka, but surely there had been others, men driven by ambition or the desire for power. She looked at him, his face creased with age but still young compared to the countless years he had lived.

The sound of a greeting in a language she did not recognize interrupted her reflection. In the darkness, she made out the shadow of a man coming up the road followed by the bleating of a flock of goats. Goron called back, inviting the man to approach. An older man entered the limits of their firelight, wearing the simple tunic and headdress of a goatherd, his skin darkened from spending hours in the sun but his hair whitened with the years.

Inviting the old man to sit by the fire, Goron began conversing with him in Kukrili, the *lingua franca* of the Merouin Caliphate. Noticing the confusion on his companions' faces, Goron translated.

"He asks if we are planning to dig for treasure here. I told him we were scholars researching the ancient kings of Hikuptah," the warrior explained. "He believes there is little difference between a scholar and a grave robber. I will ask him whether he has heard if Manoueka has begun his excavation."

"Yes, yes," the old man exclaimed in response to Goron's question. "You Douraadii. I talk Douraadii very good. Other Douraadii far side of town. He pay many men for dig. You pay?"

Slipping back into Kukrili, the two chatted for a few minutes, the goatherd explaining and gesturing, before Goron translated. "It seems Manoueka is exploring an area about half a day east of here. If we had continued on the road we had been traveling this afternoon, we would have come to another road that led to more tombs, probably those of the Twenty-seventh Dynasty. Those tombs once overlooked a great lake, built by pharaohs and fed by the canal we had been traveling along. The lake is long since dry."

The old man continued talking as Goron translated for Annissa and Iko. "Manoueka has hired many men from the city, but rumors say that he has not found much. The shepherd laughs at them because every decade or so, someone comes along hoping to find the treasure of the Mad Caliph. The locals don't believe the legends of the treasure, saying 'The Mad Caliph was mad, not stupid.' He doesn't think we will find much either. All the tombs in the valley ahead were plundered centuries ago. He says there is nothing left."

A moan rose in the distance, perhaps by a gust of wind or the cry of a coyote. In any case, the sound caused the old man to become agitated, looking around at the dark hills. His unease infected Annissa as well.

"No sleep here," the white-haired shepherd warned. "Night bad by graves. Beware *an-nathulai*."

"What does he mean by *an-nathulai*?" Iko's voice was timid with anxiety.

"It comes from Doradic *anthai thúlon*, 'the spirits of the dead', " said Goron. A shiver crept down Annissa's spine when she realized what the old man was talking about. Iko blanched at the explanation, looking to Annissa for reassurance but finding none.

Having frightened himself with ghost stories, the old man made his apologies and rose to leave, leading his bleating goats into the darkness.

Talk of dead spirits did not faze Goron. "Pay no attention to the old man's stories. You are too easily frightened by the wind. I'll keep a watch." He laughed. "That way, if any ghosts come, I'll hear them first."

Annissa rolled out her bed and lay down for the night, but it was a long time before she could get the old man's voice out of her head and sleep.

Chapter 4

Goron woke the other two at dawn. He needed to find Korefael before Manoueka and now that he knew that his rival was nearby, his determination increased. He wanted to find the tomb as soon as possible and leave the area before the wizard found out he was there. Annissa prepared a meager breakfast for the three while Goron packed the bedrolls, readying for their trek into the valley of tombs that day.

He still had not determined what to do with the stone once he found it. He knew that he should not carry it, but perhaps Annissa could be trusted with it. Before he gave it to her, he would have to impress upon her the danger of such a powerful artifact.

Breakfast finished and their belongings packed up, the three entered the ancient necropolis, Iko leading Bason past the pair of obelisks at the head of the valley. The trail declined slightly at the beginning, falling more steeply into the gorge as they continued on. Appearing to have been created by water action ages ago during a time of wetter climate, the gorge carved a steep V through the stratified sandstone.

Goron examined the walls of the ravine, judging its ability to be scaled. Once they found the tomb of Thamses, he would still have to find the air shaft he had seen in the tomb robbers' notes. The edges of the layers of rock that formed the cliffs near the top would offer easy hand- and footholds for climbing, almost like a ladder. A climber would have to beware of loose rocks, which were common when sandstone was so highly stratified. The deeper they hiked into the gorge, the wider and steeper the layers of sandstone became. At the bottom, one massive layer of red sandstone formed high walls streaked black with weathering on either side of the cliff. The trail leveled off, snaking between the two towering walls, in some spaces only wide enough for Bason with his saddlebags.

The trio was in good spirits. The sun had not yet climbed high enough in the sky to reach the bottom of the ravine, making travel relatively cool after days of sun burnt travel. Goron found the closeness of the walls comforting and protecting. He did not expect to meet bandits on such an untraveled road.

Less than a mile down the trail, the three explorers discovered the first of the open tombs. The trail widened into a broad plaza between the canyon walls. A pair of tunnels gaped from the sandstone cliffs, each large enough to fit a house. In front of the dark cavities, stone rubble lay scattered into the plaza, the broken pieces of the tombs' facades destroyed by time or defaced by religious zealots. Among the pieces of broken columns, architraves, and friezes lay toppled statues, their heads smashed to bits and scattered. Goron explained to Annissa and Iko that at certain periods in the past, followers of the Younger Gods had destroyed most of the leftover remnants of the Elder

Gods' religion, including any sculptures that their remaining followers might still venerate.

"The tombs were built in the order of the kings' reigns." Annissa read from her scroll with the notes identifying the tombs. "These first two were the richest and most powerful, so they are the largest. All the kings after these two copied their architecture. The tomb we are looking for was built by a rather poor pharaoh near the end of the dynasty, so we shouldn't expect to find anything quite this large." She surprised herself at how much she remembered from the books in the Tulkeen library.

The three continued past other tunnels, each getting smaller as Annissa had said. The facades cut into the rock surrounding the opening remained the same size, though the cavity itself grew smaller. Goron explained that boring a hole into solid rock was expensive, but wanting to appear rich and powerful, the pharaohs would cut a smaller tomb and decorate it more lavishly. Those that could afford thick bronze plated wood doors fastened them to the rock with bronze or iron ribbons, but grave robbers had removed the bronze centuries earlier, melted them down, and sold them for scrap. Later pharaohs had carved and placed heavy stone doors to deter thieves, but those had been removed as well.

Goron counted half a dozen open and plundered tombs dug into the solid sandstone before the three explorers came to another broad plaza between the cliff walls. Three tombs faced out from the sandstone here. Similar to the earlier tombs, these had a small central tunnel about ten feet square dug into the rock and surrounded by decorations of carved stone, often constructed to resemble false windows and doors. The stone of the carved facades appeared cleaner and lighter in color than the weathered red sandstone around them.

Statues and sculptures had also been carved into the facade but most had been smashed, similar to those they had seen earlier at the first tombs they had passed. A fourth wall faced the plaza but its entrance had been bricked up with large stones and any remnants of decoration of the facade had been removed, making the wall smooth and clean, more so than even the natural rock.

"This is where the tomb of Thamses should be." Annissa studied her scroll, comparing it to her surroundings. "The map describes a plaza with four tombs, Thamses's being on the northwest wall. There had obviously been a tomb here, but it appears to have been closed up solidly."

"It is likely that the Mad Caliph sealed it." Goron approached the wall and examined the stones. "I suppose he thought it would be harder to rob a tomb that no longer existed. We will need to find the air shaft and hope it was not also bricked over. Otherwise, Annissa will need to perform some spells to remove the rock and that might delay us considerably. It will be next to impossible to find the air shaft if we backtrack to the beginning of the valley and follow it out. I will climb the rock wall here and you two must take Bason back and find a trail at the top of the cliff. I will meet you there, so it should be easier to find. Iko, get my rope and Castrian spikes from Bason's saddlebags."

"Can I climb too?" asked Iko. "I'm a good climber; I climbed the tower in Synnakon after you." Immediately upon saying it, the boy stifled his next words, knowing that Goron might be angry with him for doing such a foolish thing.

The black-haired man turned to him in amazement, his dark eyes burning into his grandson. "You should not have done that. Climbing is a very dangerous business to do alone. You should always have lookouts in case of an accident. What if your knots had been faulty and you had fallen?"

Feeling guilty for shaming Iko, Goron gave him an important job to boost his confidence. He whispered conspiratorially to the boy, "I must climb alone this time. I need your help handling the ropes from the ground. You can show Annissa how to do it. When I am at the top, you must guide Bason to meet me; Annissa cannot handle a horse like you can."

Grudgingly, Iko accepted his grandfather's explanation and went to gather the climbing gear. Goron examined the stone masonry where the caliph had bricked over the tomb's entrance. The face of the rock was mostly smooth, interrupted by pits and marks where someone had tried to drill their way in, giving up after testing the strength and depth of the stone. On the rock face above him, the stone walls of the facade had been chiseled flat, giving the entire rock wall the look of a solid, evenly smoothed cliff face. Climbing would be difficult.

A mere ten yards away, however, stood the tomb of Thamses's predecessor, its false porticos and colonnades decorated with the entablature of ancient Hikuptahn architecture. While its earlier age demanded a simpler style than the later Doran or Cokan styles, the unfluted columns and unadorned cornices and architraves would provide enough hand- and footholds to get halfway up the cliff. Beyond that, a crack in the rock extended from near the top of the facade to the rim of the canyon.

After Iko brought the Melissene silk rope and Castrian steel spikes, Goron tied the cords together. He estimated he would need a hundred and fifty feet to reach the top of the cliff. Next, he fashioned a harness as he had done when climbing Manoueka's tower. Putting the rope through the ring on Bason's saddle, he asked Iko to belay for him. This time, he put Annissa on the rope behind the child, instructing her to learn from him. "It is better to have two on the line if I fall and the boy's strength is not enough," he explained.

Inspecting his bag of spikes, he remembered that he had lost many of them in his disastrous climb up the face of Manoueka's tower. Having been captured and rendered unconscious, he had been unable to retrieve any of them. Iko had gathered what he could, but many remained lodged in the wall of the tower. He would have to use those he still had sparingly.

Removing his boots, he began to climb, placing his first pin about fifteen feet up in a crack between a cornice and capital at the top of the first row of columns. This part of the climb was easy, using the narrow space between a column and the wall as a chimney. Getting past the entablatures between the colonnades would be harder, requiring him to pull his entire weight over a cornice extending past the rest of the stonework by nearly a foot.

Luckily, the age of the structure had allowed it to weather and sag in some spots. This made the rock surface rougher, forming small hand- and footholds and creating cracks between the pieces of the masonry. At the top of the column, he placed a second spike and threaded his line through it. He hesitated a second before continuing, realizing that he had to go back for the expensive spike he had left behind. He would have to do this for every spike he placed, making the climb twice as long and increasing the risk if he fell. With only one spike to break a potential fall, he would need to make sure each one was placed solidly before continuing.

The second spike placed, he backtracked down for the first and continued up. Stopping for a rest before tackling the climb over the cornice, he resolved to place the spikes closer together so he did not have to climb far to retrieve the previous one.

Taking a mouthful from his water pouch, he continued to clamber over the lip of the cornice. It was a good thing the Hikuptahn built level entablatures, he thought. If this were a Doradic structure, he would have to climb to the sloped top of a triangular pediment above the cornice. He placed a third spike, then climbed down to retrieve the second. Climbing back was more difficult the second time, and retrieving the spikes might tire him out before he reached the top of the cliff.

Resting before he continued, he discovered climbing the next colonnade was similar to the first. Sliding up between a column and wall, he placed spikes above where he found a crack and removed the one below so he would not have to climb the entire distance twice.

Crawling over the second cornice, he placed his next spike in a small crevice above him. Looking down to see the previous spike below him a few feet, he thought he would not have to climb back down to remove it if he could retrieve it from where he stood. He checked the topmost spike, hanging his weight from it to make sure he had placed it firmly. To his relief, it did not move at all.

He reached down for the lower spike to remove it, but he had set it out of reach by a few inches. Hanging farther over the lip and stretching his sinews, he could reach the metal with his fingertips. Pushing himself the extra half inch to grasp the spike, he felt his center of gravity shift over the edge.

Instinctively, he reached back to grab the edge of the stonework, but his hands had already moved beyond it. Time slowed, gravity took over, and he felt his body tumble headfirst into empty space. As he fell, the faces of his companions appeared as if he stood in front of them, their eyes wide in alarm, yelling a belated warning as their bodies went taut, pulling on the rope to check his fall. In that split second, he imagined the three of them as some kind of family, wondering if he died what would become of Iko. He knew the boy's grandmother, Aisarra, would be upset, but she would not be able to take the boy back to her convent. He did not want the child to be alone in the world. Would Annissa be able to care for him? What of her? He knew so little about her and where she came from. He had grown fond of her in the past couple of months in spite of the sad loneliness that had fallen over her since Geotheris had been slain.

Then the rope commenced its function and interrupted his fall. Time resumed its regular pace and Goron hung in the air, dizzy from spinning in space. His heart slowed, adrenaline ebbing from his veins as he gathered his wits. Noticing that he was slowly dropping on his lifeline, he looked down to see Iko and Annissa thirty feet below, straining to keep him aloft.

Reaching out slightly above him, he grasped the lip of the cornice and pulled himself up, relieving the pressure on the two at the other end of the rope below. The spike he had sought before his fall projected from the rock in front of him. Plucking it from the wall, he resumed his climb, pulling himself over the lip of the cornice a second time.

Sitting on the ledge and gathering his breath, he examined the beginning of an extended fissure running diagonally from halfway up the next colonnade to the top of the massive sandstone formation. He began the easy climb between a column and the wall to reach the beginning of the long crack. Reaching that point, he followed the crack the rest of the way, placing spikes within reach above him before removing the previous one below. In a relatively short time, he reached the top of the sandstone formation, climbing past the Hikuptahn masonry and up the natural rock face.

The rock layers became much narrower above the massive lower formation. Repeated strata of sandstone lay interspersed between thin layers of broken shale. This final stage of the climb would be the easiest. Like a giant staircase to the top of the plateau, each layer stood farther back from the previous, giving him a broad, rock-strewn ledge to start from for each climb to the next step. Goron had no need for rope from that point on.

He turned back down, yelling at his companions to release the rope and start their journey back up the valley to meet him at the top. They gathered their belongings and led Bason back up the valley. Goron drew the heavy rope up the side of the cliff face, coiling it over his shoulder at the top. Collecting the last of the silken cord, he turned and finished the climb to the top.

Chapter 5

By the time the other two reached the top of the cliff a couple of hours later, Goron had fully rested and was ready to continue. Annissa brought out the scroll she had created from the notes in the bandits' cave. The two bent over to study it while Iko waited to the side with Bason.

"The entrance to the air shaft is here, about a hundred yards back from the main entrance to the tomb." Annissa pointed at a spot on the map.

"The face of the entrance is there, behind us at the bottom of the cliff. If we walk back a hundred yards in this direction, we should find the air shaft," she said, pointing in a northwesterly direction. Rolling up the scroll, she followed Goron as he headed off in the direction she had pointed. Iko followed close on her heels with the horse.

Pacing out a hundred paces, Goron stopped. "The shaft should be here somewhere. We do not know what size it is, but be careful, it could be covered up and you would not want to fall in. Let us split up and look around. Annissa, you head in that direction. Iko, come with me this way." Being responsible for the boy, he did not want him to wander on his own in this rough country. A child unfamiliar with the desert would not be aware of the dangers of this region. Poisonous snakes and insects could be found all around and he did not know what other shafts might be in the area.

Iko tied Bason to a nearby shrub and followed his grandfather. They began a sweep in front of them, meandering back and forth to cover a wide area. After a short while, they heard Annissa shout.

Goron nudged Iko. "It sounds as if she has found something."

Hurrying over to Annissa, they found her examining a large stone about four feet square, two feet thick, and carved with Kukrili letters on the top. Wind and sand had worn down the inscription slightly. "I can make out a few letters, but I have not had much time to learn the language. Can you read it?"

"It is an inscription by the Mad Caliph." Goron translated the message, running his fingers over the inscriptions in the rock. "It warns intruders not to attempt to open it on threat of the wrath of Momadou."

"It would not be magically warded or sealed," Annissa said. "The Mad Caliph was vehemently antarkanist. It's why he buried all magical artifacts in his treasury; he would never have used magic."

"No, but you forget that priests can also cast spells," Goron countered, inspecting the stone closely, trying to figure out if it were moveable. "It may seem to the priest as if he is calling on the gods to perform magic, but the result is the same."

"That seems to be a rather abstract objection," said Annissa.

"Perhaps, but remember that questions of magical theory could be as much political as scholarly, the same as they are today." Goron stopped inspecting the stone and addressed Annissa directly. "Do not forget that both the Wanaj sect and the antarkanist controversy developed during the *monousion* debate, which the cult of Hadrianism started. Those that held to that belief maintained that all magic derived from the gods and those that did not properly venerate the gods when using magic performed a blasphemy."

"So there is no difference between the Wanajji priests and a Synnakian wizard?"

"Other than in name, no. Even the form of spells those priests and all wizards use contain invocations to the Megisitibalitsa, the Great Quadrality. The forms were developed centuries ago in the Phersi Empire, before the Younger Gods arrived. This is one argument antarkanists once used against arcane magic: that it is derived from the Elder Gods, whom they considered evil."

Goron turned to face the Mad Caliph's stone sealing the tomb's air shaft again, directing the discussion back to it. "The question we have at hand now is whether this stone is magically warded or not. Do you detect any *ousion*?"

Annissa turned her attention to the stone, searching for any evidence that the *sep* field had been altered, concentrating on the area surrounding the entrance. A faint shimmer appeared, indicating that some magic had been used, but it was very weak. "I believe the seal has been warded in some way, but I'm not sure how. The shift in the *sep* field is very weak, as if the seal has deteriorated over time. It is possible the spell has faded, but it's hard to tell."

"What will happen if we move the stone?" Iko kneeled next to them.

"I'm not certain. It's possible we will end up triggering whatever ward has been put on it, but I don't know what kind of ward it is. The patterns in the field are strange to me. I don't understand this magic well."

"Can you break it or make it melt like you did in the caves?" Iko asked.

"Yes, but that will have the same effect on the wards. Besides, it would be easier to move it; it requires less energy. Causing solid stone to flow was exhausting. Besides, I have only done it that one time and the threat was urgent then. I'm not sure I could do it again."

"Then we shall have to try to move it," said Goron, deciding for them. "If you set some protective spells around it first, perhaps that will protect us from the effects of the wards. We can harness Bason to help pull it if you have a spell that will push it away from the hole."

"But I don't know any spells to protect against magic wards," said Annissa

"It is the specific intent that is important, not the words," said Goron. "If you call on the powers of air requesting protection, it might work. Momadou's powers derive from elemental air, so we would likely need protection along those lines."

With a nod indicating assent, Annissa began chanting, calling on the spirits of air for protection. "*O póntonízuva wániz...*"

While she cast the spell, Goron slipped ropes around the large rock, tying the other end to Bason's harnesses. When that was done, Annissa began casting spells to move the seal, this time calling on the powers of earth. The stone must have weighed at least two tons. Given the weight, she would need to channel a large amount of *ousion.*

With Bason pulling on the great stone, his haunches straining, and Annissa pushing, channeling as much *ousion* into it as possible, the stone actually began sliding sideways. It only needed to move a few inches to uncover a small opening in the air shaft. It was enough to trigger the Mad Caliph's warding spell.

A rush of air exploded from the opening, knocking over Annissa, who was standing closest to the opening, breaking her concentration and kicking up a cloud of sand.

Thinking that the Mad Caliph's wards had weakened if those were the extent of the effects, Annissa picked herself up and prepared to continue. But the cloud of sand did not dissipate. Instead, it grew stronger.

The wind blasted her with sand picked up from the surrounding soil, growing in strength and expanding in area. She felt the burn of millions of fine particles scouring her skin. She stumbled away from the source of the pain, her eyes clenched against the sand.

Goron, seeing his companion's distress, pulled a scarf from inside one of Bason's bags. He wrapped it around his face and rushed into the growing sandstorm, warning Iko away from the wind.

He grabbed Annissa, who was wandering sightless in the storm, and led her quickly away from the center of the maelstrom.

Already, the vortex was beginning to break apart and diminish.

Taking a waterbag and pouring its contents into Annissa's eyes, Goron washed the sand away. As she opened her eyes tentatively, blinking away the remains of the sandy debris, Goron realized that he had never noticed her green eyes. They were quite beautiful. He had assumed, given her sandy-colored hair and tanned complexion, that her eyes were brown, green eyes being less common.

Realizing he was staring at her, he quickly looked away. "It was a djinn, a spirit of air devoted to Momadou," he explained, stowing the waterbag among the rest of the gear. "Such protections were once quite popular among the Wanajjis. Nowadays, such spells are more rare. The similarity of djinn to the Elder Gods is too great for them to ignore.

"If this was the extent of the Mad Caliph's spells on the seal, it is possible that he has placed other wards protecting the tomb, ensuring its safekeeping over the intervening decades. Those wards might have weakened over time, but we cannot count on that possibility."

Inspecting the inch-wide opening between the stone and the edge of the air shaft, Goron was encouraged. "That went well, in spite of the djinn," he said. "I don't expect we will trigger any other wards until we actually enter the tomb. We must be very careful once we get inside." Turning to Annissa, he asked, "Are you ready to continue?"

Wiping sand, dust, and water from her face, she nodded, beginning her chant once more. Taking his position on Bason's reins, Goron again directed the horse to pull on the stone. The sorceress, more determined this time, channeled more *ousion*, creating a stronger force to push the huge block.

The slab moved more easily this time, inch by inch. When it had uncovered an opening three feet wide, Goron called a halt to the endeavor. Kneeling next to the hole, he peered down. A shaft angled steeply down into the darkness below. He announced that it was large enough to enter.

"I will go down alone," he said. "You two can stay up here and keep guard."

"I don't think you should go by yourself," Annissa said. "You are more likely to run into danger inside the tomb than we will out here. What if the Mad Caliph put other protection spells on his treasure? You would be well served to have someone back you up, especially with some magic."

The swordsman could not argue with her reasoning. "It is a long way to the bottom." Goron picked up his ropes to fashion a new harness. "It is very steep. The climb might be the hardest part. Have you ever rappelled down a line before?"

"No, but I think I can learn."

Giving her a skeptical look, he finished knotting the harness around his waist and began tying it around hers. Hiking her cotton *abaya* up, he began wrapping the lines around her thighs. Checking his knots for security, he became aware that tying a harness around a woman had a different effect on him than doing so for a man. The ropes held her dress tightly against her thighs and backside, revealing an alluring, lithe figure. He stepped back, embarrassed again.

Annissa blushed as well. "Shall we go then?" she asked, turning away.

"Erm... Yes," he stammered. "I will go first and you can follow on the same line after I am down."

Showing her how to wrap the rope around the metal ring on her harness to slow her descent, he wondered why, after centuries of living, he could not ignore a woman's charms. Certainly now was not the time to be distracted, and he almost wished he had left the sorceress behind in Synnakon.

After a short lesson, Annissa declared herself confident in her ability to work the ropes. Her bravery impressed him. Few Doran women would be so bold as to attempt such a physical task.

Anchoring the line around a pair of small boulders nearby and tying it to Bason's saddle, he looped the other end through the ring on his harness and dropped it down the shaft. "Iko, when we are ready to come up,

I will give three tugs on the rope. When I do, have Bason pull us up out of the tomb."

"Watch me," he said to Annissa. He stepped backwards over the lip of the void into the darkness and hanging from the rope. "It is simply a matter of walking backward down the wall, letting the rope slide slowly through the ring," he said. "Do not let it slide too fast or you might not be able to stop it. When I get to the bottom, pull the rope back up and knot it through the ring on your harness exactly as I have."

Continuing backward, he descended down the shaft, becoming engulfed in darkness. It only took a few minutes to reach the bottom. Removing the rope from his harness, he let it go slack. He wished he had given Annissa a pair of gloves. Even with his calluses, letting the rope slide through his palms chafed. He gave the rope three tugs and it began ascending back up to the entrance.

After a few minutes, the rope fell down the shaft again. He looked up to see a shadow blocking the light from the opening hundreds of feet above. He grabbed the lower end of the rope to steady it, watching Annissa descend. She seemed to be coming down faster than she should have. He pulled the rope tight to slow her descent, but she had already lost control and was slipping down the rope freely, her hands trying to grasp the rope above her.

Reaching the bottom, she landed on top of Goron, who stood directly below her.

"That went well," he laughed sarcastically.

Picking herself up and brushing herself off, she tried to recover whatever Synnakian dignity she had left. "The rope began burning my hands and I could no longer hold on," she explained, blowing on her palms to cool them down.

The dark-haired man gave her a sympathetic grimace before turning to face the long tunnel. He pulled a torch out of his backpack.

Annissa pulled out the map she had drawn. "The diagrams of the tomb did not show very many chambers," she said. "There should be an entry hall, followed by a larger central hall, with the sanctuary at the back. The air shaft usually came off a smaller chamber to the side of the central hall, so if we follow this tunnel, we should find it."

"Let us explore," said Goron. "The treasure cannot be too far."

Chapter 6

Exactly as Annissa predicted, the tunnel led a short distance, opening to a larger hall, its roof supported by four massive pillars. Paintings of human bodies adorned the fifty-foot walls of the entire chamber from floor to ceiling. Goron's torchlight barely reached the top of the images, though it was clear that the beings' heads had been obliterated.

Goron recalled back to the time before the dawn of the Younger Gods. "These were images of the Elder Gods." His voice echoed in the vast chamber. "Each one would have represented a different deity, though one cannot tell which is which without seeing their faces. The Mad Caliph probably had them defaced in order to rededicate the tomb to his own gods."

Annissa examined them all. "I don't see any difference between them other than that some had female and some had male bodies," she said. The faces and symbols that would have distinguished the figures had been thoroughly removed. Some of the female bodies wore only a skirt, leaving their breasts bare, though that part of the image had been carefully censored as well. "Did the ancients worship devils? It's no wonder the caliph destroyed the images."

"These were no devils," Goron replied. "The disciples of the Younger Gods preached powerful sermons against them. In order to win the people over to the new religion, they condemned the Elder Gods as devils. Nowadays, they are mostly forgotten except in diluted form as evil demons in folktales."

Mulling over Goron's words after he turned away, Annissa stared a while longer at the colossal images in the torchlight, as if their faces would reappear if she stared hard enough.

Exploring the room further, they found a passage to the right leading off into the darkness, but a pair of bronze doors drew Annissa's attention to the left. "The sanctuary would be there." The sorceress pointed at the doors.

Examining the cast bronze doors, they found them divided into eight panels, four on each door, decorated with images of the Younger Gods. Oversized hinges fastened the doors to the stone walls with large bronze handles attached at the middle of each one.

The hinges looked weak, time and corrosion having taken its toll on them. "Are there any wards on the doors?" Goron asked, inspecting the hinges and handles.

Annissa examined the bronze closely, discovering the telltale signs of *sep* field distortions. The patterns indicated an unfamiliar earth-based enchantment. "There's something here," she answered. "Perhaps the caster had intended to cause the ceiling to collapse."

"That does not seem likely." Goron guessed at what the spells might unleash. During the time of the Mad Caliph, the fashion was for priests to manipulate the life forces of creatures, animating otherwise inanimate materials. "Like the djinn above, these wards are more likely to activate a spirit of some sort, perhaps a golem fashioned from the surrounding stone. In any case, can you neutralize it?"

"As I said before, I don't understand this magic. I can cast some protective wards, but they will likely have no effect, the same as the ones I cast on the tomb's seal had no effect."

"It is probably best to save your energy until we find out what we are dealing with." He reached into a small bag at this waist and pulled out his lock picking tools. Kneeling down in front of the door, he went to work on the keyhole an inch or so below the handle of the right door. Annissa decided to step back from the door while he worked, in case she was right about the magical ward.

As he inserted his first tool into the lock, a voice sounded in his head, similar to the voice he had heard when he attempted to open the great stone door in the catacombs under Synnakon.

"Do not do this. Leave it be. It is dangerous to you."

Hesitating before shrugging off the voice's entreaties, Goron continued working. He understood the danger, but knew that, if he did not remove Korefael from this hiding place, Manoueka would find the stone and use it for his own purposes. It was only a matter of time before the wizard figured out he was looking in the wrong place and discover the shard's true resting place. It took less than a minute before Goron heard the *click* of the mechanism in the lock.

Nothing happened.

Annissa let out a sigh of relief, waiting a moment longer as Goron reached out to grasp the bronze door handle. "I can still sense the energy of the ward in place," she said. "The trap is not tied to the lock."

Goron nodded in understanding as he pulled the door open, its weight groaning on the ancient hinges. "The *ousion* from it is beginning to flow," said Annissa, her voice raised. "It's like . . . water down a drain into the room beyond."

Goron steeled himself, ready for result of the spell cast centuries ago. Noticing no ill effects, he pulled the door wider, revealing a chamber beyond filled with gold, jewels, and artifacts. Approaching the sanctuary, the enchantress' eyes widened at the sight of wealth she had never seen before.

Goron let out a long, low whistle. The treasure was beyond calculation, chests full of gold and silver coins sat to one side, but the artifacts drew the observer's attention, each item displayed individually. Staves topped by gemstones the size of a child's fist lay inside, as did crowns of gold set with rubies and emeralds that no dust had touched over the centuries of their burial. Gem-encrusted bracelets, necklaces, and brooches fashioned from silver and gold lay on tables and benches. Even one small piece of the treasure would pay off Annissa's debt to the Nankisos Maholon and still leave enough to pay for a license to become a full *maholos*. She reached out to pick up a necklace.

"Touch nothing," Goron said, grabbing her arm. He set his torch into a nearby sconce to light the small chamber. "We don't know what powers might infuse these artifacts. They might also be warded against thieves." Heeding his warning, she inspected the treasure more closely, seeking the revealing evidence of *ousion* that a magical artifact would emit. "All the artifacts in the room emanate strong signs of *sep* field distortions," Annissa said.

Goron nodded in understanding. "The artifacts are powerful, to be sure. It was no wonder the Mad Caliph hid them so deep."

He continued to search the room for Korefael. Eventually, his eyes rested on a plain grey statuette of a lion resting on its haunches, about a foot and a half tall. His heart lept in recognition. The figure appeared to be fashioned of lead. It seemed out of place here, the only item undecorated with jewels or not gold.
Remembering the legends surrounding the stone and its fate, he told Annissa the story.

"It is said that the god Deihosos himself blessed the stone. Korefael has been associated with Hikuptah since the time of Aranel. According to legend, the King of Ptahmel set Korefael into a golden statue of a lion dedicated to Deihosos in the second century of the Cokan Empire. Later, the Synnakians took the statue back to Synnakon when they conquered Hikuptah. It sat in the Eterodeihon in the Apse of Deihosos for some time. Eventually, a foolish emperor sold off the riches of Synnakon in order to finance his wars against the Merouin Caliphate. It is believed that an Erminikonian merchant purchased the lion, but nobody knows for certain where it went after that. According to the legend, the merchant encased the lion in a covering of lead in order to bring it safely out of Synnakon. When the Synnakians conquered Erminikon again, the lion could not be found.

"Another legend states that the statue is cursed. It is said that the Erminikonian merchant sold the lion to a Merouin general. The general brought it back to Damash and made a gift of it to the caliph, telling him the story of gold and jewels beneath the lead covering. The caliph did not believe the general's story and had the general put to death for making a fool of him with gift of a plain lead lion. On the night the general was executed, the caliph died at his dinner, face down in a bowl of soup. Thus began the legend of the Curse of the Lion of Ptahmel.

"It appears we have found the Lion of Ptahmel," Goron said.

"It is a very powerful artifact," the sorceress said as she examined the statue. "It emanates a very strong *sep* field. But there is no discernible pattern to the eldritch energy. I cannot identify what powers it draws on. At times, the *ousion* seems to be of earth, other times of air, fire, or water. It appears to be a blend of all four and none, all at once. It is very odd."

"This statue contains Korefael inside," said Goron. "What you describe is the pattern of the stones of power. They were created before wizards differentiated between the four elements."

Reaching out to pick up the lion, he heard the voice speak to him once more. *"Do not touch it."*

Another voice spoke then. Similar to the first but slightly higher pitched, it argued for a different path. *"Do not submit to my cousin's timorous wishes. He has not the capacity to grant authority to others, but I have. It is your fate to reunite me with my brothers. You and my cousin know this. Take me from here and I will bestow on you more power than you have ever felt before."*

The enticing new voice kindled a desire in Goron to take the lion and use it for himself. With the power the stone would give him, he could gather all the other stones and prevent anyone else from using them.

"Listen not," the first voice warned. *"My cousin uses seduction and temptation. His powers would corrupt you. Any attempt to bring him and his brothers together is a step toward cataclysm."*

Shrugging off both voices' demands, Goron picked up the lion.

• • •

The magician took a moment to observe the columns surrounding the temple, a watered-down copy of the great temple of Sovopitraz, the Phersi sun god, in the royal city of Phersivauras. The capitals of the columns, with their two bulls facing away, seemed merely an add-on feature rather than a fundamental piece of the structure, as if the provincial architects did not trust themselves or the design. Furthermore, the floral ornation of the columns was simplified, resembling a Ponaji column with floral bas-reliefs rather than a stack of flowers rising to the sky in the Phersi style.

It was true that local architects in the Ponaj preferred a simpler style and most Ponaji did not worship the Phersi sun god, but the execution of the style in this building lacked any of the beauty and grandeur of the original.

His team of vilimancers, having determined that this city was closer to the center of the world than Phersivauras, had traveled north to find an appropriate spot for their endeavors. He would have preferred if the other magicians had decided to stay in the royal city or at least to perform their investigations somewhere other than a temple, but on the advice of the personal priest of the Ponaji satrap, they had agreed to use the newly constructed temple. It was more likely that the priest had wanted to showcase the new building rather than improve the chances of success for the arcane rites. In any case, if for political reasons only, his magician companions had agreed to use the temple.

He looked across the central courtyard, enclosed by the graceless columns, at the four wizards working with him, making preparations for the incantation to come. They surrounded a large gem slightly larger than his fist sitting in a brass frame. Their inquiries into the nature of the magic they intended to channel had led them to the conclusion that the new philosophy of elemental magic would allow them greater control over the forces involved. Each of the four took one of the prime elements as his own to channel as part of the unbinding ritual: earth, air, fire, and water.

He had been assigned his own role for his part in the ceremony, controlling the receiving stone. His responsibility was minor and less dangerous compared to the others, this part of the ritual being already well understood.

When all was prepared, the four gave signal to begin. He began to chant, channeling the magical substance that underlay the universe, into his stone. *"O póntonízuva..."*

• • •

As suddenly as the vision arrived, it left. The dream was specific but indistinct, as if it were some vague memory or déjà vu. He jerked his hand back from the statuette. Annissa gave him a worried look. "Are you all right?" she asked. "You hesitated a moment, as if you were in a daze."

"I am fine," he replied, pulling a thick cloth out of his bag and throwing it over the figure. He gave her an empty leather bag, well worn with use. "I should not touch this thing. Pick it up with this cloth and put it in this bag. Make sure not to touch it yourself. Who knows what powers it might unleash."

She did as he instructed, surprised at the weight of such a small figure. "What of the rest of the treasure here?" she asked. "Can we take any of it?"

"It would be best to leave it, except for a few coins. Most of it is very powerful. Grab a few handfuls of coin if you must, then we should return to the surface quickly and reseal the tomb. If anyone should find out we have opened it, they might come looking inside."

A creature came at them from behind as they faced away from the sarcophagus it had climbed out of. It struck Annissa's left side with a blow that sent her flying into the displayed artifacts, knocking over a crown and scepter. She sat dazed for a moment as the creature turned on Goron to strike again. Its brittle skin crackled as it fell upon him, its bones clattering underneath.

A wave of nausea overcame Annissa. Was it from the creature's blow or her own revulsion at the reek of death and dust from the creature?

The creature's face was no more than a withered mask stretched over the frame of its skull, a sepulchral fire shining in its eyes. It had been wrapped in a tight-fitting shroud that appeared to have been shredded away enough to free its head and allow its desiccated legs and arms free motion. Was this the *an-nathulai* the old man had told them about the night before?

Goron struggled to draw his weapon and avoid the creature's raking claws. By the time he retrieved his sword, Annissa had revived and began to chant. "*O póntonízuva...*"

Barely had she started the incantation when the creature, ignoring Goron, turned and flew at her. It gave the swordsman time to strike a clean blow on the monster's back, but the shroud, infused with funereal ointments and sacred magic, had become hard as a suit of armor.

Panicked, Annissa had no time to finish the chant before she threw up a shield of air. The rushing ghoul stopped in its tracks, blocked by the invisible obstacle.

"Don't touch it!" yelled Goron, waving her away. "Keep it away from you. It is attracted to the *ousion* in your spells!"

The creature battered the surface of the barrier between it and Annissa. As if understanding it could not break through the shield, it stopped and opened its jaws wide. A cascade of beetles poured from the gaping hole in its face. Each beetle no longer than her index finger, they crawled down the corpse's body in an unending torrent. Even as Goron pounded on the creature from behind, the flow of beetles did not stop.

The chittering beetles flooded toward Annissa, bypassing her shield on either side. She tried expanding its width, but the insect swarm flowed around it still. When the writhing mass reached her, they began climbing her legs, biting as they came. Distracted, she let her shield drop, allowing the remaining swarm to rush toward her in a wave.

The bites grew in number as the swarm climbed her body. She had to keep them away from her mouth. A horrifying thought came to her. If they crawled in her mouth, she would die.

Panicked, she lashed out with a spell. "*O póntonízuva digímaviz, awigindúd miv kelshiz wikiz!*" Almost instinctively, she relied on an earth spell, the spell form she had become most comfortable with in a fight. She imagined them all turned to one inch stones.

As soon as the thought came to her, the bugs that had been climbing her body fell away from her, clattering on the stone floor.

Some fell on other scarabs still living, crushing them, but uncounted more still swarmed around her. The flow from the ghoul had stopped, but the swarm was still overwhelming. Even as soon as the stone insects had fallen from her, others climbed over them to take their place, biting her as soon as they found open skin. She could continue turning them to stone, but she would have to do it multiple times, getting bitten each time.

Now she had bites on top of other bites up and down her legs. The pain increased, making it difficult for her to think of a new, more effective spell. She turned the next batch to stone. The clattering of the small stones on the floor eased her mind somewhat, but her panic was rising. Feeling unsteady on her feet, she began to smell smoke.

Suddenly, as if a candle had been blown out, the beetles stopped and fell away from her, like the ones she had turned to stone. These were still made of chitin, though. Why had they stopped?

The smell of smoke in the chamber grew. A black cloud billowed towards her from where she had last seen Goron.

"Get out of the room!" Goron yelled at her, running through the smoke.

Remembering what Goron had said about the coins, she grabbed a handful and threw it into the bag with the lion. Smoke filled her lungs as she ran from the room.

• • •

Goron set upon the *an-nathulai* again with his sword, but it was no use, the priests that buried this creature had done their jobs well. It was as hard and strong as iron.

Having disgorged every beetle from its mouth, the creature turned on Goron. The last straggling bugs skittered down its body, heading towards Annissa.

The *an-nathulai* moved fast as lightning, its emaciated body deceptively fast. It raked at Goron with its claw-like fingernails, grown to monstrous length by the magic that animated it.

Goron was able to keep the thing at bay, his sword parrying every swing of the creature's bony arm. The ghoul's rapid onslaught prevented Goron from landing any clean blows. Even if he had been able to strike the beast, he doubted whether the sword would cause the creature any damage. Even when parrying the creatures raking swings, the armor-like skin on its arms resisted the sword blows, not leaving a single chip or cut. He needed a new approach.

Opening himself to a flurry of blows from the creature, he swung his sword over his head, bringing it down hard on his opponent's right arm. He had judged right. The ancient dressings were hard, but brittle. The creature's arm broke clean off.

Its left arm scraped Goron's face, though, leaving four cuts the length of his cheek, drawing blood. Goron worried what kind of disease this kind of undead creature might carry. Any open wound caused by a dead body might fester and infect.

Now, the creature had only one arm, though it still had teeth, bared in a rictus. If it could get close enough, it might use them as well. Its second arm, still animated by foul magic, crept towards the body it had been separated from, each finger pulling the arm, the nails clawing at the uneven stone floor, as it if wanted to be reunited with its body.

Its one arm was the initial danger, though. It swung at him, claws like daggers. Again, Goron left himself open to deliver a sweeping blow powerful enough to break ancient, brittle bones. This time, he aimed at the demon's head. He swung with all the strength he could muster, breaking the corpse's head off at the neck. It hit the floor with a crack, smashing the side of the skull. Fire still shone in its eyes, watching Goron.

It did not stop the decapitated creature's body, animated as it was by necromancy. It came at him blind, its single arm as dangerous as ever. Goron parried the creature's arm, keeping it from raking him again with its claws.

He could try to take off the second arm, but by the looks of the disembodied arm on the ground, this creature was designed to reassemble itself. He had to keep it from coming together and stop it for good.

Again, Goron swung back for a powerful blow, this time aiming at the creature's legs, breaking its left clean off and toppling the thing over. Its bones clattered as it hit the stone floor. Stale dust rose in a cloud where it fell.

It struggled to rise, but with one arm and one leg, it could not. It crawled toward Goron, no longer as fast as it was.

Goron looked around for something to finish it off. Grabbing the torch he had placed near the door, he touched the flame out to the animated corpse. A thin tendril of fire reached out from the torch and attached itself to the fiend, catching it on fire. The salves used to embalm the corpse were flammable even after centuries. The one-legged, one-armed corpse flailed its remaining limbs as fire engulfed it, smoke filling the room. He kicked the disembodied head into the flames.

The fire did its job, destroying the creature. As its one arm and one leg stilled and the light went out of the cadaver's eyes, the chittering of beetles swarming Annissa stopped. He yelled at her through the smoke, "Get out of the room!"

The fire from the burning corpse lighting their way, he and Annissa fled, hoping the fire would do its work and finish off the fiend.

Chapter 7

It was not hard for Manoueka and his entourage to find the spot where there was a supposed excavation north of Amonkhareb. Following small groups of men heading east, then north, they arrived at two obelisks on either side of the road before descending into a narrow ravine. On the way, they had met up with Askulas, who had heard the same rumor in the city and followed its lead.

A group of men had gathered there, some standing and conversing in Kukrili, probably discussing the prospect of work. Others sat waiting, perhaps for someone to come out of the valley to offer them a job. When Manoueka arrived with Askulas, Kyrion, Kora, and his armed Ushidian guards, the crowd of local Hikuptahn men parted before them, recognizing the foreigners on sight.

The Doradic wizard recognized the foreman who had left with his crew earlier that day. "Bashr. Have you met the man who is excavating here?"

"Not one has seen him today, *Sidhi*," the sun-baked overseer replied, somewhat sheepishly. "If he is not here, it would be easily done to bring the men back to work for you. I will talk to them."

He turned to the crowd and began cajoling men, gesticulating at Manoueka and his men in an attempt to convince them to return to the other site. Many simply argued back at him.

"Kyrion," Manoueka called to his assistant, "do you understand what they are saying?"

The subordinate mage listened to the argument a bit before responding. "Their accent is very thick and they use many unfamiliar words. Bashr is trying to convince them to come back to work for you, he says that you have money and will pay." Manoueka grimaced at that, knowing how much his treasury had diminished. "The others argue that people had slept there last night. Bashr says it was simply a shepherd, but the others say there is no evidence of sheep, just a man, a woman, and a child. They plan to wait until he comes out of the valley before dark."

"Why don't they go into the valley to look for them?" Manoueka turned to Mirán and said, "Come, let's go down into the ravine. If he is there, we will find him."

"Wait, *Sidhi*," the Hikuptahn foreman warned. "Spirits of the dead inhabit in that valley. *An-nathulai*. Very perilous."

"If men will not go down into the valley, how do they expect to work for this man who supposedly is excavating in the very same valley?"

"Every man has a price, *Sidhi*."

With a cynical sneer, Manoueka left the man, heading for the two obelisks marking the entrance to the Valley of Tombs.

"Dakanun!"

Everybody at the entrance to the valley turned at the sound of the man's shout. Standing at the top of a small rise to the left, a man pointed off into the distance, yelling. *"Dakanun! Dakanun!"* The local men, understanding the language, started moving in his direction to see what was happening.

Manoueka turned to his erstwhile foreman for an explanation. "He has seen smoke, *Sidhi*," Bashr said. "Perhaps it is your rival, the other digger."

Gesturing his men forward, Bashr headed off in the direction of the others.

They traversed the desert a short distance to reach the source of the smoke. When the crowd of Hikuptahn men stopped, Mirán cleared a way to the front so Manoueka could see what was happening. To his surprise, the only person there was a single boy next to a pillar of smoke rising from an open shaft in the ground.

"Is this Goron's little brat?" Manoueka asked.

"Kora!" the boy called out. Seeing the girl among the group, he scrambled to his fallen pack to grab a paramerion sheathed near the top.

Askulas grabbed Kora to keep her from running to the boy.

Turning back to the girl's captors, Iko rushed forward, waving his blade at them. Before he reached the wizard, an Ushidian in a chain shirt and wielding a full-sized sword stepped out. With a quick sword maneuver, he slapped the knife out of Iko's hands.

The boy's eyes widened at being disarmed so easily. He tried running past the swordsman to get to Kora. "Iko, stop!" the girl yelled out at him.

The Ushidian reached out to block him, grabbing him around the waist and picking him up off the ground. The boy settled down after a minute trapped in the Ushidian's arms. Struggling was futile.

"It seems you have a knight determined to rescue you, Kora. How very touching," said Manoueka. The mage's words dripped with sarcasm as the rest of the entourage laughed along. "Let him go, Mirán. I don't think he's going to run."

The boy's cheeks flushed red with embarassment. "Let her go!" Iko screamed at him. "When Goron and Annissa come back up out of the tomb, they will show you."

"How convenient. That saves us the trouble of questioning you." He turned to Askulas and said, "The boy has confirmed that Annissa is here." Turning back to Iko he added, "I suppose they're down the shaft where the smoke is coming out?"

The boy apparently decided he had better be careful of what he said, so refused to answer the question.

"So it'll be the silent treatment, then?" He smacked the child on the side of the head, attempting to elicit a response.

At that moment, an indistinct voice came from underground. Manoueka approached the entrance to the shaft and looked down into the blackness. The flicker of a torch appeared far below. "Goron, are you down there?"

When Goron responsed in the affirmative, Manoueka cautioned him, "We have the boy and perhaps you remember the dressmaker's girl?"

He beckoned Iko to the shaft. The boy came reluctantly. Manoueka grabbed him, bent him over the edge to show Goron, and yelled, "They will not be harmed if you do as I say. I am going to send men down there to retrieve the contents of the tomb. You will not interfere or things will not go well for the children."

"Goron, help us!" Iko yelled.

The wizard laughed at the boy's feeble protest and sent him back to his guard.

Mirán and the other Ushidians had been preparing ropes to descend the shaft. At the guard leader's direction, Valád and Barász backed down one at a time into the shaft to act as an advance guard. Czoszín and Mirczóncz followed, leaving Érzopirz and Darzo at the surface to guard Iko and Kora. When he received the signal that it was safe to enter, Manoueka descended, followed shortly after by Mirán, leaving instructions with Bashr to send down Hikuptahn laborers after.

The Hikuptahn strode over to where his men were still discussing the events in hushed tones and began to prepare them to retrieve the contents of the tomb.

• • •

Climbing down the rope ladder his men had lowered to the bottom of the shaft, Manoueka shuddered at the closeness of the place. At the bottom he found the four Ushidian guards watching over Goron and Annissa, who had been disarmed, their weapons lying at their guards' feet. Goron had a cut on his forehead where one of the guards had struck him with the hilt of his short sword to subdue him, perhaps with more brutality than necessary.

"I did not want them harmed, Kosyn." Manoueka addressed Czoszín using his Doran name. "I know you want revenge for the death of Velsid and Kurlz when the fugitives killed them outside Synnakon," he said, mispronouncing his dead guards' names. "But you will have to wait longer for vengeance."

Shortly after Mirán reached the bottom, Askulas descended. Kyrion followed closely behind, appearing ill at ease at the end of the long rope.

On a word from Manoueka, the Ushidians seized Goron and Annissa and began tying them up. Askulas approached the sorceress. "You have run a long way, Annissa, but as always, it did you no good. I am here to bring you back to the Thunolohoi Maholon to answer for your crimes." He inspected the ropes that bound her, making sure she would not be able to escape them.

"So we finally meet," Manoueka addressed Goron. "It took me some effort, but I found out why you burglarized my study. The old dressmaker told me you were looking for my book, that you were following me in order to get the stone. He told me much about you and would have told me more, but he had a weak constitution and could not handle questioning. No matter, we have his grand-daughter and now we have your grandson. His grandmother will be very disappointed to find out you led him into a life of crime."

Looking over Annissa, he spotted the sack she had packed the statue in. "What is this you've found?" Manoueka took the heavily laden bag from the sorceress. Opening it, he smiled broadly, reached inside, and pulled out the Lion of Ptahmel. A few local men that had arrived at that point began murmuring excitedly among themselves, having been raised on legends of the Mad Caliph's treasure. "So you have led me to my objective," said Manoueka.

The wizard inspected the statuette, searching for the telltale *sep* flows that indicated transfers of magical energy. His face revealed his astonishment at the volume of power within the artifact.

Bashr the foreman stepped forward. "*Sidhi*, you understand what this is? Legends tell of this artifact. It is said that, under the plain lead covering, the Lion is encrusted with jewels. It is very magical, very perilous.

Many copies have been made, but this must be the Lion of Ptahmel itself. No other would be so well hidden."

"Yes, I understand well. This is the treasure I seek." Reaching inside the bag again, he pulled out a gold coin and in a fit of generosity, gave it to the sun-burnt man. "There is more in the chambers, I am sure." Mirán directed Valád and Barász to search deeper in the tomb.

"The old man is right." Goron lay on the ground, bound by his captors. "The stone is difficult to control. It might end up killing you, or worse. Do not attempt to use it."

"Do not lecture me on the proper use of magical items. I assure you, I can manage the power." At that point, Manoueka decided he would perform the *seganaion*, the ritual to activate the stone, as soon as he got the statuette back to his encampment. Having picked it up, he no longer saw the necessity of having Kyrion perform the ritual. After all, if it were as dangerous as Goron said, allowing a lesser mage access to such a powerful item could be dangerous to all involved. Besides, he did not want to provide Kyrion with any knowledge of the artifact he might later be able to use to his advantage against him. It now seemed best to keep the esoteric knowledge of the artifact to himself rather than share it.

"Mirán, get these two out of the way," Manoueka said, pointing at Goron and Annissa. "Find them a spot where they won't annoy me. Try to make them somewhat comfortable. They are going to be here a very long time."

"You mean to leave them in tomb?" Mirán was surprised at his employer's change of plans. "Demodoi wants Goron brought back."

"I'm not worried about Demodoi. With this stone, I will have enough power to protect myself. His agent is nearby. If he wants his prize, he can come here to retrieve him."

Askulas interrupted angrily, "I have been sent here to recover the woman. She is to be tried before the Thunolohon. She has a bounty on her head. I have incurred great expense coming this far to capture her, including the loss of a valued colleague. I will not have you treat me..."

Reaching into the bag he had taken from Annissa, Manoueka pulled out a small handful of gold coins, laughed, and tossed them at Askulas, who attempted to catch them. "This should pay for your expenses and then some."

Valád returned at that point. "Boss, we found much treasure."

"Excellent," Manoueka replied. "Did you find any other exit?"

"No, Boss. There is exit from main chamber, but it is filled with stone, like building. Stones are joined together." Valád faltered in his explanation. He lacked an Ushidian word for masonry and found none in Doradic.

"Yes, yes. I understand." Impatient with the Ushidian's poor command of the language, Manoueka turned to the local men. "Bashr, get some of your men down here to start hauling the treasure out. You will have to lower them down this shaft; the front entrance is sealed."

Manoueka continued into the tomb, leaving Askulas to scrabble on the floor for the fallen coins. Valád led him through the central chamber with its defaced murals, into the burial chamber. The sight of the wealth astonished him. Inspecting the artifacts, he found their power stronger than he imagined. None were as strong as the lion he held, but still stronger than any he had wielded before. He had thought that the lion would be enough to further his ambitions, but with the number of magical items in this room alone, he could become the Perkos Nankisou, the First of the Council.

When the workmen arrived, Manoueka first had them remove the burnt remains of the creature lying on the ground. They hesitated initially to touch it, but when they saw it was a dead body, they made short prayers to Deihosos, or Jasho as they called him in their language, before removing it.

Once they had gotten rid of the corpse, they carried out the treasure, starting with the coins. Encased in casks, they were the easiest to carry. Manoueka himself began wrapping each of the most powerful artifacts in finely made vestments stored with the rest of the hoard. Of superior workmanship, the cloth alone was worth hundreds of *nomastoi*, yet it was nothing compared to the value of the relics entombed with them.

The laborers carried out multiple baskets of gold, jewels, statues, wands, and scrolls. Manoueka could not believe his fortune. The wealth he found here today could allow him to become the most powerful wizard in Synnakon. Few men outside the imperial court had access to this kind of wealth and magic. He would have to plan his next steps carefully. His first would be to activate the stone he had come so far to find. That could not wait. He would study the other items later to discover their usefulness.

When the carriers had packed the last item, he ordered the indigenous men out of the tomb, leaving only himself, Mirán, Askulas, and the two guards. "In case you had not guessed, I plan on sealing you in this tomb," he told Goron and Annissa. "If you have done the kind of study I have on ancient Hikuptahn tombs, you would know that, other than the main entrance, the only exit is through this air shaft." He pointed upward to the tunnel by which they had entered. "I'm sure you realize the front entrance is sealed. While I appreciate you unsealing the air shaft, I'm afraid I will not be able to leave it open. It will get dark very soon. Goodbye." He climbed the rope ladder up the shaft and out of the tomb.

Chapter 8

Once Manoueka and Mirán had left, the two remaining Ushidians climbed after them, one giving Goron another kick in the head for good measure. A few minutes later, the ropes and ladder disappeared up the tunnel and the tomb was plunged into pitch blackness.

Lying in the dark tied to Goron, Annissa felt his body against hers, struggling against the ropes that bound his wrists. With every pull, his sinewy musculature tightened. How different he is from Geotheris, she thought of her now-dead sweetheart. A life of study had made her mage friend soft and lean. Goron had led a life of action and for much longer. His body was much harder. Quickly, she put that thought from her mind and began concentrating on how to release herself and Goron from their bindings.

She had tried struggling against the cords earlier as well, but the rope dug into the insect bites on her legs, causing pain she had not expected. Both legs burned and itched as well.

Doubtful of Goron's ability to escape by brute strength, she began chanting, "*O póntonízuva wániz. Yakúd síkam míviz.*" Upon completion of the spell, a knife formed in her hand.

"Stop moving around or you might get cut," she cautioned the warrior. Turning the knife inward, she began cutting the bonds around her wrists. Once the bonds fell away, releasing her arms, she focused on loosening the ropes binding her to Goron.

Freed from the cords, the two began figuring out how to escape from the tomb. Goron groped in the dark, searching for a torch or some other light source. Annissa sat, pondering their options.

"The crypt has one entrance aside from the air shaft we entered through," the sorceress said, remembering the map Manoueka had taken from them. "From the main entrance, one would proceed through a passageway before getting to the central chamber. Right now, both are blocked."

"Can you break the stone sealing the air shaft?" Goron lit a discarded torch he had found.

"It is too far up the tunnel for me to affect it. I'm not sure I can climb that high, especially without ropes. Even if I were to reach the top, destroying the stone block would bring rock falling down on top of me."

"The main entrance to the tomb is sealed with stone blocks, is it possible to break those stones?"

"I don't know. Shattering the rock of the canyon walls when we fought bandits took nearly all of my effort. I don't know if this is more difficult or not." The two of them traversed the central chamber of the crypt toward the blocked over main entrance. Similar to the outside, the original builders had carved intricate architectural ornamentation, though the internal structures were mostly intact. Empty pedestals indicated the earlier presence of long-removed statues. The ten-foot high entrance tunnel itself was completely bricked over with large stones. It seemed hopeless.

"This entrance is likely to be warded, like the air shaft was," said Goron. "It is difficult to know what protection the Mad Caliph put on it."

The possibility of magical protections worried Annissa even more. Her skin still stung from the sandstorm she released when she opened the air shaft earlier in the day. Inspecting the stones of the wall, she sensed no *ousion* indicating magical protections.

Goron brought the torch closer to the walled-in passageway in order to inspect the foot-wide stones himself. He judged that each stone would weigh only about one hundred and fifty pounds, heavy but still within his ability to lift. "These stones have only been lightly mortared together. Would it be possible to crack the mortar? Perhaps we could disassemble the wall. We would only need to get a tunnel large enough for us to crawl out."

Annissa doubted it would be enough. She was already tired from the climbing and the spells she cast earlier. How thick was the wall? If it filled an entire tunnel, there might be too much stone to remove. Nevertheless, she began to chant. "*O póntonízuva...*"

"It is not necessary to chant every time you wish to channel *ousion*," Goron said. "The words are merely a method of focusing the mind on the intended goal, nothing more. Try the spell again, thinking of your aim without speaking."

Annissa instinctively understood what he meant. Recently, when she had cast with great urgency, such as when she fought the bandits, it seemed the *sep* flows had begun before she even uttered the words of her spells.

She began again without speaking, using her mind alone to call on the spirits to shatter the mortar between the stones. She heard the crackling of the cement as her spell fragmented it. Her success surprised her.

"That was not bad," Goron grunted, removing the first stone from the wall. "It can be more difficult to cast without an external focus, but it is much more versatile and can be quicker. With practice, you will be able to shape *ousion* at will and on the fly."

Annissa nodded and went back to directing another *sep* flow at the thin strip of mortar securing the next stone.

The work progressed slowly. Annissa crumbled the mortar around one stone at a time. Once she had a stone loose, she crawled out of the way so Goron could remove the heavy block. In the course of a few hours, they had dug a tunnel three feet high and wide but only about five feet deep. She wondered how thick the Mad Caliph had built the wall. It had been enough to keep marauders out for over a hundred years, perhaps it would keep them in for the same amount of time.

The two had been without food for most of the day and without water for hours. Manoueka had not seen the need to leave them with sustenance; he had intended for them to die, sooner rather than later. The dust from the disintegrating mortar coated Annissa's throat. It felt as if she'd swallowed rocks. The dress Goron had bought for her in Iskander was torn and dirty. The pain and itching on her legs where the scarabs had bitten her was intensifying. Would it worsen as she fatigued?

It was not long before Goron noticed her discomfort. Bringing the torch closer, he examined her legs. Black patches radiated out from bites she had received from the beetles. "The corpse's magic lasted beyond its destruction. The insects carried a disease. Does it hurt much?"

Annissa nodded with a grimace, confirming his diagnosis.

"We must redouble our efforts," he grunted, crawling into the tunnel and picking up another stone. He carried it out of the slowly-lengthening tunnel and placed it on a growing pile of displaced blocks. "A tincture of renaskuta would cure it, but there is nothing in this tomb that will heal your wound. I had an herb kit in my pack but I left it with Bason. Manoueka has probably taken him as well. It is possible it is the *mordigenon*, the disease which Iko contracted in the catacombs under Synnakon. Renaskuta cured him, along with rest."

"We have neither at the moment," Annissa said. "Our only option is to escape this tomb." She badly wanted water for her dusty throat, but there was none to be had. She wanted so badly for them to be finished. The pain in her legs was getting to be too much to bear. Weary but determined, she turned again to the stones, channeling another flow of *ousion* to release another stone.

They continued for a couple hours longer, Annissa breaking up the mortar that held the blocks together, then trading places in the narrow tunnel with Goron so he could remove the heavy stone she had loosened. At long last, Goron gave a shout from inside the tunnel, "We have breached the outside!"

Before his words had finished echoing off the walls of the entry passageway, a figure materialized at the other end of the tunnel in the torchlight in front of Annissa. Brown-haired and light of skin, he dressed in Ushidian fashion. He wore a short blue tunic over leggings, finely embroidered at the collar and cuffs and bound with a colorful embroidered belt. Though Annissa would not have been able to recognize that the style was older, harkening back to a time before

Ushidians had entered the empire, she recognized his clothing as that of a richer man.

"I am seeking Goron." The man's voice had a low timbre, sonorous but not melodic, with a thick Ushidian accent.

"I am here." The answer came from behind him as Goron exited the tunnel. "It has been a long time, Témopirz. I see Demodoi has not given up the hunt."

"He will continue hunting until he has answers he is seeking," the Ushidian responded, turning to face the unarmed swordsman. "If you are not coming calmly, I am empowered to use force."

"You know I cannot do that," answered Goron.

At Goron's refusal, the villain appeared behind Annissa, grabbing her hair. She did not see him move from where he stood between her and Goron. He held a long hunting knife against her throat, the sharp, curved edge pressing against her jugular. Her pulse throbbed against the knife as her heart raced.

"Perhaps you are willing to come with me in exchange for life of your latest bitch. Or is she meaning as much to you as all other whores you have abandoned in your lifetime?

"He has told you how old he is, yes?" he asked Annissa. "Have you wondered at number of other women he has lain with before you? Are you wondering where they are now? Perhaps I end your torment now, so you are not waiting twenty, thirty years." He pressed the knife tighter against the pulsing artery, inhaling her scent as he held her close. "I am smelling blood in you. Are you knowing practice of vampyr? Goron knows. You see, your new lover has loved many women before you because he is immortal. My master is wanting to know his secret. He is refusing to explain."

"Your cult is an abomination, Témopirz. You drink the blood of innocents to gain immortality, but even that does not give you truly everlasting life, it only extends your vitality a while longer. And at what cost? Why did you not come with Manoueka during the day? Was the sun too hot for you? When was the last time you saw blue sky? You and your master have become creatures of the night, tales to frighten children."

He pointed the knife at Goron, still holding Annissa by the hair. "You will regret your impertinence, *alóze*," he said, using the Ushidian word for sorcerer.

The moment he removed the knife from her throat, the sorceress took the opportunity to act. Without speaking or thinking about which spirits to call upon, she opened a *sep* flow, channeling undefined *ousion*. Directing the *sep* at the pile of stones Goron had been building, she took them and threw them at her captor.

Caught by surprise by her silent casting, the first stone hit Témopirz in the side, knocking the wind out of him and forcing him sideways. Annissa followed, her hair still in his grip.

She directed the second stone higher, at his head. Bad aim caused it to glance off his ear, but it was enough to force him to release his hold on Annissa's hair. She moved away to turn and face him, giving her enough visibility to aim the third stone, which hit him full in the side of the head, crushing his skull. He fell to his knees facing her, a look of complete surprise on his face. After a few seconds, he fell forward, his mangled brain no longer able to hold him upright.

"Let's get out of here!" The sorceress, still shocked at what had transpired, continued the *sep* flow in a rage, directing it past Goron and up the tunnel. The ground shook slightly with the bass notes of stone fracturing and exploding out from the tomb at the far end.

Letting go of the *ousion*, Annissa relaxed, the energy seeping out of her. Lacking the urgency of the danger she had faced, she found it difficult to hold herself upright and crumpled to the ground.

Goron rushed forward, picking her up. Checking her for injuries, he held her close. "That was daring. You could have gotten yourself killed.

She slowly drew herself up to a sitting position. "I thought it was the only way out. I was not going to let him decide my fate for me." Or you, she thought, not certain how her companion would have chosen.

She tried to stand, stumbling once. She could barely move, the soreness of the disease having spread from the bites on her legs.

"Casting has weakened you," Goron said, inspecting the black spots that now nearly completely covered her legs. You need renaskuta and rest. I have to go find Manoueka and prevent him from using Korefael. He is likely to have medicines somewhere in his camp. Stay here and I will bring a tincture to you when I return in the morning."

"No. I will go with you." She did not want to rely on Goron to save her. She knew that his first priority was the artifact, not her. Her strength was ebbing. Would she survive until morning? The prospect of a hike across the desert at night was daunting, but she resolved to make the journey.

"The sooner I can find renaskuta, the sooner I will be able to help," she said, pulling herself up with his help. "You need to prevent Manoueka's ritual, but we also need to find the children."

Goron nodded in agreement. "The children will be with Manoueka during the ritual. He plans to use the blood of an innocent to activate the Stone of Power."

Chapter 9

The moon had not yet risen and the stars shone bright through the clear desert air. Though the sun had long gone down, the star-dazzled sky provided enough light for Goron and Annissa to make their way across the sands to the dry lakebed where Manoueka made his camp.

Goron worried that Annissa might not make it to the camp before the disease crept further up her legs and into her torso. Worse, her exhaustion might slow his own progress. He was determined to reach the camp before Manoueka began his ritual. The fact that the wizard had brought Kora all the way from Synnakon troubled him. Would he use the blood of an innocent to wake the stone? Did he intend to include Iko in the ritual? Such a ritual would unleash great power from the stone, but doing so risked losing control of the *sep* flows. In the hands of an inexperienced mage, the statue could destroy everything within a mile. When it came to the Stones of Power, no mage, not even Manoueka, had the necessary experience.

After traveling on it for a few hours, the road crested a rise overlooking the lakebed. Goron saw the camp below laid out in the starlight, a dark spot staining the dim, white clay of the lakebed. The wizard and his company had arranged the camp in an oblong plan with one larger tent, likely Manoueka's, at one end.

It would still take an hour to get near the site, but he dare not rush Annissa. He felt her urgency as much as he felt his own, but the disease and the extensive channeling of *ousion* had worn on her. Rubbing the pain in her legs, she gave him a determined but weary look as the two headed down from the hills to the flats below.

Approaching the edge of the camp in the dark, he spotted a pair of guards standing next to a small brazier, a fire in it to warm them in the cold desert air. They looked alert, as if expecting thieves to steal the treasure the Synnakians had removed from the tomb of Thamses.

"We need to find Kora and Iko and you need to find a tincture of renaskuta," Goron whispered to Annissa. He also needed to get to the stone before Manoueka started his ritual. Given the glow in the eastern sky, it appeared the quarter moon was about to rise, which meant midnight was fast approaching. If his ritual required the blood of an innocent, then it made sense he would attempt it at midnight to increase the potency.

"Perhaps it's best if we separate," she suggested. "I can look for medicine while you look for the children."

He gave her an uncertain look. Given her weakened condition, if she ran into trouble, she might not be able to defend herself.

"I'll be all right," she assured him. "Most of them are focused on the treasure or the stone. None will expect me to try to steal a little renaskuta. The hard part will be finding where they keep it."

"They probably have one tent dedicated to their supplies, if you can find it."

As they were about to approach the camp, another guard arrived from the left side of the tents, as if he had been patrolling the perimeter. After he approached the fire and set his gear down nearby, one of the other guards picked up his weapons and left in the opposite direction to continue the patrol.

"Let us follow that one." Trailing the patrolman in the darkness, Goron led the sorceress across the lake bed around to the side of the encampment. When they were out of sight of the two guards next to the brazier, they headed directly into the camp, sneaking between the tents behind the departing sentry.

With a finger to his lips to signal that they should not speak, Goron moved forward to get a view of the center of the camp. They had entered between what appeared to be the guards' tents, lined up and facing each other across a broad central lane. To their left, the light from the sentries' fire shone behind a tent at the end of the lane. To their right, the lane opened up into a larger courtyard lit by a ring of sconces. At the center of the ring, Goron could make out figures preparing for the wizard's invocations.

Manoueka stood on a dais at the center of the courtyard. The lion statuette sat on a pedestal in front of him, Korefael enameled inside. Kora and Iko stood in front of that, chained to a short obelisk engraved with arcane symbols. A table stood to the mage's left, holding the necessary material elements of the casting. The wizard directed the preparations, giving Kyrion or another person tasks while he oversaw the planning.

Annissa touched Goron's shoulder, the weary look in her eyes telling him that she saw the children and encouraged a rescue attempt. With a nod, she withdrew in the other direction, ducking into a nearby tent, her own search taking precedence.

The sorceress gone, Goron turned his attention back to the ritual preparations. He needed to rescue the children, but also to prevent Manoueka from completing his ritual.

He circled around the back of the main tent, hoping to get a better view from the other side, only to come face to face with one of the Ushidian guards.

The guard stopped short upon seeing Goron, apparently not expecting anyone to be standing there. Drawing his sword, the guard began yelling in Ushidian and charged.

• • •

Mirán surveyed the camp. Manvecze wanted nothing to be left to chance when he performed his *seganaion*, the magical ritual translated to "awakening". Valád stood nearby, shifting his feet back and forth, kicking at clumps of dried mud.

"Look alive, cousin," he said in their native tongue. "We must keep our eyes open. If anything goes wrong this evening, Manvecze will have our heads."

"There is nothing happening here," Valád responded, kicking another clump of dried mud. "We are miles from anywhere and can see anything coming all around. Is it necessary for us to watch this wizard gather his ingredients?"

Mirán looked around. The tents that circled the camp created a courtyard between them. The center of the courtyard was well lit by torches, but it was dark beyond the tents. The light at the center made it difficult to see into the darkness outside the camp.

Czoszín, Barász, and Mirczónz all stood at the edges of the courtyard, watching Manvecze. The center of the courtyard was well attended but his sentries patrolled the outside only occasionally. Manvecze had insisted on having four guards for the ritual, one at each corner of the courtyard, but he had not started the ritual yet.

"Go make patrol around camp, cousin," he told Valád, giving him a light shove. "There is probably nothing happening, but at least you'll keep busy. You must return before Manvecze starts his chanting."

Valád hurried away, eager to be doing something other than standing around. Mirán turned his attention back to Manvecze and his preparations. The two children they had captured crouched in front of the wizard. They had taken the girl with them from Szinnakana. Her name was Kora, he had learned. She was an intelligent and well educated child.

Mirán was not clear why Manvecze had insisted on bringing her. The wizard had said she was innocent. If that were the case, why had he imprisoned her? Ushidians taught that innocents were allowed to be free. Only the guilty would be jailed.

The *perekhe* felt even more uneasy when the wizard had made a comment about using the blood of an innocent in the ritual. Did he plan on killing Kora?

Manvecze seemed to think it lucky to find the boy. He understood using the boy as a hostage in case Goron or the woman tried to interrupt the ritual, but it did not seem right to harm children to cast a spell. Perhaps it would be more tolerable if the spell were for a good purpose, but it did not seem to Mirán that the wizard had a good purpose in mind. He only thought of his own power and his own enrichment.

The sound of yelling interrupted his reflections. It was Valád, he had found something! The children jumped at the sound, their eyes widening, alert with excitement.

Perhaps this was Goron and the sorceress attempting to free them. If so, how had they escaped the underground tomb they had been sealed in? On hearing the disturbance, Manvecze stopped his preparations, looking about for the source of the noise.

Using hand signals, Mirán directed Czoszín across the courtyard from him to investigate. The wiry fighter hastened toward the exterior of the camp, charging into the dark around the corner of the main tent.

Mirán called his other two fighters to him. "Barász, Mirczónz, come with me!" he said in Ushidian. Grabbing a torch, he led them around the other side of the tent, opposite where Czoszín had gone. Manvecze followed closely behind. The wizard was far too curious for his own good, Mirán thought.

The group arrived at the rear of the tent to find Valád and Czoszín surrounding Goron. So he had escaped the tomb. Now was not the time to speculate how he had accomplished the feat. Valád had his sword out, ready to stab at Goron. His cousin had more enthusiasm than brains. At least Czoszín had the insight to realize Goron was more valuable alive.

Before Mirán could stop him, Valád charged Goron's back. The warrior stepped out of the way of Valád's charge as if he had seen him coming from behind. Goron's speed and agility impressed Mirán. His admiration of the warrior's skill grew.

"Valád, put your weapon down. We want him alive," Mirán said. "It will take all of you to subdue him," he told Barász and Mirczónz, giving them each a shove, pushing them in the direction of the fight.

Mirán watched Goron prepare to defend against four attackers as the two additional guards moved into place. His fighters had practiced together many times. He had never seen anybody escape four of them acting as a unit. But Goron was apparently not their usual opponent.

Like a fox surrounded by hunting dogs, Goron was cornered. He began to set up a grappling maneuver. Knowing that his prey's skill might be greater than his men's, Mirán did not let finish the maneuver. "Take him now!" he ordered his men. The four Ushidians sprang at Goron, hitting him high and low, bringing him to the ground.

Valád and Barász held him down while Mirczónz and Czoszín slipped a snare around his wrists. Goron struggled against the bonds, but could not break free.

The four of them carried the intruder back to the courtyard on the other side of the tent.

"Excellent work, Valád, Brash." Manvecze said. He nodded to the other two, whose names he seemed to forget. Mirán could not believe the wizard's lack of interest in the men who protected him. They had been working for him for years and he could not remember their names.

They dumped Goron on the ground next to the dais where the children still sat, chained to the obelisk. Mirán looked up at them, their faces downcast at seeing their supposed savior bound. Mirán almost felt bad for the children. He felt no such sympathy for Goron, though he felt some admiration. He did not know what Demodoi had planned for the captive, but it would be a shame for such an accomplished warrior to die in captivity rather than in battle.

Valád arrived with shackles and chains. "We should chain him more securely," his cousin said. "He has escaped us twice already. I don't want to let it happen again."

Mirán smiled at Valád's determination. He had been blamed for Goron's escape once. Twice would be too much shame for him. "We'll keep him here with us until Manvecze is finished," Mirán said. "Once this ritual is over, we can decide what to do with our captive."

• • •

The pain in Annissa's legs had spread up to her hips and deepened, as if someone were plunging a dagger into the joint and prying the bones apart. Moving caused swords of pain to radiate down her legs and up her spine.

She nearly tripped from dizziness as she moved to the nearest tent, as if a fever were beginning to grip her. If the disease were the same as the *mordigenon* that Iko had contracted in the catacombs under Synnakon, it would spread fast and she would be unconscious in a matter of hours.

The first tent she entered seemed to be an Ushidian's. He had made a bed of furs, though he had covered it with a thin cotton cloth. Apparently, it was too hot at night for the northern barbarians to sleep under their accustomed furs. The men had obviously not lived around women for a while, she guessed. It was bad enough that the owner of this tent seemed to toss his belongings wherever they might fall; the smell was worse. Was there not enough water in this camp to wash clothing?

She was unlikely to find renaskuta here. The camp was laid out with the largest tent, obviously Manoueka's, at one end with two larger tents close to his. The Ushidians' were farther away, so it stood to reason that the tent with the lowest status, the storage tent, would be opposite the largest.

Peeking out the tent flap, she checked to see if anyone stood outside. From her vantage point, she watched the activity in the central courtyard and saw Iko and Kora tied to the obelisk. She did not see Goron. The ritual seemed to capture everyone's attention, allowing her to slip out of the tent into the shadow of the next.

Slowly and patiently, she made her way to the tent at the end of the broad lane. Listening at the side to make sure no one was inside, she slipped in.

She had difficulty seeing in the dark interior, but her eyes adjusted enough to move around. If there was any renaskuta in the camp, it would be here. She found legs of lamb, barrels of wine and flour, and casks of oil, all bought locally by the looks of the symbols branded on the outside.

More promising were the small crates hidden in a corner. The labels, written in Doradic, revealed their contents to be various tinctures, ointments, extracts, and herbs. As quietly as she could manage, she began examining the contents of each case, pulling out each bottle and jar, inspecting their labels in her search for her needed medicine.

The pounding in her head made it difficult for her to focus on anything but her search. Consequently, she failed to hear the approach of two men, their voices loud enough to be heard outside the tent.

Caught by surprise when they entered, it took Annissa a moment to recognize them. Being clear-headed, Kyrion and Askulas recognized her immediately.

Before she could run, Askulas pulled out his small gem and began casting the one spell he knew well. *"O póntonízuva wániz! Yasigód kélsham mam!"* A grasping hand formed of *ousion* in the shimmering air in front of Askulas, reaching out to Annissa.

No longer afraid of the enforcer, the sorceress did not run, but before the *makaphos* finished chanting, she instinctively threw up a shield of air in front of her as she had many times since the last time she and Askulas had met. Even with her head swimming, her feeble attempt to block his attack succeeded.

Surprised at her quick response, he tried again, the hand grasping at her in the air. "It seems you have learned a few tricks, *kibona*," he insulted her in Catacalonian. Her weakened shield still blocked his grabbing attacks.

"Get out of the way, *kasso*," Kyrion ordered Askulas. "Let me show you how it is done. *O póntonízuva wániz. Yaváud udin keshaya maya.*"

The newly minted *maholos* had apparently learned many things as an unlicensed *alutsa*. Kyrion pounded on Annissa's defenses with a force of air, punching her shield back against her until the blows fell on her body.

Askulas had not given up his attempts to grapple her. Her shield reduced in size, he got a tentative hold on her, tightening his grip as she weakened and pinning her arms to her sides.

Her head reeling, she closed her eyes to concentrate and thought how easy it would be to surrender to these two. She would be brought before the Thunolohon for trial and sentenced to labor in a manufactory, weaving cheap cloth for the poor of the empire. If she were to survive a little longer, perhaps she would find some way to escape in the future.

She realized then how much she would miss Goron and Iko, having grown fond of them. She had learned much from the ancient warrior. The prospect of being separated from him set her heart to aching and told her more than she already knew.

What of Iko's fate if she were gone? Goron, for all his centuries, seemed ill-equipped to raise a child. The boy needed a more tender hand. If she were not there, he might grow as hard as his grandfather.

From somewhere far outside her, she heard a commotion. Something was happening outside the tent. Were others coming to reinforce her assailants?

The two Synnakian wizards seemed distracted, their focus drawn to the disturbance outside. Their assault weakened, giving her a chance to counter their onslaught.

Reacting slowly, she reached out her mind to her assailants, wishing for the attack to stop, for them to go away. She closed her eyes, ignoring any external distractions. She focused on her aim: for these two to vanish.

And the assault stopped. The pounding had ended. She could move freely. Weakly, she opened her eyes. Askulas and Kyrion were gone. Had they left the tent to deal with the disturbance outside? Listening closely, it sounded as if the commotion had ended. Was Goron freeing the children?

She could not worry about that right now. She had to find medicine quickly. Her vision was blurring and the pain in her legs came back, causing a wave of nausea. Emptying the meager contents of her stomach, she returned to rummaging through the medical crates for the tincture of renaskuta.

Her blurred vision making it difficult to read the labels, she discarded this vial and that in her increasingly desperate search. She began to worry that she would not find the cure soon enough.

Finally, after ransacking the fourth crate, she found three vials of the treasured tincture. How should she use it? Was it to be applied to the wound or drunk? Uncertain, she did both.

Pouring the first bottle over the lacerations on her legs, the burn of a thousand bee stings shot through the blackened veins of her infection. Not certain it would be enough, she swallowed a second bottle, the taste bitter on her tongue and burning her throat. She gagged, wanting to vomit, but she had already emptied her stomach.

Her head continued to swim, darkness closing in on her vision. Perhaps it was too late, this would be her end. The blackness overtook her.

Chapter 10

Standing on the dais the Ushidians had built, everything was in place for the *seganaion* ritual Manoueka was about to perform except some *trempious* for the children manacled to an obelisk across the plinth from him. He had found the obelisk near the false tomb unearthed in the weeks before and had drawn arcane runes on it in preparation for the ritual .

The sleeping potion was not a necessary part of the spell, but it would make the children easier to control and cause them less discomfort. The boy put on a brave face, struggling against his chains, but the girl's whimpering would distract him if she continued. Capturing her was a stroke of luck. He could have performed the ceremony without the blood of an innocent, but the extra component made it all the more powerful.

It was true that the risk of unintended consequences or surges in the *sep* flows increased with the introduction of the unpredictability and impulsive nature of a child's essence. It was a shame one of them would likely die to give his or her blood to the ritual, but he saw no other option. If the ritual demanded blood, he would have to provide it.

He had initially thought to use Kyrion as the conduit, but when he found the statue, he changed his plans. The idea to perform the ritual himself had come upon him like a revelation. The inferior mage understood enough of the magic involved that he might have been able to control of the energy streams the ritual would unleash. Manoueka did not want to give up any control. Using the children allowed him to direct the *ousion* according to his own will.

He kept Goron captive close to his right, Mirán guarding him. Manoueka did not understand how he had been able to escape the tomb he had been imprisoned in earlier in the day. Surely Témopirz should have been able to capture him. Where was the mysterious Ushidian, anyway? Manoueka hoped he would not return. The strange man unsettled him.

He had ordered Mirán to station four men around the dais facing the openings between the tents surrounding the courtyard of their encampment. They held Goron captive, but could not locate his *alutsa* companion. Had he been able to escape the tomb without her?

He paced back and forth, anxious to begin. He had sent Askulas and Kyrion to find some of the sleeping potion long ago. They should be back by now--the moon had nearly risen and midnight was close at hand. The two were probably bickering. Kyrion could not control his contempt for anyone not of Doran blood. The junior mage thought Askulas beneath him and only cooperated with the Catacalonian *makaphos* when Manoueka ordered him to do so.

Overcome with a desire to proceed, he could not wait any longer for the two subordinates. An unfamiliar longing at the back of his mind urged him to start the ritual.

He reviewed his notes one final time before the appointed moment. At the moment the crest of the moon rose over the eastern horizon, he began chanting over the Lion of Ptahmel. "*O póntonízuva wániz, digímaviz, niz, okuvuz...*"

He recited from his well-researched notes, the *ousion* emanating from the statuette. His heart rate increasing, he had to ensure he did not rush through the multiple elements of the ritual.

The spellcasting proceeded slowly and painstakingly, layering invocation on invocation. He slowly drew out the tender threads of magical energy that bound the artifact together, searching for the secret he longed to learn: how to activate and use the device.

Continuing with his incantations, his mind began more to observe the process than to participate in it. Had he memorized the charms so thoroughly that they had become second nature? It provided him an advantage to not have to concentrate on remembering the arcane language of spellcraft. He would use the opportunity to truly study the artifact and how it was bound to the eldritch *sep* field beyond the material world.

As the enchantments increased, Manoueka noticed the spells he cast differed from what he had prepared. They appeared similar on the surface, but slight variations crept into the formulae. The artifact was teaching him how to awaken it through some self-activation enchantment!

Feeling as though his excitement would cause him to rush the spells and make a mistake, he consciously willed himself to slow down. To his surprise, he chanted faster rather than slower. He attempted to stop the invocation in mid-chant but he no longer had control over his own actions. Another consciousness controlled his body, moving his hands over the statuette and ritual implements, speaking increasingly unfamiliar incantations through his mouth. The once-familiar words took on new implications as the exotic-accented intruder spoke them.

"You have become aware of me," a voice sounded in his head. Another consciousness resided within him. It had made a prisoner of his own consciousness. *"I had not originally intended to take control, but you risked failure in the activation spell. You know too little of what is needed for such an artifact to function, so I had to act in order to ensure success. Now be silent. I must finish the ritual."*

The foreign voice continued chanting, leaving him alone, detached from his body as he... it proceeded with a ritual that grew increasingly alien to him. It seemed like hours trapped in his own mind, listening to the incantations. The eldritch energy rose through his body, causing his heart to flutter. *Ousion* flowed around him in torrents, volumes he had never felt before. He realized then his own ignorance to that point. The Stone of Power within the statue had potency far beyond his own imagination and still the *sep* flow grew in volume.

At long last, his enslaved arm reached for the ritual knife to draw the child's blood. The ritual would be over soon and he would have a chance to regain his own body and perhaps capture the stone for himself.

He watched with growing anticipation as the alien consciousness directed his body to grasp the girl's arm, a look of terror on her face. He pulled her chained wrist to the plinth, forcing her palm face up above the Lion of Ptahmel. To his surprise, the knife only glided across her open palm, leaving a thin red line.

The girl cried out in pain, squirming against her chains. A slight pang of guilt for harming the child came over him. He wondered whether it was a sense of guilt that was the necessary element in the ritual.

His fist clenched her wrist as the line grew thicker, the blood seeping out of the wound. Would it be enough? Shouldn't he have cut deeper, collected more?

The seeping blood trickled down the side of her hand, a red drop hanging from it. Slowly, the red bead grew until gravity enticed it to separate from the hand it clung to, falling to the statuette below.

When the blood touched the statue, a door opened in the world in front of him. Through the prism of that door, everything that stood before him appeared to be made of endless fields of energy, blazing with the amber radiance of a thousand suns. The world appeared as fire to his eyes, shining with a prismatic brilliance, solid as stone, yet flowing like a river. It roared in his ears with the sound of a thousand voices, pressing against him like the rush of wind. The smell of ash and smoke assaulted his nose.

The fields of energy formed firey shapes on the surface of the world, disappearing as quickly as they appeared. Innumerable eyes and mouths, faces and limbs all appeared. The shapes formed into four figures striding toward him through the substance of that domain.

Each had the bodies of men but with different heads. One had the head of a lion, his roar shaking the earth. Another had the head of a bull, smoke coming from his nostrils. The third moved with the fluid grace and beautiful face of a woman. The last flew through the air on wings of an eagle.

The four figures reached out to the opening between worlds as if to close the breach. Before they could act, the foreign consciousness within him reached his arms out into the endless eldritch fields and gathered *ousion* to himself, tapping a reservoir deeper than any he had imagined, pouring a flood larger than any he had yet conceived. As if a stone held a door open, the creatures beyond were unable to seal the rupture between worlds.

The energy coursed through his body like fire, crackling with power. It spread out from him, Korefael, and the children, but flowing through them as well.

Manoueka watched amazed, unable and unwilling to stop it. The alien presence spread the energy in all directions away from him, like a fire catching, toward his terror-stricken guards. Giddy with excitement, he laughed out loud as the Ushidians fell, overwhelmed by the power coursing through them, consumed like trees in a wildfire.

The vitality intoxicated him. The glare of the flowing *ousion* blinded him. He felt alive as he had never before. Everything was quiet; all pain was gone; grass shifted in the wind on the nearby hills. Instead of ash and smoke, he smelled a sweet aroma, like the perfume of a fresh rose or gardenia combined with a hint of dry grass, like walking in a garden on a hot summer day.

Slowly, a sense of unease crept in around him. Something was happening that he could not see through the *ousion*'s glare. Something was going wrong.

The vision stopped and the world went black.

• • •

From the side of the central courtyard of the camp, Mirán watched Manvecze prepare to cast his magic. The wizard had been preparing this for a very long time and the Ushidian could sense his employer's anticipation.

As his boss had instructed, he had assigned Barász, Czoszín, Mirczóncz, and Valád to guard the corners of the courtyard to prevent further disruption. He himself guarded Goron in chains not far from where his master was about to begin his incantations. It had taken three of his men to subdue the powerful swordsman, bloodying his face and breaking ribs. Goron had not been alone earlier that day, but the sorceress with him earlier had not been found.

The *perekhe* wanted to question the intruder to find out how he had escaped the tomb they had left him in, but the ritual had to be performed at midnight. Questioning would have to wait until the morning.

Why had Askulas and Kyrion not returned? Manvecze had sent them to find some item to calm the children during the ritual. He suspected the real reason he sent them away was to keep them from seeing everything involved in the ritual. Manvecze had said he wanted to have Kyrion perform the incantations, but for some reason he had changed his mind earlier today. He seemed to be even more suspicious of other wizards than usual.

"You should not trust the wizard," Goron whispered in a raspy voice, chained and kneeling at his side. "What he does here is dangerous to himself and to you. The forces he plans to unleash are beyond his power to control."

"Silence!" Mirán ordered. "If you speak more words, I will put gag in your mouth."

Goron spoke no more, but what he had said unsettled Mirán. In fact, his own doubts about his employer had grown on this journey the more the wizard confided in him. Initially, he thought it odd to bring the girl along when they left Synnakon. Manvecze had implied that she would be central to the great ritual he had prepared and was about to begin performing tonight. He knew it was not because of any sense of charity toward the girl or guilt for leaving her an orphan. The wizard had shown no compassion when the girl's grandfather had died under aggressive questioning. Mirán had recommended letting the old man rest, but the wizard would have none of it. In the end, the physical coercion was too much for him and he died without telling them everything they wanted to know.

The two children sat shackled to the obelisk, the girl whimpering and the boy struggling against the chains. There was no chance either child would be able to break the iron bonds. Mirán had had them fashioned recently by an ironsmith in Synnakon whose work he knew to be of the highest quality.

When the crest of the moon appeared over the eastern horizon, the wizard announced that they could wait no longer and began the ritual.

The wizard chanted for a very long time in an arcane, ancient language, employing ritual implements, consuming obscure herbs and powders. The ritual seemed to take much longer than any other Mirán had seen before. He wondered what the words meant, what spirits they called on and what powers they awoke.

It seemed as though Manvecze was casting multiple spells, one after another. As he completed each, the tension rose in himself and could sense it in his men as well. The night grew silent. The girl had stopped her sobbing and the boy had stopped struggling. There were few noises other than the wizard's chanting: the creak of Mirczóncz's leather armor as he shifted his weight behind him, Goron's labored breathing as he knelt beside him.

As the ritual progressed, the wizard's voice changed subtly, rising in pitch. A strange foreign accent crept into his speech, slowing the cadence, changing the rhythm, and emphasizing different syllables. His patron's face altered, taking on a sinister, unnatural look. Was Goron right? Did the ritual unleash forces too powerful for his master to control?

A palpable tension rose in the atmosphere surrounding the dais. The hair on Mirán's arms stood on end. The air smelled dry, as if Manvecze's ritual had sucked the last bit of moisture from the desert air. The arcane runes written on the obelisk glowed with mystical energy. Some animal part of his mind registered his rising fear, but the spectacle captivated him as he anticipated the outcome.

Another incantation done, Manvecze picked up the ceremonial knife. Grabbing the girl by the arm, he pulled her toward him, her chains still keeping her bound to the obelisk and the boy.

"You must stop this," Goron said with a rasping voice. Knowing that the wizard intended the child harm, Mirán decided to act, but found he could not move. Some unknown force immobilized him, preventing him even from shifting his arm from his side. Both children seemed frozen in place by the wizard's incantations. Valád and Czoszín stood across from him petrified with horror as well. Only the wizard and Goron seemed able to move.

Realizing his captor's incapacity, the swordsman struggled against his chains next to him, but the Ushidians had mastered the art of imprisonment. Goron would not be able to free himself from his shackles to rescue the girl.

Mirán felt minor relief when the wizard only cut the girl's palm, drawing forth a small trickle of blood. This surprised him; his master had implied earlier that the ritual might be fatal to the girl. Perhaps he would draw more blood with further incantations.

The first red drop fell from her hand to the statue below and the world exploded.

A massive blast of fire burst from the lion statuette, engulfing Manvecze and Kora. It traveled down the iron chains towards Iko, but did not burn. It filled the three of them with energy that radiated outward. Their very breath seemed to be made of fire. A bright light shone from the boy's chest. The fire seemed to sweat out of their very pores. The amber light bathed the entire plaza in a golden glow but cast no shadows.

Manvecze's face revealed his own ecstasy, his eyes wide and grinning like a madman, intoxicated with power. At a signal from the wizard, the fire poured out from the children, who remained whole and unburned. Leaving them, the fire slowly spread out, not consuming the world, but changing it to fire, as if everything it touched were made of flames rather than earth, wood, and stone.

Panic rose in him as the fire spread toward him and the other Ushidians standing at the edge of the courtyard. When it arrived, a wave of pain engulfed his body and he screamed. Swords of agony thrust into every joint. Fire and ice seared and bit him. Every muscle spasmed and cramped. Never in his life, not from battle wounds or broken bones, had he felt pain as intense.

Through the pain, he watched helplessly as the fire reached Valád and Czoszín, turning them into creatures of flame, screaming with the same pain he felt. Behind him, Barász and Mirczóncz screamed as well.

Faces formed and dissipated in the fire. Unnumbered voices gibbered through the roar of the flame. Out of the sea of faces, four faces solidified: a lion, a bull, a woman, and an eagle. The faces grew the bodies of men on the surface of the flame surrounding Manvecze.

By now, the fire had spread beyond the edge of the camp, turning the tents to flame. As far as Mirán could see, the world had been transformed into, but not consumed by, the conflagration. Unable to touch the wizard, the four creatures turned towards the four guards surrounding the courtyard. The creatures moved toward the Ushidians across the surface of the inferno like the dolphins that had followed the *Morespina Ula*, visible just below the surface of the water but not emerging to take their own shape.

Reaching the four sentries standing like statues, the four creatures moved across their bodies as if to inhabit them. Their faces merged, the visages of Valád and Czoszín, Barász and Mirczóncz fused with the heads of the bull and lion, eagle and woman. The four creatures were taking form, inhabiting and possessing the four Ushidians.

The creatures were not able to complete the transformation. They were not meant to reside in the material world. The bodies of Mirán's four comrades ignited like torches, screaming with a pain beyond his own. The four creatures dissipated, expelled from the charred bodies of his subordinates and subsumed into the conflagration.

Goron moved by his side, but Mirán could not turn his head to see. His curiosity overcome by agony, he could not bring himself to care whether the warrior had freed himself. He only wished for the ordeal to end.

When he could bear it no more, when he felt he would succumb to the torment, the pain lifted and the night went quiet and dark once more.

• • •

Annissa woke from unconsciousness, strangely reinvigorated. Her fatigue seemed to have left her as if it had never occurred. Looking at her legs, the infection appeared to have disappeared entirely. Certainly the renaskuta did not work so fast. It had taken Iko nearly a full week to recover from his illness and Goron had administered the healing potion to him repeatedly over that period. She cannot have been unconscious for long. Someone would have found her.

She sat up inside the supply tent, wary that her attackers would return. Where had they gone and why had they not restrained her? They could easily have found rope to bind her in this tent, but they had not done so.

Forcing her worries from her mind, she focused on other concerns. She would need to find Goron. Hoping the warrior had succeeded in freeing Iko and Kora, she set out to leave the camp. Opening the tent flap a crack, she surveyed the scene, anticipating guards or her two Doran assailants. No one stood near her tent. Manoueka prepared his ritual at the center of the courtyard at the other end of the encampment.

To her dismay, Goron had not succeeded in freeing the children and had been captured himself. He kneeled next to the Ushidian guard boss, struggling against his chains, his face bloodied. He spoke to his captor, who barked out a reprimand. Too far away to hear them, she could not make out what either said.

The wizard stood on a stone dais in front of a short pedestal. Neither Askulas nor Kyrion were present on or near the dais. Manoueka had chained the children to an obelisk with arcane runes painted on it. Iko struggled against his chains and Kora sobbed, apparently terrified of the magician and his plans for them.

When the upper corner of the quarter moon peeked above the eastern horizon, the wizard began chanting a spell she did not recognize. The Ushidian guarding Goron shifted uncomfortably in place as if he did not want the ceremony to proceed.

With only a sliver of moon in the sky, her end of the camp remained shrouded in darkness, allowing her to slip through an opening to the outside of the ring of tents.

She moved slowly and cautiously around the perimeter, wary of patrols. Five Ushidians stood guard around the wizard's dais. Others might be present but not visible, but she had no way of knowing how many or where they were. The Catacalonian *makaphos* and Doran *maholos* were still unaccounted for as well.

Drawing nearer to the central dais, she didn't need to concentrate to feel surges of *ousion* coursing around her. The current was stronger toward the center of the ritual. Given the strength of the *sep* flows, she would not need to invoke any spirits to cast a spell, she would need only to seize the energy streaming past her.

From her hiding place behind a tent, she heard the wizard chanting. The voice sounded strangely accented and otherworldly. He did not pronounce the arcane language the same as she had been taught or had heard others pronounce it. Was this the difference between the spells of the uneducated *alutsai* and the more powerful *maholoi*? She didn't think so. She had never heard incantations performed like this. They seemed older, drawn from some long forgotten past.

Scouting out the conditions in the courtyard, she looked around the corner of her tent. She gasped, a stab of fear shooting to her heart, One of the Ushidian guards stared straight at her. Ducking her head back behind the tent, ready to run, she realized he had not moved. He did not pursue her.

She slowly peeked around the corner again, No one else looked in her direction. Manoueka was preoccupied with his ritual and the other guards faced away from her.

She examined the Ushidian in front of her. A powerful flow of frozen *ousion* surrounded him, immobilizing him. She recognized him as the guard who had kicked Goron before abandoning them in the tomb of Thamses the Great earlier that day. Though he could not move, he still saw her in front of him and recognized her. His eyes begged for help and forgiveness. She found it difficult to forgive, but her compassion overcame her resentment. With a silent nod, she promised him whatever help she could, though she did not know how to proceed.

Seizing the *ousion* surrounding the guard, she attempted to wrest it from around him. The energy had frozen in place, solid as stone. She tried gathering other, free-flowing *ousion* to use to force the frozen bonds open. No matter how she tried to grip the guard's bonds, she did not have the strength to move them.

Shrugging an apology, she silently instructed the guard to wait; she would have to figure out another approach. Goron sat a few feet away; only he and Manoueka appeared able to move. If she could free him perhaps he knew how to stop the wizard.

Before she reached her companion, Manoueka grabbed Kora by the wrist and cut the girl's hand. Annissa suppressed a shout, not wanting to give herself away to the wizard yet.

As she moved toward where Goron knelt, Manoueka completed his ritual and the world opened before her. Glowing energy flowed like fire from the statuette in front of Manoueka through Kora and down the chain that bound her to Iko. Manoueka seemed possessed, the atmosphere around him brightening as he drew power to himself. Like a ripple on the surface of a pond, the energy radiated out from him, Kora, and Iko. The fire bathed her surroundings in an amber hue but cast no shadows. Only Goron's heart glowed brighter.

The wave of revelation spread outward from the wizard, removing the veil of materiality from the world. Annissa saw the substance of the everyday world for what it was: all matter composed of *ousion*, organized and structured into patterns comprising the ordinary elements, making the building blocks of existence.

The energy passed through things and people and from one to the other in a free exchange. Faces of men and animals appeared and disappeared in the flames, gibbering unintelligibly. The commonplace distinctions between individual objects and creatures seemed misleading to her now. It was the *ousion* that was the reality, not the material of the day-to-day world.

When the ripple reached the guard before her, he burst into flame like a torch, screaming in agony. His face merged with the faces in the flames as they consumed him like firewood. Some force surrounding Goron and the Ushidian captain protected the two from turning to flame, though Mirán screamed as loudly as his subordinates. Goron seemed unfazed. It was as if something had stabilized the material world around him.

Goron's deep voice sounded in her head, but spoke with an unfamiliar foreign accent. *"Come forward and touch him."*

Unnoticed by Manoueka in his ecstasy, Annissa stepped into the conflagration, past the burning Ushidian, the smell of roasting flesh in her nose, and grasped Goron by the hand. Looking into his eyes, a profound realization swept over her. She understood how to stop the wizard's rampage. The interaction of spells and *sep* flows and how they acted on objects became obvious. It was all *ousion* interacting with itself.

The *ousion* was the natural form of the universe. The material world was only that seen by the observer. To convert the conflagration around her back to matter, she needed merely to recognize its materiality. Manoueka had broken the substance of his surroundings down to the energy it was composed of, revealing its malleability.

Seizing the material of the universe, she focused on the area around herself, Goron, and the surviving Ushidian, converting the conflagration back into the solid matter of earth and flesh and releasing the captain from his agony. Slowly, she added more energy to the solidified area, expanding its circumference.

The crazed wizard noticed her attempts to manipulate the energy he channeled. Like a child covetous of every toy in the nursery, his face flashed with rage. Drawing energy to him, he focused its full power directly on her in an attempt to convert the matter surrounding her back to the raw *ousion* it had been moments before.

Grasping more of the *ousion* Manoueka directed at her, Annissa strengthened the substance of her surroundings, turning it against Manoueka and preventing him from breaking it down to malleable energy. The *mahalos* seemed unable to increase the power he wielded beyond that of the *alutsa*, as if the shard within the statuette limited the volume of the stream.

Projecting her will outward from herself, she expanded the solidified area to the children, cutting off the flood of *ousion* from the wizard. Recovering from his own agony, Mirán quickly ran forward to the children hanging loosely from their chains. They were drenched with sweat, steam rising from them in the cool air. The Ushidian released them from the manacles and carried them away. Annissa focused on the raging *maholos.*

Manoueka directed his flow of ousion towards Annissa while she focused on solidifying the matter that surrounded him. Circling him with a ring of solid matter and strengthened by her own force of will, all the ousion he channeled intensified within his shrinking domain. Gouts of flame burst from the surface of the boiling energy.

Slowly, some of the gouts of flame within his shrinking domain formed into creatures. As the flames formed bodies that grew and diminished, Annissa counted twelve that seemed to maintain their shape to some extent. The creatures ringed Manoueka as if to create a defensive shield. Power radiated from each of the creatueres, lending their force to Manoueka's. Their efforts stopped Annissa's encroachment of their domain. The margins of the fire stabilized, as if Annissa's determination to solidify the world balanced that of the creatures in the flames.

Annissa struggled to overcome the power of the creatures in the flames, maintaining an uneasy balance between them. As she did so, the ring of twelve shrank, encircling Manoueka, as if to merge their powers into one creature and focus it all on Annissa's defenses. Somehow, without understanding why, the *alusta* knew that these twelve desired to manifest in the material world, as if it were their home and they sought to return.

The creatures combined into one another, converging on Manoueka as if to absorb him into the new, more powerful creature they made. But the *maholos* was still material, not broken down into the malleable *ousion* that comprised his domain and that of the creatures he had conjured. The union was unstable. Manoueka struggled against his intended allies, flailing in panic as they converged on him. The attempted union broke apart violently, releasing the energy of the twelve creatures in a fireball, consuming Manoueka with it.

Annissa struggled to contain the inferno within the confines of the enclosure she had created for Manoueka. The ousion around her was surging, the volumes too great for her to control.

As if subconsciously feeling her weakness in the face of the final energy burst, Iko and Kora ran to her, embracing her and pressing themselves close. With their touch, the surging flood of ousion calmed. The same volumes flowed around and through her, but now they flowed more easily.

Following the childrens' lead, Goron came and laid a hand on her shoulder, as if to tell her that she did not stand alone. Her companions could not manipulate the massive volume of ousion circulating around her and Manoueka. Only she could do it.

Since Geotheris died, she had felt empty, as if she had lost the center of her being. Now she knew that was not true. Geotheris had not given her strength any more than Goron was doing now. Since she had met him, Goron had pointed out that she already had the strength and ability to accomplish more than she ever had before. His hand on her shoulder was enough to tell her the same thing now.

Knowing that her companions stood by her, she found the strength within herself to resist the conflagration and contain the power that Manoueka's ritual had unleashed.

She focused her will on the swirling flames to reconvert them to the substance of the material world. Once again, the flames diminished, the circle shrinking until it only contained Manoueka, blazing in the center of the inferno.

Annissa, Mirán, Goron, and the children stood and watched as the flames devoured the wizard from the inside out, destroying him with the power he had craved for so long. The flames subsided, leaving only a charred skeleton on the dais where Manoueka once stood.

Chapter 11

The fires died down and the *sep* flows subsided, leaving a charred ring in the darkness around the dais where Manoueka had performed his ritual. Mirán helped Goron carry the children away from the obelisk where they had been shackled, laying them on beds in his tent nearby. Annissa followed, tending to them. Their breathing slowed to normal and they slept, relieved of the burden of carrying vast amounts of *ousion*.

Goron exited the tent to stand next to Mirán. The two of them surveyed the devastation in the light of the still burning sconces that ringed the scene. The fires had charred everything on the dais within a radius of about ten to fifteen feet of where Manoueka had stood. The firestorm of *ousion* had burned off the symbols drawn on the obelisk and burst apart the statuette of the Lion of Ptahmel. The lead and enamel pieces lay scattered, leaving an amber jewel lying on the plinth, apparently untouched by the fires.

"Do not go near the jewel," Goron warned the Ushidian. Having seen the power the item contained, he did not want to risk the possibility that it could dominate someone else. It appeared to have taken possession of Manoueka, compelling him to perform rites long ago forgotten.

The charred husk of Manoueka's body lay in a pile in the middle of the dais, his desiccated and blackened skin and tissue stretched over his burnt bones. Goron remembered the wizard's face as he died, not writhing in fiery agony, but overwhelmed with ecstasy, as if the *ousion* flowing through him were an intoxicating drug. Did he even know what was happening to him at the time?

Mirán's face registered no emotion as he surveyed the scene. Only when he turned and looked at the charred remains of the four guards did he break down and sob. The men must have been close to him, Goron reflected.

Putting his hand on the Ushidian's shoulder, Goron spoke softly, "We need to bury them." It seemed to him that he had been burying a lot of people lately.

"We always knew of danger of battle," Mirán confessed. "But not such end, not burned in fires of *maholos* gone mad. They were my friends. Valád was my cousin." He wiped away the tears and pulled himself together, accepting Goron's suggestion. "We have shovels in supply tent at end."

Érzopirz and Darzo arrived, having returned after fleeing the scene of the conflagration. The two guardsmen surveyed the damage, the shock registering on their faces. Mirán explained in his own language as best he could what had happened and pointed out their four comrades, charred beyond recognition. Goron understood very little Ushidian, having never traveled among them, so could not follow what they were saying. Darzo appeared to accept Mirán's explanation without question, but Érzopirz began to argue with a raised voice, gesturing aggressively at Goron. The *perekhe* yelled back, quieting his subordinate.

At Mirán's direction the two guards marched to the supply tent.

"I have told Érzopirz and Darzo of events," he explained. "They will bury others. They insist no one else touch bodies. They will allow you to bury wizard."

Returning with shovels, the Ushidians set to work at once, digging four graves for the remains of their friends. They would not allow Goron to dig near them, not wanting the body of the wizard that had killed their countrymen to pollute their burial site.

With a torch to light his way in search of a proper burial site, the warrior carried Manoueka's remains shrouded in a bolt of fine silk the wizard had plundered from the Mad Caliph's treasure the day before. Goron remarked to himself how little the desiccated body weighed. It was as if the very essence of the man had been burned away, leaving nothing.

He found a spot on a rise overlooking the dried lake and began to dig. If rains ever returned or Amonkhareb repaired its waterworks, this area might become a lake once more. If that were the case, Manoueka would have a view of the lake from his final resting spot on shore.

Finishing the grave, he returned to the camp as the sun rose. The Ushidians had finished their graves as well and knelt next to the mounded earth, praying to their foreign gods in their own tongue. Exiting the tent where they had laid the children, Annissa watched the guardsmen with Goron.

"The children are sleeping," said Annissa, dark rings evident under her eyes. She sat down heavily next to him. The events of the night before were beginning to catch up with her. She likely did not sleep, worrying and tending to the children. "I think they'll be all right. They don't seem to be injured in any way, as if the fire hadn't touched them at all."

"You should sleep yourself. You need rest to heal your injury." He gestured at her legs.

"It's fully healed." Seeing the surprise in his eyes, she showed him her legs, devoid of the black patches that had spread the night before. "I know it wasn't the *renaskuta* that healed it so fully, but I can't explain what happened or how it healed."

Goron inspected her skin and found no trace of either the disease or the claw marks that had caused it in the first place.

"Perhaps it was related to the ritual," she suggested. "Massive volumes of *ousion* flooded the area last night. Perhaps some subconscious wish on my part channeled it into healing me."

"That is unlikely. Since ancient times, scholars have taught that one must be conscious and form a specific intent in order to channel *ousion* properly. The sum total of all the wishes of our subconscious minds would cancel out the desires of all others. Rarely does *ousion* get channeled in such a specific manner by accident."

She thought about that and the events of the previous night, her fight with Askulas and Kyrion and their sudden disappearance. She had formed a specific intent that they vanish. Had they? "Goron, did you find Askulas or Kyrion's bodies among the dead?"

"They were not involved in the ritual. Manoueka sent them on some errand before beginning and they never returned. He apparently lost patience and began without them. Do you know what happened to them?"

"They caught me searching for the *renaskuta* last night. They captured me, nearly knocking me out before disappearing. I had assumed that they left when you attacked the others."

"My attack was less than successful," he said, his voice betraying no emotion. "Even so, I never saw those two again."

Annissa had more questions, but Mirán approached Goron and began asking questions regarding the treasure Manoueka had plundered from the tomb.

"We cannot leave so many magical items loose in the Emirate of Ptahmel." Goron knew that magic such as that contained in the artifacts was rare in this part of the world. If an untrained sorcerer found these items, his inexperience could get him and many others in trouble. "The power they contain would cause somebody to get hurt. In the wrong hands, they could be used to cause chaos or destruction. We must bring them with us."

"But there are too many," Mirán protested. "We cannot carry so much."

"We only need to take the magical items. Annissa can identify which ones." Goron looked at the sorceress for confirmation. She nodded indifferently. Turning back to Mirán, he asked, "You brought a wagon to carry everything here, correct? With a few horses, we can carry all the magic. We will leave anything non-magical."

"Leave behind gold?" asked Mirán, his eyes widening in surpise. "Perhaps we should bury it in tomb where we found it. We can come later to retrieve it."

"That would be a waste of time. The locals would find it soon enough and it would be gone before we returned. There is no need to spend precious time hiding it. We might as well leave it in plain sight for them to find." Besides, he thought, the wealth might bring a small measure of relief to the impoverished city. "Find the wagon and as many bags as you can gather. We will load the artifacts and bring them with us."

"Where are we going?" asked Mirán.

"Leave that to me for now. Trust me that it will be a safe place, but I don't want to advertise the final destination of so much magic quite yet."

Grudgingly, Mirán nodded his assent and, gesturing for Annissa to follow him, headed to Manoueka's tent to sort through the treasure, barking out an order to his men to find a wagon and round up the horses.

Goron approached the pedestal in the middle of the dais. Korefael, Second Jewel of the Kings, lay on top, the enamel and lead shards of its casing spread around it. Such a power it had over men. He did not completely understand how the shards were able to subvert men's will, but throughout the centuries he had seen them overcome with desire for the jewels. They were not beautiful in shape or color, each of them was simply a small, broken crystal, dark brown in color with streaks and imperfections inside. No jeweler would spend a second thought on them. Korefael was no different, he thought, seeing it again for the first time in centuries. If not for the eldritch power it contained, it would be nothing more than an ordinary gem of low value. It was the magic that conquered men's souls.

Finding the leather pouch he had carried the statuette in, he upended it over the stone and scooped it up, tying the sack shut with a twist of heavy twine, careful not to let it touch him.

The two Ushidians returned with the wagon and a horse to draw it. Two other horses followed behind on a lead. Goron was pleased to see that one of the horses was Bason and he appeared in good shape.

Mirán and Annissa came out of the tent, the Ushidian heading to speak with his countrymen and Annissa coming to speak with Goron. "Mirán would like to join us. He is speaking to Darzo and Érzopirz to see whether they would like to join us as well."

"I'm not sure I trust them yet. I'm sure they don't trust me." Goron handed her the pouch with the stone in it. "This is Korefael. As I said yesterday, it is very dangerous. Keep it somewhere safe. Do not open the bag and do not touch the stone. Above all, keep it away from the children."

"Do you trust me with it? What if I succumb to the same temptation as Manoueka?"

"I suspect you will not. Something seems to be protecting you; perhaps the stone would be safer with you than anyone else."

She furrowed her brow, puzzled. "What makes you say that?"

"Call it a guess. Have no fear; you will not keep it forever," he said. "I plan to bring it to a more permanent resting place. The Order of Holy Menthanu, called the Menthani by most, have a monastery in the Ponaj north of here. They know of the stones and of my own secret." The order was centuries old, far older than the religion of the younger gods. It was only later that they adopted the trappings of the newer, more familiar religion in order to avoid the persecution that befell followers of the elder gods centuries before. He did not mention that the order has never before involved itself directly with the stones, preferring instead to observe them and those involved with them.

"They will be able to keep the stone safe. The monastery sits in a small town," Goron said. "The inhabitants are descended from the priests of the order and share the order's secrets. We will be safe there from prying eyes. I do not want anyone other than you to know our destination until we are certain that Mirán and the others are trustworthy."

Annissa nodded her understanding, looking up at him. "And you trust me?"

He turned to meet her gaze with a smile. "I am not a man that gives his trust lightly, but yes, I trust you. I suspect our fates are intertwined, at least for a time. You must understand that I will outlive you as I have done many others. It is never easy for me to see my friends and loved ones grow old and die while I endure."

"You will always be better off with people that care for you." She took his hand and smiled back at him.

The sound of the Ushidians arguing interrupted them. Neither Goron nor Annissa spoke the language, so could not understand what they said. Érzopirz pointed in their direction occasionally, his body language aggressive toward Mirán. Darzo hung back more, but appeared to side with Érzopirz. Their leader seemed more defensive. Goron watched them, bemused. "I think they're talking about us."

"I don't think Mirán's followers want to follow us. He suspected they might be reluctant," said Annissa. She let go of Goron's hand and hugged herself tight. "They are still angry with us for killing two of their own. Mirán is more sanguine about it. He blames Manoueka for the whole situation. He has professed loyalty to me. I don't understand why."

"Men are often drawn to power and you control a power beyond most. You impressed him with your defeat of Manoueka last night. I suspect he will be loyal to you until he finds someone else able to surpass you."

The Ushidians stopped their arguing, the two underlings departing from their leader. Mirán came toward them and addressed Annissa directly. "Érzopirz and Darzo will not come. They will take two horses and go to Szinnakana," he pronounced the imperial capital in the Ushidian manner. "They did agree to help load wagon, but will take gold." Mirán looked at the ground in front of him. "Perhaps it is for best that they go."

Turning to Goron he said, "They are angry at you for killing of Czúlirz and Vélszid."

The Ushidian supressed his anger, but his curt sentences and narrowed eyes when he spoke to Goron gave away his true feelings.

"We will have wagon loaded with treasure, but will we raise suspicion on road?" asked Mirán. "People on road only carry crops in wagons. Road here is not trade route."

"We can buy a load of papyrus in the next village," Goron answered. "It is light and we can pile it high enough to cover the artifacts. We should also bring a bag of gold for expenses. When we get to a Rimkai Manon chapterhouse, we can deposit gold there."

Mirán seemed to accept his answer. Annissa went back to the children's tent to look after her charges. Goron and Mirán headed to Manoueka's tent to help the Ushidians unload its treasure, dividing the artifacts from the ordinary wealth. Érzopirz and Darzo loaded their horses with as much gold and wealth as they could carry, leaving the rest in the tent for locals to find. Saying their goodbyes, the Ushidians parted company, leaving Mirán behind with Goron and Annissa.

Goron harnessed Bason to the wagon. "I'm sorry to have to use you as a packhorse again, old boy, but we need a strong back to pull our load." Strapping the horse in, he fed him a dried apple Annissa had discovered in the storage tent when foraging for breakfast for the children.

His group of companions had grown larger again. He had not intended it, but somewhere inside, he felt better knowing he was not alone.

He found the children with Annissa finishing their meal. Mirán had joined them, wolfing down the last of his breakfast as well. "Are we ready to travel?" he asked his companions. "We will travel north for a week or so, then we can rest for a while at our destination."

They all nodded in agreement and began their journey.

THE END

25242620R00202

Made in the USA
San Bernardino, CA
23 October 2015